KILIMANJARO SNOW

Gaile Parkin

Also by Gaile Parkin
Baking Cakes in Kigali
When Hoopoes Go to Heaven

First published by KDP 2019
Revised 2020
Copyright © Gaile Parkin 2020
All rights reserved.
The moral right of the author has been asserted

ISBN: 9798602595697

This book is sold subject to the condition that it shall not, by way of trade or otherwise, be lent, re-sold, hired out, or otherwise circulated without the author's prior consent in any form of binding or cover other than that in which it is published and without a similar condition including this condition being imposed on the subsequent purchaser.

All rights reserved. No part of this publication may be reproduced, stored in a retrieval system, or transmitted in any form or by any means, electronic, mechanical, photocopying, recording or otherwise without the prior permission of the copyright owner.

All characters in this book are fictitious, and any resemblance to actual persons living or dead, is purely coincidental.

Cover design: Gaile Parkin

Chapter 1

THE HEART was really the only possible choice, because only the heart could tell its own story. Not one of the other shapes – not the squares, not the oblongs, not the circles – no matter how big or small, could say anything through its shape alone. But the shape of a heart spoke about love – and in the end, that was all that truly mattered.

Removing the two matching heart shapes from the kitchen cupboard reserved especially for her tins, Angel began the work that could always push any worries to the very back of her mind. She delighted in every one of the sounds of preparing her batter: the sharp crack of the eggs against the rim of her favourite blue china mixing bowl; the gentle scraping of the small grains of sugar and the soft, almost silent yielding of the flour as she scooped each of them up into her yellow plastic measuring cup; and the quick suck of the margarine behind her stainless steel spoon as she scooped it from its plastic tub. But today was special. Today – even though this cake was not being paid for by a wealthy customer, and even though Angel really needed to be counting every Tanzanian shilling that she spent – today she ignored the tub of margarine, reaching instead for the expensive block of butter softening on a plate next to the sink.

With the heavy bowl cradled firmly in her left arm where it felt like it belonged, she steadied her rather over-full weight as the wooden spoon in her right hand began to establish the strong, familiar, rhythmic beat that never failed to lift her spirits way up high. Sometimes she felt exactly the same kind of elation when she prayed in church or when the choir's singing was especially beautiful. Once or twice she had even opened her eyes after the congregation's *amen* and been unsettled to see that she was not in fact in her kitchen, her wooden spoon in her hand, and that the wood pressing against the back of her legs belonged to a pew and not a kitchen cabinet.

From time to time, somebody would express surprise – shock even – that she had failed to modernise to an electric beater. But really, how could a small machine know as much as her own body knew? How could it sense and feel the rightness of a batter in the same way that her own strong arms and expert hands did? How could it possibly bring her the deep, deep happiness that came from putting every ounce of her own energy and love into her work?

If ever Angel had more work than she could cope with alone, Titi could always put aside the family's washing or cleaning or cooking to help her by preparing a batter – but really, it was always possible for an experienced tongue like Angel's to tell a batter beaten with duty from one beaten with love.

'Girls!' she called, scooping half of her perfect batter into her second favourite bowl – white on its inside where her favourite was pale blue, and deep orange on its outside where her favourite was bright turquoise. *'Grace! Faith!'*

Her almost-teenager granddaughters appeared in the kitchen doorway, both of them so giddy about tomorrow that Angel could almost hear their excitement pinging off her cake tins. They were halfway through doing each other's hair in preparation, and Angel felt a small stab of regret about her decision to forgo the expense of a trip to the hair saloon herself. But the bright length of *kitenge* cloth that she planned to wrap around her head for tomorrow's special event would conceal her roots – wilder than the short layers of her smooth, relaxed hair, and noticeably less black – so perhaps it did not matter too much.

Right behind the girls was their younger brother Benedict, the eldest of Angel's grandsons, who set about helping her by using a finger to rub some butter around the insides of the two heart-shaped tins, while the girls giggled and argued their way through their task of choosing the two colours for the two layers of sponge. Benedict was keen enough for tomorrow to arrive – Angel was sure of that – though unlike the girls, he had a habit of keeping what he felt inside him while he gave it careful thought. But when Benedict called the two younger boys in from their play in the back yard to help with choosing the colours for the icing, the girls' excitement soon found its way into all of them, and everybody became a little dizzy and silly. Moses said the heart should be iced in bright green like a football field, then Daniel suggested black and white like a football; Benedict said red, because hearts were red, and Grace and Faith said cerise – which was the colour of a skirt in their fashion magazine – and also silver. Or even gold. Maybe purple. Or just blue. Pinkish blue. No. Yellow.

Smiling widely, Angel listened and watched, her eyes more than a little damp behind her glasses, her own heart swelling despite everything.

But now the morning's joyful pleasure in the kitchen was long over, several hours had passed since darkness had fallen, and all of the children's activity and animation had calmed into the deep quiet of sleep. Without any of the day's busyness to distract her, Angel's mood was quite different as she sat in her bed, her back against the wall, feeling uncomfortably hot and wishing she could rather be a carefree visitor to this edge of the Indian Ocean, blissfully asleep in one of the city's expensive air-conditioned hotels.

Leaning sideways to retrieve a dwindling square of ice from the glass of water on the small bedside cupboard, she slipped it into her mouth, sucking on it as she fanned her face with her notebook. The notebook was still new, and it still smelled faintly of the memory of long-burnt-out incense that the shelves in that shop still carried from their days of holding sari fabric instead of stationery and schoolbooks. Writing in it every night still felt like something new and strange, but she was determined to make it a habit, because it was going to help her to focus on all the reasons that she had to be happy.

Not that she was *un*happy. No. Not at all. But right now, challenges and changes were banging on the solid metal gate leading into the family's front yard, and there was no possibility of simply pretending that nobody was home. The gate – and her heart – must be flung open in welcome, her smile wide and true. Re-plumping the pillow behind her back, she removed her glasses and gave the lenses a good polish with the edge of the sheet, hoping that it might help her to see things a little differently.

Tonight her pen had been hesitating above the page of her notebook for a particularly long time because her husband was not at her side in the bed, his greying head propped up against his own pillow as he read himself to sleep with some or other article or report or study, presuming that his wife was busying herself with something trivial like a shopping list. He would never have thought that her notebook was for anything more serious, because she was not an educated somebody like he was. She was simply Mrs Angel Tungaraza, but he was Dr Pius Tungaraza, a learned elder who was respected as a consultant far beyond the borders of their home country of Tanzania.

Pius would have been right to think that she was writing a list, but it was certainly not a simple list of things to buy at Kariakoo market. No. It was a list of five things that she was grateful for today. People on *Oprah* had been writing such lists every day for weeks, and the habit had been helping them to acknowledge their blessings instead of simply taking them for granted, and to focus on all the lovely things in their lives rather than dwelling on any difficulties.

Reluctant to think about the difficulty that had taken Pius away from her side tonight, Angel focused on Pius himself. She had already written a reason to be grateful for him in one way or another every night since the first page of her notebook: because he was a good man; because she had always felt that she could rely on him one hundred per cent; because his strength had held the pieces of her together after the loss of first their son Joseph, and then their daughter Vinas; because he had sacrificed his plans for retirement to make sure that there was enough money to raise their grandchildren well; because he had always encouraged and supported her in her cake business; because after taking her and their grandchildren with him when he had gone for a year of work in Rwanda and another year of work in Swaziland, he had brought them all home to Tanzania, to their house here in Dar es Salaam. Putting her glasses back on, she wrote now that she was grateful that it was at least this familiar gate that she must fling open in welcome along with her heart.

And at least the gate had had a fresh coat of green paint, and the wall a coat of yellow – though Angel had already written in one of her earlier lists about her gratitude for the property looking good from the outside. Really, the entire house – a long oblong of plastered brick with just a small, corrugated-iron addition outside the kitchen for Titi's twin-tub washer and ironing board – all of it could have done with painting. But Pius was keeping a very firm hand on the family's budget.

What else could she write down ahead of such a difficult special day tomorrow? She could not simply write that she was thankful for the joy that her baking had brought her today – even though today, making the cake with her grandchildren had brought her even more joy than usual. No. The joy of her work was something that she had written about already, and each day she must find five completely new things. Struggling to find them, she glanced around the room. Across from where she sat, the wooden shoe rack leaned rather unsteadily against the wall, its top four shelves densely packed with her own prized collection, the bottom one almost empty of Pius's few large pairs now that he was away. Her eyes danced across the colours – blue, green, red, gold, silver – and she could not help smiling.

With such an enormous event looming so close in her life, could she write that she was grateful for her shiny black sandals with their kitten heels? Smart and elegant, but at the same time comfortable enough for long periods of standing and easy enough to walk in for some distance, they could – if she had no other choice – complement nearly every one of her outfits. They really were such a versatile shoe. Maybe Pius was right to tell her that she did not need so many pairs of shoes. Maybe he was right to roll his eyes when she tried to occupy a small edge of his one shelf on the rack. Maybe he was right to question her about how many pairs of feet she actually had.

Maybe focusing on being grateful for her shiny black sandals with their kitten heels was simply not right. At least not tonight.

Sighing deeply, she drummed her pen against her notebook as she looked further around the room. Possibly she could write that she was glad of the big double wardrobe with the full-length mirror hidden inside one of its doors which, if she angled it carefully, revealed her back view in the second full-length mirror attached to the opposite wall – though her gratitude was slightly diminished now that the mirror on the wall had somehow become too narrow to accommodate her entire rear view from side to side. Or maybe she could write that she was glad of the chest of drawers and of the small basket on top of it where her few pieces of jewellery glimmered in the light from the overhead bulb, bright and bare for Pius's night-time reading. She did not want to write that she was grateful that her husband had not noticed – or, if he had noticed, that he had not said – that she had put away the small framed photo of their son Joseph that had been next to the small framed photo of their daughter Vinas on top of that chest.

Like Pius, Angel was not comfortable with the modern idea of sleeping under a mosquito net – though of course there was one above each of their grandchildren's beds – so she was grateful for the screens that he had fitted to their bedroom windows to keep the mosquitoes out. But the screens had already appeared in one of her lists a few pages back, and she needed to write five new things each and every night. Really, she could not write about any of the bedroom furnitures or fittings tonight. What would anybody think, anybody who decided one day – against every rule of politeness and decency – to read her private notebook? What would they think about a woman who concentrated on being grateful for furnitures and fittings the night before such a big – such a personal – event?

With another deep sigh, she swung her legs out from under the sheet and slid her feet into her *malapa*, slipping the plastic thong of each between her big toe and the next as she stood. Nobody else in the house was awake, so there was no chance of anybody seeing her in her thin nightgown and judging her indecent, but just in case, she wrapped a *kanga* around her body, tucking the end firmly between her full breasts, lower on her chest now than they had once been. Very quietly, she opened the bedroom door, slowly allowing the light to creep all the way up the passage to the door at the far end before she began to move towards that door herself, clutching her pen and notebook to her chest as she did her best to match the silence of the house.

Behind the door on her right, the three boys slept: Benedict – very close now to his eleventh birthday – and seven-year-old Moses, both of them from her late son Joseph; as well as eight-year-old Daniel from her late daughter Vinas; all of them now her boys, her and Pius's boys. Pius said that though Moses was taller and thinner and Daniel was shorter and more solid, those two were like two halves of the same boy: where there was one, the other was beside him, their heads filled with football, their bodies constantly running and leaping and kicking. Long and lean like Moses, Benedict was a different kind of boy. Quieter and more serious, he loved to be by himself with a book or looking at an insect or a bird or a flower – though today, in charge as the eldest boy in the absence of his grandfather, he had annoyed everybody by putting his nose into their business.

Behind the door on Angel's left lay eleven-year old Faith from their daughter Vinas, and Grace – soon to become a young woman by turning thirteen – from their son Joseph. For the last two nights there had been a third bed in that room. Pius had gone out and bought it, and when the men had delivered it, Angel had left it to Pius and the girls to decide where in the room it should go. Still now, she had not even looked. The thought of it sent a shiver through her body now, as if one of the squares of ice that she had sucked had lodged itself in her heart.

Behind the third door off the passage slept Titi, the house girl who had come with Grace, Benedict and Moses when Joseph had brought them here to live five years ago when his wife had become too sick to care for them and he had been too busy. AIDS was a word that Angel and Pius had learned to say to each other, though they would never want to say it to anybody else – not about their own family. Nobody said AIDS – *ukimwi* – about their own family, no matter how much they might talk about it in general. *Sick* was the word that everybody used instead. Joseph had not lived long enough to become sick himself, because just six months after he had brought his children here to Dar es Salaam and gone back to his sick wife and his big, important job eight hundred and fifty kilometres away in Mwanza, robbers had shot him dead in his house.

But Angel did not want to think about that now. Without making a sound, she opened the door that separated the bedrooms from the lounge and made her way carefully past the smart, plastic-leather couches in the TV area, switching on a light only when she reached the far end of the room. There, on the large dining table, the bright orange cake waited for tomorrow.

Placing her notebook and pen on the table, she angled the head of the standing fan before switching it on. Then, with another sigh, she quietly pulled out a chair and sat with her back to the fan's cooling draft, closing her eyes while the part of her that did not really want to look at the cake battled with the part of her that wanted to admire its beauty and her expertise. Inside of her, she could feel the fun of making it with the children crumbling under the weight of the challenging occasion for which it had been made.

In the distance, a neighbourhood dog began to bark, and one by one several more joined in. She was glad that there was no dog making a noise in this yard, even though the firm *no* from both her and Pius continued to disappoint Benedict. She could see it in the boy's eyes, though he did not say. When at last the neighbourhood dogs settled down and there was nothing to be heard but the quiet of the night, she opened her eyes and looked at the cake.

Immediately another thing to go on the list in her notebook came to her: she was grateful that Pius had managed to phone her earlier this evening, just in time. His voice on his mobile phone from Mwanza was a loud whisper.

'Angel!'

'Pius? Where are you?'

'I'm at the house where they took her in. Listen, Angel—'

'Why are you whispering like that?'

'I'm in the washroom pretending to wash hands. Listen—'

'Pretending? Is there no water?'

'There is water. But listen, Angel. There is water. But listen, Angel You need to change your cake.'

'Eh?'

'Just a little.'

If his call had come any later, she would have had to change a lot more. As it was, she had still been able to use the letter O and the two letter Es that she had already cut out expertly from the bright yellow sugar paste, but the J, the P, the N and all the others had had to be squashed together and rolled out again so that she could cut different letters instead. If the wrong letters had already been fixed to the cake, its surface would at the very least have needed re-smoothing, and the entire process might have been just too much for her nerves. But because Pius had called in time, it had simply been an inconvenience. No, not just an inconvenience. An irritation. An inconvenience and an irritation. Those were minor things compared to what was still coming.

Angel shifted uncomfortably on her chair. That was not how she wanted to feel. Not at all. She began again to tell herself what she had already told herself too many times to count. It was not the girl's fault that her father was Joseph Tungaraza, Angel and Pius's son. Nor was it the girl's fault that her mother was somebody other than Joseph's wife Evelina. The girl herself was in no way responsible for the fact that Joseph had never once told Angel and Pius that they had another grandchild. Nor could the girl be blamed for the fact that she was an orphan now because now her mother was late, too. Of course Angel and Pius would raise her. She was their grandchild. They already had five other grandchildren to raise, but that was not the girl's fault.

Most important of all, the girl was in no way to blame for the fact that Joseph had not been who Angel had thought him to be, that he had not been the good family man she had been so proud of, that he had not been the honest and decent man she had believed him to be – the man who had got infected through being a hero, pulling injured people from a crashed and mangled *daladala* halfway under a truck, too focused on saving lives to feel the jagged piece of windscreen cutting his hand, too busy caring for the survivors to worry about their blood mingling with his own. None of that pretence was the girl's fault. But *eh!* How was Angel going to look at the girl without thinking about who Joseph had not been? How was she going to sit with the girl without letting a sigh of disappointment deflate her heart? That was the very big challenge that God had given to Angel, and she must face it tomorrow when Pius brought the girl back with him on the aeroplane from Mwanza.

Since they had first learned of the girl's existence, Angel had wept like young Moses and Daniel still did from time to time; she had allowed her thoughts to make her feel ill in the way that she sometimes suspected Benedict of doing; she had extended her lower lip and sulked just as Faith did; and she had even – once or twice, and just for the briefest moment – not bothered to care, just like Grace did about anything that was serious. But tomorrow she would take a deep breath and open her heart wide.

Today had surely been harder for Pius, eight hundred and fifty kilometres away in Mwanza on the southern shore of Lake Victoria, coping with everything by himself to save Angel from having to cope alongside him. That was certainly something that she was grateful for tonight: that Pius had gone to take care of everything so that she had not had to. She added it to her list now.

Straight from Mwanza airport Pius had gone to the school for the meeting that he had booked with the school head, *Mwalimu Mkuu* Makubi, the man who had written the letter telling Pius that he had a grandchild whose mother was lying so sick in Sekou Toure Hospital that the girl was most certainly on the verge of being orphaned. *Mwalimu Mkuu* Makubi had been ready with the account of outstanding school fees for Pius to settle, as well as a copy of the girl's school records – plus the original of the girl's birth certificate, to match the photocopy that he had stapled to his letter to Pius.

It seemed like a good school, Pius had told Angel afterwards, a good private English-medium school. Pius had been on the phone in the taxi that was taking him from the school to the factory where Joseph had been Manager, and where the girl's mother had been a secretary. That phone call had also told Angel two other things, two things that Pius had not said in any words. Number one, that he had possibly been less comfortable than he had pretended to be about meeting this new grandchild – otherwise he would have gone straight to see her at the home of the family who had taken her in. Okay, they had been expecting him there for a meal this evening, but he had not needed to wait until evening. He could have gone to meet her first, and then gone afterwards to Joseph's work to pay respects to the man who had helped him to gather Joseph's things after robbers had shot Joseph dead in his house four and a half years ago. That courtesy visit had surely not been necessary. No. It had been a distraction. It had been a delay.

The other thing that phone call had told Angel even though Pius had not said it, was that perhaps the cake should speak English instead of Swahili. After all, the girl's school was private and had educated her using English, unlike government primary schools, which used Swahili. Perhaps her cake needed to say *Welcome* instead of *Karibu*. Pius's whispered call even later from the washroom had warned her just in time about what to write after *Welcome* on top of the cake. The girl's name was not, after all, Josephine. Okay, her name *was* Josephine – it said so on the birth certificate that *Mwalimu Mkuu* Makubi had sent – but nobody actually called her that. Instead they called her Lovemore, the second name on her certificate.

So *Welcome Lovemore* said the heart-shaped cake on the table in front of Angel tonight as she counted how many things she had on her list so far – three – and tried to find two more. On Pius's desk in the corner of the room sat the family's big new telephone that was also a fax machine. Paging back through previous days' lists in her notebook to check that she had not mentioned it before, she wrote now that she was grateful for the fax machine because it meant that she and Pius would always be able to send letters to each other, no matter where he was. There was the computer, too, but that was much too modern for Angel. The fax machine was already more than modern enough, and a very big advance from their slow exchange of letters that had sometimes taken weeks when Pius had been away in Germany for his higher degrees. Back then Joseph and Vinas had still been small, and Angel had been raising them in her and Pius's home town of Bukoba – further west from Mwanza on the shores of Lake Victoria – with the help of their extended families. There had been plenty of aunts and uncles and cousins there, always ready with support and advice and assistance.

But now Pius was going to be away again, and Angel was going to have to cope on her own with six grandchildren. *Six!* First just Joseph's three that he had brought to them – Grace, Benedict and Moses – then some time later when their daughter Vinas had passed away, two more – Faith and Daniel. Now there was going to be one more still, and six was just too many for Pius to take the whole family with him on a long contract somewhere else in Africa. He was on a long leave from his job at the University of Dar es Salaam so that he could earn more as a consultant in other countries, but adding one more grandchild meant that the money from long contracts was just not going to add up to enough. Now he was going to have to leave them all here in Dar es Salaam while he went for shorter, better paid consultancies in many different places.

It was not this girl Lovemore's fault that the family was going to be split. Angel could not blame Lovemore for chasing Pius away from here. She could not hold the girl responsible for making her a lonely grandmother without her husband at her side. It was not the girl's fault. Of course not. Angel knew that. She thought for a moment about making number five on her list that she was grateful that nothing was Lovemore's fault, but it did not feel quite right.

And who was this Lovemore? What was the girl like? To Angel's shame, those were not questions that she had spent enough time contemplating. No. She had been too busy focusing on herself, too busy feeling the girl's very existence as some kind of slap to the face from her late son Joseph. She wished that she could feel more like the children. Not like Moses and Daniel, who – because Lovemore was not another brother to kick a ball around with – appeared to be indifferent. No. That would be wrong. More like Grace and Faith, who were bubbling with excitement like a soda, or like Benedict, who seemed curious and hopeful. Angel wished that she could feel in some small way genuinely welcoming. But perhaps that would come with time.

Her eyes went back to the cake that said welcome on her behalf, and recognising that she was hungry for something sweet, she moved quietly into the kitchen. There was just one cupcake left from the batch that she had baked this morning with leftover batter from Lovemore's heart-shaped cake. Smiling, she peeled the paper casing away from it, appreciating the turquoise blue of the light, moist sponge beneath its thick layer of bright orange icing. She had already written in her notebook on other nights that she was grateful for her skill as a cake-maker, for her expertise as a cake decorator, for her professionalism in running her cake business from her home, for the important contribution to the family's income that her cake business was making, and for the recognition that her cakes had already received beyond the borders of Tanzania. Could she find another reason to write as number five to complete today's list?

It came to her as she bit into the cupcake.

Sugar!

She was grateful for sugar, as simple as that. Okay, sugar was not doing her expanding hips any favours, but still she was grateful for it. Using one little finger to slide a small lump of orange icing delicately from her upper lip into her mouth, she slipped silently back into the lounge and added sugar to her list. Now she had her five.

Switching off the fan and the light, she balanced the rest of the cupcake on her notebook and headed quietly back to her bed, hoping to manage some sleep ahead of opening her heart to Lovemore tomorrow.

Chapter 2

Lovemore sits next to her grandfather as they eat their greasy *sambusas* and drink their ice-cold sodas. They met for the first time just yesterday evening, at Auntie Agrippina's house, and now they are alone together for the first time ever. Strictly speaking, they are not really alone, because they are at Mwanza airport, and the departures room is full of hot, impatient people who are waiting for the plane to Dar es Salaam that they should have been on more than an hour ago.

Part of Lovemore wishes that she could have spent this extra time on the other side of security, still talking with her best friend Rose, still delaying their goodbyes. But another part of her is excited, because sometime soon she will be on the plane that will take her to her new life, the better life that will be her doorway to the best life possible.

If you want to go anywhere in your life, you first have to get to Dar es Salaam, and then from Dar you can fly to anywhere in the world. Planes from Mwanza will take you only to other towns in Tanzania, towns like Bukoba and Musoma that are also on the edge of Lake Victoria, or Arusha, where the plane that Lovemore and her grandfather are waiting for is still sitting. The only way you can fly directly out of Tanzania from Mwanza is if you are a fish. Fish from Lake Victoria fly from Mwanza to Europe all the time.

Suddenly everybody sits a little straighter on the uncomfortable seats and looks hopefully towards the big windows where they can see a plane coming in to land. But when the plane touches the runway and they see that it is only big enough for four or six people, they all slump back again, clicking their tongues against the backs of their teeth.

'From the mines in Geita,' a woman says to nobody at all, angrily fanning her face with one of her sandals.

Hope is in the room again when another plane comes in to land, but it is very soon clear that it is way too big to be the passenger plane from Arusha that everybody is waiting for. As its engines scream, the noise of it is so loud that the windows begin to rattle, and Lovemore's grandfather gets up from his seat to go right up to the window to look. Lovemore is used to hearing those planes, but she has never seen one this close. It really is enormous.

'That's an Ilyushin,' her grandfather says loudly to the man standing next to him at the window. 'Russian made.'

'It's here for fish,' the man shouts back. 'Nile perch.'

They watch as the giant grey plane turns round, the heat from its massive engines blasting right through the glass of the window before it taxis in the other direction until it is out of view.

Lovemore's grandfather sits back down and asks her if she would like another soda, but she shakes her head no. She has already used the squat toilet in the washroom once, and it is not very clean. For now, they have run out of things to talk about, and they are simply sitting together, quietly comfortable in each other's company. He has not asked her anything about her mother, but he stayed late at Auntie Agrippina's last night, long after Lovemore and Rose had gone to bed, so she is sure that Auntie Agrippina and Uncle Steven told him everything he wanted to know before he went to sleep at his hotel. He did ask if Lovemore would like to stop at Highway of Holiness on the way to the airport to say a last goodbye to her mother, but Lovemore said no. Mama is not in the ground outside that church. Mama is in Paradise.

On the plane, Lovemore's grandfather lets her sit next to the window so that she can see Mwanza from the air. She is nervous during take-off, not just because it is her first time to fly. One of those enormous planes once crashed into the lake at the end of the runway, its greedy belly too heavy with fish for it to lift up into the sky. But their plane is light enough, and it rises up high before the side where they are sitting lowers as it makes a steep turn over the lake. Lovemore can see that the water is dotted with fishing boats and, closer to the shore, studded with islands of boulders. The one closest to the ferry jetty must be the one called Bismarck Rock, the one that looks like one of its huge rocks could unbalance and fall at any second. Lovemore points it out to her grandfather.

'Ah, Bismarck,' he says, 'Otto von Bismarck. Chancellor of the German empire, including German East Africa. You know this?' Lovemore nods her head yes, even though she means no. 'Today, that one territory that Bismarck once claimed is three separate countries.' He counts them on his fingers. 'Rwanda, Burundi, Tanzania.'

Lovemore has known her grandfather only since yesterday evening, but one thing she knows already is that he loves to give a history lesson. Last night he gave one to Auntie Agrippina and Uncle Steven, a long one about two *Wazungu* from England called Burton and Speke racing each other to find the source of the Nile river back in eighteen something. Burton said the source was Lake Tanganyika, but Speke said no, it was Lake Victoria, and long afterwards another English *Mzungu* called Stanley proved that Speke was right. When Speke first saw Lake Victoria from the boulder-covered Isamilo hills above Mwanza, all the local people knew the lake as Nyanza; it was only later that Speke decided that its name was Victoria.

The plane is over Mwanza now, and the city's rocky hills and the roofs of its shops and kiosks, many of them red with the words Coca-Cola in white, are gradually becoming smaller and further away. The plane levels out after its turn, heading towards Dar es Salaam.

'My plane to Mwanza yesterday stopped first at Arusha,' her grandfather tells her. 'When you fly from Arusha you get an excellent view of Mount Kilimanjaro, covered in snow on top. *Eh*, that icy coldness does not belong in such a warm country, yet it is there.' He lifts his hands, palms up, in exactly the way that Lovemore remembers his son – her father – doing when something did not make sense.

Lovemore knows about Mount Kilimanjaro. Coming up to every Independence Day they talk at school about the Uhuru Torch, the torch that was lit on the top of Mount Kilimanjaro at Tanzania's independence to shine freedom and enlightenment all over their country.

'Did you see the torch burning?' she asks him.

'No, no, it's a very big mountain, the tallest in all of Africa, and the Uhuru torch is tiny compared. Beside to that, it doesn't burn there constantly.'

A lady pushes a small trolley up the aisle next to Lovemore's grandfather, giving out sodas and sandwiches. Another lady squeezes past the first, on her way right to the front of the plane, holding up high a tray with two big silver-foil parcels on it. Sticking out of the end of each parcel is the blackened tail of a fish. Lovemore turns her head away quickly, trying not to have seen.

'The pilots are hungry,' her grandfather says. 'They missed their lunch break with all these delays.'

Not really feeling like all of her sandwich, Lovemore gives her grandfather half. He tries to refuse, but not very hard. Then her soda begins to make her feel uncomfortable, and she needs the toilet.

'There's a washroom right at the back,' he tells her, moving out of his seat to let her pass. 'Should I . . ? Do you want me to . . ? I can go with you, if you like.'

Shaking her head no, she gives him her best big-girl smile and makes her way to the back of the plane by herself. A man gets there just ahead of her, and Lovemore must wait her turn outside the washroom.

The two ladies who work on the plane are squatting down just near her there at the back, busying themselves with something on the floor. The trouser of one of them rides very low as she leans forward, showing the fishtail shape of a thong rising above it. Lovemore sees that they have a fish in silver foil too, a tilapia. They tear at it with their fingers, pushing blackened pieces hungrily into their mouths. Lovemore looks away and swallows hard several times, and when at last the man comes out of the washroom she bends over the toilet and vomits again and again.

At Julius Nyerere International Airport in Dar es Salaam, Lovemore's grandmother is there to meet them. Lovemore recognises her at once from her photo, so she is not afraid when she finds herself suddenly buried in the lady's warm, soft embrace before there has even been an introduction. Her grandmother is quite a bit shorter than her grandfather, and more than a little too round, but round all over, unlike Auntie Agrippina, who carries most of her extra weight on her lower half. She is dressed beautifully in a lovely skirt, blouse and head wrap, all in matching *kitenge* cloth that swirls with bright blues, greens and yellows. Wearing shiny black kitten-heel sandals and glasses rimmed with gold, she looks every centimetre the kind of lady who lives in a nice big house in Dar es Salaam, the kind of house you would find in Capri Point, the best part of Mwanza.

Lovemore was expecting a big shiny car, maybe even with a driver, but the vehicle her suitcase goes into is an old red microbus that has patches of rust. She sits in the back beside her grandmother, in the seat behind her grandfather, who battles to get the engine going.

'What is going on with this vehicle, Angel?'

'It was fine coming here, Pius. Just be patient with it.'

Lovemore watches as he reaches into the cubbyhole for a handle that he uses to wind down his window before putting the handle back in the cubbyhole. At last they get going, but the vehicle is baking hot and it cannot move fast enough to create a breeze because the traffic is very slow. Even from the plane as they came in to land, Lovemore could see the lines of traffic. She also saw how much bigger Dar is than Mwanza, and how much flatter the land. But, *eh*, its buildings are very tall and shiny!

The traffic is so slow that smaller vehicles are leaving the tarmac road and creating dust by passing them on the verge. Lovemore's grandmother coughs as a *bajaji* speeds past on its three wheels, bumping this way and that as it tries not to topple over. Something blocking the verge makes the *bajaji* try to ease back onto the tarmac, causing some loud hooting from a *daladala* packed with passengers that does not want to let it in.

'Look at this madness!' Lovemore's grandfather says, braking hard as a *bodaboda* pushes in front of them from the verge. 'Two on the back is one thing, but this?'

Lovemore and her grandmother lean forward to look at the *bodaboda*. The rear of the two passengers on the back of the motorbike taxi holds his arms out behind him, his hands gripping the handles of a wheelbarrow laden with two enormous sacks of sugar as he pulls it backwards behind the vehicle like a trailer.

'Maybe his wife bakes many, many cakes,' Lovemore's grandmother suggests.

Letting go of the steering wheel for a moment, her grandfather raises both hands, palms up, as he shakes his head and clicks his tongue against the back of his teeth.

'You are so welcome with us, Lovemore,' her grandmother tells her again, holding her hand and stroking it. 'Truly you are.' Lovemore smiles at her, trying to feel more comfortable. 'The children are so excited to meet you! They wanted to come to the airport with me, but I told them no. They're waiting for you at home. We baked a cake for you, all of us together.'

Lovemore smiles again, wishing she could feel more relaxed. But it is not easy. As nice as her grandmother seems, there is just nothing familiar about her. Her grandfather, on the other hand, is a different story, looking exactly like his son Joseph except for his greying hair and the tight stretch of his shirt across his belly. If she closes her eyes, she cannot tell which of the two of them is speaking, except that she knows that it can only be her grandfather because four and a half years ago somebody shot his son dead.

'You are so welcome with us. Truly you are.'

'Thank you, Mama-Joseph,' she says, and immediately she recognises that she has made a mistake. 'Ah, sorry! I mean *Bibi*. Thank you, Bibi.'

'Don't worry, Lovemore,' her grandfather tells her from the front. 'Look how many times I called you by your wrong name before Lovemore came automatically to my tongue.'

'It is simply a matter of getting used to it,' her grandmother tells her, squeezing her hand more tightly. 'That is all.' Her smile is very wide.

Their son Joseph used to tell many stories about them, so for the longest time they have been Mama-Joseph and Baba-Joseph in Lovemore's mind. She never knew until after somebody shot him dead that Joseph was her father – to her he was always just Uncle Joseph, her mother's friend and boss at work. To Lovemore, her grandmother is still Mama-Joseph, but she must try to make *Bibi* come automatically to her tongue, just as *Babu* must come automatically to her tongue instead of Baba-Joseph. Last night Auntie Agrippina took Lovemore aside and told her she really must call her grandfather *Babu*, otherwise she was going to be reminding him all the time of his late son Joseph, which was an unkind thing to do to an old man.

While her grandmother talks, Lovemore says *Bibi* over and over in her mind and tries not to notice the crack that has spread across part of the windscreen, or the discoloured piece of foam rubber that has worked its way out from under the top corner of the seat in front of her. Baba-Joseph is supposed to be— She stops herself. *Babu* is supposed to be a top professor at the University of Dar es Salaam. He is Dr Pius Tungaraza, a Very Important Person. That is what Uncle Joseph always used to say. Lovemore already knows that Babu is on a long leave from his job at the university; he told her that last night. But he is doing other work as a consultant in other places so that he can earn more money than the university pays, and this old microbus is not what a Very Important Person who is earning more money should be driving. What would Lovemore's mama say if she saw the state of this vehicle? Maybe it is simply what Mama-Joseph— She stops herself again. Maybe it is simply what *Bibi* drives. Babu's smart shiny car must be waiting for them at the Tungarazas' house. Perhaps it is busy getting a nice polish.

But there is no other car at the Tungarazas' house, and the house is not like any of the nice big houses back in Capri Point, the best part of Mwanza. It is not even in the best part of Dar es Salaam. How can it possibly be, when there is no tarmac on the road outside it? But at least there is a nice big yellow wall around it, and a big green gate of solid metal that does not let people look through it. That is at least a step up from the chicken-wire fence around the house back home in Mwanza where Lovemore grew up. She is barely out of the microbus when she is surrounded by what feels like a big crowd, but it is really only her two new sisters and her three new brothers, all of them younger than her. She recognises them from their photo, but their names are suddenly gone from her mind. Mama-Joseph – *Bibi!* – introduces them all, the girls Grace and Faith, and the boys Benedict, Moses and Daniel. The house girl Titi closes the green gate behind them.

There are too many people. For now, Lovemore decides to focus only on Grace and Faith, who are closest to her in age. They take her into their bedroom, and her heart sinks when she realises that it is going to be her bedroom, too. Back home in Mwanza she had her own bedroom. Sometimes Rose slept in it, too – top to tail in the same bed when they were both still tiny, and later on the mattress that pulled out from under Lovemore's bed – but it was Lovemore's room, and she could be private and alone in there whenever she wanted. Sharing a bedroom is not at all what Lovemore's mama told her to expect. But at least she does not have to share a washroom with any of her new brothers, because there is a washroom leading off the girls' room that is only for the girls.

Grace and Faith show her around the rest of the house, while Benedict follows them around trying to show Lovemore on a map of Dar es Salaam exactly where the house lies.

'So the kitchen is here—'

'Here's where we are, Lovemore, look. Mwenge is the name of our area—'

'And this room is for the boys—'

'Do you like fashions, Love—'

'And music, Lovemore? Do you like—'

'Here, you see? Look, Lovemore. Here's the airport, and this is the road you came on—'

'Later, Benedict! We're showing her where she lives now!'

'Me too! See, Lovemore, here's our road. Look.'

'Later, Benedict!'

'And this is their room—'

'But children coming in here is breaking the rul—'

'Forget the rules, Benedict, we just want to show her!'

'I want to show her, too! See, Lovemore? This is the tarmac roa—'

'*Benedict!*'

Apart from the girls' bedroom, there are only two others: a small one for all three of the boys across the passage from the girls' room, and at the end of the passage the private room for Babu and Bibi, with its own washroom leading off. At the other end of the passage, just before the door that closes the bedrooms off from the lounge, there is a small hallway to the left leading to the house girl's room and the washroom that the house girl shares with the boys.

It is not like any house back in Capri Point, the best part of Mwanza. Paint is peeling off some of the walls, and near the back door there is a plastic bucket on the floor containing the morning's rain that came through the kitchen ceiling. Outside the back door, there are no beautiful flowers or lawns kept green by sprinklers. There is simply a bare earth back yard across which Moses and Daniel, the youngest boys, are kicking a football.

The house girl has made tea for everybody – milky, spicy and much too sweet – which she serves on an old tin tray that has been scrubbed so many times that it carries only a hint of the picture of Mount Kilimanjaro that used to be on it. Bibi has made a special cake. It is shaped like a heart and iced in a bright orange colour with WELCOME LOVEMORE written on top in yellow letters. Babu must have phoned from Auntie Agrippina's last night to stop Bibi from writing the wrong name on the cake. Inside, the cake itself is in two layers, one a lovely turquoise colour and the other a light purple, with a layer of pink icing in the middle. It is beautiful and very delicious but, really, it has way too much sugar.

After tea, Lovemore goes to the bedroom to unpack her suitcase, and the house girl Titi goes with her to show her where everything can go. Lovemore knows that there is a surprise waiting for her inside her suitcase, because Auntie Agrippina, who packed it for her, told her in a whisper outside the airport in Mwanza this morning as she held her tighter than ever before. She is expecting the surprise to be maybe a pair of Auntie Agrippina's earrings or possibly a new T-shirt or perhaps a framed photo of Lovemore with Rose. But underneath the clothes inside her suitcase there is a large box, the kind of box that Mama used to have in her office at Nile Perch Plastics. You could put a thick pile of papers into a box like this and stand it up on a shelf with many other grey boxes that look exactly the same except for what you have written on its side to say what you have put inside. This box is covered in blue paper from Mama's office, and it has a label from the printer stuck to it saying FOR LOVEMORE FROM MAMA. Underneath that it used to say, in smaller letters, *You Will Be In My Heart Eternally*, only Mama has crossed that out with a pen.

Lovemore sits down on her bed and begins to cry, holding the box on her lap. Titi is suddenly still, and Lovemore knows that she has seen the box and its label. Titi slides Lovemore's empty suitcase under her bed, gives her shoulder a squeeze and leaves the room, shutting the door quietly behind her. Lovemore knows that she is letting herself down. She promised Rose and Auntie Agrippina that she was going to be strong, that her eyes were going to be too busy looking at her future to fill up with any more tears, but this reminder of Mama has been too sudden, too much of a shock. She holds the box to her chest, rocking back and forth as she weeps.

Slowly she starts to recognise that what is in her arms is a gift, a gift from Mama. Taking a tissue from the box next to her bed, she wipes her eyes and gives her nose a good blow. It does not look nice that Mama crossed out the message about Lovemore being in her heart eternally, but Lovemore tells herself that Mama must have recognised that for Lovemore to be in Mama's heart eternally is simply not possible. Strictly speaking, Mama's heart is with the rest of Mama's body, and Lovemore cannot be there, under the ground outside the Highway of Holiness church on the way to the airport back home in Mwanza.

Carefully, Lovemore opens the box, pulling its lid up with a small click as the two tiny magnets let go of each other.

There are so many things inside! Photos of Mama holding her as a baby, photos of her and Mama when she was growing up. On the back of each one Mama has written with a pencil what it shows. *Glory with Lovemore, age one month. Lovemore's birthday turning three. Lovemore's first day of school.*

There is Mama's small tape recorder from work, the one they always used for listening to cassettes at home, and there are two cassettes that have not yet been used. A thick black notebook with a large red metal spiral down its side has half a white page from the printer glued to its cover saying JOURNAL OF GLORY MATUMAINI LUTABANA. Underneath that, Mama has written, in her own handwriting, *And Letter To My Daughter*. Quickly Lovemore flips through the pages of the notebook, all of them completely covered in tiny writing, but she cannot find the letter that Mama wrote to her. When did Mama write all of this? Lovemore never once saw her doing it.

It is noticing the socks that makes Lovemore stop looking in the journal. There are four of them in the box, big grownup socks like a man would wear, each one of them fat and round like a slice from a snake.

Suddenly there is a soft knock at the bedroom door and Titi calls Lovemore's name. Without knowing why, Lovemore slams the box shut and hides it under her pillow before saying, '*Karibu*.'

Titi comes in with another cup of tea for Lovemore, and says that she can take her time with her things, but when she is ready Grace and Faith are waiting for her in front of the TV in the lounge. When Titi has gone, Lovemore opens her box again and takes out Mama's journal.

She sees now that there is a note stuck with tape to the red paper that lines the inside of its front cover. It is written on a page of the shorthand notebook that Mama always used to carry with her at work, even long after everybody already knew that she did not know any shorthand. The piece of tape is not straight, even though Mama always liked things to be straight, and the writing is a bit untidy, which was not like Mama at all.

My Darling Lovemore

If you are reading this, it means that God and Agrippina both did what I asked of them. This is what I ask of you:

1. Always remember that everything I did was for you. You were always everything in the world to me so I always wanted everything in the world for you. I loved you with all my heart since I first held you in my arms, and so did Joseph. Never forget this, Lovemore.

2. Always work your hardest and do your best to achieve your goals.

3. Don't believe any man's lies. Let my mistakes die with me.

4. Don't let me become extinct through you. When you are grown, have at least one child.

5.

But there is no number five. Maybe Mama ran out of instructions, which was not like Mama at all, or maybe she just got tired, which was like her near the end. Is this note really all there is of Mama's letter to her daughter? Lovemore reads it again. Mama loved her with all of her heart since she first held her in her arms. Taking a deep breath, Lovemore wipes her eyes and blows her nose again.

The journal notebook has lines in it like the books Lovemore writes in at school, but Mama has written tiny to fit two or even three rows of writing in between each line and the next. All of it is English, which is no surprise. Mama sent Lovemore to an English-medium primary school, and they always spoke English together at home, even in front of Mama's distant cousins Philbert and Sigsbert who did not speak very much of it, and their house girl Pritty who spoke none of it at all. Mama always said that English took you much further in the world than Swahili, which took you only as far as East Africa where you already were, so what was the point of practising it?

Lovemore begins to read.

This week at Group we had a new leader. An old leader, but new to me — she had been away for training. She told us about writing a journal to record our stories and to help us to get our thoughts and feelings out — because who are we going to burden with our thoughts and feelings outside of Group? A journal isn't something that is going to turn away or walk away or try to talk about something else.

She also told us about writing a letter to our children, things we want our children to know later in life but maybe they are too young now.

Lovemore's eyes move up to the date at the top of Mama's first page, and she counts on her fingers. She was nine back then, and now her birthday turning thirteen is coming up very soon. Again she flicks through the pages, looking for a letter to her that is more than the note taped inside the notebook's cover. Not finding it, she goes back to Mama's first page.

But if I'm going to write, why don't I save time and paper and write both at the same time? So here is my journal and my letter to my daughter together. We're supposed to start by saying who we are. I am Glory Matumaini Lutabana of Mwanza city in the Mwanza region of Tanzania. My mother and father sent me here from Ngara in the Kagera region of Tanzania to do my secondary schooling. I am the mother of one living daughter, Josephine Lovemore Lutabana. I shall tell my daughter the truth about her father on her birthday turning 10.

Lovemore — I have to tell you lies about your baba until you are big enough. Please forgive me. Don't tell lies yourself.

The lies that Mama told Lovemore about her baba were that he was a *daladala* driver and that he was late in a crash with a bus when

Lovemore was still a tiny baby. On Lovemore's birthday turning ten, Mama stopped telling her those lies, and she told Lovemore that Uncle Joseph was not just Mama's boss at Nile Perch Plastics and not just Mama's friend, he was also Lovemore's father. Mama and Uncle Joseph were always going to tell her together on her birthday turning ten, but Mama had to tell her on her own, because some time after Lovemore's birthday turning eight, robbers shot Uncle Joseph dead in his house.

Growing up, Lovemore always believed Mama's lies about her baba being late, so finding out that Uncle Joseph was her baba when Uncle Joseph was already late, it did not seem new or shocking to Lovemore that her real baba was late. She had already cried all her tears about losing Uncle Joseph, but she found many, many more tears for him inside her when she knew he was her baba. She and Mama cried together about him for a long, long time. But till today, she cannot think or talk about Uncle Joseph as *baba*, because she never once called him that. To her, he is always going to be Uncle Joseph. Mama said that was okay, it was better, in fact, because sometimes it was better for a secret to stay a secret.

It was always a secret that Uncle Joseph was Lovemore's father because Uncle Joseph had a whole other family, a wife and three children. He lived with them in a nice big house in Capri Point, the best part of Mwanza. Mama took Lovemore to see his house once, but just from the outside. They never went in. Uncle Joseph's father, Lovemore's grandfather, is supposed to have an even nicer, even bigger house here in Dar es Salaam. But Lovemore knows, now that she is in it, that somebody must have been telling lies.

Lovemore was Uncle Joseph's firstborn, so he chose the name Josephine for her. Mama chose the name Lovemore, and they both decided that her papers would know her as Josephine Lovemore Lutabana, and that everybody would call her just Lovemore. When Mama was very sick in the hospital, Auntie Agrippina arranged for Lovemore's papers to be sent here to Baba-Joseph – to Babu – and he came to fetch Lovemore in Mwanza with the name Josephine on his tongue. But Lovemore has always been Lovemore, the name that Mama chose for her.

Uncle Joseph's second child was born just a few days later than

Lovemore, another girl. For his second-born, uncle Joseph and his wife chose the name Grace.

'Lovemore!' It is Grace who calls to Lovemore now.

'Yes?' Lovemore pushes Mama's journal back into the box, hiding it under her pillow.

But Grace does not come in. '*Mimi na Faith tunaangalia TV*. Come and watch with us,' she shouts through the closed door.

'Okay!'

Everybody in this house seems happy to mix Swahili and English, even though they know English perfectly well. Mama would say that they were not planning to go very far in life.

Lovemore puts the box back inside her suitcase and zips it shut. Then she slips her small gold padlock through the two ends of the zip and locks it before sliding the suitcase back under her bed. The key to the padlock is still on its shoelace necklace under her blouse, exactly where Auntie Agrippina put it for safekeeping.

For supper that first night they crowd around the dining table at the far end of the lounge. The table has the shape of a short oval, and it is much too small. It could be bigger, but the middle part of it has been taken out, and is now a kind of desk – with a computer and a telephone-fax machine on it – up against the wall next to the door leading into the kitchen. The door leading into the kitchen is not like any door you would find in any house back in Capri Point, the best part of Mwanza. It does not even have a handle. A length of washing line has been tied through the hole where the lock should be, coming around the edge of the door and back again so that the door never shuts completely. You can push it open from this side, or you can open it from the kitchen side by pulling on the piece of washing line.

There are nine people around the table. *Nine!* Lovemore and her new sisters Grace and Faith make three. Her new brothers Benedict, Moses and Daniel are another three, making six. Then there is Bibi and Babu, and also the house girl Titi. Nine altogether. Lovemore can feel elbows in the way of her own even before they begin to eat. But how is she going to eat anything anyway, after all that tea and cake? On the table are two big pots with covers. She hopes they are not completely full and needing to be emptied.

Babu gives a long speech about how happy they all are to have Lovemore in their family and how welcome she is in her new home. When Babu has finished, Bibi gives almost the same speech all over again. Moses and Daniel begin to fidget, but they stop when their older brother Benedict gives them a hard look. Everybody claps for Lovemore and says, '*Karibu!* Welcome!' all over again, and then Bibi and Titi get up and go into the kitchen, pushing at the door that has no handle.

Grace removes the lids from the pots. One of them contains green peas, and Lovemore is not surprised to see boiled *matoke* in the other. That kind of banana was Uncle Joseph's favourite, and whenever Mama made it for him, he said it was his father's favourite, too. *Matoke* always reminded Uncle Joseph of growing up in Bukoba, further west on the edge of Lake Victoria from Mwanza.

Bibi and Titi come back from the kitchen with three plates, which they place in a row down the centre of the too-small table. On each plate is a whole grilled tilapia. Lovemore tries not to look at them.

'The fish is specially for you,' Bibi tells her.

'To make you feel at home,' Babu tells her.

'To remind you of the lake,' Titi tells her.

Swallowing hard, Lovemore smiles and thanks them. Her stomach heaving, she does her best to concentrate on helping herself to a small amount of *matoke* and peas. But when everybody stretches forward and begins to tear at the tilapias with their fingers, no amount of rapid swallowing can prevent everything from rising up into Lovemore's throat from her stomach, and she runs from the table, reaching the toilet in the girls' washroom just in time.

She is still leaning over it when she feels a hand on her back.

'It's okay, truly it's okay.' Bibi's voice sounds comforting as her hand begins to rub Lovemore's back very gently. 'A flight in an aeroplane can upset anybody's stomach, even mine.'

Lovemore straightens up shakily, and Bibi digs for a tissue from inside her bra to wipe gently around Lovemore's mouth.

'Of course your day has been too stressful, of course it has. Saying goodbye to your best friend – Rose, is it?' Lovemore nods. 'Saying goodbye to Rose, meeting all these new people in this house. Really, it can be too much for anybody.'

Bibi helps Lovemore to take off her nice clothes, the ones that Auntie Agrippina helped her to choose for her big day, and together they wrap her in a *kanga* instead. She lies down on her new bed, half in Bibi's lap, and Bibi asks what her mama used to do to comfort her when she felt sick. Lovemore shows her how to stroke her forehead in exactly the way that Mama used to, and very soon Lovemore is weeping in Bibi's arms. Bibi holds her and says it is okay, and all the time she continues to stroke Lovemore's forehead exactly the way that Mama used to.

In the morning, Lovemore feels better. She manages to laugh about boys with Grace and Faith – who really are very kind, trying their best to make her feel like she belongs – and she manages to listen like it interests her while Babu tells her about the Organisation of African Unity coming to an end and a new organisation, the African Union, coming in its place. She even lets Benedict show her things on the map of Dar es Salaam. The best part of Dar is not Mwenge, where the Tungaraza family lives, but the Msasani Peninsula, which sticks out into the Indian Ocean like a finger, in the same way that Capri Point sticks out into Lake Victoria.

But at lunchtime, everything turns bad.

Titi has made sandwiches for everybody, everybody except Lovemore. For Lovemore there is the re-heated special treat of tilapia, *matoke* and peas that she missed out on eating last night. Once again she must run to the toilet in the girls' washroom, reaching it just in time.

Again she feels Bibi's hand gently rubbing her back, and again as she straightens up, Bibi wipes around her mouth with a tissue, telling her that it is okay.

But it is not okay, and it is never going to be okay if Lovemore does not tell them.

'Ah, Bibi, there is something I must say.'

Bibi cups Lovemore's chin and cheeks in her hands and tells her no. 'You don't need to say anything at all, Lovemore. Really, it's okay.'

Gently moving Bibi's hands away so that she is able to speak,

Lovemore takes a deep breath before she begins. 'Ah, Bibi. Um . . . You see . . . Fish—' She swallows hard to stop herself needing to bend over the toilet again. 'Fish is not something that I like to eat.'

'*Eh?*' Bibi's eyes open wide, her eyebrows leap upwards on her forehead, and her mouth falls open. Taking Lovemore by the hand, she marches her back into the lounge. 'Titi, take Lovemore's plate back into the kitchen, please. Quick-quick.'

Titi's face is covered in confusion, but she moves her short, solid body as if the house is on fire, and immediately the tilapia is gone.

Everybody looks at Lovemore and Bibi, their sandwiches halfway to their mouths.

Titi returns from the kitchen. 'The fish is bad, Auntie?'

'No, no. Not at all. Lovemore just doesn't like it.'

Babu's eyebrows leap up his forehead. 'Eh! You don't like tilapia?' Lovemore shakes her head no. 'What about Nile perch?' Lovemore continues to shake her head no. '*Dagaa?*'

Lovemore puts her hands over her ears so as not to hear the names of any other types of fish that Babu might list, and she shuts her eyes tight. 'I *hate* fish, Babu! All fish! Even if I think about it, my stomach can turn.' Her hands move to her belly, where they press hard. She opens her eyes. 'Even if I smell it.'

'*Eh!*' says Bibi. 'Titi is like that with guavas.'

'Ooh, Auntie!' Titi covers her mouth with a hand.

Grace begins to giggle. '*Eh*, Titi, remember that huge basketful of guav—'

'Don't, Grace!' Babu's voice is firm.

'*Eh*, don't even *talk* to me about a guava!' Titi's hands move to her belly, the edges of her mouth move downwards, and her nostrils flare.

Lovemore recognises that she probably looks very much like that herself. 'I'm sorry,' she says. 'You cooked it specially for me.'

'We are the ones who are sorry,' Bibi tells her, giving her a squeeze and settling her back in her chair at the table. 'We didn't know.'

'But how could we know?' Babu raises both of his hands, palms up.

Bibi shrugs. 'A girl who grows up next to the lake is supposed to love fish.'

'That is a reasonable assumption.' Babu sounds like he might be about to give one of his lessons. 'But, *eh*, in my line of business I know better than simply to assume. Really, we should have done some research.'

'He means we should have asked,' Bibi tells Lovemore.

'No, I should have said. I'm sorry.'

'No need for sorry,' Titi tells her, giving her a sandwich thick with slices of tomato and boiled egg. 'It can happen.'

Yes, thinks Lovemore, it can happen. It can happen that things are not as they are supposed to be. It can happen that things are not the way you expected them to be.

But at least she is in Dar es Salaam now, and there is an international airport for planes that can take her very far from this life here in Tanzania.

Chapter 3

Lovemore stands in the passage, listening carefully. Through the open window of the girls' room, three different voices come to her from the back yard.

'A little more to the left. No, not you, Daniel! Moses!'

'Can't we just stop now?'

'Uh-uh, I can't get straight lines by myself.'

'But it's us holding the string, Benedict, you're just looking.'

'Can't we just stop now?'

'The sooner you concentrate and do what I tell you, the sooner we can stop.'

'Ah, Benedict!'

'It doesn't help to whine, Moses. Just a little to the left. No, Daniel you stay where you are!'

'Can't we just stop now?'

That is something that is going to carry on for some time. Behind the closed door of the bedroom at the end of the passage, Babu snores quietly through his short afternoon sleep, while from the opposite end of the house come the faint clatter and chat of Bibi and Titi working together in the kitchen.

Those sounds are all safe enough.

It is the closer, louder noise that Lovemore needs to pay attention to. On the other side of the door that shuts the bedrooms off from the lounge, Grace and Faith are wasting their time watching TV. When they get tired of it, they are supposed to switch off before leaving the lounge, otherwise they are going to be wasting power that Babu will have to pay for – so if the TV suddenly goes quiet, Lovemore will know that they might be coming her way. But switching off the TV before they walk away from it is not something that those girls always remember to do. They are not very good at concentrating, maybe because they are best friends as well as sisters. When Lovemore spent time away from schoolwork with her best friend Rose back home in Mwanza, their minds often used to jump from here to there, quickly moving from something serious to something to giggle about. Right now, Lovemore hopes that nothing will make her new sisters' minds wander away from remembering to switch off the TV.

Closing the door of their bedroom behind her, Lovemore bends and slides her suitcase out from under her bed. On her knees now, she hooks the small gold key out from under her blouse on its shoelace necklace, and stretching forward so that she does not have to slip it off over her head, she unlocks the small gold padlock that holds the two ends of the suitcase zip together. Unzipping quickly, she removes the box from the suitcase and places it carefully on the floor.

Stopping for a moment, she listens again. The TV noise continues, fainter now through the closed bedroom door. She re-locks the suitcase, slides it back under her bed, scoops up the box and hurries into the girls' washroom, closing that door behind her, too.

The washroom is more than just a washroom, and that is what makes looking in the box there unsafe. It has the long set of deep shelves where they keep all their clothes that do not need to be on hangers in the cupboard in the bedroom, and there is also a full-length mirror on the wall behind the door. So it is more than just the shower or the toilet that could bring in her sisters. Mostly it is the full-length mirror.

They are supposed to knock, but they do not always remember. Even now, more than two weeks after Lovemore first arrived, they are not yet fully used to the idea that somebody else could be in their washroom.

Unlike the toilet back home, this one has a lid, which means that you can sit on it even when you do not want to use it. And the lid has a nice soft cover on it, bright pink with a pretty green frill around its edge. She sits there now, holding the box on her lap for only the second time ever. *Eh*, it is so difficult to find time alone here! Lovemore does not want anybody else to see what is in the box. It is all she has left of her mama that she can hold in her hands, all that is left of her mama outside of Lovemore's head and her heart. She does not want anybody else touching it. She does not want anybody else looking inside it.

It is Mama's journal that she takes out now, keen to read some more of Mama's words. Flipping through it quickly, she notices that only the first page has a date, the date that Mama began to fill page after page with tiny writing. It is not like a diary where you write what happened each day, the kind of diary that Rose and Lovemore both started to keep in Standard Three. They soon got bored with writing in their diaries because it was so much nicer to talk to each other and to tell each other about everything that was happening, rather than writing it all down at the end of each day. Mama's journal is not that kind of diary. There is a blank line between each entry and the next, and it looks like Mama moved backwards and forwards in time, writing about whatever she wanted whenever she wanted. As Lovemore flips through, a very short entry catches her eye, just two sentences between two blank lines.

How am I going to tell Lovemore? What am I going to say?

Lovemore reads those two sentences again and again. What was Mama thinking about when she wrote them? There is no date, so Lovemore cannot be sure if Mama meant telling Lovemore on her birthday turning ten about Uncle Joseph being her baba. Maybe Mama was thinking about telling Lovemore something else, something like—

'Lovemore?' Grace is knocking on the washroom door. Lovemore slams Mama's journal shut and pushes it back inside the box.

'Yes?'

'*Mimi na Faith tunafanya* modelling! Come and show us again!'

Lovemore knows modelling from Rose's big sister Lulu, who once tried for Miss Tanzania. Lulu was Miss Mwanza, and then she competed against all the Misses from all the other towns and cities around the edges of Tanzania's part of the lake, and she won the crown of Miss Lake Victoria. That year Lulu missed out on the Miss Tanzania crown to Miss Arusha, and afterwards she started a modelling class on Saturdays for extra, and she taught Rose and Lovemore.

'Okay,' Lovemore calls, 'I'm coming.'

Standing up, she pushes down on the handle of the toilet tank to make it flush so that Grace will think that she has been using it. The flushing toilet is one of the few things Mama told her to expect here that is actually here. Back home in Mwanza, Mama replaced their squat toilet with a sit-on toilet. It had a tank for water, but there was no pipe to fill it, so they still had to scoop water from the bucket in a jug and pour it straight into the bowl, as if the tank was not there. Mama said they had moved up from squatting to sitting, and their next step up was going to be flushing. Flushing is where Lovemore has stepped up to now. In life, it is important to keep on stepping up.

Quickly locking the box back into her suitcase under her bed, Lovemore goes into the passage to join her sisters, who are taking turns practising their walk. Grace and Lovemore are both tall like Uncle Joseph, only Grace is a bit taller and thin like a pencil. She makes Lovemore look big, though Lovemore is not at all fat, she is just a bit rounder and her buttocks sit proud and high up on her back just like Mama's. But anybody who looks carefully at Lovemore and Grace together will be able to see that they are sisters. Back home in Mwanza, nobody ever looked at them together: they went to different schools and they prayed at different churches. Mwanza is small, though it is second in size to Dar es Salaam, but Lovemore and Grace never met each other there, they were never in the same place for somebody to look carefully and notice that they might be sisters. Faith does not look like them at all. She is younger and shorter and just a little too round and solid. Of the three girls, Lovemore is the only one who has a waist.

The plastic measuring jug from the kitchen stands unsteadily now on top of the head of Faith, who tries to balance it there while she walks down the passage. But every two steps, the jug begins to slide and she has to stop walking and grab at it.

'Show us, Lovemore.'

Taking the jug from Faith, Lovemore walks to the far end of the passage, towards the closed door behind which Babu quietly snores. There she turns, and positioning the jug carefully on her head, resting her left hand expertly on her left hip, she glides smoothly towards Grace and Faith as they admire her from the far end of the passage where the door closes it off from the lounge. Keeping her head up and steady as she places one foot directly in front of the other, swinging her buttocks from left to right with each step and staring straight ahead, ignoring the doorway to the boys' room on the right and the doorway to the girls' room on the left, she stops just in front of the two girls, staring over Faith's head and right through Grace, pauses for a moment to place her other hand on her other hip, then turns very carefully to her left and takes a few steps into the small hallway leading to Titi's room and the washroom that Titi shares with the boys.

'Eh!' say Grace and Faith, clapping their hands together.

'If we were village girls we would do this with a heavy load of wood or water,' Lovemore tells them. It was what Mama's mother used to do, but Mama stepped up from that.

Grace takes the jug from her. 'Let me try!'

'Try without the jug first. I told you I couldn't do a jug for weeks.'

But Grace is determined. Balancing the jug on top of the neatly plaited rows of her braids, she sets off unsteadily down the passage, both hands up near her head, ready for the jug to fall.

'Hands down,' instructs Lovemore.

'Put one on your hip!' calls Faith.

Grace stands still. Very slowly, her left hand goes down to her left hip. Her right hand stays where it is, ready to catch the jug. She sets off again at a better pace, but her feet are not one in front of the other.

'Imagine a line on the floor and keep your feet on it,' says Lovemore, copying what Rose's big sister Lulu used to say to all the girls who came to modelling class.

Grace looks down at her feet, sending the jug toppling to the floor, where it bounces forwards a few times with a hollow thud before hitting the door to Babu's room and coming to a stop, all three of them giggling. Lovemore's own giggle surprises her, coming as it does so soon after losing her mama, and so far away from her best friend Rose.

'Girls!' The voice comes from behind the door. Still today, it shocks Lovemore to hear that voice. It is exactly like Uncle Joseph's.

'Sorry, Baba!' Grace and Faith chorus as Grace bends to pick up the jug.

'Sorry,' says Lovemore, uncomfortable calling him *Babu* when the girls are calling him *Baba*. It is such a small difference – *Baba* with an *a* at the end for father, *Babu* with a *u* at the end for grandfather – but she does not want to call him *Baba* as they do. She has never called any man *Baba*. Why should she call her grandfather *Father*? It is bad enough that everybody in this house calls their pastor *Father*.

The bedroom door opens, and Babu fills the doorway, looking just like Uncle Joseph except for being a bit grey and having a stomach that stretches his T-shirt above his trouser.

'Is this a good place to be making noise when somebody is sleeping?' He is sliding his bare feet into a large pair of *malapa*.

All three of them shake their heads and say sorry again.

'Why can't you do what you were doing outside?'

'The boys are out there,' says Grace.

'And it's too hot,' says Faith.

Lovemore says nothing, uncertain about how Babu is going to react, and trying to still Mama's voice that has suddenly said, inside Lovemore's head: *What am I going to say?*

They all follow him into the lounge, where Bibi is sitting with her feet up on the coffee table, fanning her face with a magazine while she watches *Oprah* on TV. She hands over the remote as Babu sits down beside her.

Babu glances at the girls over his shoulder. 'If you don't want to go outside, sit and watch some news with us.' His thumb punches in some numbers on the remote. 'Educate yourselves about world events.'

Rolling their eyes, Grace and Faith take their places on the second of the three red-and-black couches that make a U facing the TV, while Lovemore heads for the third. But Babu and Bibi slide apart, patting the space that they create on their couch, and Lovemore goes to sit between them. When Babu has sighed out all of his irritation at being woken up, he smiles and slips an arm around Lovemore's shoulders, and as she leans in to him, she almost feels like she is small again, sitting with Uncle Joseph.

But Lovemore never sat watching TV with Uncle Joseph. Back home in Mwanza, Mama never wanted a TV, even though Uncle Joseph kept offering to buy one for them so that he could watch football when he visited. Watching TV occupies your eyes, Mama used to say, and what else can you achieve at the same time that does not need your eyes? Mama always liked to do more than one thing at a time, and she did not like anybody to be doing nothing. 'Lovemore,' she would say, 'are you going to sit around doing nothing? When you are old, do you want to be wishing you had done something with your life instead of sitting around doing nothing?'

Auntie Agrippina and Uncle Steven have a big TV, bigger than this one here, and when Lovemore was visiting, she and Rose could watch it whenever they wanted. But Lovemore was always careful not to let Mama catch her watching, because watching TV was really just the same as sitting around doing nothing. Now, here in Dar es Salaam where it is so much hotter than Mwanza, sitting around doing nothing does seem to make a lot more sense.

Babu takes a handkerchief from his trouser pocket and dabs at his forehead. '*Eh*, where is that fan?'

In this house, there is no fan hanging from the ceiling. Lovemore is sure that a fan hangs from the ceiling of every room in every one of the houses in Capri Point in Mwanza. There are surely ceiling fans, too, in all the houses on Msasani Peninsula here in Dar es Salaam.

Bibi's hand shows Babu the dining table at the far side of the room, where the standing fan is busy cooling several cakes resting on wire racks.

'I need to start decorating tonight,' she says. 'It's a big order for the DSG.'

Removing his arm from around Lovemore's shoulders, Babu leans forward and looks past her at Bibi. 'The DSG? The Deputy Secretary-General?'

'Uh-uh. The Diplomatic Spouses Group.' Bibi smiles and pats one side of her hair with the hand that is not fanning her face with the magazine. 'They're having a fund-raiser tea.'

Lovemore can understand why people order Bibi's cakes: they are certainly very delicious, though a little too sweet for her. She never had much sugar back home in Mwanza. Nearer the end it was because it was not the best thing for Mama, but before that it was because Mama did not want their buttocks to grow bigger, especially Lovemore's. The men outside of Africa may not like a woman with buttocks, and a man outside of Africa is going to be Lovemore's destiny. Bibi, on the other hand, does not worry about sugar and her own shape: she is round and soft and easy to hug, just like Lovemore has always known a grandmother should be. Rose's bibi, Auntie Agrippina's mama, has a lap that could hold both Rose and Lovemore at the same time. But Lovemore has her buttocks and her destiny to worry about, and she is going to have to be careful not to eat too much of Bibi's cake.

She can see that news and world events are not at all interesting to Grace and Faith, who are only pretending to watch; and Bibi has stopped fanning herself with the magazine and has begun paging through it instead. Lovemore is not really that interested herself, but she makes herself try to concentrate because you cannot go out into the world without knowing the world, and Lovemore is going to go out into the world. She and Rose are going to be lawyers together in New York.

That was Uncle Joseph's idea. When Lovemore and Rose were still small, he said once, when he was visiting their house and Rose was there too, that Lovemore and Rose sounded like the name of a law firm in New York. After that, every time he saw them together he would say, 'Ah, the lawyers.' Mama loved that. She made a sign saying *Lovemore & Rose* for Lovemore's bedroom door.

Back home in Mwanza, Lovemore and Mama used to listen to news on the radio. The radio took only your ears, leaving your eyes to do other things, things like mending or drawing or checking to see if their house girl Pritty had been cleaning nicely. At the same time as listening to news on the radio, Mama could even do typing at home for extra, first on the electric Olivetti golf ball that Uncle Joseph gave her to match the one in her office at Nile Perch Plastics, and then on a computer when her office changed to computers. Mama's eyes knew how to read somebody's handwriting and tell her fingers what to type without her even looking at her fingers, and at the same time she could say something about what they were listening to on the radio. She taught Lovemore how to type without looking at her hands, even though Lovemore is going to have a secretary to type for her in New York, but Lovemore has not yet learned how to listen to something else at the same time.

It was not always the radio that they listened to. Nearly every month, two or three cassettes used to come in a parcel from Auntie Agrippina's cousin Joy in America. Back when Joy's American husband threw her away like the empty bones of a fish, Joy began listening to CDs that told her that she was worth more than that and how to be successful. Every CD Joy listened to, she copied onto a cassette for her cousin Agrippina. Mama and Lovemore listened too, on the small cassette player from Mama's office, the one that is now in the box in Lovemore's suitcase under her bed.

Lovemore did not always understand everything on those cassettes, at least when she was smaller, but she loved to listen, especially while her hands and her eyes were busy putting together a jigsaw puzzle borrowed from the Indian ladies' toy library. Afterwards, she and Mama would practise their American accents so that Lovemore would be ready for being a lawyer in New York, and Mama's cousins Philbert and Sigsbert would practise their American accents, too, so that they could try to impress Rose's big sister Lulu.

Now, because of Mama, it is hard for Lovemore just to sit and watch news on TV – she always feels that there is something else that she should be doing. So it is a relief when Titi comes in from the kitchen to ask if the cakes are cool yet, because she wants to prepare the dining table for their supper. When Bibi gets up to look, Lovemore goes with her, and she helps her to move the almost-cool cakes on their wire racks to the coffee table, moving the fan with them so that Babu and the cakes can both get cool.

While Lovemore and Grace never once laid their eyes on each other in Mwanza, Lovemore and Titi did. Titi was Uncle Joseph's house girl there before she came here with the children. Lovemore did not recognise her at first, but now she does. Titi has still not recognized her, though. Maybe she never will. And maybe Lovemore will just keep quiet.

'It's goat with rice,' Titi tells her now, as they prepare the table together, 'and peas and carrots in peanut sauce.'

'She's lying!' Grace calls from the couch. 'It's fish!'

'No!' shouts Bibi. 'Stop it, Grace!' But Bibi is smiling.

Slowly by slowly, Grace's constant teasing has been turning Lovemore's stomach less and less. Next time – or maybe the time after that – maybe she will be able to smile with Bibi. Maybe. Just a little.

Angel's friend Irene, having declined the offer of more cake several times, was attempting to slice the thinnest possible sliver for herself. 'So she no longer vomits about fish?'

'Hallelujah!' declared Esther, holding out her cup so that Angel could refill it from the fresh pot that Titi had just brought.

'Thanks God none of my grandchildren is fussing about foods.' Irene's sliver fell to the side as she cut, and she used the knife to scoot it on to her plate. 'Anybody else?'

'Just small-small,' said Fatima, sliding her plate forward.

Dipping her head of white hair as she reached into her bag, Stella retrieved her small silver flask and poured some of her medicine from it into her fresh cup of tea. Everybody knew that it was probably not medicine, but nobody ever wanted to say – and nobody was going to say anything today.

'But *fish*, Angel!'

'Fish, Stella!' Angel shrugged her shoulders and shook her head. Really, to grow up on the shores of Lake Victoria without wanting to eat fish was very peculiar indeed. What on Earth had Lovemore's mother fed her? Growing up in Bukoba on the shores further west from Mwanza, Angel had been given fish all the time – fried, stewed, curried, grilled, dried, smoked, salted – and she had fed plenty of fish to Joseph and Vinas while they were growing. She had never before known anybody from the lake who did not want to eat it.

Esther signed herself with the holy cross. 'Please God when Kenneth and I have our children—'

'He needs to marry you first!' Irene reminded her.

'Yes, of course,' said Esther, adding quickly, 'and I'm not complaining about our long engagement—'

'Good!' declared Stella, reaching forward and slapping the coffee table loudly for emphasis.

'Yes,' agreed Fatima, the bright white of her smile highlighting the circles of white on her orange tie-dyed dress. 'Complaint-free tea, remember!'

'But I think we've done well so far?' Angel looked in the envelope while the others all nodded in agreement, smiling rather proudly at themselves.

The idea had come to the house this morning with Irene, worn out by the constant complaining of the daughter who lived at Irene's house together with Irene's three grandchildren, all of them busy picking up from their mother the habit of not finding anything quite good enough. Fatima had been quick to accept the idea because all that her husband ever did, now that he was retired and under her feet all day, was nag her to clear her large plastic tubs of dye away from every spare centimetre of their house, and nag her to reduce the network of washing lines laden with freshly tie-dyed cloth from at least their *front* yard. Esther, too, had been keen to try not complaining, wondering out loud whether it might not have been exactly the kind of challenge that Jesus had set for his disciples.

For Angel it had sounded like another good way to direct her mind towards her many blessings, an opportunity to talk of her surprise and joy at how enormously wide she had felt her heart opening for Lovemore when she had held the girl in her arms as she had wept that first night, an opportunity to talk about how relieved she continued to feel that she was managing – at least some of the time – not to see Joseph when she looked at the girl, not to show her any bad feelings or disappointments that were really about the girl's father. The ban on complaining also meant that she could focus on telling her friends how happy she was that Lovemore's friendship with her new sisters Grace and Faith had so far seemed easy enough, and how much Lovemore had gladdened Angel's heart by making such an effort to listen to her new brother Benedict.

But could Angel talk about how her new granddaughter seemed much more comfortable with Pius than with Angel herself? How could she do that without making it sound like she was complaining? Did she need to talk about it at all, though? Really, it was only to be expected. After all, Lovemore had had time to get used to her grandfather when it had been just the two of them on the flight here from Mwanza. In this house, Angel was just one member of this big new family that Lovemore was getting to know. Perhaps Lovemore would learn to become more comfortable with her after Pius left for Johannesburg tomorrow.

Irene's idea had put everybody into such a positive mood that

Fatima had suggested that maybe they could follow it not just today, but each and every time they met, and Stella – widow of one of Pius's oldest friends – had suggested that they should fine themselves for any complaints, and when there was enough, treat themselves to a nice lunch.

'But our lunch is far away, ladies,' Stella said now, fanning her face with her diary, the very diary that had triggered her first complaint and fine by being almost empty because she had less and less to do these days. 'We need more breaking of rules. Angel, I'm sure you can put more money in that envelope by telling us where Pius is travelling to. You don't like that he's going to travel.'

'Eh! Thin ice, Stella!' Leaning forward from across the coffee table, Irene laughed as she wagged a finger. 'Thin ice.'

'What?' Stella's pretence not to know what Irene was talking about was just that little bit too dramatic, and her smile was not quite straight. Angel made a note not to offer her any more tea in case she added even more of her medicine to it.

'And your late husband was Pius's best friend!' chided Esther.

'I only said it's nice that Angel has brought Pius back to us here in Dar es Salaam and I'll miss him when he leaves us from time to time.'

'Not *quite* the way you put it,' Irene sliced another small sliver from the cake, 'or you wouldn't have had to pay up.'

Stella folded her arms across her chest and, slumping back on the couch, declared, 'But good men are too few!'

'Complaint!' shouted somebody.

'Fine!' shouted all of the others.

Stella's mouth flew open in surprise at herself.

Laughing, Angel tapped her finger on their envelope where it rested on the coffee table, and Stella joined everybody's laughter as she dipped her head of white hair and scratched in her bag for her purse.

That night, after tying a scarf around her head to protect the pillow from the oil that she had applied to her hair, Angel settled into bed with her notebook. She had barely had time to open it when Pius came out of the washroom, his toothbrush still in his hand, and moved quickly to the small pile of papers resting on the pillow on his side of their bed. Placing the toothbrush in his mouth so that both of his hands were free to reach for and search through the pages, he furrowed his brow as he read. Then, holding a page motionless in his left hand, he hit it suddenly with the back of his right hand, rolling his eyes up towards the ceiling.

'Pius?'

Apparently not hearing her, he took the toothbrush from his mouth and headed towards the bedroom door shaking his head, the papers in one hand, his toothbrush in the other.

Angel said his name again, a little more loudly.

'*Eh?*' He turned round, and it seemed to Angel that he was surprised to see her there.

'Pius, what is it?'

Again he hit the papers with the back of his right hand, not seeming to notice that it held his toothbrush. 'I've left out an important factor. I must re-do this and re-print.' Clicking his tongue against the back of his teeth, he pulled open the door and disappeared down the dark, quiet passage with his toothbrush.

Angel re-plumped the pillow behind her back. Pius would be up till late at the computer again tonight. He was preparing for his first short consultancy, and it was an important one to him – not just because he wanted to shine so that others would rush to employ him to consult on other projects, but because it was to do with building the new African Union, the new organisation that was going to unite all of the countries in Africa. Angel herself had not yet managed to understand exactly how the new African Union was going to be different from the old Organisation of African Unity, but no doubt Pius would try to explain it to her when he had the time. He was certainly very excited about it. Angel had been anxious about him going to Johannesburg – South Africa had many guns and it was a violent country, especially for any other kind of African than a South African – but Pius had assured her that he would be safe. Just today a letter had come to him on the computer telling him about the security arrangements for all the meetings that he would be involved in, and he had showed it to Angel to ease her fears. She was still not entirely sure that he would be safe, but she decided to write in her notebook that she was grateful that there would be good security around him.

There were so many things that she could write about the lovely tea with her friends here this morning, but first she wanted to write something about the very dearest of her friends. Tomorrow Concilia would arrive back from a trip to South Africa where she was doing a degree by distance, and Concilia would be such a comfort to Angel with Pius away, a new grandchild to cope with, and a business that she needed to make busier so that she could supplement more to the family's income.

A visit from every one of Angel's other friends required her to set her work aside and to give them her full attention – both because their friendship was important and because chatting whilst working was unprofessional. But Concilia was different. Concilia felt more like family. She was younger than Angel's other friends – younger even than Angel's daughter Vinas would have been – and in the same way that Vinas had liked to do, Concilia loved to press a finger into a bowl that Angel had just finished with and to scrape it all the way round, collecting any last bits of batter or icing to pop into her mouth, all the while saying that she really shouldn't because she wanted to reduce. And Concilia was so easy to talk to about anything at all, and the perfect friend to have in your life if ever you were trying to cope with a problem. Angel had prayed every day for her to be safe in South Africa – on her own in that violent country, without any of the special security that Pius would have – and now she was very, *very* grateful that Concilia would be back tomorrow.

The next thing to go on Angel's list was something more about Pius. First thing this morning, before the ladies had come for tea, she had gone with him to the schoolbook shop that used to be a shop for sari fabric – the one where she had bought her notebook – and together they had picked out all the children's textbooks for this year. Just three sets of books, as the six children were very conveniently starting just three different school years: Moses and Daniel were together, as they had been from the start; Grace and Lovemore would be in the same class at secondary school; and for the first time ever, Benedict and Faith would be doing the same year, because Faith had fallen behind and needed to repeat. Faith was not happy, but she only had herself to blame. Okay, maybe Angel and Pius were to blame, too, for having disturbed her progress with a different education system in Rwanda and then another system in Swaziland, but Faith really did need to learn to pay more attention to her schoolwork. Perhaps being in class with Benedict would help. Anyway, it was certainly a blessing to the family's budget that only three sets of books needed paying for at the shop this morning. Angel had found herself holding her breath as Pius had removed a big wad of Tanzanian shillings from his pocket – much more money than Angel could comfortably carry in her brassiere, even if she used both cups – and counted out note after note at the till before the bookshop lady had re-counted each and every note. Only when the till drawer had opened with a loud ping and clatter had Angel finally exhaled. One more set of books would have deprived her of air for just too long, and Pius would surely have found her suddenly in a heavy pile of pink and blue *kitenge* cloth beside his feet.

She wrote now – again – that she was grateful for Pius, this time because he took such an active interest in the children's education. That was not something that could be said of every man in Tanzania, particularly when it came to the education of girls. Pius did not see educating a girl beyond primary school – or educating her at all – as a waste of money because she was simply going to marry into another family and become a mother. No. Even when their own daughter Vinas had been small, even back then, he had believed in the value of sending girls to school. How proud he had been when Vinas had qualified as a teacher!

But thinking about Vinas always made Angel sad, because Vinas was late and Angel still missed her terribly, even though it had been almost three years. She would need to find something else to think about, otherwise she would end up going to Pius in tears, and he would stand up from the computer and hold her, and in the end his eyes would be wet and he would be even more stressed about the work that she had interrupted. Taking a very deep breath, she paged back through her notebook and began to read through all the reasons to be grateful that were blessing her life. After a while, she looked up, a smile beginning to play across her lips as she thought of Pius and his toothbrush. He would leave it there, she thought, next to the computer, and reaching for it in the washroom tomorrow morning and finding it gone would spoil his whole day. Titi would find it next to the computer in the morning and not know what to think.

Giggling quietly to herself, Angel slid her notebook and pen into the drawer of her bedside cupboard and got out of bed, slipping her feet into her pair of *malapa*. Maybe Pius would be too busy to notice that she was there retrieving his toothbrush, but maybe – just maybe – he would notice her in her thin nightgown and decide that his work could wait until the morning.

The week before the school year begins, Benedict has his birthday turning eleven. Babu is away in Johannesburg helping with plans for the African Union, and Benedict is behaving like he is the boss of the whole family because he is the eldest boy. But Lovemore can see that he is disappointed that his grandfather is not there for his birthday, and she knows that it is because of her that Babu is away. She tries to make up for it by being especially nice to him, by letting him show her on the big map of Africa on the wall above Babu's desk exactly where Johannesburg is, and by drawing with him a pretend straight line between there and Dar es Salaam so that they can see that Babu's plane flew over parts of Mozambique, Malawi and Zimbabwe to get there. She even lets him tell her about his book from the library, a true story about a husband and wife who spent many years studying lions in Botswana.

Benedict has the same tall, thin shape as Grace, though Grace and Lovemore are both quite a bit taller. But Benedict is taller than Faith, even though he is younger than her, and Faith – being from a different mother *and* a different father – is a different shape entirely, much more like Bibi's kind of shape than Babu's.

There is no party for Benedict's birthday because eleven is not a special birthday. Ten is special because it is double figures, and thirteen is special because then you are a teenager. Only those birthdays can have parties here. Back home in Mwanza, Lovemore had a party for every single birthday, and so did Rose. But Benedict does not seem to mind very much that he cannot invite any friends. Maybe it is because his three older sisters and his two younger brothers are already enough people for a small party, or maybe it is because a party without his grandfather is no party at all.

Though none of Benedict's friends come for his birthday tea, one of Bibi's friends does come. After Titi opens the green gate to let a smart little blue car drive into the front yard and park next to the big old red microbus, Benedict opens the car door and waits while Bibi's friend gets out and leans her weight on a stick that she holds at her left side. It is not a wooden stick, but a silver one with a black rubber nose on its end and a ring at its top that she can slide part of her arm through so that her hand can hold on to the short bar that juts out to its side. It is not the kind of stick that you lean on if you are just old – and Bibi's friend does not look as old as Bibi or even as old as Mama – it is the kind of stick you need if you have something wrong. The head teacher back at Lovemore's old primary school, *Mwalimu Mkuu* Makubi, he had a stick just like it, and he was a polio, so Lovemore knows without anybody needing to tell her that Bibi's friend is a polio. That must be why she is hiding her legs in a trouser even though her buttocks are quite big and would look much better in a skirt. Otherwise she seems to know how to make the best of herself, because she has made herself look taller by wrapping her head in high swirls of cloth patterned in black and brown to match the rims of the glasses sitting on her nose.

Benedict shakes her hand. '*Karibu*, Concilia.'

'Happy birthday, Benedict!' Her voice is warm, friendly. 'Are you too grown up now for me to hug you?'

Bibi is in the doorway now. 'He's the man of the house, Concilia. Pius is in Johannesburg.'

'Aah! Your baba is away on your birthday? That is not good!' Concilia hugs Benedict, then she hugs Bibi and all the children, even Lovemore, and she tells Lovemore she is just Concilia because Auntie Concilia makes her feel old.

It is not a party, but it feels a bit like one. Titi makes tea for all of them, milky, spicy and much too sweet, and they eat big slices of chocolate cake with bright green icing.

Uncle Joseph never told Mama and Lovemore about Bibi's cake business because Uncle Joseph never knew. Bibi only started it after somebody shot him dead. The business is Bibi's way of earning money for the family now that she is the mother of her grandchildren. Customers can order any kind of cake at all from her, and they can look through her big photo albums full of pictures of cakes that she has already baked and decorated, some of them complicated, some of them funny, all of them beautiful.

But those kinds of cakes take a long time to make and decorate, and they are for Bibi's business. The cakes that Bibi makes for the family are much simpler, unless it is a special birthday or a very, very special occasion like welcoming Lovemore into the family. Benedict's birthday cake is simple and round with HAPPY BIRTHDAY BENEDICT piped in light blue on top of the bright green icing, and a birthday candle that plays the happy birthday tune when Bibi lights it.

Concilia has brought a birthday present for Benedict, a green T-shirt and two packets of seeds. When he takes Concilia out through the kitchen to see the vegetable garden that he is making in the bare yard at the back, Concilia takes Lovemore's hand and invites her to go with them.

'Ah, Benedict, you are so clever,' says Concilia, looking at the neat rows of bare soil. 'You must tell me if ever you have any produce to sell, I want to buy from you instead of going to the market.' She turns to Lovemore, giving her hand a small squeeze. 'I live near to here, it will be more convenient for me than the market.'

Benedict shows her the wall at the end of their yard. 'There used to be a fence there, Concilia, remember?'

'Ah, I remember the big dog!'

'Those people moved while we were away,' says Benedict. 'The new people built the wall.'

'Me, I fear big dogs,' says Concilia, shaking her head. 'How about you, Lovemore?'

'I fear all dogs, Auntie—'

'Ooh, you don't need to Auntie me, Lovemore! I told you I'm just Concilia.' Concilia squeezes Lovemore's hand again and laughs. 'You fear all dogs? Even small puppies?'

Lovemore shrugs. She has never seen a small puppy. 'I fear birds, too. *Eh*, I'm happy that nobody wanted to let Benedict have chickens!'

Benedict tried very hard to persuade Bibi and Babu to let him keep chickens in the yard. He worked out some sums that showed that it made more sense for him to keep chickens than for Bibi to buy eggs for her cakes and chickens for the family to eat from the market or the supermarket. But Bibi said no, she did not want the noise of chickens in the yard, and Titi said no, she did not want chickens messing on the washing hanging in the yard, and Babu said no, there was surely a law that said it was not right to keep farm animals in a suburb in the capital city. Benedict said Dar es Salaam was not really the capital city, Dodoma was, but Babu still said no. So Benedict is starting to grow vegetables instead.

He has marked off a piece of the yard for his garden, leaving plenty of space for Moses and Daniel to play with their football. But playing with their football is all that those two boys ever want to do, and they never want to help in Benedict's garden, even though he thinks that they should. There have been plenty of arguments about that.

'Vegetables are better than chickens,' Concilia says. 'You don't have to twist the neck of a carrot. A cabbage isn't going to run all over the yard after you cut off its head. Benedict, did you really want to be committing violence in your back yard?'

'Uh-uh.' A big shiver runs all the way down Benedict's body.

'You see? Vegetables are so much better. And you have made such an excellent garden. Now. Have you shown Lovemore where my number is written in your mama's book?'

They go inside, and Benedict shows Lovemore Concilia's name in the book next to the telephone-fax on Babu's desk, the book where Bibi writes down people's numbers. Concilia squeezes Lovemore's hand again as she tells her she is welcome to call her any time if ever she wants to talk to her about anything at all; her ears are always open for any Tungaraza. It is a landline number, so Lovemore does not bother putting it into Mama's old mobile phone. Mama used to let her phone Rose on it, but Bibi and Babu have a rule about children not talking on a mobile because their brains are still growing and something bad that comes from a mobile next to your ear can disturb a growing brain. Lovemore is only allowed to send SMS text messages to Rose, though every weekend they can talk to each other on the telephone-fax – but only for fifteen minutes if it is Lovemore's turn to phone, because Babu likes to count every Tanzanian shilling that everybody in this house ever spends. And with so many people in this house, there is never a time when nobody else is in the room, when nobody else can hear whatever Lovemore is saying to Rose.

Benedict chooses a programme about flamingos on TV, and Bibi makes everybody sit and watch it with him because it is his birthday. Lovemore does not want to look. Flamingos are big and frightening, even though the ones on the screen are on Lake Nakuru in Kenya and not in the back yard of the Tungarazas' house. Lovemore wishes that she could be in the bedroom reading some more of Mama's journal, or else at the computer on Babu's desk, practising her typing speed.

The computer is not new, but it is new in this house. Babu bought it so that he can keep in touch by email when he is away, and also because Lovemore and Grace will be doing Information and Communication Technology at school this year. Lovemore already knows how to use a computer because Mama taught her, and she can type much faster than Babu, who uses only six of his ten fingers and has to look at the keys. Grace, Faith and Benedict are learning slowly, but Moses and Daniel do not want to know. Those two are really only interested in things that they can kick, and they are not allowed to kick the computer. Bibi says that she is too old to learn something so new, and Titi says that she does not want to touch the computer except to dust it.

Lovemore pretends to be watching the flamingos, but she is looking instead at everything that is around the screen. The TV stands in the centre of a large cabinet. There are cupboards and drawers below it, while the space above it and to its left and right is divided into small compartments. A statue of Jesus stands in one of them, while the baby Jesus lies in Mary's arms in another. In one compartment there is a pile of photo albums, and several more compartments house framed photos of people in this family here and in the wider Tungaraza family in Bukoba, Bibi and Babu's home town on the western edge of Lake Victoria.

The flamingos rise suddenly from Lake Nakuru in a big surge of pink. Lovemore's heart begins to flutter like their wings, and she makes herself look further away from the screen so that she cannot see the birds even from the corner of her eye. On the wall to the left of the TV cabinet is a framed photo of Uncle Joseph and his sister Vinas, Bibi and Babu's only children, both of them late. Uncle Joseph – a young version of Babu – looks comfortably familiar, his smile friendly and warm. It is a long time since somebody shot him dead in his house, so it feels nice to see photos of him here, reminding Lovemore of knowing him and loving him when she was small. But Mama went into the ground outside Highway of Holiness only recently, and it would be just too painful to see photos of her mama on the walls here.

On the other side of the cabinet hangs a purple cloth with writing printed on it in white. The heading at the top is *Home Rules*, and underneath are teachings from the Bible. Lovemore decides to get her mind ready for the start of secondary school by trying to memorise the full list. There are only twelve, so it should be easy enough. She does not try to remember where in the Bible each of the teachings comes from, though she is certain that she could, without the noise of the TV disturbing her concentration. *Always be honest. Count your blessings. Bear each other's burdens. Forgive and forget. Be kind and tender hearted. Comfort one another.* When Lovemore has those first six committed to memory, she moves on to the last six. *Keep your promises. Be supportive of one another. Be true to each other. Look after each other. Treat your friend like you treat yourself. Love one another deeply from the heart.* With all of them memorised, she decides to make a start on learning where the teachings come from, starting at the bottom and working her way up. The last one is from two places, Peter and Corinthians, but the numbers of the chapters and verses put her off. Numbers never want to stay in her mind for long.

Lovemore is suddenly aware that her hands feel empty, idle. For a moment she thinks that she should take up knitting, like Rose's bibi, so that the time she spends doing nothing in front of the TV here is not completely wasted. But school will begin soon, and then there will be no time for knitting, and no time for TV.

She glances over at Bibi and Concilia, who are so deeply involved in a conversation at the dining table that they probably do not even know that a programme about flamingos is on the TV or that six children are in the room watching it. Seeing them together makes Lovemore miss Rose and all their shared talk and laughter. She looks at Grace and Faith, who are managing to find the flamingos interesting by commenting to each other about which one of the birds is the right shade of pink to go well with their different outfits. Lovemore longs to be part of their easy friendship, but she does not know the outfits they are talking about, and she does not want to look at the pink birds on the screen. Moses and Daniel are slumped back, half asleep, but Benedict's eyes are wide and bright.

Lovemore recognises that she is missing Babu, that she would love to be listening to one of his lessons right now. Not for the lesson itself or for anything that he might be saying, but just for the sound of Uncle Joseph in his voice, just for the look of Uncle Joseph in his face as he speaks. The things inside her box inside her suitcase under her bed, the things she cannot find any time alone to look at, those things and Uncle Joseph's voice in Babu's mouth are all that she has here of her old life back home in Mwanza.

She wishes that she could be busy listening to one of Auntie Agrippina's cassettes while she and Mama piece together a jigsaw puzzle, one with a picture of somewhere far away. Somewhere like New York, where an enormous statue holds up a torch way bigger than the Uhuru torch that was lit on top of Mount Kilimanjaro at Tanzania's independence. Or maybe Italy, where taxis are boats that men power with poles. Or maybe Germany, where people live in big castles. Or even Egypt, where women are beautiful and they wear many jewels and have many servants.

Right now, Lovemore would rather be almost anywhere else than here.

Chapter 4

Babu is at last due back from Johannesburg, and while they wait for the taxi to bring him home from the airport, Grace and Faith spend time trying to guess what gift he will bring for them.

'Something with beads,' Faith suggests, making a loop with her hand down from one side of her neck and up again to the other side. 'South Africa has nice beadwork.'

'But beads are not necessary,' says Grace. 'Have you ever known him to buy us something that is not necessary?'

'Ah, true.' Faith nods. 'Maybe clothes? Johannesburg has nice fashions.'

'Yes! Clothes!'

Lovemore joins in. 'We just got clothes. We just got our school uniforms for tomorrow.'

Grace laughs. 'School uniforms are not *clothes*!'

'No?'

Faith is laughing, too. 'No. They are school uniforms!'

School uniforms are things to wear. They are definitely clothes. But Lovemore says nothing. She is sitting on her bed, writing TUNGARAZA inside each of the new textbooks for Form One that Grace and Lovemore are going to share. Rose and Lovemore could easily have shared some of their textbooks all the way through primary, but Mama bought Lovemore her own full set each and every year. Mama always wanted everything in the world for Lovemore because Lovemore was always everything in the world to Mama.

Sprawled lazily on her own bed, Grace makes another suggestion. 'How about books? For sure he thinks books are necessary.'

'Yes,' says Faith, who is sitting on her hands on the edge of Grace's bed, kicking her feet up and down. 'Probably we'll get books.'

'We just got books,' Lovemore points out. 'We just got all our schoolbooks.'

Grace and Faith both laugh. 'Schoolbooks are not *books*, Lovemore!'

'No?'

'No!'

Schoolbooks have pages and words to read. They are definitely books. But Lovemore says nothing. Some days have been less difficult, but today the loss of her mama is weighing on her particularly heavily, and she would rather focus on what her mama wrote to her in the note taped inside the cover of her journal: *I loved you with all my heart since I first held you in my arms, and so did Joseph.* The gift that Lovemore most wants Babu to bring back from South Africa is his voice, which will remind her of Uncle Joseph holding her – and loving her with all his heart – when she was small.

A hoot sounds outside the gate, and Grace and Faith rush to get to the front yard. Titi opens the big green gate to let Babu in, shaking his hand with a quick, shy curtsy.

'*Karibu*, Uncle.' Closing the gate, she takes his suitcase from him.

'*Asante*, Titi.'

The boys reach Babu ahead of the girls. Benedict tries simply shaking his hand, but in no time at all he is clinging on to him together with Moses and Daniel. Caught up in all the excitement, Lovemore joins Grace and Faith in hugging him, too. Inside, Bibi reaches up to embrace him with her plastic icing syringe still in her hand: she is busy finishing off a cake for a customer who will collect it this evening.

There is tea and cake, but Babu asks Titi to make him a cup of Tanica instead, black. It is the same brand of coffee that Uncle Joseph used to drink, coffee from the Tungarazas' home town of Bukoba.

'*Eh*, Angel,' Babu says to Bibi, rubbing his stomach, 'a hotel buffet is a dangerous thing! You can pile your plate, then you can return and pile your plate again. Day after day! Now I need to stay away from milk and sugar.'

But he eats one of the cupcakes that Bibi has made, vanilla with some of the dark blue icing that she is using on part of her customer's cake. Bibi continues to work on that cake at the dining table while the rest of the family sit on the couches to have their tea. Babu tells them about the work that he did in South Africa, and Lovemore watches his

Uncle-Joseph gestures and listens to his Uncle-Joseph voice without even trying to concentrate on his words. Slowly the boys drift outside, first Moses and Daniel, and then Benedict.

Grace lets Babu continue for a while before she interrupts. 'Baba, what did you bring for us?' Her eyes are bright with excitement.

Even now, it still works on Lovemore's ears like a carrot on a grater to hear Babu's grandchildren calling him *Baba*. *Babu* she says silently in her head. *Babu* with a *u* at the end, not *Baba* with an *a*. He is our grandfather, not our father.

'Ah. Now.' Babu sits forward on the couch. 'You have not asked me *if* I brought you something, you have asked me *what* I have brought you. That means you suppose that I have definitely brought you something. Am I right?'

Grace and Faith both nod their heads yes, but Lovemore can see that doubt is beginning to seep into Grace's excitement.

'Well, you are in luck!' declares Babu. 'I *have* brought you a gift, the most precious gift there is.'

'Diamonds!' says Grace, her eyes shining again.

Babu shakes his head no. 'More precious.'

'Gold?' Faith looks like she is daring to hope for something unnecessary.

'More precious than that.'

'What, Baba? What?'

'Lovemore, can you guess?'

Lovemore shakes her head no. She cannot imagine a man who drives a rusty old microbus having anything very precious to give, other than the echo of his son in his voice.

'Is it in your suitcase, Baba?' Faith jumps up from the couch. 'Should I fetch it?'

'No, no, no.' Babu drinks the last of his Tanica, making the girls wait. 'The most precious thing is not any kind of object. No. It is *wisdom*.'

'*Wisdom?*' Grace looks like the word has slapped her face. Faith looks like she might be on the verge of tears. Lovemore wonders if she should try to comfort both of them with hugs.

'Yes. Wisdom. That is the most precious gift that a man can give. And beside to that, it does not take up any space in a man's suitcase, it does not add to its weight. I have brought a piece of South African wisdom for you to learn from. It is this...' Babu puts down his empty cup and clears his throat. 'If you are looking for a fly in your food, it means that you are full.'

'What?' Disappointment has flooded into Grace's voice.

Lovemore is already resigned to the fact that Babu is not the rich man that he was supposed to be. She feels nothing that he has brought them a gift that she cannot hold in her hands, that she cannot photograph for Rose to see.

'What does it mean, Baba?' Faith whines like a much younger child.

'Ah, that is for you to work out. *Eh*, Angel,' Babu looks across the room at Bibi, patting his belly, 'I should have looked for a fly!'

Looking up from decorating her cake, Bibi smiles at him. Lovemore can see the love for her husband in Bibi's eyes, and again Lovemore is aware that it is because of her that he was away.

Out of all the things that Mama told Lovemore to expect, only two are right. The flushing toilet is one, and the other is the good secondary school that is going to help Lovemore to do well enough for university. The school is for girls only, and only Grace and Lovemore are going because Faith is still doing primary and she has to go to the same school as their brothers.

In the first week of school, Grace keeps telling Lovemore how happy she is to be starting secondary with a sister, though Lovemore knows that the sister Grace would rather be starting with is her best friend Faith, and Lovemore keeps telling Grace how happy it makes her, too, though really it would be much nicer to be starting secondary with her best friend Rose. But that would mean being in Mwanza still, and Mwanza is further away from a flight to far away.

Of course, if Lovemore were in Mwanza still and if nothing had happened to her mama, Auntie Agrippina would have taken her photo with her mama on the first day, then her mama would have taken Rose's photo with Auntie Agrippina, and when their photo was printed Mama would have written on the back with a pencil, *Lovemore's first day of secondary school*. Sometimes it used to be Uncle Joseph taking those kinds of photos, but after somebody shot him dead it was always

Auntie Agrippina.

Grace is not Rose, but she turns out to be a good sister to be starting secondary with after all. Four of the girls there went to the same primary as Grace, so Grace already has friends, which means that there are already girls for Lovemore to speak to. And as soon as all the other girls in the class find out that Grace is international, that she has already lived a year in Rwanda and another year in Swaziland because of Babu's work, most of them want to be Grace's friend. Lovemore thinks maybe it is because being the friend of an international girl makes them mind a little less that their parents are not rich enough to send them to the International School on Msasani Peninsula, the best part of Dar es Salaam. Anyway, thinking of herself as international gives Grace plenty of confidence, which helps Lovemore to feel more confident herself.

She was confident enough starting primary school because she and Rose were friends even before Standard One, and then when they started school Auntie Agrippina was their *mwalimu*, their teacher. They had to remember to call her *Mwalimu* Mahingila, though, because if ever Rose made a slip and called her Mama, or if ever Lovemore made a slip and called her Auntie Agrippina, the other children laughed at them. But when they passed their Standard One and graduated to Standard Two, they got a different teacher and that problem went away.

Now Lovemore is in Form One with Grace, there is a different teacher for every subject, and there is nobody for Lovemore to make a slip and call Auntie. There is nobody for her to call Mama either, but she tries not to think about that too much. She does not want to embarrass herself with tears in front of all the other girls.

It is not the International School on Msasani Peninsula, but they do have two international teachers, teachers who need to be called *Madame* and *Miss* rather than *Mwalimu*. Their French teacher *Madame* Lumumba is from Congo, but *Madame* Lumumba's Congo is just like Grace's Rwanda and Swaziland. African international is not the same as world international, and cities like Brazzaville or Kigali or Mbabane are not the same as New York.

Their only truly international teacher is from far away in England.

Miss Brown is not like her name, she is a *Mzungu*, a white person, and she is just as new to Dar es Salaam as Lovemore is. She is tall and thin, but not like a model: her shoulders hunch forwards instead of down and back, and she looks up at the girls from a head that is always bent low, though if she were to hold it high and proud, her height would mean that she looked down on them all. Holding her head low means that the bits of her light brown hair that cannot reach as far as the elastic holding the rest of it back, those bits keep falling forwards from where they are tucked behind her ears.

Very early in the term Miss Brown has the class explore their own histories by making a diagram of their family as far back as they know. Miss Brown knows her family as far back as her great grandparents, and she draws it on the board so that everybody can see how to draw the lines that show how her great grandfather was married to her great grandmother and together they were the parents of her grandmother. All the way down from her grandmother, sideways lines connect parents and downward lines show their children, until there is Miss Brown, who does not yet have a husband or a child.

Then each girl has to draw her own diagram, except Lovemore and Grace can work together because they have the same family, and Magdalena and Mary work together, too, because they are cousins. Lovemore knows only her mother, her father, and the grandparents she lives with now, the parents of her father, Uncle Joseph. Of course, there are Philbert and Sigsbert, too, the cousins on her mother's side who lived with her and Mama in Mwanza, but Mama always said those two were so far distant that they were hardly family at all. Not knowing how she could possibly make them belong on the diagram, Lovemore decides simply to leave them out. There is nobody else she knows on her mother's side, but Grace knows all of Bibi and Babu's cousins and aunts and uncles back in their home town of Bukoba, further west around the edge of the lake from Mwanza.

When their time is up and Miss Brown asks who would like to come and draw their diagram on the board for the class, Grace shoots her hand up without even asking Lovemore, and they both have to go up to the front. Miss Brown looks at their paper with all of its names, then she looks at her watch and says they should just go from their grandparents up to now. Then she puts the other girls in pairs to tell each other about the people in their own diagrams until Lovemore and Grace have finished drawing lines and writing names on the board.

Grace begins. 'These are grandparents,' she says, pointing. 'Pius Tungaraza is married to Angel Tungaraza. They had these two children, Vinas and Joseph. Here you can see that their son Joseph Tungaraza married Evelina Wambali, and they had three children. Me, Benedict and Moses.'

Lovemore continues. 'This same Joseph Tungaraza,' she says, pointing, and then she hesitates. 'Miss Brown, I don't know how I must say. He didn't marry this Glory Lutabana. Can I just say that Joseph Tungaraza and Glory Lutabana had one child together?' Miss Brown nods, the nod dislodging some of the hair that is tucked behind her ears. 'Their child together is Josephine Lovemore Lutabana. That is me.'

Then Grace takes over. 'This Vinas Tungaraza here,' she says, pointing, 'the daughter of these Pius and Angel Tungaraza, she married somebody, but we put a question mark because we don't know his name.'

Miss Brown says a question mark is fine if any girl does not know a name, and they can always ask somebody in their family later on. Lovemore thinks about all the question marks she would have to put for her mama's parents and brothers or sisters. There is nobody she can ask about those names now.

'Okay, so Vinas Tungaraza and her husband,' Grace points to the question mark, 'they had these two children here, Faith and Daniel.'

Mama never told Lovemore to expect Faith and Daniel to be part of Bibi and Babu's household, because Uncle Joseph never told Mama. Uncle Joseph never knew, because they came only after robbers shot him dead.

Miss Brown says they have done very well, and does anybody have any questions? None of the girls has a question, so Miss Brown says she has some of her own.

'So you two had the same father but different mothers. What does that make you? To each other?'

'Sisters,' says Grace, without even thinking.

'Lovemore?'

'I think we are half-sisters, *Mwalimu*.'
'Miss.'
'*Eh*, sorry. Miss.' Lovemore has never called a teacher anything other than *Mwalimu*, except for when she made a slip back in Standard One and called *Mwalimu* Mahingila Auntie Agrippina.
'Very good. Do you see that Grace?'
Grace says nothing.
'And Grace, that girl Faith. What are you two to each other?'
'Sisters.'
Miss Brown clicks her tongue against the back of her teeth and looks at the class. 'Anybody? Magdalena?'
'They're cousins, Miss.'
'Good. Who can explain why? Mary?'
'Grace's father Joseph and Faith's mother Vinas, they are brother and sister. Grace and Faith are cousins like me and Magdalena.'
'Excellent. Do you see that, Grace?'
Grace says nothing.
'Okay. How about Faith's brother Daniel. What is he to you, Grace?'
'He is my brother.'
Miss Brown frowns, tucking her hair back behind her ears, and some of the girls begin to giggle behind their hands. Lovemore wants to giggle herself, but she is standing right at the front. She knows that Grace must be trying to be funny on purpose. All these family things you learn already in primary, and Babu told Lovemore that Grace was in the top five all the way through primary.
'Grace, let's review,' says Miss Brown, looking at their diagram on the board and taking a deep breath. 'Let's begin with something very simple. Tell us the name of your mother.'
'Angel Tungaraza,' says Grace, pointing to Bibi's name on the board.
Miss Brown's hands fly up to her ears even though there is no hair needing to be tucked back, and the girls do not even try to hide their laughter behind their hands. Standing next to Grace, Lovemore bites down on her lower lip to stop a laugh from bursting out of her.
'Come on, Grace, be serious! Can't you see that Angel Tungaraza is your grandmother?'
'No, Miss.'

'No?' Miss Brown's pink cheeks are becoming red. 'But how can you be so confused?'

'I am not confused, Miss. Angel and Pius Tungaraza are my parents. They used to be my grandparents but now they are my parents. These two here,' Grace picks up a piece of chalk and crosses a line through Joseph Tungaraza and Evelina Wambali, 'they used to be my parents, but now they are late.' Grace continues crossing a chalk line through other names as she speaks, and Lovemore closes her eyes tight as the chalk cancels out her mama. 'This Glory Lutabana is late. This Vinas Tungaraza is late. This somebody who was Vinas Tungaraza's husband is maybe late, too, but we don't know, he went away a long time ago. This whole row of parents is no longer there. We all have new parents now, these Pius Tungaraza and Angel Tungaraza. All of us used to be their grandchildren but now we are all their children, we are all brothers and sisters in their house.'

'Miss Brown,' says one of the girls, 'my aunt used to be my aunt but now she is my mother.'

'My big sister is my mother now,' says another girl.

'My cousin's older brother is his father now.'

'My aunt didn't know that her big sister was really her mother.'

'I've already had two fathers. Maybe I'm still going to get another one.'

'My father is late, Miss, so now my father's brother is my father.'

Lovemore joins in. 'I always used to call my father Uncle, Miss. I knew he wasn't my uncle, I called him Uncle Joseph for respect, but I didn't know he was my father.'

Miss Brown's face is now very red. She claps her hands together and says that is enough, and can they perhaps all agree that families can sometimes be complicated? Grace says that families can also be simple, but she says it with a big smile, so Miss Brown does not think that Grace is arguing.

That is how Grace is, it is how she sees things. It is like she is choosing to put a jigsaw puzzle together with all the pieces face down. It does not matter to her what the picture on the other side actually shows; if the pieces fit together, even if not very well, it is fine with her. And if some pieces are missing, she does not seem to mind. But Lovemore prefers to see the real picture, with all the pieces linking together neatly and properly. If a piece is lost and it leaves an empty space – like her mama – the picture just cannot be beautiful. And she certainly cannot fill the empty space with the wrong piece and pretend that everything is fine. Calling her half-siblings and cousins her brothers and sisters does not bother her at all – she and her friend Rose often used to call each other *sister* and Rose's big sister Lulu used to be like a big sister to Lovemore – but Mama is always going to be her mama, and nobody else can ever be. Not Bibi, not anybody.

It was late and Angel was extremely tired, but she could not bring herself to close the door of her wardrobe and climb into bed with her notebook to begin the task of writing today's list. Her feet in their *malapa* seemed to have grown roots, anchoring her to the floor, making it impossible for her even to turn round, to turn her back on the true masterpiece resting on one of the wardrobe's shelves.

Eh, she was so proud of this cake! And not just of the cake itself: she was also extremely impressed with the way that she had managed to keep the whole of it secret. Grace and Lovemore knew that she had been baking something special for their combined birthday party – of course they knew – but they had not managed to discover anything about it. Neither Titi nor Angel had let a single detail slip from their mouths, and Angel had managed to keep every bit of it hidden.

Okay, not *every* bit. Her excellent real-size sugar-paste sunglasses had been on a plate in the kitchen when Benedict had surprised her by coming back in just seconds after he had gone out to work in his garden – really, what kind of child wanted to wash his hands *before* plunging them into soil and mud? – but she had been quick enough to slide the sunglasses off the plate and onto the kitchen counter, so that when Benedict's glance had taken them in, he had seen them as real sunglasses, not just pretend ones for on a cake.

Angel's outstanding sugar-paste mobile phone – silver and black with bright green buttons – looked so real that it had fooled even Angel herself as soon as she had completed it. When her own phone had rung, the one she had just made was halfway to her ear, her other hand reaching for the blue sugar-paste pen she had crafted earlier, before Titi had shouted, '*Auntie!*' It had taken a long time for the two of them to be able to look at each other without bursting out in laughter at that mistake! *Eh!*

Nobody but Titi had seen Angel's superb open lipstick – bright red where it protruded from the end of the gold tube, black at its base – or her small bottle of nail polish – the same bright red as the lipstick, with a white top. In truth, the last of these had not turned out quite as well as the other pieces, because Angel had really battled to make it look like the polish was inside a bottle – but now that it was in its place amongst the other pieces on the cake board, it would certainly do. Choosing what pieces to make had been easy enough, because everybody knew that a teenager girl would carry around in her handbag exactly what she carried around in her head, except for boys.

The handbag itself was exquisite, and looking at it there on the cake board on the shelf inside her wardrobe, Angel could not help smiling very widely indeed at the quality of her work. She had baked it yesterday morning while the children had been at school, working on its intricate icing over the past two nights when they had all been in bed. It was only in the past half hour that she had finally finished the whole of it and slid it away into the cupboard where it had been secretly hiding from the world.

Pius's clothes from that shelf had been in a large plastic bag on top of the wardrobe, out of the way of small eyes. Angel could not simply leave the cake – or a pile of Pius's clothes – on top of the chest of drawers, because although the children knew that their grandparents' bedroom was private, it was still possible for one of them – usually Moses or Daniel – to come in there at night in tears, if Benedict had not been able to give enough comfort himself for the smaller boy to go back to sleep.

Thinking of a boy needing to go back to sleep made Angel yawn. Aware that she must still write tonight's list of five things in her notebook, she began, reluctantly, to swing the wardrobe door shut. But as she did so, the mirror on the inside of the door showed her the reflection of her back view in the mirror on the opposite wall. *Eh*, even her nightgown was beginning to strain across her hips now! That was definitely not something that she could feel any gratitude for.

Nor was she at all grateful that tonight she must be alone in the bed once again.

When Lovemore and Grace have the party for their birthday turning thirteen, Babu is away in Kenya, where he is organising a conference for the whole of East Africa. In charge again, Benedict has made sure that everybody has done their tasks on his list so that the party can go well. Bibi's friend Concilia is the first to arrive, and Benedict makes a point of showing her on the big map of Africa on the wall above Babu's desk exactly where Kenya is, even though everybody in Tanzania already knows that Kenya is Tanzania's neighbour to the north. But Concilia looks without rolling her eyes behind her glasses, and she thanks Benedict for showing her. Then she asks Benedict to show Lovemore on his map of Dar es Salaam where to find Concilia's house, and how to get there from the Tungarazas' house. Sure that Concilia just wants to escape from Benedict, Lovemore helps her – and Benedict – by looking carefully at his map, watching his finger trace the way.

There are boys at the party. Magdalena and Mary bring their cousin brother, Fenella has come with her older brother as well as her younger brother who is at school with Benedict and Faith, and Prisca is there with her brother and his friend Dickson, who has brought a guitar. Lovemore knows those four girls from school, and then there are a few more that Grace and Faith know from before they went away from Tanzania for Babu's work, but now they are at different schools.

Because there are boys, some of the girls spend time in the girls' bedroom applying lipstick and deodorant, and checking themselves in the full-length mirror in the girls' washroom. Lovemore lingers in the bedroom with them, anxious that nobody should pull her suitcase out from under her bed and try to break in to it.

'Have you heard?' the one called Veronica asks Grace in a whisper, looking round to make sure that all the girls in the room are listening.

'What?'

'About Scholastica!'

The one called Zawadi opens her mouth wide and sucks in a big breath. 'Oh my God. Scholastica!'

Lovemore asks who Scholastica is, and somebody tells her that Scholastica is Euphrasia's sister, which means nothing to Lovemore, as she does not know who Euphrasia is.

Grace helps her. 'Euphrasia was in our class at primary. Scholastica is her big sister, maybe in Form Two this year.' She turns to Veronica and Zawadi. 'What about her.'

'*Pregnant!*' declares Zawadi, making Magdalena suck in her breath.

'You never told us!' says Mary.

Grace's eyebrows seem very high up on her forehead. 'When? Who? I mean—'

'*Dickson!*'

Prisca tries to put a hand over Veronica's mouth. '*Shh!* We don't know!'

Magdalena's voice is a tiny whisper as she points to somewhere beyond the girls' room. 'You mean *this* Dickson? The one who is here?'

Prisca nods. 'My brother's friend.'

Lovemore is suddenly aware that all of the girls have come together in a tight circle, and that she, too, is part of it, though she does not know the girl they are talking about. Trying to feel that she belongs in that circle, she asks a question.

'Are they getting married?'

'Ah, no,' says Prisca. 'Dickson has not confessed. Maybe it is some other boy.'

'Scholastica's father has sent her away,' says Zawadi. 'She's gone to an aunt in a village somewhere, we don't even know where.'

'But it's land where they grow pyrethrum,' says Veronica, 'we know that. After her baby comes she's going to put it on her back and work the fields.'

'*Eh!*' Faith looks truly shocked. 'But she was always clever! She was going to be a doctor!'

'What about the boy?' Lovemore asks, trying to be part of the girls' excitement, but not managing to feel it because they are not her friends, not her and Rose's friends.

'Dickson?'

'*Shh!*' Again Prisca tries to cover Veronica's mouth. 'We don't know it's him! It's just a rumour!'

Veronica pushes Prisca's hand away. 'Why can't I say it's Dickson? Do you know different?' Then she opens her mouth wide, covering it herself. 'Is it your brother?'

'No! Stop it, Veronica!'

'But they are both still at school?' Mary asks. 'Dickson and your brother?'

'Yes.'

'Maybe the boy loved her,' Grace suggests, 'and now she's far away. Maybe his heart is in pieces.' Some of the girls tilt their heads sadly, while others roll their eyes. Grace continues. 'Let us go and look at this Dickson—'

'*Shh!*'

'Not forgetting Prisca's brother—'

Prisca covers Veronica's mouth again.

'Girls,' Grace tries again, 'let us go and look for any signs of a broken heart in any boy!'

The girls make their way back into the lounge in a cloud of deodorant, their lips stained red, and Lovemore finds herself thinking about Babu. She has known him for only a short time, but she already knows him well enough to be sure that the story about Scholastica would make him nervous. He does not like that he is not here for their birthday turning thirteen – he phoned early this morning and Grace and Faith pressed the speaker button on the telephone-fax so that they could both talk to him at the same time – and he does not like that he is going to be away a lot while they are growing. It is why he is sending them to a school for girls only, so that they can be safe from boys.

Babu does not have to worry about Lovemore and boys. She is not going to bother with a boyfriend until she is a lawyer in New York and she can have her destiny of a man from outside of Africa. Until that time, she will focus on working hard to get there, and she does not want any distractions from Mama's goal for her. Grace, on the other hand, is an easy kind of girl to distract. She does not even have a goal yet, she does not know what she wants to be in her life. She is not even working hard at school, because she does not really have to.

Sitting around doing nothing does not bother Grace at all.

Lovemore worries for Grace's future in life, wishing that she could help her sister by lending her one of Auntie Agrippina's cassettes, the one about finding your path. If your mama has not already told you your path, then you have to look inside your heart to find it. But Grace has not even thought to look there yet.

Their birthday turning thirteen is very special because now they are teenagers, so Bibi has made one of her special cakes from her business. It looks exactly like a tipped-over handbag lying on its side with things tumbling out of it. The handbag itself is bright pink and quilted into diamond shapes with small, silvery-white stitches. It is the kind of bag that can stand up by itself, so the smooth oblong base of it – which shows now that it is lying on its side – has a round silver stud at each corner. It lies slightly open, its pink handles falling across the light blue of the cake board, and tumbling out of it on to that same light blue are a number things, all of them made from sugar: a lipstick, a pair of sunglasses, a phone, a nail polish, an earring, a pen. There is also a necklace made up of white beads – Bibi calls them pearls – and the necklace has broken, sending beads rolling all over the cake board. Thirteen of those loose beads each carry a white candle.

Eh, the cake is too beautiful! Lovemore does not want to cut it, but Grace says they must because when you cut your birthday cake you can make a wish, and if you do not tell anybody what it is that you are wishing for, your wish is going to come true. All the way through blowing out the candles with Grace and listening to everybody singing the happy birthday song for them, Lovemore wonders what she should wish for. She wants Mama back, but wishes cannot do that and nor can prayers. Wishes cannot make Rose a guest at the party either, nor can they add another bedroom to the house just for Lovemore. When she and Grace both hold the knife and sink it into the pink quilting of the handbag, she cannot help wishing for private time alone with Mama's journal, even though she knows it is a waste of a wish.

When Grace gives Prisca's brother his piece of cake, she stands talking to him for a long time, forgetting completely that she and Lovemore are supposed to be serving their cake together, so Lovemore is left to do it all by herself. And then Grace sits giggling with Faith behind their hands about Dickson, leaving Lovemore and Titi to go around with the crate of sodas making sure that everybody has. And when Dickson plays his guitar while Prisca's brother sings, Grace sways her body, clapping the beat above her head to make both of the boys look at her. Bibi does not notice – she and Concilia are busy with a long conversation – but Babu would notice, and he would be very nervous.

The day that Babu gets back from Kenya, Lovemore enjoys having tea with him and Bibi after school. He has brought some wisdom from Kenya for them, wisdom that says that talking with one another is loving one another. Babu says that each of them will know what it means, and Lovemore has an idea from listening to Auntie Agrippina's cassettes that it is about loving each other enough to listen completely and tell things honestly. Grace must think that it means something else, because she shows Babu photos of their birthday party, but only the ones without boys. The rest are in the photo album that Concilia gave her for her birthday turning thirteen. Concilia gave Lovemore a photo album, too, and if Lovemore ever gets some private time alone, she is going to fill it with the photos from Mama that are in the box inside her suitcase under her bed.

Teatime has to be short because Babu needs to get on with using the computer and the telephone-fax for his report on the conference, Bibi needs to get back to mixing in the kitchen, and Lovemore and Grace need to get down to their homework, even if their teachers have not given them very much. Lovemore already knows about spending time at home going over the day's classwork: Uncle Joseph always used to say it was how you grew up to be somebody important. Lovemore knows that it works because Uncle Joseph grew up to be the Manager of Nile Perch Plastics in Mwanza, and his sister Vinas grew up to be Deputy to the Head Teacher, the *mwalimu mkuu*, at a school in Arusha. Nobody ever told Mama about going over her classwork at home, so she only got as far as being Uncle Joseph's Personal Assistant, but Lovemore is going to grow up to be somebody more important than even Uncle Joseph, so she needs to spend more time than anybody else on going over her classwork.

Faith and the boys got back from their school earlier, and they are already out of their uniforms, sitting around the coffee table on the four low stools that pull out from under it, busy with their books. Cakes are cooling on the dining table, so Lovemore and Grace take their schoolbags to their room, change out of their uniforms and sit cross-legged on their beds to work. It is not very long before Grace's thumbs are busy on the keypad of Mama's old mobile phone, which Grace and Lovemore now share.

'Are you not working, Grace?'

'I am! I'm doing these signs for things that are dangerous.'

'But you're using the phone.'

'Yes! I'm telling Prisca that her brother's friend Dickson shouldn't have a tattoo of a skull with two bones crossed underneath. Did you see it?' Grace rubs the top part of her right arm. 'Under his sleeve.'

'*Eh!* He took off his shirt?'

'Uh-uh, he pushed up his sleeve and showed me. Prisca's brother told me it was there but I didn't believe. So I'm telling her Dickson shouldn't have it.'

'And his tattoo is your business because why?'

Grace taps on the page of their chemistry textbook. 'It means he's toxic.'

Lovemore smiles. 'Be serious, Grace.'

'I *am* being serious!' Her thumbs are busy on the keypad. 'I'm telling her he should rather have the flames.'

'For flammable?' Lovemore already knows some of the danger signs in their schoolbook from Nile Perch Plastics. Grace must have been there, too, but maybe she looked more at the men working in the factory than at any of the signs.

'Is he not hot?' Grace puts down the phone and fans her face with her hand. 'Did you not feel like your face might be on fire when you stood next to him?'

'*Eh*, Grace!'

Grace licks a finger and touches it to her cheek. '*Tsss!*' she says, sounding like a bowl of chopped onions being emptied into a pan of hot oil.

Lovemore decides that it is time to use the new wisdom that Babu has just given them, that it is time to love her new sister by talking with her. She tells Grace that she is worth more than a boy like Dickson, a boy who may already have spoiled another girl's life by making her pregnant and getting her sent out from her home as well as from school.

'But he's hot!' says Grace.

Lovemore does not give up. She tells Grace that she deserves somebody better than Dickson as her boyfriend, somebody who will respect her and love her nicely. She tells her as many things as she can remember from Auntie Agrippina's cassettes that might help Grace not to settle for less.

Then a message comes through to Mama's old phone from Prisca, and Grace's attention is gone.

Lovemore tries to go back to her books, but she can hear Grace's thumbs on the keypad again.

'Grace, concentrate! We have homework!'

Grace is sighing loudly when Titi passes through their room with some freshly ironed T-shirts to put on the shelves in their washroom, and Grace asks her if Faith is still doing homework in the lounge. Titi says they are all still busy.

'Only because Baba is here,' says Grace. 'He's working in that room, so they can't go outside or watch TV. Titi, will you come and tell us when they finish?'

Lovemore's eyes are on their geography book, but she can feel Titi's eyes on her.

'I don't want to disturb.'

'*Eh*, there's disturbing and there's rescuing, Titi. Please rescue us when it's safe!'

Lovemore hears the soft padding of Titi's bare feet as she leaves, and then the quiet click of the phone's keyboard again. She tries her best to concentrate on memorising the picture of the solar energy flow. It shows sunlight hitting different plants and trees and the sun's energy being transferred to different animals when the plants become the animals' food. The picture has many arrows, and it is important to remember all of them and what each of them means.

It is bad enough having to share a room with Grace, and sharing books with her is even worse. Grace is clever – much more clever than Lovemore – but she is not somebody who respects books and learning; her mama cannot have listened to Uncle Joseph in the same way that Lovemore's mama did.

At last Titi comes to tell Grace that Babu is going to help Benedict with something in the garden, so Faith is switching on the TV. Grace is out of the door before Titi has even finished saying it. Lovemore feels a small flood of relief and excitement. With the girls only just sitting down in front of the TV and unlikely to get bored straight away, this might at last be a good time.

Closing the bedroom door quietly, she kneels in front of her bed and pulls out her suitcase. The key on the shoelace around her neck slips quickly into the small gold padlock on the front, the two sides of the zip whizz apart, and the box is in her hands. She hesitates for a moment. Is this the right time to put the photos into her album from Concilia? Or should she try to read more of Mama's journal and letter to her?

She knows that if she had tried really very extremely hard, she could maybe possibly perhaps have found a private moment before now to look in Mama's journal again. She wants to read more, she honestly does. But she does not ever want to get to the time when she has finished reading it, because then she will have finished hearing everything that Mama wanted to say, and Mama will be gone. If she does not read it, then she still can.

'Moses! Daniel!' Babu is right outside the bedroom window, sounding exactly like Uncle Joseph. 'There is a place for football, and a place for vegetables. What is wrong with you that you keep confusing the two?' Grabbing Mama's journal out of the box, Lovemore closes everything up and pushes it back under her bed. 'Does this fence of sticks that Benedict has built look in any way like a pair of goalposts? Put your ball away and come and help us to strengthen it.'

Sitting cross-legged on her bed again, Lovemore opens Mama's journal inside their history textbook in case she needs to hide it quickly. She opens it right near the beginning, and starts to read what Mama wrote about Auntie Agrippina, Rose's mama.

Agrippina is my best friend in the world, what would I do without her? I tell her ~~everything~~ almost everything. Our friendship started at school, we were both in Form I but I was older because Agrippina went straight to secondary immediately after primary but I didn't. We were two very different girls, we weren't supposed to become friends but we did because of our buttocks.

Agrippina lived in a nice house with a good family, she went to an English medium primary before she came to secondary, so she knew a lot of English. It was a good secondary, not the best in Mwanza but quite a bit more expensive than a government secondary. Her parents could pay because her father is an electrician and her mother is a teacher. I didn't have good English or educated parents or a nice house. She was clever, I was slow. I was shy, she was loud and confident. The only thing we both had was our buttocks. Mine stood high up on my back like two watermelons pointing up, hers hung low and suddenly wide like a motorbike was tucked sideways across the back of her pantie. Later our chests filled out and our buttocks began to look like they belonged, but in Form I it was hard because our buttocks made the skirts of our uniforms ride up higher at the back than at the front, and the boys laughed at us. In the second week of Form I two boys were making me cry and suddenly Agrippina was there shouting at them and asking them did they want her to come and sit on them? She hooked her arm around mine and led me away, and after that she was always there.

The door opens and Lovemore slams Mama's journal shut inside her history book, holding them both to her chest.

'*Eh!* I didn't know you were here,' says Titi, carrying in the girls' towels, warm and dry from hanging on the line in the sun.

'It's okay.' Lovemore clutches the books a little more tightly, aware that Mama's journal is much bigger than the history textbook, which cannot be hiding it at all well.

'*Samahani*. Sorry.'

'It's okay.'

Titi puts the towels away in the washroom, says *samahani* again, then closes the door behind her.

Lovemore waits a few seconds, then goes back to reading about Mama and Auntie Agrippina being friends.

I left after Form four and she was going to continue so we weren't going to see each other regularly, so she asked me then did I want to go to church with her and her family every Sunday? She was going to have her baptism, did I want to have my baptism too? I knew that she spent time at weekends studying the bible, but we never talked much about God other than saying we were praying to God if ever we wanted something nice to happen, and saying thanks God if ever something nice did happen. In my family we were Lutherans but we only went to church at Christmas and Easter, so going to church wasn't something that interested me. But Agrippina was my friend and I wanted to see her regularly after I was finished with school, so I said yes. Then she told me in her church the Holy Spirit sometimes came inside people and they spoke in tongues, they spoke languages they never learned in school. Being with Agrippina already made my English very good, but I always struggled in our French classes, and I thought maybe if I went to her church the Holy Spirit would come in me and make my French better or even make me speak German, and then I started to get excited about going to her church.

At that time Agrippina didn't know about where I lived, not yet. She only knew that my parents lived in Ngara and they sent me to my auntie and uncle in Mwanza for my secondary. She knew that I worked in a shop every afternoon and evening after school, and she was jealous of that because her parents didn't give her enough pocket money and they wouldn't let her get a job because she was too young and she had to concentrate on her schooling. I told her the lie that my auntie and uncle were too busy with their jobs to come for my baptism, but my employer old Mr Chowdary was going to come if he could find somebody he could trust to watch his shop.

In the end old Mr Chowdary couldn't come, but he helped me with some white clothes that he borrowed from a Mhindi lady, a trouser and a long-sleeve top so long it could have been a dress. There were 17 of us that day, 11 girls and 6 boys, all of us dressed in white from top to toe. Eh, it was like a party there at the side of the lake, there were drummers, there was a choir, there was everybody's family, people were too too happy and excited. Me I was shy and nervous without a family, but slowly everybody's excitement came inside me, and Agrippina's family made me feel like I belonged, like me and Agrippina were sisters. One by one we took turns to walk into the lake up to our waist, and Pastor held us and prayed for us, then Pastor held our one *side and somebody else from the church held our other side, then we held our nose and they helped us to fall backwards into the lake, right under the water. Eh, when I came up everybody next to the lake was clapping and cheering like I did something too too good and special, and that was how I felt inside. After that I went to church with Agrippina's family every Sunday, they fetched me in their car outside the secondary school because that was half way between where they lived and where I lived. I liked their church from the start, it wasn't like going to Lutheran church back home in Ngara, you said your own prayer out loud and you walked around while you were saying it, it didn't matter what anybody else was praying for, you didn't all just have to stand still or sit still and listen. And the music—*

Somebody knocks on the bedroom door. Quickly Lovemore places the history textbook inside Mama's journal to mark her place, and pushes both of them under her pillow.

'*Karibu.* Come in.'

Bibi comes in and sits on the edge of Lovemore's bed, leaving Titi hovering in the doorway. Bibi is holding a big, gold-coloured alarm clock.

'Lovemore, Titi and I have been talking.'

Lovemore shoots a glance at Titi. What has she been saying? Did she see that Lovemore was hiding something? Has she told Bibi about the box inside Lovemore's suitcase?

'Yes?' Lovemore can hear the nervousness in her own voice.

'We were thinking that maybe when you lived wi—' Bibi stops herself. 'When you lived in Mwanza, maybe you did your homework by yourself?'

'Yes?' Lovemore is not sure where this is going. Why is Bibi holding that alarm clock?

'We were thinking maybe it's hard for you to concentrate on your homework when others are coming in and out of your room. Are we right?'

Lovemore looks at both of them, nodding her head yes.

'Titi has made a suggestion,' says Bibi.

'Come,' says Titi, and Lovemore follows her, with Bibi behind them, out into the passage and towards the door that closes the bedrooms off from the lounge. Are they taking her to the lounge? How is she going to concentrate in there with the TV and the telephone-fax and Babu at the computer and Bibi working on her cakes, and Titi's cooking and chopping noises coming from the kitchen through the gap in the door because the piece of washing line instead of a handle does not let it shut properly?

But just before the door into the lounge, Titi turns left into the small hallway leading to the boys' washroom and Titi's own room. Titi's door is always shut, but she opens it now and all three of them squash in to a tiny room with just a small chest of drawers and a double bunk.

Titi pats the upper mattress, which is bare except for the swirl of mosquito net resting upon it. 'You can sit here to read your books if you like.' She points to the lower mattress, neatly made up into a bed with sheets and a thin blanket. 'I have my nap before you and Grace come from school, but other times you can be alone.'

Alone? Lovemore's breathing begins to quicken.

'This bunk used to be in the boys' room,' says Bibi. 'It matches the one Daniel and Moses sleep in. Here there used to be a single, but Benedict wanted the single instead of this bunk.'

Titi shrugs her shoulders and smiles. 'Me, I don't mind.'

'What do you think?' Bibi's arm is around Lovemore's shoulders. 'Will this be easier for you?'

Lovemore feels like her smile is going to tear her face in half. '*Eh!* Bibi! Titi! Thank you!'

Then they all jump with fright as the alarm clock in Bibi's hand begins to ring.

'*Eh!*' Bibi makes the noise stop. 'My cake is ready.'

Titi opens another door, diagonally opposite the one they came through to get into Titi's room from the hallway. It leads straight into the kitchen.

'Thank you!' Lovemore says again as Bibi and Titi go into the kitchen, closing the door behind them and leaving Lovemore alone in Titi's room. That cassette of Auntie Agrippina's is right: when you focus on what you want, you make it happen. But the cassette also says that you have to be careful not to focus on what you do not want, because you can make that happen, too. Now Lovemore no longer has to focus on worrying about somebody finding Mama's journal.

Going quickly back to the girls' bedroom, she slides the journal out from under the pillow with the history textbook still inside it and slips both of them into her schoolbag before taking it to Titi's room and closing the door behind her. She swings the bag up on to the top bunk, then climbs the small wooden ladder at the end of the bed and sits cross-legged on the mattress. The mosquito net is in the way, and it needs tying into a knot as she does each morning to the one that hangs above her own bed. As she is tying it, Babu's Uncle-Joseph voice comes in through the room's small window.

'Benedict, let us create a goal post for these boys at the other end of the yard.'

Lovemore opens Mama's journal and finds the sentence that she was reading about Mama going to Auntie Agrippina's church.

And the music—drums, guitar, keyboard! Eh, I felt too happy every Sunday!

Then Agrippina went away to Arusha for her teacher training, and while she was away I got my job as the clerk at the Tanzania Plastics depot, and I found a room to rent in the Pasiansi area of Mwanza, close to the road to the airport. When Agrippina came back she got a job teaching Standard I at an English medium, and after a while she said she was going to rent a room in a house where some teachers from outside of Mwanza lived, did I want to rent it with her? Eh, that was a nice way to live, me and Agrippina sharing a room, talking and laughing together late into the night. We talked about what kind of man did we want to marry, how many children did we want to have in our family, what did we want in our lives – all those things. That was when I told her the truth about me.

Mariamu was the first in that house to get married and go, and then Flora got pregnant and she went home to her family in Shinyanga. By then Agrippina was already falling in love. Steven was quite a bit older than her and he already had a young daughter Lulu, but her parents didn't mind because he was a good man, he went to their church. Steven was alone with Lulu because the lake took his wife and their baby, the ferry sank because it had too many people. Agrippina was happy to be the mother that Lulu needed.

At Agrippina's wedding I prayed that my own wedding was going to be soon, because I was already in love with Joseph. But when Agrippina was just 3 months away from delivering her and Steven's daughter Rose, I found that I was pregnant with Joseph's baby and that Joseph wasn't ever going to marry me because his church wasn't ever going to let him divorce, and anyway his wife Evelina was pregnant too. Agrippina told me about a small house to rent very close to the big house where she was living with Steven and Lulu and Steven's uncle Milton and his nephew Godbless. That small house is where I still live today, me and Agrippina are still best friends, and our daughters are best friends too.

Lovemore feels like she is back in Mama's small house in Mwanza with her best friend Rose just up the road, so it takes her a moment or two to understand that she is in her grandparents' house in Dar es Salaam, and that Grace and Faith are calling her name.

'Coming,' she calls back as she pushes everything back into her schoolbag, climbs down the small wooden ladder and goes back into the girls' room. The girls call again from the other side of the door into the lounge.

'*Coming!*' She locks Mama's journal away inside its box inside her suitcase under her bed.

Grace and Faith are sitting around doing nothing in front of the TV, where they have found an episode of their latest favourite, an American story called *Charmed*. It is about three sisters who are witches, good witches who try to save everybody from evil. Grace and Faith like to imagine that, together with Lovemore, they are like those three sisters. It is a silly idea and it is a silly story, but Lovemore perches on the edge of one of the couches to watch part of it with them because it is a story from America and she needs to know how to behave in America when she goes to be a lawyer in New York.

Everything in America is better, even the witches. Witches in Tanzania are old and ugly with red eyes, and people want to kill them because they can make bad things happen to you, things like poverty or sickness or your business not being successful. But in America witches are young and beautiful, and men want to fall in love with them. Every one of the three in the story could be a model. Maybe

Grace could one day be a model, but not Faith. Faith is never going to be the right kind of shape and her face is never going to be beautiful. It is good that Rose back in Mwanza does not want to be a model, because she has Auntie Agrippina's buttocks – but Lovemore could be. She does not want to, though. She only went to modelling class because it was Lulu's class, and because Mama said it would teach her to move with elegance, which Lovemore will need to be able to do in New York.

On the screen, one of the beautiful witches is making a spell to take her back in time to before something bad happened, so that she can stop it from ever actually happening.

Lovemore finds herself settling back on the couch, longing to go back to the time before anything bad happened to Mama.

Chapter 5

A N INFERIOR cake-maker could have taken any number of short cuts with this particular cake. Number one, they could have baked just a simple round vanilla sponge in two layers with an extra-thick layer of dark brown icing in between. Number two, they could have simply decorated the outside of the cake to look like what it was supposed to be, without bothering at all with what was on the inside of the cake. Number three, they could have crafted a small representation of the thing entirely from sugar paste and placed it as a decoration on top of a simple, ordinary cake.

But not Angel Tungaraza. No. When customers ordered a cake from Angel Tungaraza, there was no need to tell her that they wanted it to be spectacular, because it was going to be spectacular anyway. There was no need to insult her by stressing at least four times in person and then twice more – in capital letters and underlined – in the letter via the messenger with the deposit and the picture, that what they wanted was something spectacular, as though there was a danger that she might forget and make their cake inferior instead. There was no danger of an inferior cake from Angel Tungaraza. None at all. No. Angel Tungaraza was a professional somebody. Each and every one of her cakes was spectacular.

Getting up from his chair in front of the computer, Pius asked Angel if she wanted another glass of iced water. She did, as a matter of fact – the night air was hot and still – but without turning to look at him over her shoulder, without even looking up from the dining table where she was working on her spectacular cake, she told him no. Not no thanks. Just no.

When he brought her one anyway, she did not say thank you.

Right now, she was simply too angry with him to be polite to him. He knew it, and his sighs from in front of his conference report on the computer had been extremely heavy.

It was only that morning that he had finally told her about the evening in Nairobi when he had been walking back to his hotel from the Kenyatta International Conference Centre and two men on the street had wanted his wallet and his phone. Who knew what could have happened if a big group of others from the conference had not appeared exactly when they had? Pius did not have the philosophy of simply handing something over. No. He had tried to tell the two men that he was busy with a conference for all the countries of East Africa about strengthening their union through greater cooperation in all spheres, and that those two men were not helping tourism to the region as a whole by confirming Nairobi's reputation as *Nairobbery*. Honestly! What had he hoped to do? Put them to sleep? He should have given them exactly what they wanted and walked away quickly. There were six grandchildren now – *six!* – who needed him to stay alive, not to mention Angel herself. What had he been thinking?

As quietly as she could – so as not to imply any gratitude to him at all for the glass of water – she scooped out a square of ice with her fingers and slipped it into her mouth. As she sucked its cooling relief, she closed her eyes and tried to breathe slowly and deeply through her nose. She must try to put her anger at Pius aside, or it was going to spoil her cake by making it less spectacular than she fully intended it to be.

Okay, the two young women who had ordered the cake were certainly not *trying* to insult her. They were simply excited about their party – and Americans could become very easily over-excited. She had seen that on TV. These two *Wazungu* worked at the American Embassy – the new one that had been built with every kind of security after the car bomb at the old one out on Bagamoyo Road had killed eleven people in 1998 – so perhaps their nerves were on edge, too. The very same day, another bomb had killed more than two hundred at the American Embassy in the middle of Nairobi in Kenya.

But Angel did not want to think any more about Nairobi in Kenya. Her thoughts about that place had been like pieces of broken glass inside her head since that morning, when Pius had told her what had happened to him there.

Very quietly, she scooped up another square of ice and forced herself to focus on her cake.

She had very nearly finished, and it was very nearly exactly like the picture that the two *Wazungu* had sent via the embassy's messenger. A cheeseburger was not something that Angel had ever eaten herself, though of course she had eaten chips. Almost everybody in Tanzania had eaten *chips mayayi* – the chips omelette that was so very popular from restaurants to road-side kiosks – and these chips that she had baked from yellow-coloured vanilla biscuit dough to go alongside her cheeseburger cake were big, fat and long. The cheeseburger itself was many times bigger than anything a man could hold in both hands and fit between his jaws. Its bottom-most layer was a round of vanilla sponge covered in bread-coloured sugar paste, and sitting on top of it was a layer of expert sugar-paste lettuce leaves in not one, not two, but three different shades of green. Then came a thick round of chocolate sponge expertly dabbed with three different shades of dark brown icing sugar, its upper and lower edges rounded off to make it look just like a much larger version of the patties of minced beef that Titi prepared for the family from time to time. Next there was a large, flat square of bright yellow sugar paste, laid over the top of the iced surface of the chocolate layer, its four corners extending beyond it and draping down its sides. That she topped carefully now with her large white rings of sugar paste onion, and finally some rounds of sugar paste tomato slices that she was particularly proud of. Anybody could want to pick those up and put them into a sandwich or a frying pan, not recognising that they were made of sugar.

It was late, and she did not want to pause for too long to admire her expertise before she moved on. Now she must make the seeds to go on top of the domed round of vanilla sponge – covered in sugar paste to look like the top of a bread roll – which she would add to the cake as soon as the seeds were securely on it. Rolling small pieces of yellow sugar paste between finger and thumb required very little concentration, and when Pius sighed loudly yet again, it threatened to undo the better mood that Angel's cake had brought her.

She steered her mind to the phone call that she had received today from Agrippina, the mother of Lovemore's friend Rose in Mwanza. They had spoken only once before, when Pius had phoned Agrippina to say that Lovemore was safely here and was busy unpacking her suitcase. Angel had taken the phone from Pius then and thanked Agrippina for taking care of Lovemore when her mama had died, and for looking after her for the nearly four months it had taken for Pius to complete his work in Swaziland before bringing the family back to Tanzania. They had not spoken for long that time, because Agrippina had sounded tearful underneath her friendliness. Angel remembered wondering if she herself had sounded like somebody who was trying a little too hard to seem cheerful despite everything.

'Pius is so like Joseph,' Agrippina had told her on the phone today. 'When he came here for her, I thought he was Joseph grown old. *Eh!* At every opportunity I checked myself in the mirror to see was I maybe grown old too?'

'I used to look at Joseph,' Angel had told her, 'and see my Pius young.'

'Lovemore must be refreshing his loss for you now, my dear. It is very hard for you.'

'And for you, Agrippina. Was Mama-Lovemore not your friend?'

'My very best friend, since school. There is no day when I don't miss her. Still today something can happen and I think of telling Glory about it, then after some minutes I remember that there is no more Glory to tell.'

'*Pole sana*, Agrippina. So sorry.'

'*Asante*, Angel.'

'You know, Mama-Lovemore could have called on us for help the very moment we all lost Joseph. She didn't have to struggle on her own.'

'*Eh*, that is something I told her, Angel. I told her! But she feared that you would want to take Lovemore from her, raise her as your own. Lovemore was all she had left.'

'*Eh!* I can understand that.'

'My dear, I hope you don't mind if I call you from time to time like this? It's just that Mama-Lovemore is late and you are Bibi-Lovemore…'

Continuing to roll small pieces of sugar paste into seeds as she ignored the irritation of another sigh from Pius, Angel recognised that the many questions that she had about Mama-Lovemore would have to be asked very carefully. Even after the pain of Glory's loss had dulled, Agrippina was not going to want to say anything bad about her best friend since school. And obviously there were bad things to say, because Glory had done sex with another woman's husband, which no good woman would ever think of doing. But there must have been good sides to Glory for a good woman like Agrippina to keep her as a friend. Angel would have to sit on her curiosity, at least for now.

Pius's sighs were growing louder and more frequent now, and Angel was finding it increasingly difficult to be in the same room as him. Very quickly, she fixed her seeds to the upper surface of the cheeseburger's lid, then she leaned it up against the rest of the burger at an angle – one edge of it resting on the cake board – so that all the layers of her cake, with her beautiful slices of tomato on top, were on display. Finally she filled her plastic icing syringe with sugary red and squirted a trail of tomato sauce – ketchup, those *Wazungu* had called it – over the chips before creating a bright pool of it next to the burger.

Then she rose from her chair silently so that Pius could not hear that she had finished with her work and mistake that for an opportunity to tell her his excuses one more time. All day he had been defending what he had done, telling Angel that giving those two men his wallet and his phone would not have changed their lives or improved their lives or developed them in any way. Really, Pius must stop trying to change, improve or develop everything that he saw. What if those men had decided that the only way to take his wallet and his phone was to take his life, too? Had Pius given any thought at all to how that was going to change, improve or develop anything for his own family?

Normally Angel would have cleared the dining table of everything but her finished cake, taking everything else into the kitchen for Titi to find and wash. Normally she would have stood for a while and admired her work, inviting praise from anybody else who happened to be around, before taking a beautiful photograph of it for her album. But not tonight. Tonight she simply slipped silently out of the room without a single word to Pius, and headed for the bedroom.

Today I am grateful!
1. because nobody shot Pius dead
2. because Agrippina and I are going to become friends
3. because my cheeseburger cake is <u>SPECTACULAR</u>

4. because it looks like Lovemore is growing attached to Pius ~~*at least*~~
5.

When Angel came out of the washroom after splashing cold water on her face countless times, Pius was sitting on the edge of their bed, turning his wallet over and over in his hands. He looked up at her, his eyes damp.

'Angel, I'm so sorry!'

'Ah, Pius.'

'I'm so, so sorry!'

'Those are the words I've been waiting to hear.'

Angel sat down next to him, and let him put an arm around her.

'I was a fool,' he said.

'Yes.' It was what Angel had been telling him all day.

'I made us some warm milk and honey,' he said, nodding towards the two mugs on the small bedside cupboard. Then he took a deep breath and handed Angel his wallet. 'Do you not remember, Angel?'

Angel turned the wallet over and over in her hands, not knowing what it was that she should be remembering.

'Do you not see what it is made of?'

The finger that she rubbed over it found only the smoothness that had come from wear.

'Fish skin,' Pius told her. 'Nile perch.'

'*Eh!* It was Joseph's!' She gave it back quickly, remembering that it had been a gift from the owner of the factory where Joseph was Manager, and that it had been found empty in Joseph's house after the robbers had shot him dead there.

'Those men in Nairobi,' Pius paused to wipe his nose on one of Angel's tissues from beside the bed, 'I didn't want them to take Joseph away from me. Not again.'

Angel slipped the arm closest to him around his back, and the other arm around his middle. 'Ah, Pius,' she said quietly.

'Even now, Angel. Even after what we know now.'

Angel squeezed him as tightly as she could without her hands being able to find each other around him as they used to when the two of them had first been in love.

'Even now,' he repeated quietly, matching the tightness of her squeeze.

All of the anger that had propelled Angel through the day was suddenly gone, and she felt drained, exhausted.

'I'm sorry, Angel. I was such a fool.'

'Yes.'

'I'm going to buy another wallet. Put this one away. Benedict can have it when he's grown.'

'Yes.'

When they let go of each other, they reached for their milk and honey, sipping it together in a silence that was at last comfortable once again.

Secondary school is hard for Lovemore, even after all of the extra that Mama sent her for back home in Mwanza. Extra maths after school every Monday and Wednesday helped her to pass in the top ten in her class, but now it is a different kind of maths, and it is difficult. Grace finds it easy, so Babu and Bibi have said that Grace must help Lovemore with her maths for half an hour after school each and every day. Grace does not like the idea, but Babu says it will mean extra pocket money for her.

Only Lovemore and Grace get pocket money, and they get it because Babu says that the beginning of secondary school is the right time for young people to start learning some financial responsibility, and also because Bibi says that girls their age need to be able to buy what they need at the pharmacy, when the time comes. Until the time comes, Grace is spending her money on things like nail polish and bracelets, and it is always gone within hours of it leaving Babu's wallet or Bibi's bra.

Once Grace failed to budget for airtime for Mama's old phone and then used up all of the credit, so it was not possible for her and Lovemore to send their daily SMS text to Bibi to say that they were leaving the school gates and starting their walk home, and Bibi worked herself up into quite a state about their safety. The girls' school is nearby, and it is much quicker for them to walk than for Bibi to drive through the traffic to fetch them. But Bibi does drive Faith and the boys to and from their primary, which is quite a bit further. Faith and Benedict take turns with another phone that goes with them to the primary for just in case, and the just in case is usually on Bibi's side because the old red microbus does not always want to start.

Lovemore is much more careful than Grace with her pocket money. She rolls her Tanzanian shillings up neatly and tucks them away into her purse, keeping it locked safely in her suitcase under her bed. It will stay there until she needs it, first when the time comes for buying pads at the pharmacy, and then for her degree in law – because, really, that is not something that her grandparents who live in a broken house and drive a broken vehicle are going to be able to afford.

When their pocket money was first handed over, Faith was not happy about not getting any herself.

'But what about me, Baba?'

'Are you attending secondary school?'

'Uh-uh. But I'm a girl, Mama. Please!'

'Faith, when you need some pocket money, you will get it.' Bibi patted Faith's shoulder.

'Aah! Mama!' Faith stuck out her lower lip. 'It's not fair!'

'How is it not fair?'

Faith seemed surprised by Babu's question. 'Grace and Lovemore get, and I don't.'

'Benedict doesn't get,' Babu pointed out, 'and nor do Moses and Daniel. In order to be fair, do we not need to give them pocket money, too?'

'No, Baba, just me.'

'I see,' said Babu. 'So you are not actually concerned about fairness at all?'

'What?'

'Well, if we were to give pocket money to you but not to the boys, you wouldn't mind. Yet that is not fair.'

Catching Lovemore's eye over Faith's shoulder, Babu gave her a wink. *Eh!* Uncle Joseph used to do that over Mama's shoulder when Lovemore was small, and it always made her feel like she and Uncle Joseph were on the same side, that the two of them knew things – shared things

– that nobody else did. Babu's wink over Faith's shoulder excluded Faith – excluded Grace and Bibi, too – and made Lovemore feel like it was just the two of them.

'But they're boys, Baba,' said Faith.

'I see. So you think it's okay to treat girls one way and boys another? *Eh*, Angel, this child is undoing so many years of struggle! How have we let this happen in our own house?"

'I don't know, Pius. It is not the way we have raised these children.'

Faith lowered her head, shuffled from foot to foot, and said no more.

Since then, Lovemore has watched the disappointment settling deeper into Faith's eyes each month as the pocket money comes only to Lovemore and Grace. It is not a good look on a not-pretty face, and it only gets worse when Grace starts getting extra for helping Lovemore.

Faith needs help herself. She has fallen behind, and this year she is in the same class as Benedict – though she is a year older than him – and that does not sit well with her. It is going to mean an even longer wait until she can join Lovemore and Grace at secondary and start getting pocket money herself.

On the Sunday when Babu has to go to Ethiopia for six whole weeks, Bibi says that they should all say special prayers in church for him to be safe while he is away for all that time, and also for his safe return. Mama would be impressed with the Tungarazas' church – not with their religion, but with the church itself. It is the cathedral that stands tall near the railway station on Sokoine Drive, looking out over the Indian Ocean and the harbour and the jetty for the ferry to Zanzibar. The Germans finished building it a hundred years ago, but it does not look old. On the outside it is cleanly pale grey and white with orange tiles on its roof, and on its right-hand side it has an enormously high steeple that looks like it reaches all the way up to Paradise, which this church calls Heaven. Inside, the building seems even taller, with towering archways pointing up. What Mama would like best about it is its name: it is called St Joseph's.

Highway of Holiness back home in Mwanza is also a cathedral, but it is much smaller and lower than this, its front and roof a patchwork of corrugated iron sheets attached to the bare brick of its side walls. Inside it there are white plastic chairs nearer the front and a few wooden benches nearer the back, all of them on a bare earth floor. But it is a popular church, and on Sundays there can be too many people, and the pastor or the bishop will lead the service in the yard outside the church. Inside, there is not a single picture; there are only cloths and flowers for decoration.

When Lovemore first came to Dar es Salaam, Bibi said she would go with Lovemore to an Assemblies church if Lovemore wanted, and even the whole family could go there with her from time to time. But Lovemore said she did not mind going to a Catholic church with the Tungarazas. She knows from one of Auntie Agrippina's cassettes that God is not inside any church, He is inside her and everybody else, so it does not matter where she goes to pray. She has not yet felt the Holy Spirit inside her like Mama used to, and what happens inside St Joseph's is much calmer and more orderly than what used to happen at Highway of Holiness, but at least while Lovemore is inside St Joseph's there are beautiful pictures for her to look at.

Right at the front behind where their pastor – their 'father' – stands to talk and to read from the Bible, there are three tall, thin panels of pictures, all of them made up of coloured pieces of glass put together like a jigsaw puzzle, and along either side wall are three more big glass jigsaw-puzzle pictures, each of them round. Those are the ones that Lovemore likes best. They remind her of two of the puzzles that she and Mama borrowed from the Indian ladies' toy library back home in Mwanza: one had a picture of Jesus having his last supper, and the other was round, divided into six panels like slices of cake, with each panel showing how people do fishing in different parts of the world. Lovemore's favourite panel showed fishermen in Vietnam using big black cormorant birds to catch the fish for them, the water around the men and the birds and their tiny boats shimmering with the pink evening light of the sky. But that puzzle came before Lovemore hated fish, and before she began to fear birds.

The round picture in St Joseph's that she decides to focus on today is framed, just like the other five, by ten half-circles, each of them patterned with leaves and flowers against a red background. The picture inside the large circle shows the three kings coming to see

Jesus just after he was born. Mary sits holding Jesus on her lap, while a man in a long red cloak kneels before her, offering up a box which Lovemore is sure contains gold. The kneeling man has taken off his gold crown and placed it on the ground. Waiting to the left is a king wearing mostly green, only this king does not have a crown. Instead he wears on his head the kind of wrap that Concilia likes to wear. This one is green above a narrow band of gold bearing a red jewel at the front. While the other two kings are bearded, this one with the green headwrap is clean-shaven, his skin darker than the other two. With his straight black hair, he reminds Lovemore of the beautiful Egyptian queen in another of the jigsaw puzzles from the toy library, so maybe he is from Egypt. In his right hand he clutches the ends of three thin red ropes that suspend a small gold pot from which come puffs of grey smoke. That must be the gift of frankincense. Right at the back, behind the first two kings, stands a third, a man with a beard and a crown who is holding up what looks like a perfume bottle, which must be the gift of myrrh. In the background above them all is a gold star with a long golden tail, the star that has led the kings to Jesus.

Dressed in lovely blue with a simple pale purple cloth on her head, Mary sits holding the baby while Joseph stands behind her, bending low and looking over her shoulder to check that the baby is okay. Not for the first time since learning that Uncle Joseph was her father, Lovemore wonders about him looking over Mama's shoulder as she grew up, checking that she was okay. Her mind is very far away from the church she is sitting in, so she jumps with fright when somebody starts playing the organ. It is an ordinary-looking keyboard with pedals like in a car, but the sound that it makes comes from somewhere else entirely, from right up at the back where massive pipes magnify its sound to fill the entire church. Somebody marks the beat with a tambourine, while two others bang on different kinds of shakers. At the front, the singers in the choir raise their voices high, and at last St Joseph's feels a little – though only a little – like Highway of Holiness. There is no drum kit being pounded, and Uncle Steven's nephew Godbless – skinny as a pencil – is not there blowing his trumpet so powerfully that God must be blowing it through him, and Mama is not standing there next to Lovemore. But Bibi is on one side of her and Babu is on the other, and somehow, in a small way, that feels okay.

On Sundays the traffic in Dar es Salaam is never as bad as it is during the week. Bibi has a cake to bake, but it can wait until this evening, so instead of calling for an air-conditioned taxi to take Babu to the airport, Bibi drives him herself in the old red microbus. All the children go along too, so that they can spend every last possible minute with Babu before he goes to Addis Ababa in Ethiopia for six whole weeks. Titi stays behind at the house, and Lovemore chooses to stay there with her. She knows that she is going to feel Babu's absence – he is the only person in this household who feels familiar, who really feels like family – but she is feeling strong today, and she is not as stressed as the others about his being away for six weeks because she was already without him for nearly thirteen years. Besides, she wants to stay in for her weekly phone call with Rose.

Rose answers on the second ring. 'Lovemore?'

'Rose!' The sound of her best friend's voice lifts Lovemore up like the joyous singing in Highway of Holiness.

'Ah, my sister! How are you? How is everybody?'

'Fine! Fine! And you and everybody?'

'Fine, too. Lovemore, they chose me and Katherine for school choir!'

'Ah, a lot of congratulations, Rose! Did I not tell you they were going to choose you?' Lovemore is genuinely happy for Rose, but she finds herself wishing for some exciting news of her own to match it. She offers up Grace's news instead. 'They chose Grace for a scene from a play for Dialogue Night.'

'That is good news! Please tell her well done. What is the play?'

'Oh, it's nothing.' Lovemore does not want to waste all of her fifteen minutes with Rose talking about Grace. 'It's nothing important.' Truly, it is not an important play: the man who wrote it is not from anywhere in Europe or America, he is a Nigerian from West Africa.

'You should try drama club, too, Lovemore. Are you really not going to do anything outside of class?'

'Uh-uh. I need to concentrate on my lessons, otherwise I'll never make it to be your partner at Lovemore and Rose.'

Rose laughs. 'We have many years till then. And when we're lawyers, we don't want to be dull girls, we need some play along with our work.'

'Now you are sounding like your mama.'

'Ooh, guess what! Mama is starting a new business.'

'Ah, please tell her well done! What is it?'

'A catering hire. You know Godbless plays in a band for weddings?'

'Mm.'

'The people always hire the band and also a vehicle for the band to play on in the wedding-car procession. If the people don't have money for a full open pick-up, they go for one of those *bajajis* that's an open pick-up at the back and a motorbike at the front—'

'*Eh!* I get nervous when I see people trying to stand on the back of those.'

'*Yes.* Especially Godbless. But on those *bajaji* ones he kneels. The wind could blow him over at any time.'

'It's only the weight of his trumpet that prevents it. Is he still skinny like a pencil?'

'Mm, but Lovemore, he *eats! Eh!* Mama and I are so jealous with our buttocks! Anyway, her new business will hire out vehicles and bands together, and also marquee tents and plates and cups and that. Everything that you need for your occasion, Mama's company will supply it. Lulu and everybody at the saloon can also do your hair and your make-up if you want. Drinks can come from Walk on Water—'

'Ah, now I'm missing everybody there!' Mostly Lovemore is missing Mama, who would be so proud of Auntie Agrippina for putting so many pieces together and finding a way to do so many things at the same time. 'Please say my hellos.'

'Of course.' Rose begins to giggle. 'Has your teacher got a bra yet? What's his name?'

Lovemore laughs as she thinks about the too-fat teacher who wobbles and sweats at the front of the science room. '*Mwalimu* Masabo. No! And his breasts are still the biggest in our class whenever Pamela Pima is at home with her period.'

'That Pamela Pima is backward! Is her mother from the village?' Rose already has her period, and she has never missed a day of school because of it. When Lulu was still at school she did her best to be allowed to stay home every month, doubling over and clutching her stomach while moaning loudly, but Auntie Agrippina always just gave her a tablet and made her go to school. Now that Lulu is busy managing Three Times A Lady saloon, she never needs a tablet.

'Maybe Mama-Pamela is from the village, but I don't know.'

'When we are lawyers we must make a law for pads to be free for all girls. Village up to city, everywhere.'

'That is an excellent idea.' Lovemore likes it when she and Rose focus on their future. One of Auntie Agrippina's cassettes tells you seven things you must do if you want to be effective, and one of them is about knowing where you are going with every step that you take. 'Maybe schools must provide them.'

'Excellent. I'll add that to our list.'

They have been making their list for some time now. Lovemore suggests another thing to add. 'How about a law saying more lady teachers must qualify to teach physics and chemistry? We have to have *Mwalimu* Masabo and his breasts because there is no lady physics and chemistry teacher for us.'

'Ah, no, here we want to hold on to *Mwalimu* Shuma for physics and chemistry! He is too handsome! One of the boys in Form Four asked a Form Three girl out, and she told him no because he is not *Mwalimu* Shuma!' The shock of such an idea makes Lovemore take in a loud gulp of air. 'And the other day at break me and Katherine overheard two boys talking about another girl they like, and then they asked each other but what is the point, they cannot get her, they are not *Mwalimu* Shuma. No, Lovemore, let us not make a law that might take *Mwalimu* Shuma away from us here.'

'Okay.' Lovemore tries to imagine the girls at school wanting their boyfriends to be like *Mwalimu* Masabo, or even wanting *Mwalimu* Masabo to be their boyfriend – but it is too difficult.

'Lovemore, I have a secret!'

'*Eh!* Is there a boy you like, Rose?'

'No! I like physics and chemistry!'

'*Eh!* But you're a girl!'

'I know!'

'Is it because of *Mwalimu* Shuma?'

'Katherine asked me that, but no, I don't think so.'

It does not sit well with Lovemore that Katherine is part of every conversation with Rose now. She shifts their conversation away from any possible mention of the girl who has taken her place in Mwanza. 'Prisca brought us news at school this week. Scholastica has delivered.'

'That one who was sent away for getting pregnant?'

'Mm. Scholastica's sister Euphrasia knows nothing, but Prisca heard the news from somebody who knows somebody who knows somebody. That somebody doesn't know if it's a girl or a boy. *Eh*, Rose, Scholastica is just one year older than us!'

'Ooh, can you imagine my mama if ever that was me?'

'Uh-uh-uh.' Auntie Agrippina would surely sob hard enough to make her buttocks shake very violently.

'Lovemore, should we make a law that such a mistake must not lock a girl outside of schooling?'

'*Eh!*' Rose's suggestion sparks an idea in Lovemore. 'Let us write a letter to *Fema* about making such a law! It will be many years before we can do it ourselves, and up to that time there will be many Scholasticas.'

All the girls love to read *Fema* magazine when it comes to their school because it talks to young people about important topics without dancing around those topics in the way that parents and grandparents do. Sometimes Miss Brown will photocopy an article in English from the magazine for them to read and discuss in class, though *Mwalimu* Kikoti has never used any of its Swahili articles in their Swahili class. Perhaps it is because *Mwalimu* Kikoti is just too old to talk about such things. Miss Brown once read out for dictation one of the magazine's letters to Dear Auntie about a relationship problem, and the girls had to pretend that they were Auntie and each of them had to write a helpful reply.

'Excellent!' says Rose. 'Which of us will write the letter?'

Lovemore thinks about all of her schoolwork. 'You write it, Rose, you are better.'

'Ah, Katherine is better still! Me and Katherine can write it together.'

'Okay.' Lovemore takes a deep breath. 'But maybe you can read it to me next week before you send it to *Fema*?'

'Okay.'

Katherine's name does not come up again for the rest of the

conversation, and afterwards Lovemore feels excited. Whoever writes the letter, maybe it can make a difference for girls like Scholastica. This is much bigger than Lovemore and Rose simply writing laws on a list; this is the beginning of their careers as lawyers.

With the girls' bedroom all to herself, Lovemore sits on her own bed to read some more of Mama's journal. As she opens it, her eyes automatically do the scanning that Miss Brown has been teaching all the Form Ones to do, and she sees one of the blank lines that mark the end of one entry and the beginning of the next. It is very near the bottom of a right-hand page.

What have I done? What have I done? I have ruined everything. I have wasted everything. <u>Everything</u>.

Lovemore turns the page. What she reads there looks like the beginning of a new entry. Miss Brown would be proud of the way she skims that entry to see if it is about what Mama did that ruined and wasted everything, but it is a happy story about Lovemore and Rose when they were tiny. Turning back the page, she reads again those few small sentences. Whatever they mean, they make Lovemore feel more than a little shaky.

She puts the journal down and opens her physics book instead. But the procedures for determining the volume of a stone by the displacement method cannot hold her attention for very long, and she opens the journal again, finding the entry that follows the last one that she read, the one about Mama and Auntie Agrippina being friends.

I love my house. The brick part is small, just 2 bedrooms, but 2 more rooms and a second small washroom are added on off the kitchen with zinc walls and a zinc roof. When Agrippina first told me about it and I went to look, I knew that if I used all the money in my savings I could afford to furnish it, but then I couldn't start my own business, and I wanted to start my own business because old Mr Chowdary always told me your own business is the only way to make good money. So I asked Joseph to help with the furnitures and the rent for me and our baby until my business was running. Then I used my savings to buy and stock a kiosk, and I wrote to one of my distant aunties in Ngara, an in-law of an in-law, and I asked her did she have sons who wanted to come and work in my kiosk in Mwanza? She sent me her son Philbert and her nephew Sigsbert. They share one of the zinc rooms, and the other is for our house girl Pritty.

My kiosk is Friends in Deed, on the edge of Mwanza on the road to the airport, just next to a petrol station. We pass it in the Nile Perch Plastics daladala on the way to work and back again every day, and if I want to check on something I can ask the driver to drop me there on the way back from work. Sometimes he even stops there long enough for the people from Nile Perch Plastics to get out and buy something before he takes them the rest of the way back into town. On a Friday the men in the daladala want to buy beers. We have Tusker, Safari, Kilimanjaro, Serengeti, Balimi — every kind of Tanzanian beer. A little further is another kiosk, one in the shape of a giant black Coca-Cola bottle standing upright, but that one is too small, it only has Tusker and Kili. If the day is hot, the daladala stops at Friends in Deed because everybody wants to buy a nice cold soda. On another day maybe somebody wants to buy a cigarette or matches or salt or sugar or rice. They can call to Philbert or Sigsbert to bring what they want to the window of the daladala, they don't even have to get out.

Philbert and Sigsbert know the Nile Perch Plastics daladala and everybody inside it, they always give a small discount. That is how to keep your regular customers coming back to you when they could buy from any other kiosk or shop or bar. Old Mr Chowdary taught me that at my first job in his shop, and I taught it to Philbert and Sigsbert. A small discount doesn't matter, you can get it back quickly from the higher price you ask from a difficult customer or from a customer who is too full of beer to notice, or from a stranger passing through. Everybody coming in to Mwanza from the airport has to pass Friends in Deed. The pilots and the engineers from the big planes that come to take the Nile Perch fillets to Europe don't always want to sit and drink every night at their hotel, sometimes they want to go somewhere else and they stop at the kiosk for beer as they pass. Or they come to buy beer to drink in their hotel room because the price at Friends in Deed is better than the price at the hotel bar.

Philbert and Sigsbert take their turns at the kiosk, they keep it open from very early in the morning until late at night so that everybody who stops for petrol can always buy something from them too. It's only on Sunday that they close. Everything they know about running a business is what I learned from old Mr Chowdary. Sometimes they are both at the kiosk together, because otherwise when will they see each other? They are both good boys, they never try to touch Pritty. For a long time they have been in love with Agrippina and Steven's daughter Lulu. Lulu came from a different mother so she doesn't have Agrippina's buttocks, she was almost Miss Tanzania. There are many young men in front of Philbert and Sigsbert in the line, but that doesn't matter to them, they only compete against each other. If Philbert goes to Change is Gonna Come barbershop and has the $ shape of a dollar sign shaved at the back of his head to impress Lulu, Sigsbert goes to Electric Chair barbershop and has the shape of a light bulb bleached at the back of his. Lulu always looks and says something nice, but me and Agrippina know it's only because she's interested in hairdressing, it isn't because she's interested in those boys.

Agrippina is interested in buying the saloon where Lulu is training. She already owns Walk on Water, the small bar next to the lake where all the fishing boats come in, and Agrippina Fashions near the bus stand, and now she wants to own Three Times A Lady beauty saloon too. That is Agrippina, she wants to spend her abundance buying all of Mwanza. Me, I want to spend mine getting Lovemore out of Mwanza, getting her closer to her lawyer office in New York.

Agrippina's Steven doesn't believe in abundance like me and Agrippina, he doesn't even want to listen to Agrippina's cassettes. Every day he goes to his job at the fish factory where he takes Nile perches, cuts every piece of flesh off their bones and makes the neat fillets that will go to Europe. Before the Nile perches even get to Steven somebody else has already removed the skin for selling to make belts and shoes for people with too much abundance, and somebody else has already taken all the insides out and found the precious swimming bladder for selling to the Chinese for their soup or to the English for filtering their beer and wine. Outside the factory, Mwanza people can buy the leftover skeleton bones and heads, the fish frames.

Steven puts the fillets into the plastic trays from Nile Perch Plastics that can sit one on top of the other, he makes sure that no fillet is touching any other fillet, and then the trays go straight into an enormous walk-in freezer that blasts the fillets frozen in just a few minutes. Steven fears that freezer. Agrippina says sometimes he wakes sweating in the night because he has had a dream about being locked inside it. Once he even cried because in his dream he *was inside the freezer with all the fish and when he stopped banging on the door and turned round, he saw his first wife and baby who were late in the lake when the ferry sank. Agrippina wants him to listen to her cassette about fear but he doesn't want to. He doesn't want to try to find a job that doesn't have a freezer, he doesn't want to try to move up to a job at the fish factory where he can wear a nice suit instead of rubber boots and a plastic apron. Agrippina thinks he likes to cut at the flesh of those fish because those fish feed on other fish and even on their own babies, so what is to stop them feeding on his first wife and his baby at the bottom of the lake? Maybe he doesn't want to raise himself up to a higher job because he wants to keep plunging a knife into those fish. So Agrippina doesn't mind that he isn't ambitious, not really. Me, I would mind.*

<u>*Lovemore*</u> *– Don't marry a man who isn't already at the top or at least trying by every means to get to the top. And be careful of a man who was married but now his wife is late. A late wife remains a woman who can be in a man's dreams, she can still control his life.*

While Babu is away in Ethiopia, Lovemore tries to fill the days and weeks with schoolwork, though Grace is always pestering her for help with learning her lines for the dialogue.

'You're so good at memorising, Lovemore. How do you do it?'

'You just have to concentrate.'

'Please concentrate with me.'

'Concentrating is something you do by yourself.'

'Please, Lovemore. I need somebody to be the girl.' Grace has been given the part of a man in the dialogue because the other girls in drama club have breasts. 'I can't just talk to myself. It won't take long.'

'But you're supposed to be helping me with my maths.'

'Help me with my lines then I'll help you with your maths.'

'Help me with my maths then I'll help you with your lines.'

Grace helps her with her maths, but all the way through she practises phrases or sentences from the play.

'My heart bursts into flowers with my love.'

'Let us concentrate.'

'Bush-girl you are, and bush-girl you will always be.'
'We are doing algebraic operations.'
'Ignorant girl, can you not understand?'
'Stop it, Grace.'
'You have a smaller brain than mine.'
'Grace!'

When their half hour of maths is over, Lovemore is surprised to find that the Nigerian has written an interesting scene, even though he is only a Nigerian. Grace is Lakunle, a very educated man, a teacher. Lakunle likes a girl called Sidi, but she is a village girl who is ignorant. She does not mind to carry a bucket of water on her head even though it spoils her neck, and she does not mind to be casual with her *kanga* so that men can catch sight of her breasts. Lakunle wants her to marry him so that he can educate her and modernise her, but Sidi would rather become an additional wife to a traditional man. Sidi does not understand the importance of stepping up in life. The traditional man will pay bride-price for Sidi because she is a virgin, but Lakunle will never pay bride-price because paying bride-price is out-dated and degrading and all the other negative words that he can find in his Shorter Companion Dictionary.

That is just the scene that Grace and a girl in Form Three are going to act on Dialogue Night, but Lovemore thinks that maybe – maybe at the end of the school year when all her Form One schoolwork is behind her – maybe then she would like to read the whole play by this Nigerian.

Lovemore and Grace have finally taken out each other's extension braids, the ones that were put in all that time ago to make them look beautiful at their party for their birthday turning thirteen, and now they have come to the saloon because their hair needs treating. Grace is growing her hair and is having it relaxed, while Lovemore is having a cut that is going to take very little time to deal with every day. They could have come to the saloon in a *daladala*, but with the traffic it was quicker to walk.

Lovemore closes her eyes, enjoying the slow, rhythmic feel of a pair of hands massaging her scalp as she half sits, half lies with her head leaning back over a basin. In the background, she can hear Grace chatting, without ever seeming to pause for a breath, to the woman who is applying her relaxer. There are other voices, and there is music from the radio, but Lovemore tries not to listen. Instead, she imagines that she is in Three Times a Lady back home in Mwanza, and that it is Rose's big sister Lulu who is massaging her head.

She can almost hear Lulu laughing and joking with one of the other hairdressers about Mama's cousin Philbert, who came in earlier to bring her a *sambusa*, but only because Mama's cousin Sigsbert came in yesterday to bring her a small bag of bite-size *maandazi*. Lovemore can almost smell the spice and oil of the three-cornered parcel of potatoes and peas wrapped in pastry, as another laughing voice tells Lulu that those two young men cannot love her – not serious-serious – if they bring her snacks that are going to give her buttocks like her mama's. Everybody in the saloon knows Auntie Agrippina because Auntie Agrippina is the owner, and everybody laughs.

Lulu stops massaging, and aims a gentle jet of warm water at Lovemore's head, working slowly from her forehead round to the nape of her neck on one side, and then again on the other. Lovemore hears the lady at the next basin telling the girl washing for her that she is here from Bukoba for a wedding, and asking for advice on the best barbershop in Mwanza for her husband and her teenage son. Best Exclusive for your husband, the girl advises, and for your son, Electric Chair or Change is Gonna Come. The door of the saloon opens with a small tinkling of bells and a sudden gust of hot air. It is Mama, here to fetch her. Lovemore sits up as Lulu wraps a towel around her head.

But it is not Lulu, and it is not Mama.

Bibi is in the doorway, pulling Faith behind her. There is a towel around Faith's head, and Faith is crying. Not just letting tears fall, but wailing like a small child. Everybody in the saloon is suddenly silent, their sentences unfinished, as they turn to look.

'My daughter needs help,' Bibi says to nobody in particular. Lovemore can hear the distress in Bibi's voice, even on top of Faith's wailing. There is a slight shake in Bibi's hands as she unwraps the towel from Faith's head. A lot of Faith's hair seems to be missing, and the rest of it is orange–dull and brownish, but unmistakeably orange.

A shocked *eh!* echoes throughout the saloon.

'Bleach,' says Bibi, still to nobody in particular, though everybody is looking and everybody is listening. 'Jik.'

'Ooh!'

'Uh-uh-uh!'

All of the hairdressers are suddenly like a team of emergency doctors on TV. They rush to put Faith in the chair that Grace gives up for her, and they gather around her head, examining the extent of the damage and discussing the best course of treatment. All of them talk at once, while everybody else in the saloon is silent, listening. Even Faith is quiet now, except for some sniffing. Lovemore gives Bibi her own chair at the basin, and Bibi perches on the edge of it, anxiously looking at the group of women around Faith. Lovemore rests a hand on Bibi's shoulder, but Bibi does not seem to notice. At last all the hairdressers agree: all of Faith's hair will have to come off. They cannot shave her head, because the skin is too raw and inflamed, but they will cut as close to her scalp as they can.

Gradually the saloon returns to normal. Another chair is found for Grace so that her relaxing treatment can be completed, Lovemore has a few minutes under the dryer, and everybody seems to find their way back to the sentences that they did not finish before. One of the assistants brings tea with extra sugar for Bibi and Faith before going out to the pharmacy for some soothing antiseptic cream for Faith's scalp.

All of Faith's hair is gone and the cream is being applied when a very dignified-looking lady enters the saloon with a tinkling of bells and a gust of hot air. A vision of coolness despite the heat, she wears a simple but elegant sleeveless dress in a single pale blue colour, carrying on one arm an expensive-looking handbag that matches her expensive-looking shoes. Lovemore is certain that the lady's house can only be on Msasani Peninsula, the best part of Dar es Salaam. Her hair is greying, but even now she could still be a model. Maybe she was even Miss Tanzania once. Lovemore would love to have cheekbones as sharp as that.

'Angel?'

'Ah, Mrs Wimana!' Bibi gets up from her chair and approaches the lady, taking her hand. 'Thank you again, you were so kind to bring us here!'

'No, no. What else could I do? You had an emergency at home, your vehicle wouldn't start. Of course I was going to help.'

'But I'm so embarrassed, Mrs Wimana! You are my customer!'

'But am I not also a woman, Angel? Am I not also a grandmother?'

'That is true, Mrs Wimana—'

'Do I not also have hair?'

'Yes, indeed.'

'Of course I was going to assist. Are you ready now?'

'I think so, yes.'

All of them get into Mrs Wimana's big, smart, air-conditioned car, and she drives them back to the Tungarazas' house. Bibi sits up front, while Lovemore and Grace sit on either side of Faith at the back. Faith is still snivelling, and Grace does her best to comfort her.

'It's not that bad,' Grace whispers.

Lovemore thinks it really is that bad. There are thin tufts of dirty orange and patches of raw baldness. A woman can look beautiful with her head completely shaved, especially when it is shaved because she is mourning her late father or her late husband, and when she is carrying her head high despite the grief that is weighing the rest of her down. But there is nothing beautiful about Faith right now.

'You can wrap your head like Concilia does,' Grace whispers to her. 'Nobody will see.'

Bibi is talking quietly with Mrs Wimana at the front. 'Really, I don't know what possessed that child.'

'She was looking for some attention, Angel, that is all.'

Bibi sighs at the front, and Grace whispers at the back. Lovemore feels like they are in St Joseph's and they are not supposed to be talking because everything is very serious. All she wants to do is giggle. She dares not, though, and that makes her want to even more. She remembers the time in Standard Four when *Mwalimu Mkuu* Makubi came into their classroom to say that he was going to wait there at the front until the child who had hidden the school bell confessed. Sitting in the nervous silence of that classroom, Lovemore and Rose had begun to giggle – not because they were guilty, and not because they thought that a missing school bell was in any way funny – but because

Mwalimu Mkuu Makubi's anger made the silence so very stressful. Laughing was the very last thing that they should do, but it was the only thing that they could do.

That is how it is for Lovemore now, sitting on the back seat with Faith between her and Grace. She feels Faith's distress – she would feel even more distressed herself if her own head looked like that – and she knows that poor Bibi has had the most terrible shock. She would hate either of them to think that the nervous giggle building up in her means that she is laughing at them. And Mrs Wimana is a Very Important Person – Bibi introduced her as the wife of a retired ambassador – and she is also a customer who happened to be at the house ordering a cake from Bibi when Faith decided to bleach her own hair with Titi's Jik. Under no circumstances can Lovemore be disrespectful by laughing in Mrs Wimana's smart, expensive car. Laughing is the very last thing that she should do, but it is the only thing that she can do. Leaning forward so that Mrs Wimana cannot see her in her mirror, she covers her face with her hands. She does not make a sound, but she knows that Faith and Grace must be able to see her shoulders shaking.

Then she hears a kind of snort. Ah, please let it be Faith crying and not Grace laughing! The snort turns into a giggle, and Lovemore holds her breath, trying not to let the laugh that she is holding inside her explode out of her. The giggle is louder now, and it is coming from the front. When Lovemore raises her head, she sees that it is coming from Mrs Wimana.

'I'm sorry, Angel! But it *is* funny! The look on your face!'
'And on yours!' says Bibi, her voice beginning to fill with laughter.
Mrs Wimana is struggling to speak. 'And your house girl!'
'I know!'
'She sounded like she was giving birth to a fully grown warthog!'
Lovemore is laughing out loud now, and so is Grace. Faith is at least smiling.
'I didn't know…' Bibi slaps her leg a few times before she is able to continue, 'I didn't know who needed my help, Faith or Titi!' Bibi turns round and rubs Faith's knee, trying not to laugh. 'I'm sorry, Faith, it's only that—'

'It's okay, Mama!' Faith giggles. 'That sound—'

Mrs Wimana does her best to imitate the sound of Titi giving birth to a fully grown warthog. Bibi joins in, and then Faith. Lovemore feels like she might be on the edge of becoming hysterical, and Grace sounds like she already is.

'I didn't see her!' A tear is making its way down Mrs Wimana's cheek. 'Faith was coming up behind me, I didn't see her. I looked up from your album of cake photos as Titi came in from the kitchen. She saw Faith, and then—'

Mama and Faith make their warthog-delivery sound again, and Lovemore doubles up, seriously afraid that she might wet her pantie like Rose did once when they both laughed too hard.

'Then you...' Bibi gasps for breath, 'you jumped up like the chair was covered in ants!'

'The chair fell! It was chaos!'

A *bajaji* that has overtaken Mrs Wimana's car by using the unsurfaced verge to their left tries to force its way back on to the road in front of them, and Mrs Wimana slams her hand down on the hooter. Lovemore joins everybody else in making the sound of Titi giving birth to a fully grown warthog.

When Mrs Wimana hoots outside their gate, it is Benedict who opens it to let them drive in. His face is anxious, his words heltering and skeltering as Moses and Daniel appear from round the side of the house, covered in dust from the bare earth at the back.

'Faith! Are you okay? And Mama? Mrs Wimana, *karibu*, I have a gift of small carrots from our garden for apologies to you. Grace! Lovemore! Can you put milk on for tea?'

'Where's Titi?' Bibi asks him. 'Is she okay?'

'Mm.' He slides an arm round Faith's shoulder, his eyes growing very big as they sweep over her head. 'She was crying, then I made her a nice cup of tea and she started to feel better. She's lying down. I think we must leave her to rest.'

'Good boy, Benedict.' Bibi pats his shoulder. 'Good boy.'

Giving Bibi a smile that seems to light up his whole face – his entire body, even – Benedict ushers them all inside. Lovemore hears him quietly chiding Faith for frightening Bibi and Titi, and for disrupting

Bibi's business with her customer.

'That is not how we behave in this house, Faith.'

'I'm sorry.' Faith's voice is tiny.

Titi appears suddenly in the doorway to the kitchen, and Faith goes to her and lets her examine her head.

Mrs Wimana looks at them and begins to giggle. Bibi joins her, and when Grace does, too, Lovemore cannot hold back. A slow smile begins to spread across Titi's face, and Lovemore is certain that before the pot is even filled with milk, Titi will be persuaded to let them all hear exactly how it sounds for a warthog to give birth.

Chapter 6

THE TUNGARAZAS are finishing their breakfast one Saturday morning when the telephone-fax on the computer table rings. Lovemore is closest to it, so she picks up the receiver.

'Hello?'

'Let me guess. Is it Lovemore?' Concilia's warm, familiar voice sounds excited.

'Hello, Concilia. How are you?'

'*Eh*, I'm very fine, thank you. I hope everybody there is well because I'm rushing and I don't have time for individual enquiries.'

Lovemore smiles. 'We are all well.'

'Good. Is your bibi there?'

'Mm, hold on.' Lovemore offers the phone to Bibi, but Bibi's hands are sticky with margarine and jam, so she tells Lovemore to push the button that puts the phone on speaker.

'Concilia! Hello! We are on speaker and others are here.'

'No problem, Angel, this is not a private matter. Listen! Do you have today's *Citizen*?'

'Uh-uh. I only see a newspaper when Pius is here. He is the one who buys.'

'Aah! Still in Ethiopia?'

'Still! But he'll be back soon.'

'Very good. Listen! Do you know a brand of icing sugar that calls itself Kilimanjaro Snow?'

'Uh-uh.'

'It's very new. To launch itself it's organising a national competition for cake decorating!'

'*Eh!*' Bibi is on her feet now, wiping her hands on a paper serviette. 'Seriously? You are not joking with me?'

'I promise you, Angel! It's in today's *Citizen*.'

'Read it to me,' says Bibi, and everybody gathers around the telephone-fax to listen, Moses and Daniel standing on chairs behind their taller brother and sisters as if they think that being able to see the machine will help them to hear.

'Right.' The sound of rustling paper comes from the small speaker on the telephone-fax. 'Kilimanjaro Snow superior icing sugar is proud to announce its launch with a nation-wide hunt for the best cake-decorator in all of Tanzania—'

'It's our mama,' say several of the children.

'Auntie, it's you,' says Titi.

'*Shh*,' says Bibi, nodding her head yes, 'let us listen.'

'Ah, Angel, somebody is going to be here at any moment, I can hear the gate opening. Let me just skim and tell you. In the first round, twelve winners in each region … second round one per region … finals at the New Africa hotel in Dar es Salaam … Listen, Angel, I'm going to fax, see? Right now! Let me say my goodbyes!' The low buzz tells them that Concilia has rung off.

'*Eh*, we must end,' says Bibi, and Lovemore presses the button to end the call.

Nobody moves.

'Bibi, this competition is for you!' Lovemore has not seen any cakes more beautiful than Bibi's.

'You are the winner, Auntie.'

'They don't even need to have the competition, Mama.'

'Already you have won.'

'Nobody is better than you, Mama.'

Smiling widely, Bibi pats the side of her hair with one hand.

The telephone-fax rings, and they all stare at it while they wait for Babu's Uncle-Joseph voice on the answering machine to tell the caller to leave a message or send a fax. Then an inner whirring begins, and a page from the tray gets scooped up into the machine before it slowly stutters out the full announcement from Kilimanjaro Snow. No sooner is the page in Bibi's hand than the phone rings again.

Bibi snatches up the receiver. 'Concilia? … *Eh*! Pius!'

Bibi puts the page down on the dining table without even seeing that its corner has gone into the tub of Blue Band. Lovemore scoops it up and wipes the margarine off its corner with a tissue. While the others wait for their turns on the phone with Babu, she reads through the announcement. In round one, Bibi will have to submit six photographs of six different cakes that she has decorated herself. Once she has been chosen as one of the twelve winners in the Dar es Salaam region, she will decorate a wedding cake and have it assessed by a team of judges. When the judges have declared her wedding cake the best in the Dar es Salaam region, she will need to decorate a cake that represents Tanzania, and all the other regional winners will be brought here to the New Africa Hotel to compete against her. The top three will all win baking and decorating equipment and a year's supply of Kilimanjaro Snow, and there are different amounts of prize money. Lovemore cannot believe her eyes when she sees how much the winner will get! It is a very good prize indeed. Not nearly enough for a smart new vehicle to replace the old red microbus, it will certainly buy a handle for the door into the kitchen, some roof tiles to stop the leak that drips into the kitchen, and a good coat of paint for every room in the house. All the rules can be found on the Kilimanjaro Snow website or on leaflets that are available at any post office.

'Lovemore! You're next!'

Babu prefers to speak to them one by one because on speaker everybody tries to talk to him at once, and Babu does not like chaos. Faith is busy with her turn, and she is telling him about the note that she brought home from school yesterday saying that she does not see the board very well.

'No, I do sit near the front, Baba … But I can see! … Mm … She's taking me next week.'

Lovemore knows that Faith does not want to go to the optician next week, and that she does not want to get glasses. Grace has told her that if she has to get glasses she can make people not notice them by taking off her head wrap so that they stare at the damage to her scalp instead, but that has not helped. Faith finishes her turn without telling Babu anything about the Jik.

Taking the phone from her, Lovemore recognises that only some of the excitement in her chest is for Bibi and the cake competition. The rest is for herself, because she is about to talk to Babu and listen to his words in Uncle Joseph's voice.

Early in the following week, Lovemore finally gives up on trying to memorise unicellular rhizopods and their use of pseudopodia (singular: pseudopodium), and gives in to the temptation of Mama's journal. She has resisted for a long time, partly because reading it can leave her feeling upset and shaky. That makes her need Mama to be here to comfort her, which only reminds her again that Mama is no longer here – and that upsets her even more. But another part of avoiding reading it is about worrying about getting to the end of it. Reading some of it each and every day would mean that she would soon arrive at Mama's last ever entry, and after reading that she would have no more of Mama's words left to read. That would be like losing Mama all over again.

But she wants to read more so that she can feel close to Mama – and that temptation is very strong.

Making herself comfortable on Titi's top bunk, she opens the journal and finds where she finished reading last time.

After the Nile Perch Plastics factory was built we needed only a small part of the big old warehouse, so I said to the younger Mr Desai why don't we divide it into smaller units? If a house has only 1 big room it can be right for only 1 family, but when you divide it into 2 rooms it can be right for 2 families. What if there are some small businesses that want to rent smaller spaces to store things? The younger Mr Desai said maybe it was a good idea, he was going to put his feelers out. His feelers came back and told him that many businesses sometimes needed a space for something. So builders came in and put some wooden walls to make six units for rent down one of the long sides of the warehouse. Each unit has its own outside door for renters to lock with their own padlock, and the unit at the far end, the long one that goes all the way from one side of the warehouse to the other, that one has a big roller door if anybody wants to store vehicles. The back wall for the smaller units goes almost down the middle of the main warehouse, so Nile Perch Plastics still has plenty of space.

Most businesses rent a space from us on a short term, but the Chinese rent one of the smaller units permanently, they keep freezers in there for their swimming bladders. When their freezers get full, they pack their frozen swimming bladders into some Nile Perch Plastics polystyrene foam boxes and take them to other freezers in Dar es Salaam where they keep the fins from sharks. No person can smell that there is anything from a fish on the Nile Perch Plastics compound, but there is one big bird that knows, a marabou stork. Eh, that bird is too ugly! It sits on top of the outside wall of the compound and it watches the side of the warehouse. If ever anybody goes near one of the outside doors it jumps down on to the ground and follows them in case they are bringing swimming bladders to put into the freezers. It can even chase a person or try to take what a person is carrying. Those Chinese hate that bird but they love it because it is also like an extra day watch.

When we began with renting out the warehouse units the younger Mr Desai told me that my idea was excellent, that it was further confirmation that he was right to hire me as his clerk in the beginning, even though he saw very quickly that I was only pretending to know how to write shorthand. Eh, I never knew that he knew that I didn't know shorthand! I always went to him with my pen and my shorthand notebook and I wrote down a few words of what he was saying, but really I was concentrating hard and making myself remember every word. Joseph didn't know for more than a year that I was pretending, then one day he looked at my shorthand notebook and he started to laugh. He bought me a small tape-recorder and some blank cassettes. But by then I was used to remembering every word of what anybody was saying, I didn't need the tape recorder. I have it with me at work for just in case, and it goes home with me every night so me and Lovemore can listen to the cassettes that come from Agrippina's cousin Joy in America.

As soon as everything at Nile Perch Plastics was running well in Joseph's hands, the younger Mr Desai left us and went to start up a new factory in Kenya, Samaki Accessories. That factory takes the skins of Nile perches and tilapias and makes them into all the things that people usually make from the skin of a cow or a crocodile. Every few months the younger Mr Desai comes back to check on us at Nile Perch Plastics, and every time he comes he shows us something new from Samaki Accessories like his belt or his shoes or his wallet. Those are very special things to see in Mwanza because they go to Europe or America, they are too expensive for us here.

<u>Lovemore</u> – I am too sorry about that marabou stork, see?

Lovemore tries not to think about that marabou stork, but the harder she tries, the more impossible it becomes to think about anything else. In her mind, she goes right back to that day.

It is the school holidays, and Auntie Agrippina has brought Lovemore and Rose to Nile Perch Plastics to see how everything works. Lovemore has been in the office part before, but not in the factory part, the part where they make things. Rose has never been there at all, and she is excited to see a framed photo of her baba, Uncle Steven, on the wall in Uncle Joseph's office. Strictly speaking, only the people who know Uncle Steven can see that the blurry man right at the back is him. It is the picture for November from the Nile Perch Plastics calendar, the picture that shows Nile perches at the fish factory being packed for going to Europe. Visitors are not allowed at the fish factory because of hygiene, so Auntie Agrippina cannot take the girls there to see how everything works. Visitors are not allowed in the Nile Perch Plastics factory, either, but Uncle Joseph is the boss, and he is doing a favour for Mama, his Personal Assistant.

When they go into the factory part with Uncle Joseph, Lovemore and Rose hold hands. Auntie Agrippina would like to stay chatting with Mama in Mama's office, but she goes into the factory with them because the girls are only seven and she wants to be sure that they are safe. There are signs all over the factory that tell them to be careful because things are dangerous.

Uncle Joseph lets them hold in their hands the tiny white plastic pellets that come from Tanzania Plastics in Dar es Salaam. They weigh almost nothing, and feel like sand in Lovemore's hand. Somebody measures some of the tiny pellets into a big machine and presses a button that steams them. When they come out just a few minutes later, they have grown into big white beads. They are very hot, so Lovemore and Rose must not touch, no matter how much they want to. When the beads are cool and dry, they will go into an enormous open sack just like the other sacks that hang in a corner of the factory.

'They need to rest here,' Uncle Joseph tells them, patting one of the sacks, 'because, really, they have been through a lot. In just a short time they have grown up to forty times the size that they were. Have you girls ever had too much to eat and your stomach is just too full?'

Uncle Joseph clutches his belly, while Lovemore and Rose nod their heads yes. 'You see? Then what do you do to get comfortable?'

'Burp,' says Lovemore, giggling.

'Fart,' says Rose.

'Girls!'

'No, it's okay, Agrippina, the girls are right. These beads need to fart.'

'Joseph!'

'What do you want me to tell them, Agrippina? That the beads are unstable and that they have an internal vacuum that needs to be equalised to atmospheric pressure to avoid implosion?'

Auntie Agrippina smiles. 'You are right, Joseph. I'm sorry.'

'Okay, so we leave the beads here to fart for two days, and then they are ready for moulding into shapes.'

They watch as some of the beads that have finished farting are placed into another machine before the machine adds steam and pressure like when you are ironing your clothes. When the machine opens, it has made boxes like the ones Uncle Steven packs with frozen Nile perch fillets. Those boxes will protect the fish pieces all the way to Europe on the plane. Then they watch as another machine turns more beads that have finished farting into cups for hot and cold drinks.

Before they leave the factory to go back into the offices, Uncle Joseph gives Lovemore and Rose a cup each.

Rose sniffs hers. 'It doesn't smell like fart,' she whispers to Lovemore.

Lovemore puts her nose to hers. 'Uh-uh.'

In the small kitchen, there is a treat for the girls: two ice creams on sticks that Uncle Joseph bought on his way in to work. Taking them out of the freezer part of the small fridge in the office kitchen, Mama helps to peel off the paper before sending the girls outside to play while Mama and Auntie Agrippina have tea with Uncle Joseph.

Lovemore is excited to have an ice cream. It makes her feel like she is at somebody's birthday party. As they enjoy their treat, she and Rose wander around the outside of Nile Perch Plastics. The old warehouse is huge, and they can see a man loading boxes inside. The man waves to them, and they wave back. It looks nice and cool in there, so Lovemore feels tempted to go in and chat to the man for a few minutes. But Mama has told them not to go into the warehouse, so instead they move round to the side, where the warehouse is making a shadow. Rose stops to shake a small stone from her shoe, so Lovemore is quite a few steps ahead of her when it happens.

She thinks that the sound behind her is Rose running to catch up, but when she turns it is something else entirely. The bird is enormous, as tall as Lovemore as it runs towards her on its grey legs, its black wings spread out wide. From its white chest rises an ugly bald neck and head, its long pink beak aiming straight for Lovemore. Lovemore and Rose start screaming at exactly the same time.

Lovemore runs, and the bird runs after her. She turns to run a different way, but the bird is there. It attacks her again and again with its huge beak. Without even thinking, she keeps her arms up to protect her head. Above her own screams she can hear a lot of shouting. Mama's voice is there, and also Uncle Joseph's. There is a confusion of legs and arms, and at last the bird is gone, running ahead of the day watch until it flies up on to the high compound wall and glares down at everybody.

Uncle Joseph scoops Lovemore up into his arms and holds her until she stops screaming, then he carries her inside and sits her on the counter in reception. It is only then that Mama can hold her. The reception lady has already run to fetch the first aid kit from the kitchen, and when she comes back with it, she and Mama take a good look all over Lovemore's arms and the rest of her body. Rose is holding on to Auntie Agrippina, who is trying to wipe the tears from Rose's face.

'Ah, Lovemore,' Uncle Joseph says, 'I'm so sorry. That damn marabou stork! Glory, did you not warn the girls to stay away from it?'

'Don't blame me for this! The younger Mr Desai has told you to chase that bird away. How many times?'

'It's not too bad,' the reception lady says, dabbing on some stinging red ointment that hurts Lovemore more than the stork did. 'I think it's mostly shock.'

'Tea,' says the tea lady, and she goes to the kitchen to make some.

Lovemore feels much better after a cup of tea, but Uncle Joseph gives Mama the rest of the day off to look after her. When they go out of the building, the man from the warehouse, the reception lady and the tea lady go with them, forming a wall of people around Lovemore and Rose to protect them from the stork as they make their way to Auntie Agrippina's car.

'Mr Tungaraza is so good with children,' the reception lady says to Mama. 'Look how he took care of your daughter.'

'Mm.'

'It's because he has three of his own,' the tea lady tells Auntie Agrippina.

'Ah.'

'He is a good man,' the warehouse man says to all of them, and all of them agree.

Safely inside Auntie Agrippina's car, they stop at the Nile Perch Plastics gate to thank the day watch for the part he played in saving Lovemore.

'*Eh*, that bird!' he says, shaking his head and rolling his eyes. '*Pole sana.*'

'*Asante sana*,' they all say back to him.

Then he looks towards something behind the car and tells them to wait. Auntie Agrippina looks in her mirror and the rest of them turn round to see. Uncle Joseph is hurrying towards the car with Lovemore and Rose's polystyrene foam cups that started out as tiny plastic pellets.

Just a few days after taking herself back to when she was attacked by the marabou stork, something happens that feels to Lovemore like a kind of revenge – not against that particular marabou stork, but at least against birds in general. She is at the computer, typing a letter that Bibi is dictating to one of her nephews in her home town of Bukoba. Bibi is at the dining table, decorating a cake. Mama could do a number of things at once and keep them all separate in her mind, but that is still something new for Bibi, and it is not going well.

'What have I just said?'

Lovemore reads to her from the computer's screen. 'I'm thinking of you especially today because of the cake I'm making. I'm remembering that girlfriend you had while you were studying here at UDSM. That's the University of Dar es Salaam—'

'Ah, no, Lovemore, I was telling *you* it's the University of Dar es Salaam. He already knows that.'

'Oh. Okay.' Lovemore deletes that sentence before continuing to read Bibi's words back to her. 'What was her name? Something with a T. Tania? Tina? Anyway, the one who was deaf. But I don't know if I should say the word deaf.'

'No, Lovemore, that part is not for in the letter, that is just for me. What do you think? Should I say the word deaf?'

'Was she deaf, Bibi?'

Bibi clicks her tongue against the back of her teeth. 'Sometimes it is not right to say something. Sometimes it is better just to suggest it, or even not to suggest it.'

Lovemore thinks about it. Not about what Bibi has just said, but about how not to say *deaf*. 'If I can put her name, he will remember that she was deaf, then you don't have to say. Can you not remember it, Bibi?'

Bibi clicks her tongue against the back of her teeth a few more times, and Lovemore is not sure if Bibi is trying to say the name but getting no further than the T it begins with, or if Bibi is angry with herself for not being able to remember. While Bibi is trying to remember, Lovemore thinks ahead to the next few sentences that Bibi is going to dictate. They are going to be about the cake that Bibi is busy decorating, and that is going to make not saying *deaf* very difficult, because the cake shows all the letters in the deaf alphabet. How is Bibi going to talk about it without talking about it?

The cake is for Concilia, who is Bibi's very best friend – better than the one called Irene who, when the family was coming back to Tanzania from Swaziland, made sure that the tenants were gone, the house was clean and the fridge was full; better than the one called Fatima who has her own tie-and-dye fabric business at her house so she understands when Bibi is too busy for visitors; better than the one called Esther who tells Bibi every Sunday at church that the Tungarazas are in her daily prayers; and better even than the one with white hair called Stella who is always disappointed when Babu is away or out, and who falls asleep where she is sitting after two cups of tea. Bibi does not mind when Stella goes to sleep – she just tiptoes back to the dining table and gets on with her cakes – but whenever Titi clears away Stella's cup of tea, she puts it to her nose and gives Bibi a hard look. Whatever that is about, Bibi waves it away with her hand. Stella's late husband was one of Babu's best friends, so Bibi is never going to ask her to go and sleep in somebody else's lounge.

Bibi's best friend Concilia has ordered this cake for the deaf children at a primary school where children with nothing wrong learn alongside deaf or blind or autism children. They have their classes separately, but at break time they all play together. The school is on Msasani Peninsula, but Concilia says this school is nothing like the International School that is on that peninsula. It has no swimming pool or library or sports field or international teachers, and there can be more than one hundred children in a classroom with just one teacher. That is not how it is at the International School.

For the cake, Concilia gave Bibi a photo of the deaf alphabet that is painted on an outside wall of one of the classrooms so that all the children can learn it, not just the ones who need it because they are deaf. It shows how to spell each letter with your fingers, and each letter and finger-picture is in black on a white background. Bibi does not like to use too much white on a cake, and white with black writing on it is very ugly for her, so she is making a colourful deaf alphabet instead. She has made five strips of sugary colour to go across the surface of the cake, and she is busy drawing on to the strips the letters and fingers. There is a light purple strip with letters and hands in dark blue, a pale blue strip with letters and hands in red, and a pale green strip with letters and hands in purple. As soon as Bibi has finished drawing green letters on to the yellow strip, she will work on the last strip, the red one that she will draw on with white. Twenty-six letters do not fit equally into five rows, so Bibi is evening things out with four red heart shapes, one in each of the rows that is not red.

Lovemore is sure that Concilia will love the colourful cake, even though Concilia does not wear very much colour herself. Mostly she dresses in black or brown, and even when she wraps her head, the cloth is never bright. She is very friendly and kind to everybody, but her clothes say that she does not want anybody to notice her. Maybe she does not want anybody to notice that she is a polio.

'Bibi, what would Concilia say?'
'Hmm?'

'Would Concilia say *deaf?*'

Looking up from piping green letters on to the yellow, Bibi nods her head yes. 'But that is Concilia. Concilia will never try to say something without saying it. She will never dance around a word instead of using it.'

While Bibi goes back to drawing green icing on to the outline of fingers that she drew earlier with a pen that no longer has any ink, Lovemore thinks about Concilia dressing in such a way that she does not stand out but using words in such a way that she does.

'No, my letter is from me, not Concilia. I don't think I want to say *deaf*. Let us find a way to talk about Tiny—' Bibi lifts up her plastic icing syringe just in time for her surprise not to mess up the green fingers that are showing the letter T. '*Eh!* Tiny! That is her name! Tiny! Write *Tiny*, Lovemore.'

Lovemore turns back to the keyboard and makes some deletions. 'Okay,' she says, then begins to read to Bibi. 'I'm thinking of you especially today because of the cake I'm making. I'm remembering Tiny, that girlfriend you had while you were studying here at UDSM.'

'Good. Now how am I going to talk about this cake? I suppose I can say it's an alphabet for people like Tiny. Or do I need to say anything at all if I enclose a photo of the cake? But what is that noise, Lovemore?'

Something is happening in the back yard.

'*Auntie!*' It is Titi's voice.

Lovemore follows Bibi through the kitchen and out into the yard, where next to the high back wall Moses and Daniel are both half squatting, each of them holding one of Benedict's feet as they try to lift him. Titi is telling Benedict to get down, but he is not listening.

'Tell them, Auntie.'

'Benedict, get down! Boys, put him down!'

All three of them do as Bibi says.

Benedict looks upset. 'They shot a crow, Mama!'

'Shot?' Bibi looks suddenly afraid, and starts to make gestures about coming inside. 'With a gun?'

'Uh-uh, a stone,' says Moses. 'Maybe from a catapult.'

'It was sitting on top of the tree,' says Daniel, pointing across the wall.

'And you are trying to climb the wall because why?'

'Maybe it's hurt, Mama. Maybe it needs help.'

'*Mambo?*' A man's voice comes from the other side of the wall.

'*Safi.*' Bibi and Benedict answer the man together.

'There is nothing that can help this crow now.' A pair of hands appears over the top of the wall, and then a head with thin white hair that looks like a dusting of icing sugar on top. 'I got it right on its head.'

Grace and Faith have wandered out to join them now. Lovemore is delighted that there is one less bird in the world, but Benedict looks distressed. 'Why? Why did you kill it?'

'Benedict, first we greet,' says Bibi. 'Hello, Mr Kapufi. How are you?'

'Mrs Tungaraza, I am well.' His eyes sweep over everybody in the yard. 'I can see that everybody here is fine. Is Tungaraza well?'

'Very well, thank you.' Bibi does not mention that Babu is still away in Ethiopia, that he was supposed to be back already but he extended his stay there by another ten days, and that everybody is very disappointed. 'And Mrs Kapufi?'

'Fine, fine, thank you.'

'Mr Kapufi,' demands Benedict, 'why did you kill the crow?'

'Ah, it is what we are asked to do. These house crows are pests. Have you not seen the big traps that have been put up at the markets to catch them?'

'It has been on the news,' says Bibi.

Titi takes a towel off the washing line and begins to fold it. 'Is a crow good to eat, *Bwana*?'

Mr Kapufi's face looks like something under his nose suddenly smells very bad, like he shot the bird last week and now it is rotting at his feet. 'Do you want to eat something that has already eaten the rubbish that everybody has thrown out into the street? That is what these crows are eating now, now that they have already eaten all of our other birds.' He looks down over the wall at Benedict. 'If you care about birds, you need to be killing house crows. I can make a catapult for you if—'

'Yes!' cries Moses.

'Please!' cries Daniel.

'Stop it!' Benedict tells them.

'Mr Kapufi, thank you,' says Bibi, 'but here we are non-violent.'

'Non-violent? Ah, like that Gandhi.' Again Mr Kapufi's face begins to show a bad smell under his nose. 'That Indian. These house crows are Indian, too. Invading us. Taking everything. Growing fat on what is ours.'

Lovemore is not sure what Mr Kapufi is saying about crows from India and what he is saying about people from India. She liked him at first because he got rid of a bird, but now she is not so sure. The two Mr Desais, the Indian owners of Nile Perch Plastics, were always very good to Mama, and very kind to Lovemore.

Bibi looks uncomfortable. 'Titi, is it not time for tea?'

'Always, Auntie.' Scooping up the basket of folded washing, Titi heads for the kitchen door.

Bibi turns away from Mr Kapufi. 'Have a good day,' she tells him.

'And you.' His head disappears behind the wall. 'Greet Tungaraza for me.'

'Thank you. And our hellos to Mrs Kapufi.'

'Yes. Thank you.'

Back at the computer, Lovemore suddenly has an idea. Bibi should rather dictate into Mama's small cassette recorder, the one that is inside the box inside Lovemore's suitcase under her bed. But she cannot get it now because the girls have drifted back to their room, and she does not want them to see her box from Mama or anything that is inside it. She will fetch the cassette recorder when she gets the chance, put in one of the blank cassettes that are also in the box, and show Bibi how to use it.

There was a lightness about Angel tonight as she carried her heavy albums of cake photos from their place in the TV cabinet to the dining table. It was not a physical lightness. No. She still needed to worry about the seams of her smart skirts where they strained across her hips, and she still felt so much more comfortable in a loose-fitting T-shirt with a *kanga* wrapped around her and tied loosely at her waist. The lightness was a feeling inside her, and it felt a bit like happiness. Okay, not happiness – Pius had been away for far too long for her to feel any happiness at all. What was it then? Perhaps it would become clearer to her when she concentrated on making tonight's list later on.

Carefully moving aside the two cakes that she had just completed – a large, tall square of coffee-flavoured layers alternating with chocolate layers, and a big round of vanilla sponge that she had decorated to look just like a pizza, both of them spectacular but neither of them in her top six – she settled down at the table to start looking through her albums. Over the days since Concilia had phoned with news of the competition, the children had come up with many suggestions of which six cakes she should choose as her entry for round one. There was still plenty of time – the closing date was far away to give the news time to spread to every town and village in the country, to give people time to bake and photograph six cakes, and to give the entries time to navigate their way through the postal system – but Angel wanted to make a start by choosing her top twenty or twenty-five possible choices. Maybe even her top thirty.

Then she remembered something, and went back to the TV cabinet for what she had hidden away from the children's prying fingers after Lovemore had given it to her today. Okay, Lovemore hadn't *given* it to her – something that had belonged to her late mother would have been much too precious to give – but she had been kind enough to let Angel use it. A Dictaphone, Pius had called it when she had described it to him over the phone earlier this evening. Lovemore had suggested that Angel could use it for dictating any letters that she wanted Lovemore to type for her. Angel was certainly glad of that, because Lovemore was not very good at taking dictation herself. The girl became easily muddled about the clear difference between Angel's words for a letter and her words in general. Really, Angel would not be surprised to find that Lovemore had typed – in the middle of a letter – an instruction to Titi to heat some milk for tea. The tape recorder would certainly help Lovemore to be clearer, but it would also help Angel, too. She had begun to notice things that she was grateful for during the day, and maybe if she could speak them into the tape recorder as she noticed them, by the time she got to her notebook she would find that her list had already written itself.

She could say something about that right now, for her number one. Seated at the dining table with the fan cooling her back, she held the small machine in front of her with the microphone on one of its edges pointing to her mouth, just like Lovemore had showed her, and began to speak. 'I am grateful for Lovemore's tape recorder,' she said, unsure why she had chosen to use her professional voice, the one that she used with her customers.

Then, keen to hear how it sounded, she put the tape recorder down on the table and pressed play. There was a faint squeaking, but there was no sound of her voice. Through the see-through part of the front panel she could see that the cassette was definitely moving round. She found the volume switch where Lovemore had showed her, but still she could not hear her voice. When she pressed stop and the button made a loud click, she realised that she had failed to press the red button that said record. *Eh*, how glad she was that Pius was not here to see her mistake! He would have laughed at her gently enough – but really, she would have preferred not to be laughed at in any way at all, especially by a much more educated somebody like Pius.

She pressed firmly on the red button, its sharp click sounding very like the crack of an eggshell against the rim of a mixing bowl, and said again into the microphone, 'I am grateful for Lovemore's tape recorder.' Again it was her professional voice – but perhaps that was the right sort of voice to use for talking to a machine.

She rewound and pressed play, and this time her voice was way too loud for a silent house at this time of night. She scrambled for the volume control, rewound and listened again. It sounded like her, but – even with taking into account that it was her professional voice – it also sounded strangely unlike her.

While she was thinking of Lovemore and her tape recorder, another reason to be grateful came into her mind. Making sure to press the red button for its satisfying click first, she told the machine that she was grateful that things had become easier between her and Lovemore. She said it very quickly, as though any delay in saying it might make it no longer true. It was a fragile ease, but it was definitely there. Right from the start, Lovemore had seemed less comfortable with Angel than with Pius, but now her comfort around Angel had definitely been growing. Perhaps it was because Pius had not been here to draw Lovemore to him like a dhow caught in a current, or perhaps it was because asking for Lovemore's help with typing letters had made the girl feel useful to Angel and allowed her to feel needed, to feel wanted. Angel hoped with all of her heart that she had never made the girl feel *un*wanted.

Putting the machine aside for the moment, Angel began to page through her albums, stopping occasionally to examine one of the photos in detail. Very soon, it became clear that she was going to need some way of marking the cakes that were definite possibilities, so she returned to the drawer in the TV cabinet for Pius's block of yellow squares of paper that could be stuck and unstuck to pages. Pius did not like waste, so she tore a sheet into narrow strips so that each sheet could mark five cakes.

As she paged and marked, she stopped briefly to tell the machine that she was grateful that – so far – there did not seem to be any shortage of work for Pius. He had gone to Addis Ababa in Ethiopia to help with preparations for the new African Union parliament that was going to be based there, and even before he had finished that job some coffee growers had contracted him to stay on and help them. It could not be good coffee – good coffee came from Bukoba, Angel and Pius's home town on the western shores of Lake Victoria – but that did not matter. Nor did it matter – really – that more work for Pius meant that he was away from Angel for longer. What mattered most was that Pius would come back, and that he would come back with American dollars that would – along with the Tanzanian shillings from Angel's cake business – take care of their grandchildren as they grew.

Continuing to page and mark, she imagined how Pius had gone about getting the additional work with the coffee growers. Angel would have met them by chance and taken the opportunity to help them to have the idea that they needed her, that nobody else in the world would do, and that they wanted – more than anything – to pay her a great deal of money. But that was not Pius's way. No. Pius was much more direct, more deliberate. He would have submitted a proposal with headings and charts and statistics, and then he would have met with them in a good suit to negotiate a contract and his fee. That was Pius's way and it worked for him – just as Angel's own way of being a professional somebody worked for her.

There were so many cakes for her to choose that she was in danger of using up all of Pius's sheets of sticky yellow, even with tearing them into tinier strips. Was having too much choice something she could give thanks for? She had already been grateful for the competition on many pages of her notebook – because she had the skill to win all the way up to the national level; because the competition would give her something to focus on instead of Pius's absence; because everybody in her family had already told her that she was the winner; because Irene, Fatima, Esther and Stella had simply assumed that she had already won, and had started to make suggestions of how she could spend her prize money; and because Agrippina had sent her an SMS text message from Mwanza to say that that she was going to pray in her church for Bibi-Lovemore to win rather than anybody from the Mwanza region.

So why not be grateful for having this many spectacular cakes from which to choose just six – *six!* – for round one?

She said that into the tape recorder and then rewound and listened from the beginning. It felt very strange to listen to herself, and she found herself wondering uneasily if what she was doing might not be called talking to herself. *Eh*, that was a very bad sign in an older person! Stella had been visiting Irene just the other day, and when Irene had come back into her lounge after using the washroom, she had thought that Stella was talking into her mobile phone, but then she had seen that there was no phone in Stella's hand.

'I'm telling you Angel, she was talking to herself!'

'*Eh*, but maybe your house girl—'

'Uh-uh! Out at the market! Nobody there but me and her!'

'What did she say?'

'No, I didn't hear. But she was saying something. And nobody in the room but her!'

'*Eh*, Irene, do you think it was maybe Deogratias?'

'*Deogratias?* Deogratias her husband who has been late these however many years? Angel!'

'No, I'm not saying he was there, I'm saying maybe Stella thought he was. She was talking to *him.*'

'*Eh!* Talking to somebody long late, talking to herself, this way or that she is having a problem in her head. I'm telling you, Angel!'

Angel decided to give up on the challenge of choosing her six cakes for tonight. She tidied everything away, switched off the fan and the light and went through to her bedroom with the tape recorder. Then she completed her list in her notebook before preparing herself for bed.

As she settled down under the sheet, she thought again about the lightness that she had been feeling. If she could hear Pius snoring quietly beside her, or if she could reach out and touch him, she would recognise it very clearly as happiness. But it could not be that. Was it joy? No. How could she feel joyous with Pius away in Ethiopia, and with the whole of Kenya in between here and there? No. It could not be as strong as joy.

She lay on her back for a while, imagining Pius settling down for the night far away, and she remembered a conversation that she had had with him just before Lovemore had come to stay. They had been in the kitchen, and Pius had rolled his eyes at the heaps of *ugali*, fruit, vegetables, chicken, fish and meat from the market that Titi and Angel had been trying to find room for in the cupboards, the fridge and the freezer.

'The girl is just one more mouth to feed, Angel. Just one more mouth. She is not a horde of refugees who have eaten nothing but leaves for weeks.'

'But is she not a kind of refugee, Pius? The kind that has to move from one part of their own country to another?'

'You mean an Internally Displaced Person?'

'Exactly. She is internally displaced.'

'IDPs are not people who simply move, Angel, they are people who are forced to flee. Is there a war going on in Mwanza? Is she fleeing here from armed men there who are attacking or harassing her? No. She is just a child who is coming to live with her grandparents because her parents are late.'

'But she is being displaced.'

Pius had shrugged, raising both his palms in the air. 'I cannot argue with that.'

'Internally. In this country.'

Pius had rolled his eyes. 'It is not a refugee we are housing, Angel. The girl is part of our family.'

Lying in bed now without Pius, Angel saw that of course Lovemore had never been any kind of refugee. No. The person who had been internally displaced was Angel – displaced internally inside herself, knocked sideways by having to accept that she was not in fact who she had thought herself to be. She was not a good mother who had raised a decent, honest, loving son. She was a grandmother not of five, but of six, and the sixth – a complete stranger – had needed a place to stay in Angel's heart. Confused, angry, ashamed and overwhelmed, part of her had fled from herself. She could see that now, now that she had regained her balance and come back to herself.

For a few minutes she imagined that she was matching her breathing to Pius's as he lay in his hotel bed far away.

Home, she thought, finding at last the word for the lightness that she was feeling. She had been away from herself, and now she was home.

Smiling gently, she rolled very sleepily onto her side.

Chapter 7

Babu is still not back from Ethiopia when Grace asks Titi at breakfast one school morning if she can clean the toilet in the girls' room with something that will kill ants. 'Please, Titi. You know I don't like insects.' Grace shudders, turning her mouth down and flaring her nostrils.

Titi pauses, her slice of bread and peanut butter halfway to her mouth. 'Ants? But no.' She shakes her head. 'For ants I boil a lot of *pilipili* in water and then I spray the water. If I spray that *pilipili* water on the toilet, what is going to happen to your parts when you sit?'

'Ooh!' Rolling her eyes behind her glasses, Bibi puts down her cup of tea. 'Even after chopping *pilipili*, if you touch your eye? *Eh*, it burns! Girls, you don't want your parts burning like that!' Bibi squirms on her chair, her eyes shut tight, her lips clamped together like a tweezer.

If any of the girls uses the toilet during the night, they are not supposed to flush, because when the water tank re-fills, it makes a loud moaning sound that will wake at least the other two girls and possibly everybody else in the house. Maybe even Mr and Mrs Kapufi, the neighbours at the back. During the noise of daytime, the sound is not at all loud, but somehow the night's silence and darkness magnify it. The girl who gets to the toilet first in the morning will sometimes find another girls' night-time urine still there.

'I've seen the ants,' Lovemore tells Bibi. She makes a circle with one finger pointing down. 'Down inside the toilet bowl, all around the edge of the urine. I think they're drinking it.'

'*Eh!*' Bibi and Titi look at each other.

'*Sugar!*' They both say the word at exactly the same time, Bibi clutching a hand to her chest, Titi putting a hand to her mouth.

'Ooh!'

'Uh-uh-uh!'

Lovemore, Grace and Faith look at Bibi and Titi. The boys, having their breakfast on the stools pulled out from under the coffee table, continue to chat, unaware that at the dining table Titi is blinking very rapidly and Bibi is mopping her brow with a tissue from inside her bra.

'What?' It is Grace who asks.

'Ooh, girls!' Bibi continues to mop. 'One of you is having sugar! *Eh!* Sugar is a very bad thing.'

Lovemore knows that sugar is a bad thing for her buttocks, but still there is sugar in their tea and in their cake. If it is a very bad thing, why is it there?

'What, Mama?' Faith is looking alarmed.

'Sugar in urine,' Titi says, shaking her head. 'That is the first sign.'

'Then it is on to injections,' Bibi says. 'You know your old Auntie Geraldine in Bukoba?' Grace and Faith nod their heads yes, while Lovemore shakes her head no. 'Her husband was late from sugar.'

'We are going to be late, Mama?' Faith looks close to tears.

'No!' says Titi, her eyes wide.

'Please, God,' says Bibi, making her church's sign of the cross in front of her, 'there has been enough lateness in this family. No. Nobody is going to be late, not as long as we nip it.' She plunges her tissue back into her bra. 'We will start to nip it tonight.'

Before they go to sleep that night, Lovemore, Grace and Faith each urinate into a polystyrene foam cup – maybe even one that was made here in Dar es Salaam at Tanzania Plastics, the father company of Nile Perch Plastics in Mwanza – leaving their three cups in a neat line on the washroom floor, up against the wall near the toilet. Grace's cup is nearest the corner, then Faith's, then Lovemore's.

In the morning, Faith is the first one in the washroom. After she has flushed, she calls Lovemore and Grace in to have a look. There is not a single ant in Grace's cup, and one floats dead in Faith's. But there is a ring of black inside Lovemore's cup where ants are drinking.

'Ah, Lovemore!' Grace puts an arm round Lovemore's shoulders.

'Sorry,' says Faith.

Inside Lovemore, emotion begins to well up. She does not want her sisters' pity. She does not want their sympathy. Okay, there is the possibility that one day she is going to need injections, and maybe one day she could even die from sugar like old Auntie Geraldine's husband. But that is not going to happen, because they are going to nip it. There will be no more sugar in her tea. There will be no more cake for her. And Lovemore could not be happier. She has always found the tea in this house much too sweet, and the amount of cake here has always made her fret about her buttocks growing and ruining her destiny. The ants have given her an excuse, and she is very grateful. If her sisters were not here, she would walk around the washroom giving thanks and prayers to the Lord as if she were in Highway of Holiness.

She wishes she could tell Mama that Mama was always right to keep her away from sugar because she needs to keep away from it for bigger reasons than her buttocks. Mama is not here, but Mama's journal is. As soon as she possibly can after school that day, Lovemore sits on Titi's top bunk and carries on reading Mama's words.

I never knew about all the fish in the lake before the two Mr Desais made the calendar. It came on the plane from Dar es Salaam with the older Mr Desai, and when everybody important in Mwanza came with the directors of all the fish processing factories for the official opening of Nile Perch Plastics, everybody got a calendar for the coming year, even me. Me and Lovemore used it at home until all of that year was finished, then we took it apart and stuck the pictures up on the walls of the lounge room. The pictures are on the walls of Nile Perch Plastics, too, but in big frames with glass. Ours at home don't have frames or glass, and when Lovemore stopped loving to see pictures of fish on the walls of the lounge room and Pritty helped me to move them to the kitchen, some of them tore too badly and had to go.

We have January still, the photo of the lake from high up in the air, with the words printed underneath that say that Victoria is the biggest lake in all of Africa and only Lake Superior in North America is bigger. It says our lake is just as big as Ireland or South Carolina, but it doesn't say where are those places, so anybody who isn't educated isn't going to know. Lovemore knows. Even from when she was small she could show people where is the Kagera river coming from Rwanda in the west to bring water to our lake, and where under the clouds over the northern part the Nile river is taking water from our lake all the way to Egypt. On the ground in our daily lives the lake looks just like any water with fishermen and their boats on top and the busy fish market on the edge, but in that photo from up in the sky the way God sees it, the lake looks deep and dark like a face that's hiding secrets. From up above God can't see any lines showing where is another country to the west and north of the lake called Uganda and where is another to the north and east called Kenya, He can't see any lines across the lake showing this 6% belongs to Kenya, this 43% is Uganda's and this 51% belongs to Tanzania. God can't see those lines but He knows they're there because He made men and men drew those lines.

September used to be Lovemore's favourite, a big picture of a tiny fish called a Nyerere cichlid, named for our first ever president, Mwalimu Julius Nyerere. Eh, that little fish is too beautiful! Its head and the front part of its back fin are bright blue, its body is yellow with black stripes going from up to down and its tail is red. Joseph used to make a story for Lovemore about that fish, a story about a sudden storm of lightning in the blue sky that started a fire on a fishing boat in the lake. All the Nyerere cichlids used their tails to flick water on to the flames. They got a bit too close to the fire and the heat made their tails glow red, but the little fish succeeded to put out the fire and saved all the fishermen, and that's why if any fisherman catches a Nyerere cichlid in his nets by mistake, he always saves it and throws it back into the water.

Lovemore used to love that story, she loved when Joseph tossed her from this knee to the other for the storm on the water, and when he lifted her up on her side so she could flick her legs from her knees for the fish flapping water on to the flames with their tails, and when he threw her into the air for the fisherman saving the little fish from his net by throwing it back into the water. But really why a fisherman throws a Nyerere cichlid back is because it isn't a good fish to eat. Sometimes some Wazungu come with small nets on long poles to catch Nyerere cichlids and other tiny fish for people far away to put into glass tanks of water like in the picture for July that tore too badly, but for us here it isn't a useful fish.

Dagaa is really the only useful tiny fish for us, their picture was April and it didn't tear when we moved it, but later because of what Joseph did I tore it into more tiny pieces than the number of dagaa in the picture. In the front of the picture there was a hand holding a small pile of fresh dagaa, silvery white with pale orange fins and tails that you could almost see through. Behind in the picture hundreds of dagaa were lying on the ground waiting for the sun to dry them. They were still silvery white, the sun hadn't yet dried them brown. The writing at the bottom said a very long name for dagaa and said a dagaa was like another fish called a sardine. The April dagaa picture used to be on the wall of my office at Nile Perch Plastics, but after what Joseph did I moved it to his office and I took his September Nyerere cichlid instead. I still love to eat fresh dagaa, but for as long as my life continues I will never again eat a dried one or allow a dried one into my house. Pritty, Philbert and Sigsbert know that I mustn't find one here, but they don't know why. Only Agrippina knows, and she didn't even tell Steven.

Steven is in the November picture, but only the men in the front of the photo are clear, the ones near the back are blurred and Steven is right at the back. The men are busy packing frozen Nile perch fillets into polystyrene foam boxes from Nile Perch Plastics and weighing the boxes. They have on their white overalls, their white plastic aprons, their white plastic hats like the more pretty ones that ladies put on to save their hair when they are taking a shower, and their pale yellow rubber gloves. The tabletop is silver, the Nile perch fillets are pale pink, and the Nile Perch Plastics boxes are white, so everything in the photo is pale except for the men's faces and their arms. Two of the men are smiling, their teeth as white as the Nile Perch Plastics polystyrene foam boxes. November is also on the wall at Nile Perch Plastics but it was never on my wall at home because I gave it to Steven as soon as that year was finished.

February is a fisherman coming bent from a boat with a Nile perch nearly as big as himself across his bare shoulders. Everybody who sees that picture knows that he is going to go home with the smell of that fish in his skin for weeks. The writing at the bottom says the Nile perch never used to live in Lake Victoria, Wazungu put it there in the 1950s, and it says the long word for the fish and also sangara, our word for it here. There is another Nile perch in August, a Mzungu is standing next to one hanging up from a big hook through the bottom part of its mouth. The man has his hand held high, holding above the hook to pretend like he is strong enough to lift a fish that is bigger than himself, but really his smile is just lying, you can see the rope from the hook is wrapped tight around the high branch of a tree. The writing at the bottom says that Wazungu come from everywhere in the world to fish in our lake because no other fresh water fish is bigger than a Nile perch. To the Wazungu the fish are a sport, but for us they are our life.

May is my favourite fish, the tilapia. A pretty young woman has a big *red plastic bowl of them on her head, and she's holding one in her hands and smiling for the camera. The one she's holding is nice and big, almost as long as her head and fat and round like her face, and every time I look at that picture I start to think about a nice grilled tilapia or a spicy tilapia curry or a delicious stew of tilapia, onions, garlic and tomatoes.*

<u>Lovemore</u> — Do try to like fish again, more especially tilapia, it is a good food and too delicious. But always stay away from dried dagaa.

Mama does not have to tell Lovemore to stay away from dried *dagaa*. It was the first kind of fish to make everything rise up in her throat, and she cannot shake from her memory the reason why. She closes her eyes, and it is almost like she is there all over again.

Auntie Agrippina and Uncle Steven have fetched Lovemore and Rose from their friend Katherine's party for her birthday turning nine, and on the way home they stop at the big fish market next to the lake. Auntie Agrippina parks her yellow hatchback next to a low wall, leaving just enough space between it and the car for Uncle Steven to get out, and they go to negotiate prices for fresh *dagaa* to fry for customers at Walk on Water, Auntie Agrippina's bar.

Lovemore and Rose wait quietly in the car, exhausted from all the games at the party, and Lovemore holds both of her hands to the pain that is growing in her stomach. Mama warned her not to eat too much cake because sugar is bad for her buttocks, but it was so deliciously creamy and chocolatey, and Mama-Katherine kept offering her more, so what could she do? She wishes she had said no, because now her stomach is hurting, and though she is worn out from the party, her mind feels like it is still running around in Katherine's yard, racing to finish all of Mama-Katherine's games and puzzles first so that she can win the prize and make Mama proud.

The market is noisy and busy with people and trucks, and everywhere she looks men are pulling *trollis* and shouting, but still she jumps when a man right next to her open window shouts loudly. As he shouts again and raises his arms, the smell of old sweat and wood smoke hits her face like a slap. Then the man climbs up onto the low wall next to the car and shouts again, this time getting an answer from a man with a *trolli* some distance from the other side of the car. His feet on the wall are right at the level of Lovemore's eyes, and if she were to stretch out her arm she could touch his filthy toes where they stick out from a pair of sandals more than one size too small. The sandals are old and broken, one of them held on to his foot by a piece of plastic bag, and one of his big toes has a cut that is oozing blood and pus. One hand over her mouth, the other still on her stomach, Lovemore finds herself unable to look away from that toe. Then the sound of the man emptying his nose comes, and a large blob of yellow slime falls to the side of his other foot, part of it hitting his small toe and hanging there. He jumps down in a rush of his smell and runs to talk to the man with the *trolli*.

Lovemore swallows hard. She tries to concentrate on working out how many Nile perches there could be on another man's *trolli* as he pulls it up the small slope towards them, shiny with sweat. Many of the Nile perches are longer than Lovemore is tall, and Lovemore imagines the man growing too tired to pull and letting the *trolli* unbalance on its two wheels, sending all of the fish sliding off the back of it. How many of them would slide to the ground? Fifteen? Twenty? How much they must weigh!

Auntie Agrippina and Uncle Steven come back, followed by another man pulling a *trolli* with three sacks full of fresh *dagaa*. Lovemore thinks the three sacks do not really need a *trolli* or a man – Uncle Steven could carry one and Auntie Agrippina two – but when they are loaded into the boot of Auntie Agrippina's hatchback she can smell exactly why they did not want to carry them. The third sack does not want to fit in the boot, so Rose has to squash up against Lovemore so that it can share the back seat with them.

Lovemore is very glad that she is between Rose and the window rather than between Rose and the sack of fresh *dagaa*. Her stomach is feeling bad, and it begins to feel even worse when she sees the same man again, the one with the bad toe and the too-small sandals, as they are driving away from the market. He and another man are standing on top of an enormous pile of dried *dagaa*, helping more of them to slide off the back of the truck that is tipping them out on to the ground.

'These people!' says Uncle Steven, sitting close to the passenger door as he always does so that Auntie Agrippina's buttocks can have the edge of his seat as well as the whole of the driver's seat. 'Do they not have any standards of hygiene? People are going to put those *dagaa* in their mouths!'

'Those *dagaa* have already been lying on dirt to dry in the sun,' says Auntie Agrippina.

'Exactly!'

'Who is going to know the hygiene of them here today when they arrive in a nice packet somewhere far from here?'

'Not as far as Europe,' says Uncle Steven, shaking his head. 'If a team of inspectors from Europe was coming to this market with their white coats and their clipboards, and they were seeing those men standing on those *dagaa* without any rubber boots and gloves, *eh!* And the *dagaa* on the bare ground!'

'Immediately I would have to drive those inspectors to Bugando Hospital to be treated for fainting and shock,' says Auntie Agrippina. 'I would have to leave you here with Rose and Lovemore and our nice fresh *dagaa*.'

They laugh then, but Lovemore cannot laugh with them. She cannot help imagining being left there to look at the man's dirty feet dripping blood and pus and slime onto the dried *dagaa*. She cannot help imagining some of it going into somebody's mouth. She does not imagine it going into her own mouth, because she knows it is never going to happen. She is never going to eat a dried *dagaa* ever again in her life. Never.

'No, those are not for Europe,' says Uncle Steven. 'Congo, maybe.'

'Congo,' Auntie Agrippina agrees, swerving to avoid a load of pineapples that is slipping off a *trolli*. 'They have a taste for it there.'

Pushing down on the pain in her stomach with both hands, Lovemore tries hard not to think about somebody in Congo eating those dried *dagaa* that are coated with dirt and blood and pus and slime. She makes herself concentrate instead on the large mound at the roadside that looks like a small anthill covered in banana leaves. The chaos of interwoven leaves make a kind of fridge for keeping cool the *matoke* piled up underneath, to stop them from ripening too quickly. The *matoke* are from Bukoba, the town on the western edge of the lake where Uncle Joseph was born, and where he lived with his parents and his sister until they all moved to Dar es Salaam when he was twelve. Before somebody shot him dead, Mama often used to come here to buy Bukoba *matoke* for Pritty to cook especially for him, though now that he is late she still sometimes comes to buy them. *Matoke* do not grow well around Mwanza, they are a kind of banana that grows much better around Bukoba.

Concentrating on *matoke* and Uncle Joseph helps Lovemore not to think about dried *dagaa*, and she manages to keep all her party food inside her until Auntie Agrippina drops her back home.

Still today, Lovemore has to turn her head if ever she sees any dried *dagaa*. Mama really does not need to tell her in her journal that she must stay away from those tiny fish. But remembering Mama not wanting them in the house, Lovemore is suddenly very aware of Mama's absence, and it makes her feel a bit like the empty syrup tin collapsing in on itself in *Mwalimu* Masabo's experiment to demonstrate what happens when air pressure outside is greater than air pressure inside. She closes the journal and pushes it away under her schoolbooks, blinking quickly to keep her tears from falling.

'Lovemore?'

It is the tiniest whisper, and she is not completely sure that she even heard it. She listens, holding her breath.

'Lovemore?'

This time the tiny whisper comes with an almost silent tapping at the window.

Benedict is there, one finger of his left hand on his lips to show her that she must be quiet, his right hand beckoning her to come. Slowly, quietly, she makes her way down the small wooden ladder to join him at the open window.

'There are butterflies,' he tells her in a whisper. 'Look.'

Lovemore does not want to look at butterflies. 'Uh-uh,' she whispers, her nostrils flaring as she shakes her head no.

'They're so beautiful, Lovemore! Tiny! Please look.'

Despite herself, Lovemore shifts so that she can see Benedict's vegetable garden, a bright patch of green the complete opposite of the bare earth of the rest of the yard. It looks so much like the jigsaw puzzle from the Indian ladies' toy library with a picture of an oasis in a desert, that for a moment Lovemore would not be surprised if Benedict wanted to show her camels rather than butterflies. But the butterflies are there, tiny as Benedict said, dancing on pure white wings across his plants like bits of ribbon and confetti at a wedding.

'*Eh!*' Lovemore whispers. 'They could be baby angels!'

'Mm,' agrees Benedict, turning briefly to smile at her.

'Are they baby butterflies?' she asks.

'You don't know the life cycle of butterflies and moths?'

Lovemore shrugs. Maybe they did it at school and she learned it for a test, but now she has forgotten. 'Are they eating your vegetables?'

'Uh-uh. I put food there for them. Water with leftovers of what's inside mango peels to make it taste nice.'

For a long time they stand there, Benedict outside, Lovemore inside, watching and whispering. It makes Lovemore feel like they have a secret together, like when Uncle Joseph used to whisper with her about what should they get for Mama's birthday.

'Did you show the others?'

'Uh-uh. Grace and Faith don't like insects, Moses and Daniel don't care.' Sadness scratches the words in his throat.

The two of them sigh together.

He is busy telling her in a soft whisper that Bibi made a cake like a butterfly for his birthday turning ten, when a larger butterfly swoops down from over Mr Kapufi's wall, and they both suck in their breath. It has so many colours! Blue, red, yellow, white. Then there is another just like it, dancing with the tiny white ones over Benedict's garden before disappearing down into it.

Lovemore can hear the smile in Benedict's whisper as he tells her they have found his gift of food.

When the two big ones come up out of his garden and disappear back over the wall, he wonders in a whisper if their food is finished. 'Maybe I should give them more. So many have come!'

'Will they not fly away if you go there?' Lovemore does not want them to be gone.

'Um … if I can be slow and quiet …'

Leaving Lovemore at the window, he walks like he is in slow motion on TV. The butterflies ignore him, flying around and over him when he bends down and retrieves what looks like the lid of a jar. As he holds it in his hands, a butterfly lands right on it, and he looks over at Lovemore, his eyes shining brightly. Lovemore feels so excited that she can hardly breathe.

Then another butterfly rests lightly on the top of his ear. *Eh!* Lovemore's mouth flies open. Very slowly, without moving the angle of his head or neck, he twists from his waist to look at his reflection in the kitchen window, then he swivels slowly back, his mouth a reflection of Lovemore's as they look at each other, motionless, breathless, for what seems like several minutes.

Then Moses and Daniel burst into the yard from the kitchen with their football, making a great deal of noise that sends the butterflies scattering in fright, and everything changes. Benedict is suddenly a different boy, a boy who is in charge while his babu is away. Leaving him to argue with them about whether or not they have finished their reading and learned their spellings, Lovemore turns away from the window, feeling quite the opposite of *Mwalimu* Masabo's empty syrup tin collapsing in on itself.

When Babu comes home at last from Ethiopia after nearly two months away, everybody talks to him excitedly at the same time, creating exactly the kind of chaos that he does not like. He goes to his bedroom for a wash, and stays there for a very long time.

'But we have already not had him here for two months,' moans Benedict, who is looking tired after so much time as the boss of everybody in the house. 'Why is he making us wait for him for even longer?'

'You know why,' says Bibi. 'You know he doesn't like so much noise from all of us.'

'He must be tired,' says Lovemore, disappointed to be waiting this much longer to squash up next to him as she used to with Uncle Joseph.

'Exactly,' says Bibi. 'When he comes for his supper, you need to take turns.'

It must be hard for Bibi. Babu has been away from her for so long, and now they have all driven him away to his bedroom.

Babu is clean and refreshed when he finally comes back in and settles heavily onto one of the couches. Everybody seems too afraid to speak to him in case he goes back to his room. Lovemore is sure that Grace and Faith are anxious for their gift from him, even if it is only wisdom.

Slowly he begins to talk of his work in Ethiopia helping to prepare the way for the new African Union to be launched there in July, and of the work he stayed on to do with Ethiopia's coffee industry. Bibi interrupts him to say that coffee from Ethiopia cannot possibly be as good as coffee from their home town of Bukoba, and Babu smiles, raising his eyebrows and tipping his head to one side uncertainly.

At last he gives them their gift. 'In Ethiopia they say that when you are in love, a mountain becomes a meadow.'

'What does it mean, Baba?'

Babu sighs heavily. 'Ah, Faith.'

'Think,' Bibi tells her. 'Think.'

'Put your new glasses on,' Babu tells her. 'Maybe if they were on your nose instead of inside their case they would help you to see.'

Babu seems tired for another few days before he is back to himself. One evening about a week after his return, Lovemore is coming into the lounge from the bedrooms to see if she can help to prepare the table for supper when somebody begins knocking at the big green gate. Titi and Bibi are busy in the kitchen, and Babu is busy printing at the computer, so Lovemore goes to the gate herself.

'*Hodi!*' calls a young man's voice on the other side.

'*Karibu*,' Lovemore says, not yet knowing if the man really is welcome.

'Grace?'

'Lovemore.' At least he is not a stranger. She slides back the bolt and pulls at one side of the gate.

Dickson is standing there with a small bunch of flowers. In his smart black trousers, white shirt and red tie, he looks quite different from the boy who came to their birthday party with a guitar and a tattoo, possibly the father of Scholastica's baby.

'*Karibu*,' she tells him again, and he comes in.

Babu is in the doorway now, looking at Dickson.

'*Shikamoo*.' Dickson shows respect for Babu in his greeting.

'*Marahaba.*' Babu's response is automatic.

'I'm happy to meet you, Dr Tungaraza.' Dickson extends his hand, and Babu shakes it uncertainly.

'Babu, this is Dickson,' Lovemore tells him. 'He was at the party for our birthday turning thirteen.'

'I see. Come in, Dickson.'

Lovemore can see that Babu is not happy. He looks at Lovemore with a big question mark on his face. Lovemore's face gives him a question mark back, and she shrugs her shoulders.

Inside, Bibi is putting knives and forks on the dining table. Dickson greets her respectfully and gives her the flowers that he has brought. Bibi looks delighted and confused at the same time. As Babu offers him a seat on one of the couches, Lovemore runs to the girls' bedroom to tell her sisters what is going on. Grace is in the washroom, but Faith rushes into the lounge to see. Coming in behind her, Lovemore sees her bend and whisper something into Babu's ear. Faith goes to the dining table and whispers to Bibi, too, before joining Babu and Dickson on the couches. Lovemore follows Bibi into the kitchen.

'Honestly!' Bibi is saying to Titi in a loud whisper. 'How can you forget that you have invited a friend for supper?'

'And I have not cooked anything special!' Titi is stirring a big pot of *ugali*.

'And me in a T-shirt and *kanga*. How can you forget to ask permission from your parents before you invite somebody? Lovemore, did she tell you?'

'Uh-uh. But why did Faith invite him?'

'Faith? No, it's Grace who invited him.'

Lovemore feels hurt. Why did Grace not tell her something this big?

'Auntie, if I cut some fruit to have after, I think it can be enough.'

'Good, Titi.' Bibi fills an empty peanut butter jar with water for the flowers. 'Why does a boy bring flowers to a girl's mother?'

'Are they boyfriend-girlfriend, Auntie?'

Bibi fixes her eyes on Lovemore. 'What do you know?'

'Nothing, Bibi, honestly. I am also confused.' Lovemore cannot hide her disappointment. 'I'm her sister, but I'm not the sister she told.'

Grace seems excited and nervous during supper. The table is not big enough for a visitor, so Titi and the boys eat at the coffee table, sitting on the four stools that pull out from under it. It is a simple meal of *ugali* with a sauce of tomatoes, onions and spinach from Benedict's garden. Lovemore is sure that it is delicious, but the hurt that she feels turns all of it into polystyrene foam in her mouth, and she can hardly be bothered to shape any more of the *ugali* into a small ball with a dip in it to scoop up some sauce.

Babu is firing questions at Dickson, which Dickson is doing his best to answer. Seventeen. Form Three. Dar es Salaam, just like his father and his father's father. Singer-songwriter. Guitar.

'Actually, Dr Tungaraza, I'm already running my own business.'

Babu's hand pauses on its way to his mouth with a ball of *ugali* and sauce. 'Oh? What kind of business?' His face looks hopeful.

'Marketing.' A blob of sauce is working its way slowly down Dickson's tie.

'Marketing what?'

'Sodas. At the end of each and every workday I am at the intersection of Sam Nujoma and Bagamoyo with cold sodas for the workers going home. They are hot, they are tired, they are stuck in traffic, and I am there at their window with exactly what they need.' Dickson smiles proudly. 'Saturdays I can be there, too, or at any other intersection.'

'I see,' says Babu.

'That is very good,' says Bibi. 'I have my own business, too.'

'Yes. Your cake for Grace's party was very magnificent.'

'It was my party, too,' says Lovemore, not wanting this feeling of being left out to be made any worse.

Dickson apologises to Lovemore and then talks with Bibi about her business. Lovemore looks at Grace, who is obviously excited, but she has not said very much, leaving Babu and Bibi to talk to her guest. That is not polite. Faith looks much more excited than Grace, almost breathless. Those two girls knew about this, and they did not tell Lovemore. She wants to phone Rose. Not from the telephone-fax here in this room, with everybody listening, but privately from the phone that used to be Mama's, while she sits on the top bunk in Titi's room. She does not care what the phone can do to disturb her brain while her brain is still growing. For the whole of the rest of the meal, all the way to the end of the sliced pineapple and mango, she tries very hard not to cry.

After Dickson shakes everybody's hand and goes home, everybody fires questions at Grace in the same way that Babu fired questions at Dickson. Grace looks shocked, her mouth open.

'But, Baba, *you* invited him, not *me!*'

'*Me?* What are you talking about? Have you lost your mind?' Then, his eyebrows shooting up, he turns to Bibi. 'Angel, please tell me I have not begun to lose my mind. Did I invite that boy and then forget?'

'No, Pius, no.' Even as Bibi tries to reassure Babu, she is looking distressed herself.

Grace is playing a very bad game, confusing Babu like this. Titi's mouth hangs open in shock, and Benedict, Moses and Daniel watch with big eyes. Faith must know the truth about Grace inviting Dickson; the two of them planned it all without telling anybody else. Lovemore looks carefully at Faith. whose eyes are very bright. She definitely knows something.

'Tell us the truth, Grace!' says Babu. 'Why are you lying to us?'

'I'm not lying, Baba, I swear it!'

'Tell us the truth right now!' Babu is filling with an anger that Lovemore has never seen in him before. 'Don't play games with us!'

'Baba, I didn't invite him. I didn't know he was coming.' Her breathing is getting faster, shallower. 'I haven't had any contact with him since Prisca came with him to my party—'

'*Our* party.'

'Ah, sorry, Lovemore. *Our* party.' Grace is very close to crying. 'I swear it, Baba. I swear it on the grave of our mama in Morogoro!'

'Don't, Grace.' Bibi tries to stop her.

'I swear it on the grave of our baba here in Dar es Salaam!'

Bibi tries again. 'Stop it, Grace! Look what you are doing to your brothers!'

Moses is crying now, and Benedict is trying to comfort him, though tears are in Benedict's eyes, too.

'Stop it, Grace!' Babu echoes what Bibi has said. 'Do you think any of us in this family needs any reminder of who we have lost?'

Bibi plunges her hand under the neckline of her T-shirt to retrieve a tissue from her bra. She takes off her glasses and wipes her eyes. Faith is wiping her eyes awkwardly with the edges of the sleeves on her own T-shirt. Lovemore cannot help crying herself. She does not want to think about Babu fetching Uncle Joseph in Mwanza after somebody shot him dead, and bringing him here for burial.

In the chaos of emotions, Titi surprises Lovemore by quietly taking charge. 'Uncle, Auntie, maybe you need to sit. And, girls, you too. Try not to speak again until you are calm, okay? Boys, come with me.' Titi takes them through the door that leads from the lounge into the bedrooms.

'Deep breaths,' says Bibi, sounding a little like one of Auntie Agrippina's cassettes.

All of them are silent as they sit around the dining table breathing deeply. Next to Lovemore, Faith is doing the opposite, her breaths coming quicker and shallower, until she opens her mouth and begins to wail like a small child.

'Faith?'

Faith battles to get enough air. 'Baba, it was me.' She wails some more. 'I wanted you to be angry with Grace!'

'What are you talking about?' There is still anger in Babu's voice, and he is sounding more and more like Uncle Joseph shouting at Mama for not warning Lovemore and Rose about the marabou stork

Grace sobs out loud. 'Faith! Why?'

'I didn't know we were all going to cry,' Faith wails.

Bit by bit, she manages to tell them. There was a day when Bibi could not fetch her and the boys from school because the microbus did not want to start, so Bibi sent an SMS text message to say that they should come home in a *daladala*. When the *daladala* stopped at an intersection, Dickson was at the window with cold sodas. He asked Faith about Grace. How was Grace? Did Grace have a boyfriend? What music did Grace like? He did not ask how Faith was or if Faith had a boyfriend or what music Faith liked. He took the phone that went with them to the primary school, and he entered his number, telling Faith that Grace should call him. The boys were sitting nearer to the front of the *daladala*, so none of them even saw that Dickson was there.

Faith decided not to tell Grace or to give Grace his number. Instead, she began to send him SMS text messages herself, pretending to be Grace. But there was nobody to tell about what she was doing – she could not tell her best friend, her sister Grace – and it became boring. Then Grace wanted help learning her dialogue from Lovemore, not Faith, and Faith decided to continue pretending to be Grace sending SMS text messages to Dickson, and later she decided to embarrass Grace and get her into trouble by sending a message to Dickson saying that Babu was inviting him for supper. She thought it would be funny, but instead they all cried.

'You see?' Babu tells her sternly. 'A hen that hatches a crocodile's egg is asking for trouble.'

Faith apologises to everybody who is at the table, and then she goes to apologise to Titi and the boys. It is already late, but Babu makes Faith write a letter to Dickson – not an SMS text, a proper letter – confessing to what she did and apologising to him. She is not allowed to go to bed until the letter is finished, no matter how late it gets.

The dim light of the candle was hard on Angel's eyes as she wrote tiredly in her notebook. The candle waited always on top of her small bedside cupboard, ready for just in case, but tonight it was not a power cut that had made her light it. No. It was Pius. When she had come out of the washroom in her nightgown, ready to climb into bed, the room had been in darkness and Pius had already been in a deep sleep. She had not wanted to disturb him with the bright overhead light, but she had also not wanted to go to sleep herself without first making her list. She had done it every single night and it had become a habit as important and natural to her as brushing her teeth.

She had already written on previous nights that she was grateful that Pius was back safely from Ethiopia, that he was back with her and the children, that he was once again beside her in their bed. She wrote now that she was grateful that he was getting a good night's sleep. Really, it seemed that his work in Ethiopia had exhausted him and he still needed plenty of rest until his strength and energy were back. Actually, both of them needed their strength for the stressful time that was heading slowly their way like a large truck without any brakes, because the time would inevitably arrive when it would be five years since robbers had shot Joseph dead in his house. How would it feel to remember and mourn their son this year, now that they knew that he had not, after all, been perfect? Okay, he had never been *perfect*. He had been clever enough for university but he had never wanted to go, even though Pius – with so many degrees himself – had done his best to try to persuade him. Joseph had chosen to get a job in a factory here in Dar es Salaam instead. It never sat well with a man when his son did not respect the path that his father had cut for him, when his son wandered off on his own along a narrower path, ignoring his father's call. But Pius had forgiven him. Joseph had got promotions at the factory, and then there had been the opportunity to be Manager at a new branch of the factory in Mwanza, and Joseph had said that he wanted to go because he had missed the lake since his childhood in Bukoba. Missing the lake was something that Angel and Pius had understood, so they had forgiven him for wanting to move so far away from them. Then there had been the girlfriend, Evelina, and the rush to marry her so that Joseph could take her with him to Mwanza. A hasty wedding to a girl the family did not know was not an easy thing for a mother to cope with, but Angel had forgiven him. How proud she had been that her son was going to have such an important new job! When Joseph and Evelina had given them three perfect grandchildren – first Grace, then Benedict, then Moses – he had appeared perfect again in their eyes.

But how would they remember and mourn him this year, now that they knew about his relationship with the girl's mother, and now that they knew he had hidden their firstborn grandchild from them? How was grief going to feel with so much anger and disappointment mixed in? Would those new feelings dilute their grief or add to it? Or would their anger and disappointment simply make their grief different, in the same way that adding some yellow colouring to blue icing made it green? It was still icing, thought Angel, it was still as sweet – and the blue was still there, really. All that had changed was how it looked. But what did that mean? If her grief was really just the same – if Joseph was maybe really just the same – did it mean that loving him still was okay? That loving him and not loving him were perhaps the same thing? *Eh!* It was a confusing question, and really it was a question for an educated somebody, but Pius was very deeply asleep – and if she woke him she would have to scratch out number one on tonight's list in her notebook, which was about being glad that Pius was getting a good night's sleep.

Sighing deeply enough to send the candle's flame into a precarious flutter, she decided to move on to number two. Faith was causing trouble. What Angel could be grateful for was that her five other grandchildren were not. That was what she wrote, that she was grateful that five of the children were not causing trouble. Faith had never been like this before Lovemore had come to stay, so it was tempting to think that it was actually Lovemore who was causing the trouble. But no. Lovemore was a good girl, very serious about her schoolwork and very helpful to Angel with the computer. Much to her own surprise, Angel had found herself grateful that Lovemore was here – she had even written that down in her notebook a few nights ago. Okay, the girl was a bit strange, but strange in the same sort of way as Benedict, preferring to spend time alone with books rather than jumping around making noise with the others. Concilia said that Faith was probably feeling left out now that Grace and Lovemore were spending so much time together – which they obviously must, being in the same class at the same school – and that Faith was acting out to get back Grace's attention, or to get attention from anybody at all. Faith must never again act out the way she had tonight, inviting that young man to supper and upsetting Grace to the extent that she had sworn on both her parents' graves. *Eh,* it had been the most terrible end to a very difficult evening!

But what could be done about Faith? Angel and Pius needed to talk through some ideas together – and Angel found part of herself wishing that Pius was *not* getting a good night's sleep right now. Really, it was bad enough not being able to talk things through with him when he was away. Having him here with her but not here with her was very difficult indeed.

She took a sip from the glass of water next to her bed, careful not to let the melting squares of ice clink together loudly enough to wake Pius. Earlier today she had spoken two items for her list into

Lovemore's small tape recorder, but she could not play the cassette back now, not with Pius lost in the sleep that he needed so badly. Fortunately, speaking those items into the tape recorder seemed to have recorded them into Angel's memory, too, and she put her glass down next to the candle and wrote the first of them as number three. She had been thinking this for a while, but she had avoided writing it down because it had not seemed quite right. The truth was that she was grateful that it was Lovemore who had sugar. Okay, sugar was not a problem she would wish on anybody – but if anybody in this house was going to have sugar, Lovemore was the one who could handle it best. That girl actually *liked* to drink tea without sugar – it was how she had been raised. Imagine! What kind of mother was that? And Lovemore did not mind when everybody else ate cake and she had none. The girl had told herself that not eating cake was better for her in terms of her buttocks, and she seemed to believe it. Angel had not tried telling herself the same thing about her hips. She knew that she would never believe it – and anyway, who would want to order cakes from somebody who did not eat cakes herself? Uh-uh. That would certainly be the end of her business.

The second thing that Angel recorded on the cassette and in her memory was that she was grateful that she could not possibly be responsible for giving Lovemore sugar. Sugar was not a problem that happened suddenly. No. Concilia, Irene, Fatima, Esther, Stella – each one of them had assured her of that, and Pius had looked it up on the computer to confirm it. No. That girl had come here with that problem already – eating Angel's cakes had definitely not been the cause of it.

The fifth thing for Angel's list was very exciting. She was grateful for the new customer sent to her by Concilia's mother. Angel had never seen this customer – the director of the bank where Mama-Concilia worked – because he had ordered over the phone, being too busy to come to the house. Normally Angel insisted on meeting with a customer and talking with them face to face over tea, so that she could fully understand what their cake was celebrating, how it should look, and how far she could push them on the price. But this customer had already known exactly the cake that he wanted – he had instructed his secretary to send photos to Lovemore on the computer and she had printed them for Angel – and today his driver had brought a very thick envelope containing the deposit. The cake must look exactly like the very expensive sports car in the photos, except that it must be yellow where the one in the pictures was red, and its number plate must spell out the man's name.

When Pius had seen the pictures he had whistled and then laughed at the price that Angel had planned to quote.

'Seriously, Angel? Treble it at least! Even multiply it by four!'

'Eh?'

'I'm telling you, Angel, a man who directs a bank and wants a Porch – even just a Porch cake – that man is having very big dollar signs in his eyes.'

'Dollar signs in the eyes are not the same as dollars in the pocket, Pius.'

'Do you think the director of a bank doesn't have dollars in his pocket?'

'But I don't want to scare him away by charging too much.'

'Ah, Angel. Let me tell you about the kind of man who drives a Porch or even dreams of driving any car like a Porch. He does not want to drive a microbus like ours, though it will get him from A to B just the same in our traffic. Is he a man who cares about his family and bothers with budgeting for them? No. Only two people can sit in that car – him and his girlfriend. And he attracts that girlfriend by showing off how much money he has, by driving around in a Porch. Now, do you think such a man wants to show your cake at his party and boast about what a bargain it was? No. He wants to tell everybody how expensive it was. Angel, he does not value inexpensive things. If you charge him your low price, he will think you are offering him something inferior. Multiply it by four.'

So Angel had taken a big chance and multiplied her price by five, and her customer had bargained her down to her original price multiplied by four, and today he had sent the deposit, which was already her original price multiplied by two.

Despite the upsetting way that the day had ended for the family, despite her new worries about Faith, Angel could not help smiling as she slid her notebook, pen and glasses quietly into the drawer next to her bed and blew the candle out.

Babu has decided that there is too much noise and chaos in the lounge for him to get any work done at the computer, so he has had a carpenter make a small, low table for him to use with his laptop in the bedroom. He sits on his bed with his back supported by a pillow against the wall and his legs stretched out, the small table across his lap. Bibi says that it is only right that a man of his age should have his feet up, and Lovemore is aware that a woman of Bibi's age should have her feet up, too. Having six children to care for at their age is certainly not what they expected. It must have been hard enough when Uncle Joseph brought Grace, Benedict and Moses to stay when their mama became ill. Then Faith and Daniel came. And now Lovemore is here, too.

Lovemore goes to take a new colour cartridge for the printer from Babu's supply in one of the drawers in the cabinet under the TV.

'Lovemore!' moans Grace.

'You're in the way!' whines Faith.

Shutting the drawer quickly, Lovemore removes herself from between her sisters and an episode of *Friends*, a series about six friends who live in New York. She likes watching it herself because it shows her how her own life is going to be when she goes to live there, and the kind of people that she will meet. Instead of drinking tea at home, the people there go to a café for coffee – not coffee like Tanica, where you just add water from a kettle, but a special kind of coffee that comes out of a big machine that hisses and spits behind the counter – and they spend a lot of time sitting around doing nothing. But the six friends are not lawyers, so Lovemore knows that her own life in New York is going to be busier than theirs. She has been listening to the TV without being able to see it from where she has been sitting in front of the computer, and it is not an easy TV show to listen to without seeing, because you really have to see the friends' faces to know how they are feeling, and funny things happen that you need to see for yourself to understand why they are funny. Grace and Faith laugh out loud again as Lovemore unwraps the printer cartridge, peels off the protective tape and clicks it into place. While she waits for the printer to be ready, she listens instead to Concilia, who is taking her turn at helping Bibi to choose her six photos for the first round of the Kilimanjaro Snow competition.

'You are still using film? Seriously?'

'It's what I know, Concilia. Pius has the new kind, but it travels with him.'

'No, Angel, truly you must digitise. It's the way now.'

'I know. I do. But I'm not comfortable. Anyway, sending photos of cakes for round one is silly. Who is to say that I have made the cakes in my photos myself? Somebody else can even send a photo of one of my cakes and say that she made it herself.'

Lovemore clicks on PRINT, and the printer goes into action.

'True. What about this one? This is better than that one, don't you think?'

'*Eh*, I wish I could send a whole album!'

'Mm. But do you not think there are some who will battle to have any photos at all to submit?'

'Uh-uh. If ever you spend this much time creating a beautiful cake that other people are going to cut to pieces, you take a photo of it first. Believe me, Concilia, you have a photo of every cake that you have ever made.'

'No, what I mean is there are probably people who want to enter but they have not yet made six special cakes.'

'But those people are not yet ready for a national competition.'

Lovemore takes the page out of the printer tray and hands it over. 'The entry form, Bibi. The rules are there, too.'

'Thank you, Lovemore. You see, Concilia? I don't need to digitise, I have Lovemore.'

'There are example cakes on their website, Bibi.'

'Ooh, let us look!'

Bibi moves a chair so that Concilia can sit next to Lovemore, while Bibi herself stands behind them. Lovemore clicks away from the home page that calls Kilimanjaro Snow *The Icing On The Top* and has a photo of Mount Kilimanjaro with its snowy peak and also another photo of a chocolate cake with a dusting of white icing sugar on top. She opens up a page that has six photos of cakes arranged in a semi-circle above a big brown envelope with the address written on it that people must use for sending their photos.

'Ooh.' Bibi leans forward between Lovemore and Concilia.

'Aah,' says Concilia.

'Mm.'

The cakes in the pictures are extremely beautiful. Some of them even look much too complicated to be real cakes. Lovemore does not want to say that at least two of them look better than any cake that she has seen in Bibi's albums. Bibi and Concilia do not seem to want to say anything at all. At last Concilia tries.

'But, Angel …'

'*Eh!*'

'Angel, do these not look like professional cakes to you?'

'Professional?'

'Yes. I mean—'

'Concilia, you know that *I* am a professional somebody.'

'Yes, I know. What I mean is do they not look like a business has made them?'

'Mine is a business.' Bibi has taken off her glasses and is polishing the lenses with a tissue from in her bra.

'Of course, Angel, don't get me wrong. I'm talking about a big business, many, many people. This one here,' Concilia points to the photo of the cake that looks like a vase stuffed full with flowers, 'this lily, for an example. Making this was the job of one person. Maybe it was all he did over one day or even two, making this lily. Meanwhile somebody else had the job of making this rose, not even every rose here, just this one rose. Each and every flower was the work of one person in this big, big business. Do you not think?'

Bibi puts her glasses back on. 'You are right, Concilia. These are not even the kinds of cake they are looking for in this competition.'

Lovemore points to another of the cakes. 'You could make this one, Bibi. Maybe a whole team of people made it, but you could make it by yourself.'

'That is true.' Bibi rests a hand on Lovemore's shoulder, and for the briefest of moments it feels to Lovemore like Mama's hand congratulating her for getting her typing speed up.

'You should have a website, Angel, a place where people can see photos of your cakes.'

'*Eh!* They can see them in my albums when they come.'

'But how do they know to come?' Standing up, Concilia uses the back of Lovemore's chair in place of her stick as she moves back to her seat at the dining table.

'Somebody tells them.' Bibi sits down again next to Concilia. 'Your mother told you, and you came.'

'Yes, but things are becoming different now.'

Going offline so as not to occupy the phone line or to run up the bill, Lovemore returns to another page and clicks to print it.

'I'm too old now, Concilia, I can't change the way I do things.'

'No, Angel, you don't need to change anything, you simply have other people do new things for you. I know nothing at all about how to make a website, but I have one that is ready to go live as soon as I have my doctorate. A young man called Ibrahim did it all for me. I can send him to you.'

'I don't know, Concilia.'

'Think about it. But right now we must get on with choosing your six most excellent cakes.'

Lovemore gives Bibi her page from the printer that shows all the different regions of Tanzania in different colours. When she first looked for the map it was to show Bibi where her competitors in the final round of the competition were going to be coming from, but now that they have all seen the photos of cakes on the Kilimanjaro Snow website, she does not think that any of them is still completely sure that Bibi will be in the final. Bibi and Concilia both have a look.

'Ah, here is Kagera region. Bukoba, our home town, mine and Pius's, that is in Kagera region.' Bibi's finger lingers over the pale orange shape down the western edge of Lake Victoria before it moves to the purple shape along the lake's southern edge. 'Mwanza region.'

'And the islands are regions, too, Bibi, Zanzibar, Pemba and Mafia.'

Underneath the map it gives the population of each region. The Dar es Salaam region – a small blob of grey on the edge of the Indian Ocean – has more people than any other, then the island of Zanzibar, then Mwanza.

'How many people altogether?'

'Bibi, I'm not good at adding big numbers.'

'Ah, you will learn to add big numbers when you count your money in your New York law office.' Concilia's comment makes Lovemore smile. 'Count with me.'

There are close to forty million people in the twenty-one regions. That is a great deal of competition for Bibi's cakes.

'Maybe people in some of the regions are not interested in baking cakes,' Bibi says nervously.

'Maybe they're not good at it,' Concilia says.

'Maybe they don't have ovens,' Lovemore suggests. Mama never had an oven, just an electric two-plate.

Lovemore really should be getting back to her schoolbooks, but instead she sits down at the table. All three of them work together to choose Bibi's six best ever cakes to get her through round one, at least.

Chapter 8

Bibi leans forward from the seat behind Lovemore and Babu. 'What speed are you doing, Pius?'

Babu glances at a dial near the steering wheel. 'I am not exceeding, Angel.'

'But it feels fast.'

'Ah, you have become used to the slow pace of traffic in Dar. We cannot create a wind like this there.'

'That is true,' Bibi says, settling back between Grace and Faith, and patting her head wrap firmly as if to check that it has not been blown off.

The boys are further back in the microbus, and the noise of the wind makes it impossible for Lovemore to hear what they are talking about, or even if they are talking at all. If the microbus had air-conditioning, all of its windows would be closed, and the side of Lovemore's hair next to the front window would not be going in every direction like ants running from Titi's *pilipili* spray. But the engine of the microbus is old, and it battles even to power its radio. Air-conditioning would be just too much for it.

Lovemore shifts away from the window towards Babu, so that he can hear her voice more easily. He has already asked her too many times to repeat what she has said, and she does not want him to become irritated.

'I hope Titi is having a nice time, Babu.' Titi is spending the day with her friend, a house girl who works in the same street as the Tungarazas.

'She deserves a day off. We all do.'

Titi cooks and cleans and washes and irons for so many people. Pritty, the house girl who worked for Mama back home in Mwanza, only had to do those things for Mama, Lovemore and Mama's cousins

Sigsbert and Philbert. Lovemore used to think that life was hard for the house girl doing all those things for Rose, Lulu, Auntie Agrippina, Uncle Steven, Milton and Godbless, but Titi has two more people than that. Titi certainly deserves a day off.

Babu deserves a day away from his laptop – he has been so busy writing documents and reports and proposals in his bedroom that it has almost felt like he is away – and Bibi certainly needs a break from mixing and baking and decorating. Lovemore has been taking advantage of the school holidays to revise absolutely everything that they have covered in class so far. Before, Mama would fill her school holidays with every kind of extra lesson that anybody was willing to teach her, but Lovemore has to take care of herself now, because paying for extra is not something that the Tungarazas believe in. She has been working very hard indeed, and she, too, deserves a day off.

Grace and Faith, on the other hand, have done nothing but take time off. They have practised modelling, they have practised applying lip liner before applying lipstick, they have painted each other's nails, they have visited Prisca, they have been to see a film with Magdalena and Mary, they have gone shopping with Fenella and her mother, and they have stared at the TV for hours on end. Grace has read some parts of her library book out loud to Faith, but neither of them has opened a schoolbook.

Moses and Daniel have watched football on TV and played football in the back yard. Lovemore has heard Benedict outside in his garden, but she has not seen him except at mealtimes, though once or twice he has argued with Moses and Daniel for the remote because he wants to watch a programme about animals that is on at the same time as some sport that they are watching.

Babu is not right that they all deserve a day off, but Lovemore decides not to disagree with him because he seems so happy to be taking his family for a day out. Instead, she tries to make him even happier by inviting him to give her one of his history lessons. She asks him to tell her about Bagamoyo, the town they are heading for, out on the open road north of Dar es Salaam.

'Ah, that town is very important in Tanzania's history – actually in Tanganyika's history, because we have only been Tanzania since

Tanganyika united with Zanzibar in 1964. You know that?'

Nodding her head yes, Lovemore prepares herself for a lovely long session of listening to Babu's words with the sound of Uncle Joseph in his voice.

'Everybody should be hearing this, but with the noise of this wind, *eh!* I'll tell you, Lovemore, then you can tell the others while we have our lunch.'

Lovemore sits up a little straighter. 'Okay, Babu.' She wishes she was more like Mama, who could memorise everything that somebody said and then write it down later without missing out a single word. It was a skill that Mama had to use at work because she only pretended that she knew shorthand. When it comes to memorising, Lovemore is good, but Mama was excellent.

'Babu, I struggle at remembering dates, see? Numbers never want to stay in my head.'

'That's okay. You remember the story and I'll add the dates.'

To Lovemore's surprise, it is quite an interesting story. At the beginning of the story, Bagamoyo was just a small trading centre for fish and salt on the edge of the Indian Ocean, and then Arabs arrived and everything changed, because the Arabs came for slaves. People were stolen or bought from all directions deep inland, and they were brought to Bagamoyo, where the Arabs locked them up until the tide was right for ships to take them to the slave markets on the island of Zanzibar. The town also became the centre for trading in ivory, because the people who went inland in all directions to hunt elephants brought their trophies back to Bagamoyo.

Some *Wazungu* explorers from England and Scotland came to Bagamoyo to start their journeys inland to look for where the Nile River began – not just Speke, who found that the river began at Lake Victoria, but others called Burton and Grant and Stanley. The one called Livingstone was carried back to Bagamoyo late from malaria – without his heart, because his heart was buried in Zambia – and his body waited in Bagamoyo for the tide to be right for a ship to take him all the way to the church in England called Westminster Abbey where he lies today.

By then, Indians had also come to Bagamoyo to live alongside the Africans and the Arabs, and everything was peaceful up until the Germans arrived. The Germans decided to make the town their headquarters in East Africa, and they tried to start registering everybody's property. An Arab called Bushiri led a rebellion, and he even brought in soldiers from Sudan and others from the Zulu people in South Africa to help with the fight. But the Germans in Bagamoyo had soldiers sent over from Germany to fight back, and that was the end of the rebels. Then Germany bought the rights to the land from the Sultan of Zanzibar, and that was the beginning of German East Africa.

But Bagamoyo was not the headquarters of German East Africa for long, because it did not work very well as a port. Further south at Dar es Salaam the water was much deeper, and so the headquarters moved to there. Now Bagamoyo is a small town again, but with an old history and a new college for all kinds of arts.

Bibi leans forward again. 'Pius, are we going to leave Kaole for after, like before?'

'Yes. Let's do it exactly as we did it.' Babu clears his throat.

Bibi extends a hand and gives Babu's shoulder a squeeze. Letting go of the wheel with his left hand, Babu covers Bibi's hand with his own. After Bibi has settled back again, Lovemore can see that Babu is not happy about something. Maybe some of the people that the Germans shot dead in Bagamoyo were his ancestors, or maybe he does not like stories about people being shot dead because of what happened to his son Joseph.

'Would you like some water, Babu?'

'Thank you, Lovemore, but we are nearly there.'

In Bagamoyo, Babu takes them first to the mission compound of the Holy Ghost Fathers, and that is where they get out of the microbus to stretch their legs and drink the last of the water and sodas that they bought from Dickson at the intersection of Sam Nujoma Road and Bagamoyo Road before leaving Dar es Salaam. Dickson wanted to give Babu a special price, but Babu insisted on paying in full because one of the Tungarazas had already taken advantage of him. Lovemore saw that Faith did not once lift her eyes to look at him. Perhaps she was too ashamed of what she did to look at him, or perhaps she was hoping that Dickson would not recognise her in her glasses – which are only on her nose when Babu is around, and only because Babu insists. Outside of the microbus, they use the side mirror to check their hair: Faith's – still very short and rather patchy since the Jik – is as fine as it can be, Lovemore's needs shaping a little on one side, and quite a bit of Grace's needs tucking back under the band that is meant to be holding it back. Bibi adjusts her head wrap, pulling it forward a little on her forehead.

They all have a look at the original Holy Ghost Church – Tanganyika's first ever Catholic church, which Babu says the fathers built in 1872 – and also at the place where the fathers housed the child slaves whose freedom they managed to buy. There is a Catholic museum in the compound, but they just look at it from the outside because the entrance fee is too much for a family of eight. Outside of the mission compound, Babu points out the small Anglican church where the late Dr Livingstone waited without his heart for the ship to take him back to England.

Babu parks near the market and they walk together around the town. Men keep approaching them, offering to be their guide, but they do not need any of those men because they have Babu. Babu already knows that the building called the Bagamoyo Tea House with its beautiful carved wooden door from Zanzibar was there even before the Germans came. He knows that the big double-storey was where the Germans had their headquarters, but before the Germans came it was the home of one of the Sultans of Zanzibar. He knows that the building housing the Department of Antiquities used to be a slave prison, and that an underground tunnel leads from it all the way to the beach where the boats used to come to fetch the slaves. And he knows what used to happen at the hanging tree in the grounds of the Badeco Beach Hotel, even before he shows them the sign that says: *Here is the place where German colonialists used to hang to death revolutionary Africans who were opposing their opressive rule.*

Babu does not like that the sign has missed out one of the Ps from oppressive, and he says that it is important to get details right. That makes Lovemore nervous. She will have to get all the details right in the story of Bagamoyo when she tells it to everybody later over lunch.

When Babu shows them a three-storey building in the middle of town he gets excited, because it was Tanganyika's first ever international school.

'Like the one on Msasani Peninsula?' Lovemore asks him.

'Ah, no, Lovemore – though that one is called the International School of Tanganyika, because it pre-dates our modern Tanzania. This one began in the late 1800s, when we still had our own kind of apartheid.'

'Like in South Africa, Baba?' It is Benedict who asks.

'In a way. At the time there was no other primary school with three floors. But this was built with three floors. Why do you think?'

'Everybody wanted to go to the international school,' Lovemore suggests. 'It needed to be big.'

Babu shakes his head. Grace and Faith simply shrug, while Bibi takes a seat on a large rock in the shade and says nothing.

'Boys?'

Daniel just makes a face, but Moses suggests that the man who built it was rich.

'He was very rich. But that is not why.'

Benedict makes a suggestion. 'If it was like apartheid, was it a floor for each race?'

'Yes!'

'Well done!' Bibi calls from the rock in the shade.

'African children had the ground floor, the middle was for Arab and Indian children, and white children had the top.'

'*Eh!*' says Lovemore. 'But why did the *Wazungu* have to climb all the way to the top for their lessons?'

'When they are not good with the heat,' says Grace. 'Look at Miss Brown, Lovemore, she is ever complaining about how hot it is. Now imagine if she had to go up and down stairs.'

Lovemore does not know of any primary school with more than one floor. Their secondary has two floors, but Miss Brown never has to go upstairs because her classroom is on the ground floor. 'She couldn't manage,' she says to Grace. 'Babu, did the white children have white teachers?'

'I'm pretty sure they did.'

'*Eh,*' says Grace, 'the rich man who built this school did not like

Wazungu!'

'Was he a Tanzanian?' asks Faith.

Babu takes a deep breath before he speaks. 'There was no Tanzania when this school was built, right? But no, he was not a local man. They say he was an Indian, actually from the part that is Pakistan today. He became wealthy here from organising caravans to go for slaves—'

'The slaves went in caravans?' Daniel is excited now. 'Like those ones we saw in Swaziland, Baba?'

Babu rolls his eyes. 'We are talking about a time before there were cars.'

Bibi is laughing as she gets up from her rock, using a hand to dust down the part of her smart skirt that stretches tight across her buttocks. She puts her other hand on Babu's upper arm. 'This is a lesson for another time, Pius. All that everybody needs to understand now is that this school is like a cake. The bottom level had to be strong, it had to be made of the very best ingredients, otherwise it could not carry those other layers on its shoulders.'

'Exactly,' says Babu. 'Well said, Angel.'

Back at the market where the microbus is parked, people are selling tomatoes, onions, Irish potatoes, mangoes and bananas, but long ago they sold people there. Babu asks them all to think about how those people felt when they were being bought and sold.

'Close your eyes and imagine,' Bibi tells them, and they all close their eyes. At least, Lovemore thinks that they all close their eyes, but she has closed her own eyes so she cannot be sure what anybody else is doing.

Bibi continues. 'Imagine you are still small, and you are standing on a platform so that everybody can see you. You are almost naked so that everybody can see your body, see how strong you might be. Maybe they even touch you.'

Babu takes over. 'You watch as everybody tries to decide how much you are worth. You are young, so you can work for many, many years. That makes you worth a lot. They start to offer money—'

Lovemore opens her eyes, and Babu continues, not noticing. Lovemore does not want to imagine any more. She knows from Auntie Agrippina's cassettes that you must not visualise bad things because visualising things is what makes them happen. When you close your eyes and imagine, the things you imagine need to be good. She is wondering whether or not she should interrupt, when Benedict begins to sob.

'Ah, ah, ah,' says Bibi, holding him tight.

'You see?' says Babu. 'It was a very bad thing that happened here. Very bad.'

Benedict wipes his eyes with the tissue that Bibi gives him from inside her bra. Lovemore can see that his tears have embarrassed him, that he does not want to look like a small boy in front of his smaller brothers, but she does not know what to say to him that will not make it worse. She places a hand gently on his back, resting it there very briefly.

They walk down to the beach, where the tide is very low. At first it looks like many people are walking on the water, but when Lovemore looks more carefully she sees that the water is just very, very shallow. People have had to leave their boats way, way out, and now they are walking across the long distance of shallow water to get to dry land.

'Look, Lovemore, a fish market!' Grace has still not given up her teasing, but she does not have to point out the fish market, because Lovemore has already smelled it and is already moving as far away from it as possible. To empty her mind of fish, she concentrates instead on the slaves who walked across the water to the boats that would take them to Zanzibar. Some of them would work on the clove plantations there, but others would be sold again at the slave markets, and then they could be taken anywhere else at all. They would never come back here to their families – and their families were not even here in Bagamoyo, they were somewhere far inland.

It was all very unfair.

Slowly, Lovemore becomes aware of it being a different kind of unfair, not the same kind of unfair as Babu not being the rich man she expected him to be, nor the same kind of unfair as Lovemore having to share a bedroom with Grace and Faith, nor even the same kind of unfair as Mama being late before Lovemore's birthday turning thirteen. No. It is a much bigger kind of unfair. She is trying to work out what it is that she really means, when Babu slips an arm around her shoulders.

'*Bwaga moyo,*' he says to her, softly. 'Lay down your heart. That is what Bagamoyo means. Lay down your heart here, because your freedom is gone forever. Lay down your heart here, because they are forcing you onto a boat to far away, and you will never come back here to your home country. Lay down your heart here. Bury it here.'

'Like Livingstone's heart was buried in Zambia?'

'In a way.' Babu gives her shoulder a squeeze. 'Come. Let us go to Kaole.'

Kaole is five kilometres back towards Dar es Salaam, which is strictly speaking on their way back, so Faith insists on taking her turn to sit up front next to Babu. Lovemore takes Faith's place with Bibi and Grace in the row behind. They turn off the tarred road on to a gravel road, and every now and then Lovemore can see the sea through a break in the trees to her left. The road is not very good, so in parts they have to go slowly, which nobody likes because all the windows are shut against the dust and the microbus is starting to feel like an oven.

'A crocodile farm!' Moses shouts from the row behind as they pass a sign on the right-hand side. 'Baba, can we go?'

'Please Baba!'

'*Please!*'

'We'll see,' Babu shouts back from the front. 'Maybe on the way back.'

There is a village at Kaole, but that is not where Babu takes them. They go instead to the ruins of a place that was built before Bagamoyo's history, way back in the eleven hundreds. It was a holy place then, with the first ever mosque on the mainland – though of course there were already mosques on the island of Zanzibar at that time.

Everybody is hungry when they arrive, so they decide that they will have their lunch first, before they look at the ruins. Taking turns to use the small washrooms, they sit at one of the tables under a tree to eat the sandwiches that Titi packed for them before going off to spend the day with her friend. Titi wrapped them in silver foil and put them into a plastic bag inside another plastic bag along with a few plastic bottles of water that spent the night in the freezer, so the sandwiches are nice and cool. There are also some boiled eggs, and inside an old biscuit tin are seven of Bibi's cupcakes – not eight, because Lovemore cannot have sugar.

'Let us eat our sandwiches,' Babu suggests, 'and have our cake after we have looked at the ruins. Lovemore can tell us the story of Bagamoyo while we eat our cake.'

Lovemore does not know whether or not to feel relieved. She has more time now to revise the story in her head, but she also has more time to be nervous about getting the details right.

Babu goes into the office to pay, and comes back saying that they are insisting on giving them a guide.

'Just like last time,' Bibi says, her eyes looking without seeming to see.

'Just like last time,' says Babu, reaching for Bibi's hand.

'You were here before?' asks Grace, not even bothering to swallow first her mouthful of sandwich, thick with bright red tomato from Benedict's garden.

'Mm,' says Bibi, not saying anything to Grace about talking with her mouth full.

'A long time ago,' says Babu, his voice soft.

The way they are behaving makes Lovemore think that maybe they came here on their honeymoon. Though why would you come to see ruins at the very beginning of your marriage? Okay, Babu does enjoy history, but if he brought Bibi here to give her one of his history lessons on their honeymoon, their marriage would definitely not have lasted as long as it has. Anyway, they married in Bukoba, more than a thousand kilometres inland on the western edge of Lake Victoria, so they would not have come all this way just to see the leftovers of some old buildings.

The guide shows them the remains of the old mosque, just some broken walls and a stairway leading up to nothing that is left. At the well beside the mosque, Babu has them all line up in a row while the guide takes their photo on Babu's camera: Babu at one end, then Lovemore, Grace, Benedict, Moses, Daniel and Faith, with Bibi at the other end. They all put their arms around each other and squeeze in close as the guide steps further and further back to get them all in. Then they all bunch up close for another photo, the boys kneeling down at the front.

The guide tells them that the well is very special. Over the centuries, it has never once run dry, and over the centuries it has never once become salty, even though the sea is very close. It is most definitely a miracle. He lowers a green plastic bucket on a rope, then hauls it up brimming with water. All of them line up to have some of it poured into their cupped hands so that they can feel how a miracle tastes in their mouths. The water is clean and cool, and Lovemore holds it in her mouth for as long as she can before she swallows, wanting most of all the miracle of Mama resurrecting. One of Auntie Agrippina's cassettes used to say that everybody deserves a miracle – but Lovemore cannot help thinking that when all those people were being forced onto the boats at Bagamoyo with chains around their necks, no miracle came to stop it from happening.

Grace nudges Lovemore's elbow. 'Look!' She is pointing to a small, low building with just a doorway and no windows. Made of the same kind of coral stone that the guide says was brought here from somewhere else, it is one of the few buildings that still has a roof. 'Do you not recognise it?'

Lovemore shakes her head no, sure that she has never seen it before.

'It's on our history textbook! On the cover!'

Lovemore shakes her head again, not sure that she has ever really looked at the cover of their history book.

Babu laughs. 'Ah, Grace, I'm sure Lovemore can recognise many pages from inside that book, pages that are unfamiliar to you.'

'*Eh!*' Grace pretends that Babu has offended her, but really she is laughing.

They are looking at old graves now, and one of them is a double grave for two lovers who died on a boat on the Indian Ocean. Almost overwhelmed by a sudden sadness about Mama and Uncle Joseph lying in different graves in different cities, Lovemore wants to reach for the support of Babu's strong hand, but Bibi is telling him that the sun is too strong for her, that she is going to go back to the table under the tree and wait there for them to finish.

'Let me come with you, Angel. The children will be fine with the guide. Benedict, you are in charge.'

Benedict pushes out his chest and looks for a moment like he might be about to give Babu a salute. Lovemore watches Babu and Bibi as they walk slowly back to the table under the trees. Babu slips an arm around Bibi's shoulders. It is not something that anybody ever saw Uncle Joseph doing with Mama, not even Lovemore.

Moses and Daniel begin to throw small stones at each other and Benedict tells them to stop it. The guide takes them down a short, sandy path to where there used to be a port before mangrove trees invaded it, and now they cannot even see the sea behind the thick growth of trees. The name *Speke* on a sign catches Lovemore eye, and she reads: *This ancient port there is no stairs or even a building like what you see in modern descent ports, but for Natural vegetation of Mangroves. Explorers like Burton and Speke who were trying to find Dr. David Livingstone used the port of Kaole to penetrate to the interior.*

Ah, that is wrong! Those *Wazungu* used the port of Bagamoyo, it is in the story that Lovemore is going to tell everybody while they eat their cupcakes. She will have to check with Babu before she begins.

The guide wants to show them some other things, but really they are all tired of looking and listening. They head back to the table under the trees, but only Babu is there. Perhaps Bibi is using the washroom. Lovemore tells Babu what the sign says, and Babu says it is wrong, but the guide says it is right.

'Where is your evidence?' he demands of the guide.

'*Mzee*, it is written on the sign.'

'*Eh!* Anybody can write anything on a sign. I can take a sign now and write on it that this place fell to ruins because everybody in Kaole village converted to… to…' Babu waves a hand in the air, as if he is choosing which mango to pluck from a tree, 'to Buddhism.'

'*Mzee!*'

Lovemore can see Grace rolling her eyes and Moses and Daniel trying not to laugh. Faith and Benedict are struggling to open the old biscuit tin, which has become wet and slippery in their fingers from the melting bottles of ice. Lovemore places a hand on Babu's shoulder to show him that she is confident that he is the one who is right.

'No, I can write that on a sign. Then somebody else can look at that sign and say, yes, it is true, it is on a sign. But it is nonsense. *Nonsense!*'

'No, *Mzee*, that sign at the old port,' the guide points, 'it is by the Department of Antiquities.'

'And my sign is by Dr Pius Tungaraza, holder of degrees from

Makerere University in Uganda and the University of Munich in Germany. Do you like cake?'

'*Mzee?*'

'Come. Sit! You can eat my cake.' Babu pats his stomach. 'It will do me good not to have it.' Benedict pulls out a chair for the guide, who perches nervously on the edge of it. 'Good. Let us together tell these children the story of Kaole and Bagamoyo.' Babu turns to Lovemore, patting her hand where it rests on his shoulder. 'This is a story that you already know. You don't need to hear it again, especially not with any incorrect details. Please go and check on your bibi for me. She went to look at the baobab.'

Relieved that she does not have to tell the story after all, Lovemore scoops a cupcake for Bibi from the tin and follows the signs to the baobab tree. The signs are not really necessary, because the baobab is enormous and there are no other trees anywhere near it. As she walks, she wonders what has put Babu in the mood for an argument with the guide after he seemed so happy earlier, so in love with Bibi. Maybe it is just because Babu has been home for a while now, and maybe he prefers to be away at work. Lovemore suspects that he might be a little bit bored at home, with nobody there quite as interested as he is in his work or the other things he likes to talk about, and nobody very fascinated by his history lessons. Maybe he is just arguing with the guide for the sake of having a serious conversation with somebody.

It is very hot, there are no trees for shade on the way to the baobab, and the chocolate icing on Bibi's cupcake is beginning to shine and slip. If Bibi was finding the sun too hot earlier, why did she come all this way? Lovemore finds the answer in the cool, deep shade of the baobab, and she finds Bibi standing on the far side of it, her back leaning up against its gigantic trunk. Her eyes are closed, her glasses in her hand. Lovemore can see that she has been crying. Very gently, she touches Bibi's arm.

'Vinas?' Bibi's eyes fly open.

'No, Bibi, it's me. Lovemore.'

Bibi puts her glasses back on. 'Oh.' The tiniest hint of disappointment is like a shadow in Bibi's voice. 'I'm sorry, Lovemore, my mind was far away.'

'It's okay, Bibi. Babu sent me to check on you. I brought you your cake.'

Bibi smiles and takes the cake with a sigh. '*Asante*. You know, if my skirt was looser I would sit on the ground right here and eat it.'

'Can you not, Bibi? You can slide down the tree to the ground.'

Bibi tries sliding a small way down the smooth trunk, walking her feet forward. 'I suppose. But how will I get up?'

'I can pull you, Bibi.'

Once they are both on the ground, Bibi peels the paper case from her cupcake. '*Eh*, I hope I am not angering any kind of god by eating here.'

'Bibi?'

'Some people used to use this tree as a church. They used to come here to pray for rain.'

The shade of the tree does not feel at all like the inside of St Joseph's, but Lovemore can imagine it might feel a little like Highway of Holiness if Godbless was sitting high up in the tree blowing on his trumpet and if others were up there beating some drums. The tree is surely big enough to hold an entire choir.

'You have been here before, Bibi.'

'Yes.' Bibi takes a bite of her cake, chews slowly and swallows. 'We came here once, Pius and me, with Joseph and Vinas. Joseph was your age, Vinas a little younger. *Eh*, it was far to come in those days, there was no tar on the roads and the roads were bad, but Pius wanted to look. The guide took our photo next to the well.'

'That same well?'

'Mm. All four of us drank from it. I think all four of us expected a miracle. We were so young then.'

For a long time Bibi says nothing, and she does not even eat her cake. Lovemore thinks about the photo that today's guide took of all of them in a row: Lovemore, Grace, Benedict and Moses in place of their son Joseph in that old photo; Faith and Daniel in place of their daughter Vinas. Babu and Bibi would surely rather have Joseph and Vinas with them now in place of all their grandchildren.

'Bibi, I'm sorry I'm not Vinas.'

Bibi looks at her like she has just said that Speke set out from Kaole when everybody in the world knows that he set out from Bagamoyo. 'But Lovemore, there is no sorry, none at all! You are part of our Joseph, part of us!' She reaches for Lovemore's hand.

'Ah, Bibi.'

Bibi gives Lovemore her cupcake to hold while she takes off her glasses and cleans the lenses with a tissue from inside her bra. 'You must not think like that. You must not think that you are not my daughter simply because you are not my daughter.' Bibi puts her glasses back on, and they are both quiet again as Bibi finishes her cake.

Lovemore thinks about what Bibi has said. Yes, she is part of Uncle Joseph. She is part of Mama, too, and Mama and Uncle Joseph both loved her with all of their hearts since they first held her. Lovemore herself is the place where Mama and Uncle Joseph held hands and walked arm in arm – where they do that still. They are together forever in her, it does not matter that their remains lie in different graves in different places.

Then an idea comes to her. 'Bibi, do you still have that old photo? The one at the well?'

'Mm, in one of our albums.'

'May I see it?'

'You want to? It's old. Black and white.'

'I'd love to see it, Bibi!' Lovemore has never seen a photo of Uncle Joseph as a child. 'If you like, we can put it in a frame together with today's photo.'

Bibi looks uncertain for a moment, but then she begins to smile. 'Okay. Yes.'

'It can go in the cabinet with the TV.'

'*Eh*, I was thin then. Okay, not *thin*. Help me up, Lovemore.'

Lovemore pulls hard, and slowly Bibi rises. They help each other to dust the soil from their buttocks.

'Ooh, come! Let us go and tell Pius about your lovely idea.' Bibi takes Lovemore's arm, and they begin to walk.

'We must make space in the cabinet for another frame, Bibi.'

'Yes?'

'Mm, also with two photos inside. Can you guess it?'

'*Eh*, Lovemore, this sun is too hot for guessing.'

'The competition, Bibi! You and your winning cake at regional level, and you and your winning cake at national level, in the final.'

'Ah, Lovemore!' Bibi is shaking her head, but her smile is very wide. 'From your lips to God's ears!'

'To God's ears, Bibi.'

When they get back from the baobab to where the others are sitting, Babu and the guide are still giving one of Babu's history lessons.

All of the history has made Moses and Daniel too sleepy for the crocodile farm, so they head straight back to Dar es Salaam. Bibi falls asleep leaning over sideways towards Lovemore, and Lovemore shifts closer towards the open window, the wind full in her face. She keeps her eyes closed, opening them only as Babu slows to pass through the small towns and settlements that Lovemore failed to notice coming the other way because she was too busy memorising Babu's story of Bagamoyo. Zinga, Kerege, Bunju. The names slide past her, but only one name stays in her mind. Bagamoyo. Lay down your heart.

Finally she understands why Mama crossed out what she wrote on the box that she left for Lovemore: *You will be in my heart forever.* Mama laid down her heart in Mwanza when she went to Paradise, never to return. She did not want Lovemore to be laid down there, too, together with Mama's heart. She wanted Lovemore to go somewhere better without laying down her own heart, without leaving her own heart behind. Because when you go without your heart, somebody can even kill you and you do not care because you are already dead.

Leaning the other way, Lovemore rests her head on Bibi's as she thinks about all the people who walked across the water towards the boats with chains around their necks, already dead.

Joseph was too too nice to me all that week, then he told me at lunchtime on the Friday that he was going to come after football on Saturday afternoon, and I must make sure it was just me and him because he had something important to say to me. He squeezed my shoulder when he told me he was going to come, so I smiled all the way home in the Nile Perch Plastics daladala because I knew surer than sure it was going to happen at last. He was going to say he loved me more than Evelina, he was going to leave her, and he was going to come to me and be our daughter's father. Me, Lovemore and him, we were going to be a family together in a nice big house in Capri Point.

It was no problem to make sure we were going to be alone. Agrippina was taking Lovemore and Rose for a birthday party for somebody at school — I don't remember who — Philbert was shopping for the kiosk and Sigsbert was manning it. There was only Pritty, and I told her that after serving the coffee she must go to her room, she must stay there until I called her.

When he came he was straight from football, dirty and smelling, but I didn't mind. Steven often came home to Agrippina smelling of fish from the factory, but he was her husband so she didn't mind how he smelled as long as he didn't smell of another woman. I didn't mind about Joseph smelling of playing football because he was going to be mine. He wasn't going to be my husband, because his church wouldn't let him divorce from his wife, but he was going to be mine. He was nervous while we waited for Pritty to bring our coffee, he was walking up and down instead of sitting next to me on the couch. Steven was nervous when he asked Agrippina to be his wife, Agrippina said he fidgeted in his chair and stood up and sat down for more than an hour before he managed to ask her.

When Pritty closed the kitchen door behind her, I told Joseph to come and sit. He sat down opposite, on the chair, not next to me on the couch, so I moved his cup across the coffee table towards him. I knew he was too too nervous because he didn't even want to look at me in my eyes. He said Glory 3 — maybe even 4 — times, and each and every time he said Glory, I said yes. Then he jumped up like when Steven asked Agrippina, and he came to sit next to me.

Him — Glory, there is something I need to say to you.
Me — Yes?
Him — Eh!
Me — What?
Him — Eh, Glory!
Me — What? What is it that you need to say to me?
Him — Glory, I have received a red card.
Me — What?
Him — I went offside, and now I have received a red card.
Me — A red card? You are telling me about your football?
Him — No, no, no. Eh! Glory. I played away from home. I went offside.

Now I've been given a red card, a penalty.

Me – Why are you talking to me about football?

Him – It isn't football I am talking to you about.

Then he was quiet and I took a sip of coffee while I thought. If he wasn't talking to me about football, he was talking to me about something else, something that he needed to make comfortable by pretending it was football. I had another sip of coffee while he breathed and sighed beside me, and then I understood. His home was with Evelina, and he played away from home with me. Now his penalty was she told him to go.

Me – So Evelina knows?

Him – What?

Me – Evelina knows?

Him – Yes.

Me – How? I mean who told her?

Him – Who was going to tell her but me?

Me – Eh, Joseph!

I held him in my arms then, very tight, and he held me just as tight. At last he told her! He found excuses all the time while Evelina was carrying their firstborn Grace, telling me he was going to tell her after she delivered. Then there were more excuses, and then she was pregnant with Benedict, and after that he couldn't tell her because Benedict's constitution was sickly just like hers, and then she was carrying Moses. But now Evelina knew! And now Joseph belonged to me! I began to cry.

Him – Don't cry, Glory. There is no need for these tears. Everything is going to be OK.

Me – Eh, Joseph!

Him – I promise you everything is going to be OK.

Me – Yes.

Him – Everything is going to be fine.

Me – Eh, Joseph, I can't believe it!

Him – Don't cry, Glory. I'm a strong man. I'm fit. I can still survive for many, many years.

Me – What?

I let go of him then. I wasn't sure what it was that he was telling me, but it didn't sound like he was telling me that we were going to be a family and live together in a nice big house in Capri Point.

Him — The doctor says it can be up to as many as 20 years before I need the medicine, even if Evelina is already sick.

Me — Evelina is sick?

Him — Yes. You know she hasn't been well.

Me — But I didn't know she was sick!

Him — I'm telling you now!

Me — What exactly are you telling me, Joseph? Tell me again, from the beginning, and tell me straight. And if you tell me anything about football I swear in the name of God I will hit you.

He moved back to the chair then, and he told me straight. When Evelina was carrying their lastborn Moses and I was refusing him because he was supposed to be leaving her instead of putting another baby in her belly, it was then that he found somebody else, a woman who was visiting from Congo to buy a truckload of dried dagaa to sell back home. A common trader! Not even a woman who was decent! He even said he told himself it was better for me and Evelina that it was just a visitor, not a Mwanza woman who was going to be complicated. But, eh, that woman was too too complicated. She gave him a very serious gift, and he gave it to Evelina.

And maybe he gave that same gift to me.

He told me straight without talking about football, but still I hit him. When he left, I slammed the front door so hard that our two cups of cold coffee shook on their saucers. Some of the coffee from his full cup spilled over the edge into the saucer and splashed on to the white crochet cloth. But I didn't call for Pritty to come and clear the coffee and soak the cloth, I just stood at the window and watched him walking away to his car.

I could still smell his smell in my nose. I remember I tried to think if he came to me from an important match or if he just went for practising before he came to tell me that a trader woman from Congo was going to take his life and maybe mine also. There was some dried mud on the back of his football shorts, on the left side, like the ball hit him there, and I remember hoping the ball hit him hard. But he wasn't walking like a man who was hurting, he looked like a man who was going home for a shower after football and then out to drink beer with his team.

Near his car he stopped to greet Bismarck and Milton who were going on their way to start their night watch jobs, Bismarck at Nile Perch Plastics and Milton at a shop in Liberty Street. He made them laugh by doing a silly dance with a football that wasn't there, then he and Bismarck acted like they were boxing each other, and they laughed again.

I looked at him then, and it was like I was putting on a pair of glasses that was helping my eyes to see clearer than clear for the first time since I met him. I saw that he wasn't big and important and cost-effective like a Nile Perch. He wasn't tasty and sweet like a tilapia. He wasn't even shiny and nice to look at like a Nyerere cichlid. Now I saw he wasn't like any of those things. He was like a tiny dagaa fish that lay in the dirt on the ground until the sun dried it out and it could go with many handfuls of others to a Congolese trader woman for almost nothing. At that moment, standing at my window and watching him, that was the moment when I stopped loving him. That was the moment when God finally gave me what I prayed for.

He got into his car without turning to look at the house, but if he did he wouldn't see me because it was evening then and the light was starting to go. He began to drive away very slowly because of the bad road, and I saw that one light at the back of his car wasn't working. I didn't run out to tell him, I just stood where I was at the window, and I tried to think did I know anybody who might have a friend in the traffic police?

When I told them that last part in Group, some of them laughed and some of them nodded, then afterwards one of them gave me her phone number for next time because her brother is in the traffic police. She told me that very quietly because nobody likes anybody who is in the traffic police. I can't write her name or her story here in my journal, and she can't write my name or my story in hers. Our names and our stories are our own, and outside of Group they are private.

Chapter 9

On Saturday Babu has to leave for a long trip away to Chad in central Africa, but on Friday evening he drives the whole family to Lovemore and Grace's school to watch Dialogue Night. Bibi looks beautiful in a tight green satin dress with rhinestones around its neckline, Babu is smart and handsome in a suit and tie, Titi is in a pretty floral dress, and Faith and the boys look like they are dressed for a special mass at St Joseph's. But Lovemore has to wear her school uniform, because that is what the school has said. Grace would have to be in her school uniform, too, if she wasn't acting in a dialogue. In fact, Grace has probably been in her school uniform all afternoon, because she stayed at school instead of walking home with Lovemore when lessons were over. There are not very many other girls in uniform, because the whole school could stay late yesterday to watch the dress rehearsal. Lovemore decided not to stay, but to watch it with her family tonight instead.

Mwalimu Mkuu Moshi buzzes around like an insect from mothers to fathers. 'Ah, Dr Tungaraza! How honoured we are to have a man of your distinction here with us. And Mrs Tungaraza, *karibu sana*. Do you have our programme? Lovemore, fetch programmes from Miss Brown.'

The list on the programme shows that first there will be a scene from *Romeo and Juliet* by William Shakespeare, and then there will be a dialogue in French called *La Hyène et La Cigogne* – which Lovemore is not looking forward to because a *cigogne* is a stork – and a dialogue called *Fisi na Mbuzi*, which everybody knows means a hyena and a goat. After that, and before the final dialogue – Grace's from *The Lion and the Jewel* by Wole Soyinka – there is something in German called *Die Hyäne und Die Krähe*, which Babu – who knows German because he studied for two of his degrees in Germany – says is about a hyena and a crow. Hearing the German in Babu's mouth, in Uncle Joseph's voice, she wonders if she made the right decision not to do German herself. Not many of the girls have chosen it – French is much more popular – and the classes are small. But how nice it would be to speak German with Babu at home, just Lovemore and Babu, with nobody else able to understand or to interrupt.

'So many animals!' says Benedict, his finger running down the programme, his eyes shining brightly. 'Look, Lovemore! Look, Baba! Even a crow!'

'*Eine Krähe*,' Babu says, patting Benedict's shoulder.

Lovemore gives her brother a smile, though she could do without the crow. And the stork.

The programme says that the German, Swahili and French dialogues are all by Aesop, an Ethiopian who was taken to Greece as a slave. Lovemore hopes that the Ethiopian has done as well as the Nigerian who wrote Grace's dialogue.

Their school is not the International School on Msasani Peninsula, so there is no hall and instead they sit on chairs where the girls usually stand for assembly, when it is not raining, to listen to *Mwalimu Mkuu* Moshi talking to them from the raised veranda outside her office. Tonight Faith is not happy that *Mwalimu Mkuu* Moshi directs her to sit on the ground in front of the chairs with her brothers and all the other smaller children, while Lovemore gets to sit on the chairs with Babu, Bibi and Titi.

After *Mwalimu Mkuu* Moshi has welcomed everybody to Dialogue Night, the small dramas begin. A girl from Form Four is Juliet, while Romeo is a girl from Form Three with large buttocks that strain at the back of Romeo's jacket. The English is hard because a real Englishman wrote it – maybe it is the kind of English that Miss Brown uses when she speaks to other people back home in England rather than to girls in Tanzania – but Lovemore can understand that it is a very romantic story about a girl and a boy who love each other but their families do not approve. If Faith was sitting next to her, Lovemore would whisper in her ear that it is like Dickson and Grace, and Faith would whisper back that maybe it is like Dickson and Scholastica.

After everybody has clapped and some men have whistled and

women ululated, two girls from Form Two come on to the veranda-stage, one with a big cardboard cut-out of a hyena, the other with a big cardboard cut-out of a stork. Lovemore does not want to look at the stork, so she focuses on the hyena. In French, the hyena and the stork talk together in a friendly way about what a lovely day it is, and the hyena invites the stork to come home with him for a meal, which the stork is very happy to do. The hyena serves only soup, which he can lick up easily himself, but the long beak of the stork means that she can eat none of it. The hyena pretends to be sorry, but as soon as the stork has gone, the hyena laughs. Somebody from drama club runs on to the stage and says, '*Quelques jours plus tard*,' and the hyena and the stork are back again, talking happily about what a lovely day it is. The stork invites the hyena for a meal, and serves only some tiny fish like *dagaa* at the bottom of a narrow-necked jar, which the hyena cannot reach, though the stork can. The hyena is angry, but the stork asks him what did he expect? If you treat people badly, they will treat you badly too.

Suddenly the stage is full of drama-club members singing a song about treating people well so that they will treat you well in return, and then the hyena is back again, this time with a goat, and they are both speaking Swahili. The hyena falls off the edge of a desk and then talks angrily to himself about being in a hole that he cannot climb out of. The goat appears at the top of the hole and asks the hyena what he is doing down there. The hyena says he is storing lots of food in the hole because a big famine is going to come, and they have a conversation about the last famine that swept the land, killing so many animals. The conversation leaves the goat very worried, so the hyena suggests that the goat should jump down into the hole with him to be sure of having plenty to eat. As soon as the goat does that, the hyena jumps on to the goat's back and climbs up on its big horns to get out of the hole. The goat is angry because there is no food in the hole, and now he is stuck down there, unable to climb out. The hyena tells the goat he should never take advice from somebody who is in difficulties.

Drama club members sing a song about choosing carefully who you listen to, and then the hyena is back, with a crow, and this time they are talking in German. Lovemore does not want to look, because the hyena is eating a large cardboard fish, but she has to look because she cannot understand the words. It seems that the crow is asking for some of the fish, but the hyena does not want to share. While they talk, the hyena keeps a foot – or rather, the Form Three girl playing him keeps a foot – firmly on the fish. Somehow the crow persuades the hyena to dance, then grabs the fish and flies up into a tree, which is a desk with a branch lying across it. The crow holds the fish in its beak, shaking its head no while the hyena talks and talks, then at last the crow opens its beak and begins to sing, and the fish falls to the ground, where the hyena snaps it up. The crow shouts angrily at the hyena as it runs away with the fish.

Drama club members sing a song about not trusting people when they flatter you, and then Grace is on the stage in a suit and tie, with all her hair scraped back, and Fenella is there with her, wrapped in a *kanga* and about to swing a bucket of water up onto her head. They act out the dialogue exactly as Lovemore has rehearsed it over and over with Grace: Grace wants to marry Fenella, but Fenella is not interested in an educated somebody who is too ignorant to pay bride-price, so they argue and Grace insults Fenella by calling her a bush girl whose brain is smaller because she is a girl. On the edge of her seat the whole way through, Lovemore wills Grace to get all her words right – which Grace almost does, except for missing out *archaic* and *humiliating* from the long list of words for bride-price from the Shorter Companion Dictionary. When Fenella asks why Grace persists and Grace says, 'Faith', Lovemore wishes that Faith was sitting next to her so that they could nudge each other with their elbows, but Babu nudges her with his, and she nudges him back.

The dialogue is fast and funny, and many times Grace and Fenella have to pause to let the audience stop laughing before they continue, and when it ends with Fenella calling Grace mad and saying that she is going to turn all the students at school mad, too, the audience is on its feet, clapping and whistling and ululating, and Lovemore feels her chest swelling with pride.

All the way home in the microbus, Bibi and Babu tell Grace over and over how proud of her they are. Lovemore has said it to Grace, too, and so have Faith and all of their brothers, but Lovemore can see that it means more to Grace when Bibi and Babu say it. Lovemore is never going to be in a play herself, and even when she is a lawyer in New York Bibi and Babu are not going to be sitting in the courtroom clapping and whistling and ululating. Maybe if she can come first in class – maybe even if only in one subject – maybe then they will feel proud enough of her to say.

When the banging at the gate begins, Titi comes through from the kitchen wiping her hands on a cloth, and makes her way to the gate. The banging continues all the way up to the time she gets there.

'Really!' says Bibi, taking a photo of the cake that she has just completed, a Noah's Ark full of animals for a birthday turning four. 'What kind of young man is Concilia sending me?' She puts her camera down on the dining table, next to the cake.

'Maybe it isn't Ibrahim, Bibi. Maybe it's somebody else.'

Bibi looks at her watch. 'But it's time.'

The boys are out in the back yard – Benedict working in his garden, Moses and Daniel kicking their ball around – and Grace and Faith are sulking in their room because Bibi has said there must be no TV during her meeting. There is no TV during any of Bibi's meetings, but her meetings are usually with customers who have come to order cakes, or from time to time with friends who might want to talk about adult things without any children being around. Bibi has asked Lovemore to attend this meeting with her because Lovemore knows computers better than anybody else in the house apart from Babu, who is away in Chad.

The two of them watch through the window as Titi swings one side of the gate open and the front wheel of a bicycle appears. But it is not really a bicycle, because it has two wheels at the back instead of one, and a seat that looks like a chair. Its pedals are high up where the handlebars should be, and the rider is using his hands to power them. The rider seems to think that it is some kind of motorbike, because he is wearing a red crash helmet.

Bibi goes out to greet him, and Lovemore follows. She sees that his legs wither away to almost nothing beyond the bottom of his long khaki shorts, and she knows at once that he is another polio.

Taking off his crash helmet, he reaches for the pair of wooden crutches strapped lengthways along his vehicle, and in no time at all they are tucked under his armpits and he is up on them, shaking first Bibi's hand then Lovemore's. His face is young and handsome, his eyes kind behind his glasses.

'*Karibu*, Ibrahim. Are you going to manage with these three steps?'

'I'm fine, Auntie.' Even faster than Bibi and Lovemore, he is up the three steps and into the lounge, moving quickly on the crutches as if they are his legs.

Lovemore pulls out a chair for him, and as he slides himself down onto it, Titi goes into the kitchen to make tea.

Ibrahim's eyes are on the cake that is waiting on the far end of the dining table for the customer to fetch it later today, the pairs of bright sugar-animals crowded onto Noah's Ark looking more like they come from a cartoon than from the Serengeti National Park, because the child is only four. 'Ah, this is one of the very famous, very beautiful, very delicious cakes Concilia has told me about.' Ibrahim's words make Bibi smile, patting one side of her hair with a hand. 'But that is an old kind of camera, Auntie.'

'Ibrahim, I am an old kind of woman.'

He smiles, his smile going all the way up to his eyes. 'That is no problem, Auntie. It is easy to make old photos new, it is simply a matter of scanning. I can scan all of your photos for you, no problem. I am at your service.'

'Thank you, Ibrahim.'

'No problem.' From a large canvas bag slung over one shoulder and across his chest, he takes out the kind of notebook that Mama used to carry with her at work even though she did not know any shorthand. Clipped on to the notebook is a pen. 'Now. What kind of website are you having in your mind?'

Bibi hesitates. 'Ibrahim, it is not really me who is having a website in her mind, it is Concilia.'

'Ah.'

'But Concilia is right, Bibi. It's important to become modern.' Lovemore looks from Bibi to Ibrahim, who looks back at her through shining eyes, a small smile playing on his lips. Her face feels suddenly hot. 'I mean … um …' She looks down at the table.

'No, I know,' says Bibi. 'I know.'

'Auntie, it's no problem. You are not my first client to be unsure of becoming my client. Many people have come to me not knowing why they are coming to me, but always they are happy later. One hundred per cent guaranteed.'

Titi comes in from the kitchen with three cups of tea and two slices of cake on the scratched old tin tray. She makes sure that Lovemore gets the right cup, then puts cake in front of Bibi and Ibrahim before getting back to whatever is keeping her busy in the kitchen.

'You don't take cake?'

Lovemore shakes her head no. 'I have sugar.'

'*Eh!* My granddaddy was having sugar. *Pole sana.*' He cuts a mouthful of cake with the side of a teaspoon. 'Very sorry.'

'It's okay,' says Lovemore, glad that she is not eating cake, sure that she would embarrass herself in front of him by dropping it from her teaspoon onto the table or into her lap. She is angry with herself. She has noticed Ibrahim, noticed him as a boy in the way that Grace notices boys, and she is not supposed to notice any boy – any man – until she is in New York. It will be easy for her to meet the right kind of man when she is a lawyer there. Ally McBeal on TV is a lawyer in Boston, which Lovemore has seen in Benedict's atlas is very close to New York – maybe even as close as Bagamoyo is to Dar es Salaam – and Ally McBeal never has a problem meeting men. There are plenty as clients and plenty more working in the law firm with her. Okay, one of the partners at Ally's firm is called Richard Fish, and Lovemore could never be interested in a man called Fish, let alone marry him and become Lovemore Fish, but there are surely many other family names in New York. Lovemore and Rose have not yet discussed if they are going to have men working with them in their offices, but even if they decide not to, there will be men all around them, the right kind of men for Lovemore's destiny. Ibrahim is certainly not her destiny, and she should not be noticing him.

'Mm, very delicious!'

'Thank you, Ibrahim.' Bibi washes down a mouthful of cake with a sip of her tea. 'You know, usually it isn't me who is the client. Usually it's me asking my customer many questions so that I can see what kind of cake is right for them.'

'You can ask me questions, Auntie.' Bending his head over his cup, he sucks in a big, noisy slurp of it. Then he lifts his head and slides his glasses back up on his nose by raising his left nostril in an ugly sneer.

The effect on Lovemore is instant. It is like one minute he had a tattoo of flames on his arm to stamp him as dangerous, and the next he is simply a young man made ugly by his manners.

Bibi sips her tea delicately. 'Tell me about your granddaddy, the one who was having sugar.'

'Mm.' At least he swallows his mouthful of cake before he talks. 'His home was Zanzibar. He had a job with the British, actually he was the colleague of Freddie Mercury's daddy. You know Freddie Mercury?'

'Uh-uh.'

'Queen,' says Lovemore. 'He sang in a group called Queen. Grace and Faith were dancing when they sang on TV just the other day.'

Bibi shakes her head. 'No, I don't know him.'

'Very famous, Auntie, all over the world. But late now. Zanzibar was his native country. Anyway, my daddy and Freddie were the same age, though Freddie wasn't yet Freddie Mercury, he was still Farrokh Bulsara.'

'You knew Freddie Mercury?' For the first time since she taught her sisters modelling, Lovemore feels like she might have something that will impress them. She has drunk tea with somebody who knew somebody famous they have seen on TV.

'Uh-uh. But my daddy met him when he was still Farrokh. They didn't go to the same school or anything because Freddie went to school in India, a British school there, but sometimes our two families met because of stamps.'

'Stamps?' Bibi sips some more of her tea.

Lovemore is too excited to drink hers.

'Mm, in my family we collect stamps. Freddie's daddy and my granddaddy both collected stamps from the commonwealth, and Freddie, too. My daddy is still collecting, he is specialising in Africa, more especially pre-independence.'

'*Eh!* He should meet my husband Pius.'

'Yes?' Ibrahim's eyes are bright behind his glasses. 'He is also collecting pre-independence?'

'No, not stamps, but he likes the history of Africa.'

'Very good.' Bending his head over his cup, he slurps some more, then he lifts his head and slides his glasses back up his nose by raising his left nostril.

Lovemore wishes it could be somebody other than Ibrahim that she is going to tell her sisters about, the person whose daddy knew somebody famous.

'*Mama!*'

They hear Benedict's voice before he even comes into the kitchen from the yard. The door from the kitchen swings open, and Benedict is there, clearly upset. Bibi introduces him to Ibrahim before she lets him speak.

'Mama, Mr Kapufi just killed another crow!'

Bibi clicks her tongue against the back of her teeth. Lovemore feels torn between the urge to comfort her brother and the urge to rejoice because there is one less bird anywhere near her.

'Ah, *pole sana*,' says Ibrahim. 'An Indian house crow?'

'Mm.'

'*Eh*, but he is doing a favour to our other birds. That house crow, that *corvus splendens*, it is devastating all our natural birds. You know?' Benedict nods his head yes with a sulky expression. 'Really, it is the fault of the British, because the British, when they were in charge of Zanzibar, they requested those crows from India. They wanted the crows to clean up Zanzibar by eating all the rubbish. But now the crows have come here in our city, and *eh!*' Ibrahim shakes his head. 'They are not here as cleaners, they are here as killers.'

Benedict sighs. 'I know.'

'You like birds?' Benedict nods his head yes. 'Then you must come to my house. Me and my daddy, we are saving the birds of Dar es Salaam. Almost our whole back yard,' Ibrahim spreads his arms wide, 'it is an aviary, a big cage where all our own birds can fly free and the crows can't get them.'

'*Eh!*' Benedict looks very impressed.

Ibrahim counts on his fingers. 'We have our little sparrows, we have our paradise flycatchers, we have our sunbirds—'

'When can I come, Ibrahim?' Benedict sits down at the table.

'No, no, Benedict!' Bibi waves the back of her hand at him. 'We are having a meeting about internet, you two can talk some other time.'

Benedict stands up. 'He's putting food for the crows, Mama, then he shoots them with his catapult.'

'What Mr Kapufi does in his own yard is his own business, Benedict.'

He sighs. 'I know, Mama. I do know.' He gives Ibrahim a big smile before going back out through the kitchen.

These days it is very difficult for Lovemore to look at Benedict without seeing the black-and-white photos in Bibi's album of Uncle Joseph as a boy. Their faces are very similar, their long, thin bodies identical. She wants to go after him, to tell him sorry about the crow – because *he* is sorry about it – the way that he told her, on the day her cup was full of ants, sorry about her sugar – because he thought *she* was sorry about it. She wants to go after him and sit quietly with him in his garden, waiting for his upset to go and for butterflies to come.

But she stays at the table, where Ibrahim is making her feel uncomfortably confused. She wants to dislike him because he likes birds enough to protect them, but she cannot dislike him because he has just been very kind to Benedict – and really, protecting the vulnerable from attack is a very good thing to do, even if it is birds that Ibrahim and his daddy are protecting. Her heart is warming to him again when he bends, slurps his tea, then sneers his glasses back up on his nose, chilling her heart at once.

'*Eh*, you know birds,' Bibi says to him.

'That is my speciality in stamps, Auntie. Birds. I have nearly every kind of bird on my stamps, but not *corvus splendens*, the house crow. No country is wanting a picture of that bird on their stamps, it has no beauty at all. It is just a pest.'

'My Pius told us a story about having a meeting in the garden of one of the hotels here, and a crow came and sat on the table next to them and stole a packet of sugar, one of those small packets for one person. Really, what was that crow going to do with it?'

'Tear it open, Auntie, and eat it! *Eh*, I hope it gave that crow sugar like my granddaddy had.'

'Ah, you were telling us about your granddaddy in Zanzibar.'

Ibrahim swallows a mouthful of cake. 'Mm. In 1964, in Zanzibar's revolution, many Arabs and Indians were getting killed. Freddie Mercury's family were a kind of Indian, they were Parsis, so they fled to England. Friends advised that my granddaddy should come here to mainland with his family because he was married with a Christian, and things were uncertain. Here on mainland we can marry another faith, it doesn't matter, but Zanzibar is more strict.'

'It is not the first time for me to hear that,' Bibi tells him, finishing off her piece of cake.

'So my daddy finished his growing up here on mainland, and he became a history teacher. He married with another history teacher, my mummy. Me and my four big brothers, we are all in computer. Two are doing computer repair, one is having an internet café, one is teaching computer, and me, I am doing websites.' His tea is too low in his cup now for him to slurp it where it sits on the table, so he picks it up and slurps.

'That is good,' says Bibi, 'having the whole family interested in the same thing.'

Not for the first time, Lovemore is aware of Babu and Bibi being interested in different things and of the big gap between them in their education. Babu has all his degrees, but Bibi only went as far as completing school.

Ibrahim picks up his pen again. 'Auntie, let us begin. What is the name of your business?'

'Its name?' Bibi looks confused. 'No, my business has no name.'

'No name?' For the briefest of moments, the expression on Ibrahim's face suggests that Bibi might be incredibly stupid.

Lovemore rushes to defend her. 'People come to order cakes from Bibi, not from her business. She is her business.'

'I see. So it's called Angel Tungaraza?'

'Well, no,' says Bibi, 'it isn't called anything.'

'Ah, Auntie, for a website your business needs to have a name. Take my business for an example. How are people going to know about my business if it has no name?'

'But, Ibrahim, I don't know the name of your business. I only know that Concilia sent you to me.'

Ibrahim reaches into his large canvas bag for a business card, which he hands over to Bibi. 'This is what I am calling myself, The Web Maker. That is what interests people, more so than Ibrahim Abdullah. Who is Ibrahim Abdullah? Nobody knows what he does. But The Web Maker, everybody knows that he makes websites, and that he is the only person to go to for that because he is *The* Web Maker. There is no other. Now. What are people going to know about a business called Angel Tungaraza?'

Bibi shrugs. 'Nothing, I suppose.'

'Yes. So your business is needing a name. That is something you can think about over time.'

Over the next half hour they talk through what Bibi wants her website to be able to do, and what information needs to be on it. Lovemore takes notes, because she is the one who will type the information for Bibi's website. They are just finishing off when Grace and Faith wander in. They do it casually, as if they have forgotten that Bibi is having a meeting, but Lovemore knows that they have come on purpose to have a look at the young man that Concilia has sent. Lovemore introduces them and tells them that Baba-Ibrahim knew Freddie Mercury.

Grace is immediately impressed, her handshake threatening to unbalance Ibrahim from his chair. '*Eh!* I'm sure you listen to his music all the time!'

'Ah, no. Well, my daddy listens sometimes, but low volume in case a neighbour hears. Freddie's lifestyle?' He shakes his head, clicking his tongue against the back of his teeth. 'Liking boys? Uh-uh, it is not approved. But me, I like the songs of Queen.'

'Me too,' says Faith.

'Me too,' says Grace, more loudly, and then she begins to sing, gyrating her body slowly to the beat, 'We will, we will rock you!'

Smiling up at her from his seat, Ibrahim claps his hands. 'You are good!'

Lovemore does not like that Grace has stolen his attention. She gathers her notes and stands. 'Thank you, Ibrahim, I think you have given us plenty to work on. Plenty to think about.' It feels wrong to her, like Mama might feel if she found herself ending one of Uncle Joseph's meetings at Nile Perch Plastics. Ending a meeting is not the business of the person who is taking notes.

Fortunately, Bibi seems keen to end the meeting, too. 'Grace, you are showing off.'

Standing up, Bibi reaches for Ibrahim's crutches where they are resting on a chair behind the table, and hands them over to him. In one swift move the crutches are in his armpits and he is up on them. In an instant Grace's face moves from the excited adoration of meeting somebody who knows somebody famous, through shock and all the way to disgust. Even as Lovemore sees it, she hopes that Ibrahim's eyes are somewhere else.

Bibi has definitely seen it, because when Ibrahim is settling himself back on to the seat of his vehicle outside, she says something that Lovemore knows is meant to make him feel good.

'Thank you for the meeting, Ibrahim. Really, we have enjoyed meeting you. I hope there is a nice girl appreciating you for the fine young man that you are?'

'Ah, no, Auntie.' He pats his withered legs. 'Girls are not interested in boys like me.'

'Surely they can see beyond!'

He shrugs, strapping on his red crash helmet. 'It is hard for people to see beyond, Auntie. Look at Concilia, she is so very lovely, but,' he pats his left thigh, 'she has no husband.'

Bibi looks suddenly uncomfortable. Lovemore knows that gossip about others is not something that Bibi likes at all. 'There will be somebody for you, Ibrahim.'

Glancing at Lovemore, he smiles, and Lovemore is suddenly uncomfortable, her face hot, though his face does not look at all attractive inside the red crash helmet.

'Thank you, Auntie. Call me whenever you are ready, I am at your service twenty-four six, just not on Fridays.'

Lovemore opens the gate for him. As he pedals out using his hands she sees that he has painted THE WEB MAKER and his phone number in white on the back of his red helmet.

It took every last drop of Angel's inner strength to harden herself against Grace's red eyes and wet lashes. That girl in tears could sometimes pull Angel's heart to pieces and make her look beyond any bad thing that Grace had just done. It had been like that from the moment Joseph had first placed Angel's firstborn baby grandchild in her arms – and knowing now that Grace was not in fact the firstborn had done nothing to change it. But right now Angel could not simply give in to loving the girl with no ifs and not a single but, because Pius was away in Chad and could not be left with the job of disciplining her.

'Number one,' Angel said again, a little more forcefully, marking it on the small finger of her left hand with her right index finger.

Grace gave her nose a good blow then took a deep breath. Her voice, when it came, was that of a much smaller girl. 'Number one, I interrupted your meeting.'

Angel moved on to the ring finger of her left hand. 'Number two.'

Grace squirmed uncomfortably. 'Number two, I made a bad face when I saw—'

'Uh-uh. That is number three. Number two!'

'Number two, I flirted with a boy.'

'*Flirted? Eh!* No, Grace, that was not flirting. No. Flirting is about looking then looking away, it is about lowering your gaze. There is nothing about showing off or being indecent in flirting. It is how I attracted my Pius.'

'But these days, Mama—'

'Uh-uh! Don't try to tell me about these days and those, Grace. There was no flirting here today. No. Today you behaved like an indecent girl. Number two!'

Grace sighed. 'Number two, I behaved like an indecent girl.'

'Number three!' Angel pushed down hard on her middle finger.

'Number three, I made a bad face when I saw Ibrahim's legs.'

'His *difficulties*, Grace.'

'Okay, his difficulties.'

'And how do you feel about yourself now because you did numbers one to three?'

'I feel ashamed, Mama.'

As Grace settled in front of the computer to write her letter to Pius about why she was ashamed of herself today – not just a list, but a proper letter – Angel settled on one of the couches to go through her diary and be sure of all her cake commitments for the next few days. One or two of them were slightly complicated, and she would need to sketch them first on her squared paper to get an idea of the best shapes to bake and how best to piece them together. After that, there was her list to write in her notebook, so she had plenty to keep her busy until the time that Grace's letter was typed, printed and faxed, and they could both go to bed.

Angel wished she could be sure that Ibrahim had not seen how badly Grace had allowed her face to behave, but unfortunately he probably had. It was only that he was used to such things, and he knew how to hide his feelings well.

Angel had wanted very badly to tell him something that would have made him feel better about himself, but she had managed to hold her tongue. It would have been so easy to say to him that he must not give up hope of finding love, that he must not think that the reason why Concilia was on her own was because people could not see beyond her leg and her stick. If he could understand that perhaps there could be a different reason, then maybe he would be able to concentrate on making himself more attractive in other ways – ways like learning to drink his tea more politely and decently. But Angel had held her tongue about Concilia, and she was very glad of that because being confidential was a cornerstone of her business. When her customers came to order their cakes, they often told her so much more than how their cake should look and what occasion it was for, and they did that because they understood that anything they said to Angel was completely confidential. Sometimes they were sad because somebody was going away or somebody was retiring or they were remembering somebody who was late. Sometimes they were happy because somebody was having a birthday or somebody was getting married or somebody had achieved something special. Sometimes they wanted the very biggest cake, or the most complicated cake, or the most expensive cake, but sometimes they wanted something very simple, and then Angel could help them to understand that what they really wanted was something a little more expensive than that. It was safe for them to tell Angel about anything at all because Angel would never tell. Never. If ever she gossiped about anybody – a customer, a friend, anybody at all – people would hear about it and they would lose their confidence that her business was confidential.

Glancing up from her place on the couch, Angel recognised that she was sitting in the very spot where her friend Stella sat to drink her tea and fall asleep. It was not Angel's usual place. No. Normally she and Pius sat on the middle couch of the U shape, the one directly opposite the TV – but now she was on the side one that had its back to where the bedrooms were, so that she could keep an eye on Grace at the computer.

'Are you making progress, Grace?'

'Mm.'

'Good girl.'

Angel wondered how Stella was feeling now, after what they had all done for her earlier this week.

They had been phoning one another for days about what to do.

'It's gone too far now,' Fatima had said.

'Seriously, can we simply look the other way?' Irene had asked. 'Can we? Seriously?'

'It is our Christian duty to act,' Esther had declared.

'And our duty as friends,' Angel had agreed.

Finally Irene had phoned with an idea of what they should do. 'We need to intervent her, Angel. Did you not see it on *Oprah*?'

'*Eh*, I don't know when I last had time for TV!'

Esther had been waiting outside the children's primary school at starting time, and Angel had driven with her towards Stella's house. On the way, they had seen Fatima climbing out of a *daladala* and given her a ride for the last hundred metres or so. They had found Irene already there, paying the driver of the *bodaboda* that had brought her.

Stella had been extremely happy to see them, though surprised and confused. '*Eh*! Did I forget you were coming? Such things can happen when you're old! But *karibuni*, you are all very welcome! Let me have Anna make us some tea!'

'Ah, no, my dear! I am still so full of my breakfast.'

'Ooh, I am swimming in tea!'

'Thank you, Stella, but I must cut down on my morning tea, otherwise I cannot get through lunchtime prayers without needing the washroom.'

'Forgive me, my friend, I don't want to be rude by declining, but *eh*, look at how my seams are straining!'

'Let us sit, Stella.'

'Mm. Let us talk.'

Angel had got tips from Concilia, which she had shared with the others over the phone, and Irene had summarised them into a few short, sharp instructions that she had sent to all of them by SMS text, so they had all known exactly how to proceed. But still, it had not been easy.

For more than two hours they had intervened her, gently but firmly.

'Ah, my friend! I feel it as an honour that you are comfortable enough in my home to close your eyes, but while I'm getting on with my cakes I'm anxious! *Eh!* I want to keep checking that you are simply asleep, because, really, I don't ever want to find that you are late, especially in front of the children.'

'It's after your second cup that I feel you drifting from me, my dear, and for me that is a loss because I so love it when you are with me!'

'We think your medicine is not from the doctor, Stella. We think it is from the collection of your late husband.'

'Ooh, and Jesus *never* turned water into anything stronger than wine.'

'I always knew when my Pius had been drinking with your Deogratias, he did not come home the same man. Uh-uh. Once he failed to come home at all! Do you remember that time, Stella? You came to my house in a taxi, left them together with that bottle at your house.'

When Stella had at last put aside her denials and begun to cry about Deogratias being gone and her days stretching ahead of her as empty as a president's promises, it had been time for the easier part of their intervention, the part that had been about helping her with their ideas of how to fill her time. And they had not left until every one of them – including Stella – had sworn that they would all do the same for any one of them if ever the need should arise.

That had been an exhausting morning, though uplifting in the end, and it had helped Angel to recognise quite how absorbed in her family and her business she had become now that Pius was away as much as he was. Normally it would have been Angel herself who had seen that Stella's problem was in need of attention, it would have been Angel herself who had called the others to action, it would have been Angel herself who had checked in with Stella on every day that followed. Really, Pius's absence was having a very big effect on who she was able to be.

Tucked into the back of Angel's notebook was the letter from Pius in Chad that had arrived today via the fax machine, and she unfolded it now to read it again. The two pages were covered in his small, neat handwriting, so familiar to Angel from the days when he had been a student far away in Germany. His voice on the page sounded busy and stressed today, just as it did back then – yet how much had changed since those days!

Wondering now how Grace's letter to Pius was coming along, Angel got up from the couch and went to the dining table, where cakes were cooling for decorating in the morning. She saw at once that what was on the screen in front of Grace was not a letter but photos of boys with microphones and guitars.

'Grace!'

Grace's body jumped, and suddenly the boys were gone from the screen. 'Sorry, Mama!'

'Concentrate! Do you want us to sit here through the night?'

'No, Mama. Sorry.'

'Read me what you have written so far.'

Grace squirmed on her chair. 'It's private, Mama. Nobody is supposed to read anybody else's letter. You and Baba always tell us that.'

'That is true. But this is a different kind of letter. When Baba made Faith write a letter to Dickson after her silly game of inviting him here for supper, Baba read Faith's letter. He needed to be sure that she was confessing and apologising, not just writing any other nonsense.'

Grace sighed heavily. 'Let me finish first, Mama, then you can read.'

'*Sawa*. I can wait.'

On her way back to the couch, Angel paused to look again at the two photos in the new gold frame in the TV cabinet, the reminders of the two times when the family had drunk from the miracle well in Kaole. She took it back to the couch with her to look at it carefully. *Eh*, how like Joseph as a boy was Benedict now! But how different inside! While Benedict loved animals and plants, Joseph as a boy had been interested in machines and how they worked, to the extent that Pius had thought he might become an engineer. When Angel looked at this young Joseph, this one here in black and white, her feelings were not at all complicated. No. She loved him with no ifs and not a single but – and, really, she did love him still. It was only that she did not love how he behaved, hiding away his firstborn, cheating on his wife Evelina.

When Pius had last seen Evelina, he had been convinced that she was close to the end of her days. He had visited her in hospital when he had gone to Mwanza for Joseph's body, and she had been so very weak. She had been in hospital before, and that was when Joseph had brought the children to live here with their grandparents, but she had rallied and been discharged to go home to Joseph. For people who were sick with AIDS it could be normal to be admitted and discharged, admitted and discharged, but Pius had doubted that Evelina would ever be discharged again. She had been, though – they had learned it from the doctor at the hospital who had been keeping Pius informed – and they had waited for her to be strong enough to phone the children. But that had never happened. Her funeral had been hard on all of them, coming so soon after they had buried Joseph.

But Angel did not want to think about that now. She returned the twinned Kaole photos to their place in the TV cabinet, in front of the matching gold frame that was waiting for her winning photos from the competition. She had not wanted to risk making anything bad happen by buying it before she needed it, but the frames had been on a special at the shop, and if she bought one she could get the second for half price. Pius was a man who loved a good bargain – if he had been here instead of in Chad, he would definitely have told her to go ahead and get both frames.

It had been a very long wait, but next week the Kilimanjaro Snow people would at last announce the winners of round one in each and every region of Tanzania. Angel was not happy that Pius would not be back by then. She would have loved to have him at her side when she heard that news, good or bad. The high quality of the cakes on the competition website had certainly knocked her confidence for a while, and she was sure that everybody had grown very tired of her showing them photos and asking if they thought this cake was more impressive than that, but in the end she had been happy with her final six choices: the pink handbag with things spilling out that she had made for Grace and Lovemore's birthday party; the big round football with its pattern of black and white hexagons sitting on a field of grass – not just easy, lazy, flat green sugar paste covering the cake board, but small worms of icing looking like actual blades of grass, with a stripe of white worms looking like blades of grass painted white for the edge of a football field; the bright tipper-truck with small sweets cascading off its back as it tipped; the Christening cake in pure white with beautiful, complicated pink roses and delicate green leaves as well as the baby girl's name; the cleverly worked basket brimming with Easter eggs; and finally, the wedding cake made up of five cakes circling a sixth central cake on a special gold stand, each one of them spectacular in bright yellow and orange.

 Angel had debated hard – with herself as well as with anybody else she could persuade to join in – about whether or not to include the wedding cake. Not just because she would have to make a wedding cake for round two if she was chosen as a winner in round one, but because that particular wedding cake was already famous from appearing in a magazine. Pius had told her that if she chose to include it, she must not, under any circumstances, send along with it a photocopy of the article in which it appeared. It was a national competition, he told her, a Tanzanian competition. Pictures in a South African magazine of Angel and her cake for a wedding in Rwanda were not going to make Tanzanians want her to win a Tanzanian competition. In the end, Angel had decided to include the wedding cake as one of her six without any mention of the magazine article. That cake still meant a lot to her, and it really was very, very beautiful.

 Neatly straightening the frame of the two Kaole pictures in the TV cabinet, touching briefly the waiting competition frame behind it, Angel thought of Lovemore, who had had the idea for both of the frames. What a comfort it had been to have that girl beside her during the meeting with Ibrahim today! It had made Angel far less nervous that Ibrahim was going to say computer vocabularies that she was not going to understand. Those were vocabularies that Lovemore understood – and Pius, too, whose name and photograph were on a website for independent consultants in Africa.

At the computer, Grace was now sitting on both of her hands, her mind obviously somewhere very far away. *Eh*, that girl! Shaking her head, Angel went to sit next to her in front of the screen, otherwise the letter to Pius would never get finished and they would never get to bed.

Faith is asleep, but Grace could finish her letter to Babu on the computer and come into the room at any moment, so Lovemore takes Mama's journal into the washroom and settles herself on the brightly frilled cover of the toilet seat to read.

In Group they tell us we must forget about our could-haves and our should-haves because our past is not something that we can change. But I have a very big could-have and should-have, and something that big is very difficult to forget about. The year that Joseph made his wife pregnant with their lastborn, the boy called Moses, I could have changed everything, I could have made everything better for me and Lovemore, I could have made everything OK. Everything.

Many times that year I didn't go straight home after work. I asked the driver of the Nile Perch Plastics daladala to drop me at the airport road, and when the daladala turned right to take the other workers back into town, I waited for another daladala or a bodaboda to take me left towards the airport, as far as Highway of Holiness. Inside, one or two people walked in small circles praying in quiet voices, one or two more spoke their prayers in big loud voices as they walked here and there and somewhere else. Me, I don't know how was I walking or how was my voice inside that church. Those things didn't matter to me or to God, what mattered was what I was asking from God in my prayer. I was asking for a way out of where I was stuck, I was asking for a way to stop loving Joseph so much, to stop loving him at all.

Once upon a time I had the hope and expectation that me, Lovemore and Joseph were going to live as a family in a nice big house in Capri Point, with a brother or a sister for Lovemore. After Lovemore, Joseph always insisted that

I must take contraceptive pills. His church said the pills were wrong, but Joseph said it wasn't him who was taking them, it was me, and my church didn't mind so much. There were times when I only pretended to take the pills. Joseph put three more babies in my belly, but he never knew because they never stayed there for even three months. I never told him that I failed because I was too ashamed. He knew I told it to other men to keep them away from me, and he said he loved me for doing that. But he didn't know it was real, he didn't know it was true. I didn't want him to know I really was like a fish floating dead on the top of the lake, a fish that nobody was going to touch because everybody knew it wasn't going to be worth eating. If he knew, then we were never going to be a family in a nice big house in Capri Point. I wasn't still expecting that, but I couldn't stop hoping for it because I couldn't stop loving him. That year I walked and I prayed and I walked and I prayed, and over and over I asked God to stop me loving Joseph because I couldn't stop myself.

One afternoon that year, a man came to Nile Perch Plastics in a taxi with a letter for the younger Mr Desai, who was there for introducing a new system. After the younger Mr Desai drank tea with him, he took the man to Joseph, then Joseph brought him to me. His name was Dieudonné. He was the accountant for a Mhindi businessman in Dar es Salaam, and all his holidays he spent looking for his family all over Tanzania, they were lost since they all fled from trouble in Rwanda when he was a small boy. His Mhindi boss in Dar es Salaam told him in Mwanza the younger Mr Desai could help him, but the younger Mr Desai didn't know Rwandans, and Joseph didn't either. Some years Agrippina had a Rwandan child in her Standard I class, so I invited him to come home with me after work so that Agrippina could help him.

When we got into his taxi together, everybody who was getting into the Nile Perch Plastics daladala looked at us, and Joseph looked at us as he got into his own car. Joseph's face wasn't happy, but what could he say? He is the one who asked me to help that man. Dieudonné didn't have lodgings in Mwanza yet, so I said he was welcome to sleep in our lounge room on the mattress from under Lovemore's bed. I wasn't afraid of him as a stranger in our house, his eyes were kind behind his glasses and a person without a kind heart doesn't spend all his holidays looking for his family he lost when he was small. Anyway, Philbert or Sigsbert was going to be at home with us while Sigsbert or Philbert manned the kiosk. I took him to see Agrippina, 3 houses away on the next corner, then I went home to make sure everything was clean and tidy for our visitor and to tell Pritty to prepare extra food.

He came back from Agrippina's house with Lovemore's hand in his, and he was talking to her like she was the only person in the world he wanted to talk to, though she had only 4 years and though he was excited about other things because Agrippina was helping him, and members of the Rwandan community in Mwanza were going to meet with him tomorrow. He stayed at our house for 3 nights until he had to get back to his job in Dar es Salaam, but he found that his family wasn't in Mwanza. Somebody told him that there were Rwandan women cooking for the men who were mining for gold at Geita, so the next time he had enough holiday, he was going to go there. I told him Geita was more to the west, he was going to pass through Mwanza to go there, he must come and stay again if he wanted. I also told him next time he should also go further than Geita to my home village Ngara, because the border with Rwanda is close there, and when I was a child we always met people from Rwanda and Burundi who were waiting there for home to be a safe place to go.

When I listened to Dieudonné telling me about his lost family, I thought a lot about my own family. I knew where they were, but I never went there, not since they put me on the bus to come to Mwanza for secondary school. I didn't want to tell him that, because not seeing his own family was eating him up like the Nile Perches were eating up every other kind of fish in the lake.

For a long time after Dieudonné went, Joseph kept asking me questions. Why did I let him stay at my house? Where did he sleep? What did he want with me? Did I tell him my story about not being able to carry any other child? I liked that Joseph was jealous, it showed that he loved me. But it didn't stop me trying not to love him.

One day later that same year I went home from work and Dieudonné was sitting in the lounge room playing with Lovemore and laughing with Philbert. Eh, I was too, too happy to see him! He brought a gift for Lovemore, a jigsaw puzzle with a picture of Mount Kilimanjaro, and he was showing her how to put it together. I didn't know then because that was the first jigsaw puzzle that ever came into our house, but 500 pieces was a very big puzzle for a child as small as Lovemore. We all helped her to put it together, me Dieudonné and Philbert, and Pritty too after supper. It was like we were a family.

In my bedroom that night, I wrote a letter to my big sister Edna, the one closest to my age. I told her I had a daughter and a good job in an office with air-conditioning, and I was fine. I asked how was everybody? I put the address of Nile Perch Plastics if anybody wanted to send a letter. On the envelope I wrote her name and where in Ngara Dieudonné could find her. He took it with him after breakfast the next morning, after Lovemore held his legs and cried because he was going.

Joseph was angry that Dieudonné came again, he was sure Dieudonné was trying to be my boyfriend. I told him about our lovely evening together and about Lovemore crying when he went. Joseph didn't like that, I could see that he wanted to shout, but he couldn't because we were at Nile Perch Plastics and the younger Mr Desai was there for auditing. We argued about it in whispers in my office while we pretended to be searching through some box files for an invoice that was lost.

Him – Why are you doing this to me, Glory?
Me – What? What am I doing to you?
Him – He wants to pull down your pantie and you are encouraging him.
Me – He doesn't want to pull down my pantie, he never tried to touch it.
Him – How can you take another boyfriend when you already have me?
Me – Maybe what I want is a husband, not a boyfriend.
Him – Is he going to marry you?
Me – Are you going to marry me?
Him – Eh, Glory, you know it's complicated.
Me – It's not complicated for Dieudonné.
Him – Eh!
Me – Five years ago you told me you only married Evelina because she pretended she was pregnant, she didn't want you to come to Mwanza without her. You told me you were going to leave her because I was the one you wanted. Then you made both of us pregnant! Then you made her pregnant again! Why don't you just tell me straight that you are never going to leave her and we are never going to be a family with our daughter? Why don't you just tell me the truth and let another man be my husband?
Him – You are not going to belong to any other man!

Then he put his hand inside the collar of his shirt and he pulled out his Catholic cross, the one that hit me in the teeth again and again every time we did sex, and he held it tight in both his hands, pulling on its chain around his neck.

Him – I swear by this, Glory, I swear by this and by the holy Virgin Mary I will leave Evelina by the end of this year. On my parents' lives I swear it to you now. By the end of this year you, me and Lovemore will be a family. I would swear it on my knees except Mr Desai could come in.

I believed him because I wanted to believe him, because I couldn't stop myself loving him.

After 10 days Dieudonné came back for 1 night on his way back to his job in Dar es Salaam, and he brought a letter for me from Edna. She said our parents were late now but our sisters were fine and all were married. I was welcome to bring my daughter to meet her cousins. She put a phone number if I wanted to talk. I wasn't sure if I wanted to talk, but I was glad that my sisters were no longer strangers, I was glad that Dieudonné couldn't think that I didn't care that I had a family. His family wasn't in Geita, and they weren't in Ngara. I could see that he was disappointed, and after Lovemore and Pritty and Sigsbert went to bed, I stayed up to talk to him.

He told me that finding his family was more important to him than anything, it was like he couldn't do anything else with his personal life until he found them. Even if he heard for sure they were all late, at least then he would know, and then he could make plans for starting a family of his own. Then he told me that he hoped more than he ever hoped before that he was going to find his family in Geita or Ngara, because then he was going to be able to talk to me about did me and Lovemore think we would like to be his family? But that wasn't something he could ask any woman until his search was finished. Then he said he was sorry that he even said anything to me, it wasn't fair, he shouldn't have said, it was only that he was too too tired and too too disappointed, it wasn't right for him to disappoint me as well.

I told him I understood why he couldn't love anybody yet, and I said it made my heart very happy that he could think of me and Lovemore like that. Then I told him he mustn't worry about us because in fact there was a man who was coming to be with me and Lovemore by the end of the year. He shook my hand for congratulations, then we talked of other things. One thing we talked about was what his name means, it means given by God. I told him he was going to find his family one day, and then he was going to be a gift from God to the woman he was going to marry.

 I didn't see that Dieudonné was a gift from God to <u>me</u> until the end of the year came and Joseph wasn't going to leave Evelina because she was pregnant with their boy Moses. What I prayed for from God was a way out of where I was stuck, a way to stop loving Joseph. God gave me Dieudonné, and what did I do? I refused God's gift. I should have told Dieudonné that I was going to wait for him to find his family. I already knew how to wait for a man, me and Lovemore could have waited for him until he was ready. That is my could-have and should-have that is just too big for me to forget about, it doesn't matter what they tell us in Group.

 The next April, the April of 1994, there was big big trouble in Rwanda, the radio said many many thousands were dead, and Edna wrote to tell me Ngara was full of refugees. All the time the old warehouse at Nile Perch Plastics was full of things from the airport that were waiting for trucks to take them to where the refugees were staying in big camps. I was glad that Dieudonné was safe here in Tanzania instead of in his own country, but Joseph kept telling me I had a lucky escape from Dieudonné because he was a Rwandan and Rwandans were people who killed each other. I refused Joseph all the way through Evelina's pregnancy, and even after Moses was born early in July. I continued to refuse him, and I still refused him after our office Christmas party when he came to my house very full of beer and he begged me on his knees and cried into my lap spoiling the lovely red satin dress that the lady in Liberty Street made for me.

 Then in January of 1995 my phone rang at Nile Perch Plastics and it was Dieudonné. Eh, I was too too happy to hear his voice! He said he was phoning everybody in Tanzania who helped him when he was looking for his family, he was phoning to say his thankyous and his goodbyes. Rwanda was a better place now and many Rwandans were going home, even Rwandans who left there many years ago. Dieudonné was going home to see if his family was going home.

 That phone call made me wake up from the dream that I was still dreaming, and the very next day I decided to stop refusing Joseph.

 <u>Lovemore</u> – God will answer your prayers. Don't make yourself blind to His answer when it comes.

Lovemore closes Mama's journal with a breath that comes out of her from somewhere very deep inside. She remembers Uncle Dieudonné, and she remembers that very first jigsaw puzzle. Maybe it is a long-forgotten memory of the kindness in Uncle Dieudonné's eyes behind his reading glasses that is drawing her to Ibrahim.

Anyway, if Mama had not been blind to God's answer to her prayers, if she had decided to love Uncle Dieudonné instead of Uncle Joseph, that Congolese trader woman who came to Mwanza for dried *dagaa* would never have been able to make Mama sick and take her away from Lovemore.

Chapter 10

LOVEMORE AND Grace have just arrived home from school when Bibi's mobile phone begins to ring. Suddenly, everything in the lounge becomes like somebody has pressed pause on the remote. Having looked up from their schoolbooks around the coffee table, Faith and the boys are completely still, their pencils in their hands, their eyes on Bibi. Titi has stopped dead in the doorway from the kitchen, the scratched old tea tray in her hands, her eyes wide. Even the steam from the cups of tea on the tray does not seem to move. Just inside the front door, Grace and Lovemore keep absolutely still, their schoolbags shrugged only halfway off their backs. Without seeming to breathe, Bibi stares at her mobile phone as it rings on the table next to the cakes that are cooling on their racks.

Then it is like somebody presses play on the remote, but only for Bibi, who snatches up the phone and puts it to her ear. 'Hello, Angel Tungaraza speaking.'

Completely still, Lovemore watches as Bibi's eyes widen, her mouth falls open, and she says 'yes' twice into the phone. When Bibi says a loud '*eh!*' and pats the side of her hair with the hand that is not holding her phone, Lovemore knows. So does everybody else, and they gather around quickly and quietly, anxious to hear the news that Bibi has waited so long to hear. Bibi says '*asante sana*' many times through her widening smile, and continues to pat her hair until the end of the call.

'I'm through round one!' she says to everybody, her eyes shining brightly. 'I'm a regional winner! They loved my cakes, every one of them!'

As Lovemore takes her turn hugging Bibi, she is aware that the person Bibi would love most to be hugging right now is Babu. But Babu is still away in Chad, and Lovemore still feels bad that it is because of her that he is away at all. She gives Bibi an extra tight squeeze, and it feels good when Bibi squeezes back.

'A lot of congratulations, Bibi.'

'Thank you, Lovemore.'

'You're going to win, Auntie, all of it.'

'One step at a time, Titi. Next I have to make a wedding cake to get me through round two.'

But Bibi does not have to make the wedding cake very soon. Round two is going to be judged by a small team who will move around the country from one region to the next, starting in the west and moving all the way across to the east, so Dar es Salaam will be quite near the end of their list, just before the islands of Zanzibar, Pemba and Mafia. There is still plenty of time for Bibi to work on her design and to start becoming nervous for the next round.

Bibi tries sending an SMS text message to Babu with her good news, but it does not want to send. While she is trying again, Lovemore changes out of her uniform before using Mama's old phone to send a message to tell Rose, and when she has finished, Bibi is still trying to get her message through to Babu. She has obviously got it through to her friends, though, because messages for her keep coming to her phone from people who are not Babu.

Towards the end of their tea there is a hoot at the other side of the gate, and Titi goes to see who it is.

'*Eh!*' says Grace, jumping up suddenly from the table and rushing towards the girls' room. 'It must be Mama-Fenella.'

Grace will be sleeping over at Fenella's house so that they can practise their three emotions for drama club. They have invented their own two-girl piece over the past few break-times, and now they are going to show Fenella's mother. Fenella's mother works part time as a secretary at TBC, the Tanzanian Broadcasting Corporation, so she will be able to see if the girls' piece moves well from happiness to anger to sadness, and she will be able to help them to get it perfect before they show it to the others at drama club tomorrow afternoon.

Lovemore has seen their piece. In it, Grace tells Fenella that she has met a boy and that they are falling in love. Fenella is excited for her, and tells her how happy she is with her own boyfriend. As they exchange more details, they discover that they are both talking about the same boy. They become angry with each other, and then they turn their anger on the boy and decide to go and confront him together. On the way, they recognise that they have both lost their boyfriend, and they begin to cry. The story was Fenella's idea, not Grace's, and so far Grace has not seen that it could have been the story of her mama and Lovemore's mama.

Titi is just shutting the gate behind Grace when the telephone-fax rings. Lovemore is closest, so she picks it up and says hello.

'Lovemore?'

'Auntie Agrippina!'

'Ah, Lovemore! How I love to hear your voice!'

'Me too, Auntie Agrippina!'

'But Lovemore, I cannot dally. Is your bibi there? I want to give her my well-dones.'

Lovemore hands the phone over, watching and listening as Bibi pats the side of her hair and says 'thank you' over and over, her smile very wide. It feels good that Bibi and Auntie Agrippina are becoming friends, that Lovemore's old life in Mwanza and her new life in Dar es Salaam are finding more connections.

Later on, Bibi has a customer for her cakes, which means that Faith and the boys cannot do their homework around the coffee table and must move to their rooms instead. Faith is even worse than Grace at concentrating, so Lovemore moves from doing her homework on her own bed and goes to sit on the top bunk in Titi's room. After several minutes of battling to understand surface areas of cones without Grace's help, she hears a quiet knock on Titi's door leading into the part of the house where the other bedrooms are. It is probably the boys, wanting to pass through to the kitchen and then to the back yard, unable to go through the lounge because of Bibi's customer. It is wrong to treat somebody's bedroom like a passageway, and Lovemore is not going to let them. Besides, the whole point of working in Titi's room is that nobody will disturb her there.

She stops herself from saying an automatic, polite *'karibu'*.

The door opens, and it is Faith. Her glasses are not on her nose, but that is no surprise. Faith only wears them when somebody tells her to.

'Lovemore, do you want to do modelling in the passage?'

'Not now.' She lifts her maths book so that Faith can see it. 'I'm busy.'
'Please?'
'Uh-uh.'

Instead of going away, Faith leans on the door handle and draws circles on the floor with one foot. *'Please?'*

'Shouldn't you be doing homework?'

'I've finished.'

'But I'm still busy.'

Instead of going away, Faith looks at her hands as she shapes the thumb and first finger of each of them into a circle and puts the two circles together like two links of a chain. Then she does the same with her thumbs and middle fingers. Lovemore lets her get only as far as her ring fingers.

'Faith, I'm not going to say yes.'

'Please!'

'No.'

Tearing her chain-link fingers apart angrily, Faith sticks out her lower lip and stomps heavily away, slamming the door behind her.

Lovemore wonders for a moment what life was like for Faith before she and Daniel came here to live with their grandparents, before Faith had Grace as a sister. Faith must have been eight or nine when she came here with her younger brother Daniel, and Grace was ten when Faith came. Grace had already been living here for two years with her younger brother Benedict and her youngest brother Moses, and both girls must have been relieved to get a sister. But how was it for Faith before, when it was just her and Daniel with their mama in Arusha? Lovemore knows from Uncle Joseph that Faith's mama – his sister Vinas – was a teacher, second in power to the *mwalimu mkuu*. Maybe a teacher is exactly the kind of mama that Faith needs, somebody to stand over her while she works. If Bibi and Babu lived in a nice big house on Msasani Peninsula, they would be paying for Faith to have her own private tutor.

Lovemore goes back to trying to understand surface areas of cones in her maths book, but it is even more difficult now, because Faith has broken her concentration. She has the full set of schoolbooks because Grace has taken no work with her to Fenella's. Should she move on to revising first aid for victims of snake and arthropod bites and stings? Or maybe she should focus on drainage patterns and water bodies. Underneath all the schoolbooks is Mama's journal. Just five minutes with that could surely do no harm. She opens it to where she finished reading last time, but before she begins to read, she recognises that she needs the toilet. Putting a pencil in the journal to mark her place, she closes it, climbs down the wooden ladder and heads to the girls' room.

Faith is sitting on her bed, painting her fingernails bright red with one of the nail polishes that Grace has wasted her pocket money on. All of Grace's nail polishes are bright red, but Grace is convinced that there is a big difference between each one and the next. Faith barely acknowledges Lovemore as she passes through the room to use the washroom, and when Lovemore has finished, Faith is no longer there. The phone that used to be Mama's is on Lovemore's bed, so she decides to send a quick SMS text message to Rose to thank her for telling Auntie Agrippina about Bibi's win, and to tell her that Faith is annoying her particularly this afternoon. When no answer comes within a minute a two, Lovemore thinks that Rose is probably at one of her extra lessons.

Back on Titi's top bunk, she tries to open Mama's journal at the page where she left the pencil, but the pages are stuck together. She looks to see what is there, but the light is bad. Holding it towards the light of the window and peeling the pages a little way apart where they are stuck, she sees something bright red. She sniffs it. It is definitely nail polish. Looking up and through the window, she sees Faith talking to Titi at the washing lines in the back yard. Within seconds, Lovemore is down the wooden ladder and right through the kitchen, holding Mama's journal tightly in her right hand.

'Faith! You read this!' She has never heard her own voice so loud. Her heart is pounding in her chest like the set of drums at Highway of Holiness.

'No, I didn't.' Faith cannot look at her.

'Yes, you did! The pages are stuck with your nail polish!'

Faith hides her hands behind her back.

'*Shh*, Lovemore! Auntie is busy with a customer, you—'

'Nobody is supposed to read my private things, Titi! *Nobody!*'

'Yes.' Titi's voice is a loud whisper. She gives up on the washing and puts her hands on her hips. 'But there are many in this house. Why are you accusing Faith?'

'You did it, Faith, you know you did!' Lovemore is aware that her voice is so much louder than Titi's.

'Uh-uh!'

'Show Titi! Show her your nails!'

Faith's hands remain behind her back. 'I don't have to!'

'She looked inside here and she smudged.' Lovemore shows Titi where the pages are stuck. 'Look at her nails, Titi, this is the colour!'

'*Mambo!*' Mr Kapufi's hands and his icing-dusted head are above the back wall. Is there trouble here?'

'It's okay, Mr Kapufi!' the voice is Benedict's, from the small window of the washroom that Titi shares with the boys. 'There is no trouble here. Thank you for your concern.'

'Okay. As long as there is a boy here to control the girls.' Mr Kapufi's head and hands disappear behind the wall.

Lovemore is on the point of calling to him and asking him to pelt Faith with stones from his catapult when Bibi appears in the kitchen doorway.

'Girls!' Her voice is the same loud whisper that Titi has been using. 'What is going on here? I have a *customer!*'

Faith begins to cry. 'Lovemore is accusing me, Mama!'

Taking a very deep breath, Lovemore forces herself to talk quietly. 'Faith looked in my private notebook, Bibi. I was in the washroom and she went into Titi's room and looked. Now my pages are stuck with her nail polish. Look.'

Bibi looks. 'Faith, show me your nails.'

Faith shows her. The polish on the first and middle finger of her right hand is smudged right off her nails and onto the sides of her fingers.

'Lovemore is right to accuse you, Faith.'

Crying more loudly now, Faith points her smudged first finger at Lovemore. 'She's doing sex with a boy, Mama, she wrote it in her diary!'

'No, I don't believe you, that is not the Lovemore that I know. Titi, is it the Lovemore that you know?'

'No, Auntie.'

'What is inside anybody's diary is their business, Faith, not yours. A diary is private, it is confidential. Nobody ever has the right to look. And Titi's room is private, too, you have no business going in there. As soon as my customer has gone, you are going to sit at the computer and write to your baba about why you are ashamed of yourself today.'

Bibi goes back inside to her customer, leaving Faith outside to apologise to Lovemore and Titi. When the apology finally comes, Lovemore accepts it, but only because Benedict tells her to from the window of the washroom. But she cannot forgive Faith, and she cannot forget what Faith has done. Nobody was supposed to touch Mama's things, and now some pages are stuck and some of Mama's words are lost.

When Bibi's customer goes, Faith hates it that she needs Lovemore's help with the computer, and Lovemore hates it that she has to help Faith. When Faith has mastered enough to be able to email Babu about her shame, Lovemore goes back to Titi's room. She is surprised to find Titi in there, because usually at this time Titi is in the kitchen.

Titi pats the top bunk and Lovemore sees that she has made it up nicely with sheets and a thin blanket. 'You can sleep here sometimes if you like. Me, I don't mind.'

Lovemore is so grateful to Titi that she offers to help her in the kitchen, and it is only after supper that she is able to climb up again on to Titi's top bunk. Desperate to read more of Mama's words before any more of them get lost, she opens the journal to the first page that is not stuck to another with nail polish.

One morning early in July of 1996, Evelina came to Nile Perch Plastics in a taxi with her three children. She brought a big cake for everybody because Moses was having his birthday turning 2. Everybody was too too happy to have cake, but me I was wondering why did she really come? She never brought a cake when their daughter Grace had her birthday turning 1 or 2 or 3 or 4 or 5 or 6 or 7, she never brought a cake when their son Benedict had his birthday turning 1 or 2 or 3 or 4 or 5, she never brought a cake when their son Moses had his birthday turning 1, but now she brought a cake for his birthday turning 2.

Everybody passed through my office to go into Joseph's office to fetch a piece of cake and to take it away again on a small paper plate. I was busy eating a small piece at my desk and asking God not to let it affect my buttocks when Evelina came out of Joseph's office with Moses on her hip and Benedict's hand in hers. She stood right in front of my desk and she stared hard at me. She never said a word, not even one. I felt too too uncomfortable, so I stood up and I reached across my desk to take the birthday boy's hand. I wished him a very happy birthday and I said his mama must know we were very grateful for the cake we were having for his birthday. Evelina stared at me still, and she said nothing. I don't know if I ever before felt uncomfortable like that. My face had a smile but my armpits were wet even though the air-conditioning was on. Then I asked Benedict did he want to come with me to the kitchen to see did we have any sodas? That was when Evelina talked, but she didn't talk to me, she said to Benedict and Moses that their baba was going to take them to the kitchen to look for sodas, and then Joseph came from his office with Grace, and he said to Evelina there would be sodas surer than sure if he knew they were all going to come, but now they just had to hope.

Eh! I thought then Evelina knew about me and Joseph, I thought she wanted me to know that she knew. Then I thought maybe Joseph didn't tell her about the Congolese trader woman, maybe she thought it was me who gave to Joseph what he gave to her. That was too too unfair, I was never with any other man like that, Joseph was the only one. I wanted to tell her right then and there that it wasn't me, but I could see that Joseph's smile wasn't quite right, I could see that his armpits were very wet inside his shirt. I didn't want to break his marriage, I didn't love him any more, I didn't want him. Anyway, I knew I mustn't say anything at Nile Perch Plastics because then everybody was going to know what we did and what we had, and both the Mr Desais were going to find out, and then maybe me and Joseph were going to lose our jobs.

My armpits stayed wet and I kept having to go to the washroom to wash them again and to put more powder there, even after Joseph took early lunch to drive his family back home again. Then at lunchtime I heard Margaret and Doris talking about Evelina, she did the same thing to both of them. When they went into the kitchen to look for sodas, Evelina stood with Moses on her hip and her arm around Grace's shoulders, and she stared hard at Doris without saying a single word, she made Doris feel too too uncomfortable. Then when Evelina was waiting for Joseph to come and drive them home, she stood in reception with her arms around Benedict and Grace with Moses on Grace's hip, and she stared hard at Margaret, she never said a word. Eh, I knew then that Evelina didn't know! She thought it was a woman at Nile Perch Plastics, but she didn't know which one.

For the next few months I kept remembering that day, and every time I remembered it I became a little bit more angry. Evelina came to show every woman at Nile Perch Plastics that she was Joseph Tungaraza's wife and that those were the 3 children that she gave to him, a girl and two boys. She came to tell us all that she was more important than any one of us. She came to show us all — even Joseph — that she could come with the children to her husband's office whenever she wanted, she didn't have to phone me first and ask me to schedule a meeting in his diary. But if she was really so important and so clever, then she would know which woman it was, she wouldn't need to come fishing at the office to see who was going to bite at her hook.

One Saturday that December Joseph took his and Evelina's children to Saa Nane Island to see the animals, and that made me angry because he knew that Lovemore wanted to go ever since the jigsaw puzzle with the picture of hippos. He said he was going to take her and he was going to hold her hand so that she didn't need to fear any of the birds or animals. But he never did take her, then he told me he was going to take his other children on Saturday like he didn't even remember that he was supposed to take Lovemore. Before I even knew surer than sure why I was asking, I asked him was he going to go for the whole day? He said no, they were only going to go for the afternoon because Evelina wasn't well and he didn't want to leave her at home by herself for too long, he was going to take them after their lunch and bring them back in time for their supper.

Agrippina didn't think my idea was good, and at first I also didn't think it was good. But when that Saturday morning arrived I didn't care if my idea was good or bad, I was going to do it. I wasn't yet sure if I was going to do all of it, but I knew I was going to do the first part because I already told Lovemore the night before, and I wasn't going to disappoint Lovemore the way Joseph was always disappointing her. So me and Lovemore we dressed in our best clothes because we were going to look at how was your life when you worked hard and you did your very best and you had lots of abundance.

When you had lots of abundance you didn't go in a daladala or on a bodaboda, you went in your own car or in a taxi, so we went in a taxi to Hotel Tilapia in Capri Point, the best hotel in the best part of Mwanza, and we had our lunch there. We sat at a table on the big balcony veranda where we could see a nice view of the lake, and we shared a starter, a main course and a dessert. When you had lots of abundance you didn't have to share, but one of us was a child with a small stomach and one of us was an adult with buttocks that didn't need much food to make them seem too big, so it was better to share. We talked about many things, the lessons Lovemore was learning at school, the things I was doing at work, the lessons we were both learning from Agrippina's cassettes. All the way through we used our American accents, the waiter didn't even try to speak to us in Swahili.

All the way through I kept looking at the lake. We were sharing our ice cream with chocolate sauce when I saw the boat with Joseph and his other children heading off for their visit to Saa Nane Island. I knocked my soda over on to the cloth then and the waiter came with extra napkins to mop it up, so Lovemore's eyes and ears were on the table instead of on the boat and the sound of its engine as it crossed from the left of our view all the way across to the right and then out of sight. When I saw that Joseph had his arm around Grace in the boat I knew that I was going to do the second part of my idea.

Outside the gate of Tilapia Hotel a few taxi drivers wanted to help us. I told Lovemore to choose which car she thought was the best, because when you had lots of abundance you always chose the best. Joseph's house was easy enough to find, I knew where it was because the younger Mr Desai used to live there, and back when it was just me and the younger Mr Desai at the big old warehouse, he once had to stop at his house to run inside to fetch some papers when we were on our way together to a meeting at one of the factories that processed fish.

The taxi driver waited for us on the road while we walked up to the big blue gates with their pattern of fish and stood there holding hands. Lovemore asked were we not going to go inside to say hello to Uncle Joseph? I told her that when you were big and important and the manager of a factory, people didn't come and knock on your door without an appointment or an invitation. I told her we were just going to stand there together and look at how was your house when you had lots of abundance, she must look carefully and imagine such a house for herself the way one of Agrippina's cassettes said we should imagine clearer than clear the things that we wanted to make real in our life.

We stood there quietly outside the big blue gates, holding hands and looking at Joseph's house behind the iron-paling fence. It wasn't really Joseph's house, Joseph was renting it from the younger Mr Desai, but that didn't matter, it was where Joseph lived.

We could see through the gates and through the iron-paling fence that every window of the house had a white nylon curtain across it like it was a hair saloon for ladies, and at last the edge of one of those curtains moved. After a minute a house girl came round from behind the house and asked us did we need any help? I told her no, I was just showing my daughter the kind of nice family home she could have in her life if she was more clever than her mama, and while I was saying that I saw the edge of the curtain move again and I let go of Lovemore's hand and I put my arm around her shoulder, staring hard at that curtain.

We got back into the taxi then, and the driver took us slowly along the streets of Capri Point, all the way up to the top of the rocky hill and down and around, stopping to show us the views of the lake on the other side of the point from where Hotel Tilapia was, stopping to show us the houses that used the big boulders in their walls and the houses with 2 levels and even 3. Lovemore asked were the houses in New York as big as the ones in Capri Point? And I said I was sure they were even bigger and even nicer in New York because everything was bigger and nicer in America, it was the only country in the world that had a lake that was bigger than ours. Our lake was called Victoria, but America's lake was called Superior because that's what it was.

Joseph didn't take Lovemore to Saa Nane Island that afternoon, but I gave Lovemore a lovely afternoon myself, so she didn't mind when I left her at home with Pritty and Sigsbert and her crayons so that I could go to church. I didn't want to spend more money on a daladala all the way to Highway of Holiness because I was going to go there with Agrippina the next day anyway, so I went instead to the Assemblies of God near Kirumba Stadium. Many people were praying there and it was already very loud, so I didn't care how loud I was as I walked all over that church asking God to forgive me. Eh, I felt too too bad for hurting and upsetting a woman who was sick, just so that I could show her that I knew all along, meanwhile she didn't, and that all along meant right from the start because my daughter was just as big as hers.

God didn't let me sleep well that night, and in church the next day I cried *when I asked again for forgiveness. I told Agrippina it was the worst thing I ever did, and Agrippina reminded me that she told me not to do it but I did it anyway. I thought it would make me feel good, but in the end it only made me feel cruel – and I didn't really think that God should forgive me, even though I asked. Agrippina let me borrow again the cassette that spoke about forgiveness, and I listened to it alone in my room while everybody else slept.*

A few days later Evelina needed to go back into the hospital again, so that was where her children said goodbye to her when Joseph drove them to go and live with their grandparents in Dar es Salaam.

<u>*Lovemore*</u>*: If you try to show somebody that you are better than them you will only show yourself how small is your heart.*

Tucking Mama's journal safely under the pillow of her new bed on Titi's top bunk, Lovemore settles down for the night as Titi comes back in from the washroom, ready for bed herself.

This is not what Mama intended at all, Lovemore sharing a tiny room with Uncle Joseph's house girl. But Lovemore would rather be with Titi, who has shown her so much kindness, than with Faith, who is surely steaming like a pot of *ugali* in the girls' room all by herself.

Chapter 11

When Rose calls, Lovemore cannot remember when she last heard her so excited.

'Lovemore, I have such a news!'

'What?'

'Is your bibi there?'

'She's in the kitchen. Why?'

'Call her, Lovemore. Put the phone on speaker.'

Bibi comes through from the kitchen cradling a bowl of scarlet icing in her left arm and a wooden mixing spoon in her right.

'She's here,' Lovemore tells Rose, after pressing the speaker button.

'Ah, Bibi-Lovemore, are you well?'

'Very well, thank you, Rose. And you?' Bibi continues to beat, making sure that there are no lumps.

'Very fine, thank you. But Bibi-Lovemore I have such a news!'

'Yes?'

'It is about the Kilimanjaro Snow, the competition.'

The spoon in Bibi's hand stops beating. 'What about it, Rose.'

'My sister Lulu, at the hair saloon, one of her clients, a new lady, not one that Lulu has done her hair before, she was talking on the phone, and Lulu could hear the person she was talking to. You know that can happen sometimes, Bibi-Lovemore?'

'That is true,' says Bibi, putting the bowl of icing down on the dining table. 'I have heard both sides of somebody's conversation before.'

'Yes. So Lulu was listening and the client was saying to her friend that she is a winner in round one.'

'Eh!'

'But Bibi-Lovemore, it seems that she was cheating in the competition!'

'Cheating?' Bibi pulls out a chair, turns it to face the telephone-fax and sits. Lovemore does the same. 'How?'

'They were laughing on the phone about round one, they said it was easy to send photos. The lady sent photos of cakes she never made.'

'*Eh!* I knew that was going to happen! Did I not say, Lovemore?'

'You said, Bibi.'

'But it's not the end of my news! Next weekend is round two here in Mwanza, she is planning to cheat for that, too. She said the judges will never suspect!'

'*Eh!* Is she going to show them somebody else's cake?'

'But how, Bibi? Nobody is going to give somebody else their cake to show!'

'Lulu couldn't hear any more than that. We're sorry, Bibi-Lovemore.'

'Ah, no, there's no reason for sorry. Please give my thankyous to your sister, Rose.

'We're not through this side, Bibi-Lovemore. Mama has a plan. I don't know what, but she says we must leave everything in her hands.'

When Bibi goes back into the kitchen with her bowl of scarlet icing, Lovemore picks up the receiver and takes the phone off speaker. 'Thank you, Rose, that was a very important news.'

'Are we off speaker now?'

'Yes.' Lovemore glances over her shoulder. Only Moses and Daniel are in the room, but they are concentrating hard on the TV. Still, she lowers her voice. 'Did your mama find out anything about my Auntie Edna?'

Lovemore's mama never mentioned to Rose's mama her sister Edna, the one she wrote to back in Ngara after Uncle Dieudonné made her feel differently about her family, but Auntie Agrippina was going to see what she could find out. Lulu already asked Philbert and Sigsbert, but those two were from family too far distant to know anything about Mama having a sister.

'Ah, yes. She spoke to the lady at reception at Nile Perch Plastics. That lady said sometimes a letter would come for your mama from Ngara. One came earlier this year, so that lady put it inside another envelope together with a letter saying that unfortunately the person it was for was late, and she sent it back to the address on the back of the envelope.'

'She didn't keep that address?'

'No, I'm so sorry. Mama says the best we can hope is that Edna writes to Nile Perch Plastics to ask for more information. The reception lady knows now to call Mama if she does.'

'Please tell her thank you, Rose.'

'Ah, my sister, I'm so sorry.'

Lovemore can hear in Rose's voice that she understands how disappointed Lovemore is. At first she thought she should contact Edna just to tell her that her sister Glory was late. But now she would like to meet her mama's sister, her mama's family, just to see something of her mama in somebody else. She is ready for that now. Here she sees her baba all the time in Babu – and more and more in Benedict, now that she has seen photos of Uncle Joseph at Benedict's age. One day she will finish reading Mama's journal and there will be nothing of Mama left. How lovely it would be to see her in somebody else's face! But there is nothing more she can do now, except hope and pray that Edna contacts Nile Perch Plastics again.

The following week Rose sends a message to Lovemore to say that the cheating lady won again in round two, so it seems that whatever plan Auntie Agrippina had, it simply failed to work. That is what Bibi and Lovemore think all the way up until after supper the following evening, when Auntie Agrippina phones for Bibi. Bibi puts the phone on speaker so that Lovemore can hear, too.

'My dear! I have such a big news! Nansi Ngeleja, that is our cheat here in Mwanza. She was on the radio, she is in the newspaper, she is loving to be famous. I sent somebody to her house with an invitation for her to come and be honoured and celebrated with a free manicure and pedicure at Three Times A Lady. She made her appointment for this afternoon, and she came with a friend. A friend was never part of the offer, but that was okay.'

'Ah, Agrippina, your business has suffered a loss!'

'No, we'll make it up quickly, Angel, no problem. We gave them sparkling wine from Walk on Water, that's another of my businesses, and I made sure that Nansi and her friend felt honoured and celebrated because the sparkling wine was being served to them by the owner of the saloon, that's me, and their manicures were being performed by Lulu, that's the manager, and their pedicures by the assistant manager. All the time I was checking that they were comfortable and I was filling up their glasses. I also fed them chocolates that were a gift to me from a parent at my school. I don't eat chocolates myself, Angel. My buttocks!'

'Ooh, my hips!' says Bibi, clutching Lovemore's arm as she laughs.

'Uh-uh-uh. Anyway, those ladies were very soon no better than the men who fall off their chairs late at night at Walk on Water. It was like they forgot that Lulu and I were even there. They were knocking their glasses together and laughing, and shushing each other because they wanted to talk secrets, but they were still very loud. Then Nansi said this is how her life is going to be like when she wins all the money in the final, everybody is going to be her servant. Her friend made a toast to judges being stupid, then Nansi made a toast to judges not knowing the difference between cake and cardboard, and they laughed so much they—'

'Wait, Agrippina. Cardboard?'

'My dear! It seems that Nansi doesn't know baking at all, though she can decorate. Her cake was no cake at all, it was a cardboard box!'

'*Eh!*' Bibi's grip on Lovemore's arm is now so tight that Lovemore pulls on Bibi's fingers until she lets go. Bibi does not seem to notice.

'Auntie Agrippina, did you see the cake?'

'It was in the newspaper! I'm going to post it to you. Obviously it's more than one box, it's for a wedding. It looks very good to my eye, Angel, but your eye will see it better. If you don't know that it isn't cake, then maybe it's a cake that's good enough to win for the Mwanza region.'

'Ah, Agrippina, that is too bad.'

'Are you going to tell somebody, Auntie Agrippina?'

'I was thinking not to tell, Lovemore. What are the competition people going to do? Everybody took their cakes home after the judging on Saturday, there is no evidence now. They will think I'm making up stories because I'm jealous. And if I tell them I invited Nansi to my saloon and fed her alcohol to try to get the truth, that could be the end of my business.'

'Ooh, Agrippina, you cannot put your business in danger! No! I'm also thinking that telling could put the whole competition in danger. If there is any possibility that the judges can be embarrassed, maybe the Kilimanjaro Snow people will simply decide to cancel.'

'Uh-uh-uh.'

In the end, Auntie Agrippina, Bibi and Lovemore all agree that the best thing to do is to let Nansi Ngeleja come to Dar es Salaam for the finals and to let her embarrass herself at national level. At least Bibi knows that the finalist from the Mwanza region is not going to win the prize, which makes Bibi's own chances of winning that little bit higher.

The following Saturday morning, Benedict lets Concilia in through the big green gate and brings her inside, where Lovemore is at the dining table with Bibi and the girls, finishing a cup of tea. Benedict tells the boys to turn off the TV because there is a visitor, and Concilia hugs each of them in turn, as she does every time.

'Moses, you are ever taller! Daniel, you are smart and clean today! No football? Grace you are lovely as ever! Lovemore, your hair is shining beautifully! Faith, where are those glasses you look so good in? You must wear them! Angel, you are a joy as ever!'

'*Karibu*, Concilia! Sit! Let me make some nice fresh tea for us.'

'Ah, thank you, Angel, but no, I have actually come in search of an accomplice, or even some accomplices. I'm going to do something naughty.'

'*Eh?* Something naughty? That is not the Concilia that I know!'

'Ah, then maybe you don't know me, Angel!' Concilia's smile is very wide. 'No. This week I finished everything for my PhD, every last thing!'

'Serious? Now you are Dr Concilia?'

'Uh-uh, not yet. But soon, I hope.' Still smiling, she holds up both hands, crossing two fingers on each. 'This week I printed, I copied, I bound, and yesterday afternoon I sent.' Her hands turn again and again, the palms brushing against each other with each turn. 'Even now as we sit here, the copies are on their way to Cape Town in the hands of DHL. My supervisor at the university is going to receive them on Tuesday or Wednesday.'

Standing up from the table, Bibi claps her hands together. 'Ooh, we must have tea and cake to celebrate!'

'No, Angel, but thank you.' Concilia's hand indicates for Angel to sit down. 'No, when I woke up this morning I decided that I want to have ice cream.'

'Ice cream?'

'Mm, at Sno-Cream. Maybe a tall sundae with ice cream and cream and nuts and strawberry sauce.' Her hand hovers about half a metre above the tabletop. '*Tall!* Or maybe something with bananas sliced down their length, with ice cream and cream and covered in chocolate.' Now her hands are wide apart on the tabletop. '*Big!* But I cannot eat ice cream alone.'

Lovemore remembers eating ice cream and chocolate sauce with her mama on the balcony at Tilapia hotel.

'Ooh, no! Eating ice cream alone is a very sad thing, almost as bad as eating cake alone. Cake is for celebrations. You cannot celebrate alone.'

'No. So I'm looking for somebody to come to Sno-Cream with me.'

Daniel and Moses get up from their couch at the TV and move towards the dining table.

Bibi does not seem to have noticed. 'Could Mama-Concilia not go with you?'

'*Eh!* Things are better between us, Angel, thanks to you. But not so good that we can go and eat ice cream together. Not yet.'

'*Pole sana.*'

'It's okay. We'll get there. Slowly by slowly.'

Bibi pats her sides. 'Ice cream is something I enjoy, it's only that I'm watching my hips.'

'I know you're watching your hips, Angel, and I should be watching mine, too. But my hips will still be there for me to watch tomorrow, and today I'm going to be naughty and eat ice cream. I was thinking that maybe one or two of the younger members of your family would like to come with me?'

'Me!' say Grace and Faith, both at the same time, and just half a second later Moses and Daniel are jumping up and down and shouting the same word over and over.

'*Shh!*' Bibi covers her ears.

Benedict looks worried. 'But we're going to the library, Mama. I want to change my books.'

'Oh,' says Grace. 'Me too.'

Concilia looks surprised. 'You, Grace? You are liking books?'

'Stories about teenagers. Magdalena and Mary at school, they had one, then I found a whole shelf at the library.'

'That is good.'

'Yes, we're going to the library,' says Bibi, 'but not Lovemore and Faith. Those two prefer to concentrate on their schoolbooks.'

That is not completely true. Lovemore prefers to concentrate on her schoolbooks, so she does not want to distract herself with other books from the library – and anyway, she has Mama's journal to read. But because Lovemore has chosen not to distract herself from her schoolbooks, Babu and Bibi have decided that Faith should not distract herself either. Lovemore knows that Faith would rather be exploring the shelf in the library that Grace has found.

Bibi continues. 'Titi is off today. She has a friend, a house girl down the road. I was going to take Faith and Lovemore with us anyway, they cannot stay here alone.'

'Ah,' says Concilia, 'is that because they cannot be here without an adult, or because they cannot be alone together?'

Feeling uncomfortable, Lovemore looks down at her hands. 'We are fine together,' she lies. She has still not forgiven Faith for touching Mama's journal.

'Lovemore can't have sugar,' says Faith. 'She can't go for ice cream.'

'Of course she can,' says Concilia. 'Lovemore, not everything there is sugar.'

'I can have sugar,' says Moses.

'Me too,' says Daniel. 'Can we go, Mama?'

Bibi shakes her head.

'*Please?*' both of them speak at once, whining like children smaller than they are.

Daniel turns to Concilia. 'At least take me,' he pleads. 'Only me!'

'*Eh!*' Moses punches Daniel's arm, and Daniel punches him back.

'*Boys!*' Bibi almost never shouts.

'Stop it!' says Benedict. 'That is not how we behave in this house!

And we have a visitor!'

Lovemore can hear that he is trying to speak to them in the same way that Babu would, and for the briefest moment she wonders if Uncle Joseph used to boss his younger sister Vinas around when he was small and Babu was away in Germany for his studies.

Moses aims a sulky kick at Daniel's ankle, and Daniel prepares to kick back.

'Boys! Stop it!' Benedict's Babu voice – his Uncle Joseph voice – is firm. 'That is not how we behave!'

Concilia stands up, leaning heavily on her stick. 'Ah, Angel, I don't want to bring war to your home, especially after your cake helped to bring peace to mine. Maybe I should go and eat ice cream by myself.'

'Uh-uh, no, you need people to celebrate with. Please take the girls.'

Faith wants to sit in the front of Concilia's smart blue car, but Concilia says that of course Lovemore should have the front seat because she is older. That is not how it works in the Tungarazas' old red microbus. They are supposed to take turns to sit up front, but somebody always tries to argue about whose turn it is. It is no better when Babu is home, because Bibi always prefers to sit in the back where it is easier to get in and out, so the front seat is still there to argue over.

Concilia's car is very smart inside, not like the old red microbus. Its gear is different; not a ball on a long stick that has to be negotiated into different places while the driver presses down on a pedal. Instead it is short, squatting inside a shiny kind of box that says P, R, N and D. Concilia squeezes both sides of the oblong on top of it, moving it from next to P to next to R without needing to press her foot on a pedal. The microbus has three pedals, but this car has only two.

'Now,' says Concilia, reversing carefully as Benedict holds the gate open. 'Let us see how much traffic there is.'

Lovemore watches Concilia's feet on the two pedals. Both of them seem to work okay. *Mwalimu Mkuu* Makubi at her old school in Mwanza used to have a driver, and Lovemore always thought it was because he was a polio – but maybe it was just because he did not know driving. Anyway, there must be different kinds of polio, because *Mwalimu Mkuu* Makubi and Concilia are not the same kind of polio as Ibrahim. Concilia squeezes the gear handle again and slips it next to D. At the end of the Tungarazas' dirt road, they turn onto the tarmac.

'It's not too bad,' says Lovemore.

'Ah, not yet! Just wait! I'm sure you didn't see traffic in Mwanza. Not like here.'

'Uh-uh.'

Concilia presses a button on the shiny black dashboard that is not faded to a greyish brown and full of cracks like the one in the microbus, and cool air begins to fill the car.

'And in Arusha?' Concilia looks at Faith in her mirror. 'Was there traffic there?'

'Sometimes,' says Faith, 'but not like here.'

'Dar is the worst,' says Concilia. 'Ah, here we go.'

They slow to a crawl as the long line of vehicles ahead of them tries to join a very busy road, and as they inch closer, the noise of the traffic gets louder. Back in Mwanza, people used to wait their turn, but here in Dar everybody just goes. Concilia does that too, edging her car right across the traffic that is coming from the side and making it let her through so that she can push her way in to the line of traffic going the other way on the other side. And there they sit, moving forward just a few centimetres at a time. Any vehicle that can escape from the line of traffic does so, moving on to the dusty verge and rattling along beside the line, sending up a cloud of dust that settles onto pedestrians and whatever any roadside stalls are trying to sell. Motorbikes speed past them on the verge, and *bajajis* too, their one front wheel and two back wheels bouncing about on the uneven surface, any passengers sitting in the back holding on tight with fear in their eyes.

Near the traffic lights men come to their windows with sodas and nuts and sunglasses and phone-chargers and any other possible thing to sell. Lovemore hears the loud click of Faith's glasses case closing, and when she turns to look, Faith is adjusting her glasses on her nose.

'Can you see Dickson?'

Faith cranes her neck in all directions. 'Uh-uh. Maybe he's on the other side.'

Lovemore tries to see, but too many sellers are weaving between too many vehicles. She hears the click of Faith's glasses case and knows without turning that her glasses are off again.

A tiny boy leading a too-thin blind woman, old and bent over like a broken pencil, approaches Concilia's window, rattling some coins in a scratched and battered tin can. Concilia presses a button and her window goes down, letting in a blast of hot air. Reaching somewhere under the dashboard, she pulls out a few shillings and feeds them into the child's can before pressing a button to close the window again. The windows are not like that in the old red microbus: those windows need cranking open, and if you are the driver you first have to take the handle from out of the cubbyhole and position it correctly before you can crank it round and open the window. You have to remember to put the handle away again afterwards, otherwise it is going to fall off and get lost.

Sighing deeply, Concilia drums her fingers on the steering wheel. 'Girls, it's going to take a long time to get to that ice cream. Shall we play a game to pass the time?'

'Okay,' says Lovemore. A game is going to be much better than just looking at the traffic.

'*Sawa*,' says Faith.

'Right! I know a good one, it's called same or different. What it is, we try to find all the ways the three of us are the same.'

'We're not the same,' says Faith.

'Ah, you'll be surprised. I'll start. I'm a Tanzanian.'

'Me too,' says Lovemore.

'And me.'

'Good! We are all the same. Your turn, Faith.'

'What must I say?'

'Say something about yourself and we'll see if we're same or different.'

'Oh. Okay. Um … I'm a girl.'

'Me too,' says Lovemore.

'Ah, not me! I am a woman! You two are the same, but I'm different. Your turn, Lovemore.'

Lovemore thinks carefully, then she says, 'I'm a female.'

'Me too,' says Faith.

'Yes! And me! We are all the same. My turn again. I need glasses.'

'Me too!'

'Aah!' says Lovemore. 'Now you two are the same and I'm different.'
'Your turn, Faith.'
'Okay. I have two sisters and three brothers.'
Lovemore finds herself smiling. 'Me too!'
'Ah, no, now you two are the same and I'm different! Lovemore?'
Lovemore giggles. 'I have buttocks!'
'Yes!' cries Concilia. 'Me too!'
'And me!' says Faith, and Lovemore can hear the smile in her sister's voice.
'My turn.' Concilia hoots at a *daladala* that is pushing its way in too close. 'I'm a hard worker.'
'Me too,' says Lovemore.
'Um,' says Faith, 'I try.'
Lovemore turns to look at her. 'No, you *are* a hard worker! You do extra all the time.'
'Only because Mama and Baba make me. And Benedict.'
'Did I say anything about *why* I work hard?' asks Concilia. 'No, I just said that I'm a hard worker.'
Smiling, Faith shrugs. 'Okay, I'm a hard worker.'
'You see?' says Lovemore. 'We are all the same.'
'Your turn, Faith.'
'Um … I love cakes.'
'Yes!' cries Lovemore, meaning more that she loves the look of Bibi's cakes than their too-sweet taste.
'We are all the same! Girls, this road is like the parking area at Julius Nyerere airport. I'm going to try going a different way, it's a longer way, but I think it might be quicker.' Concilia pushes her way in to another lane, and turns off the tarred road. 'Is it Lovemore's turn or mine?'
They continue with their game as Concilia weaves her way around traffic on tarred roads and bumps and dips on dusty roads that have no tar. Concilia has a bra, but Lovemore and Faith do not. Lovemore and Concilia have a small tape recorder, but Faith does not. Faith and Concilia like fish, but Lovemore does not. All three of them love pineapples, all three of them love mangoes.
'Girls, you know what? While we're on this side of town, do you mind if we stop at a school quickly? It's only a little bit out of our way.'

The girls say they do not mind. Lovemore certainly does not mind sitting for longer inside Concilia's comfortable, icy-cool car. And anyway, she is in no hurry to get to the ice cream that she cannot eat because it has sugar.

'Thank you, girls. I just want to check on one of the boys there, and have a word with the major.'

'The major?'

'Is it the army, Concilia?'

'Salvation Army. The school is at their compound, they're funding it. Matumaini School.'

'Matumaini?' Lovemore feels sudden tears beginning to sting in her eyes. 'That is my mama's name. Glory Matumaini Lutabana.'

'Aah, it's a lovely name.' Concilia reaches out and gives Lovemore's knee a squeeze. 'For a person and for a school.'

'Hopes,' says Faith. 'In English it's hopes.'

'Mm. Hopes.'

At the gate of the compound, Concilia speaks to a soldier and he lets them in. She drives along the straight, neat driveway and parks under a tree next to a low building. The girls are going to bake in the car, even with the windows open, so Concilia says they should go and find somewhere cool to sit while they wait for her. She is not going to be long.

They find a narrow strip of solid shade cast by a row of classrooms and sit on the ground there, their backs leaning against the classroom wall. From the building on the other side of the driveway, two young girls emerge, pink-skinned and blonde-haired. But they are not *Wazungu*.

'Albinos,' whispers Faith. 'Benedict had a friend like that in Swaziland.'

Lovemore looks at them carefully, never before having seen one this close. 'They're different,' she says. 'But still they're girls like us. We're the same.'

'Mm. And they're Tanzanian like us,' says Faith.

'And all of us go to school.'

'Yes.'

'Hello!'

A voice to their left makes them jump. It comes from a tiny person, a girl maybe Faith's age who looks like something very heavy has fallen on her from a great height, ramming the top half of her down onto her bottom half and condensing her to half her height. When that happens to somebody in the cartoons that Moses and Daniel watch on TV if there is no sport to watch, the squashed person can always shake himself out or stretch himself back to who he was before. This girl has not done that, but she does not seem to mind. Her smile is very wide.

'It's hot out here,' she says to them. 'Come inside, it's much cooler.'

Lovemore and Faith stand up, and Lovemore feels enormously tall as she follows the tiny girl into the classroom. The girl's short, stocky legs do not bend, and she shuffles along on shoes that are where her knees should be, swaying her body from side to side with each difficult step.

'Hello! *Karibuni!*'

Inside the classroom are two more children, a boy maybe Daniel's age in a wheelchair, and a girl whose legs down from her knees are not her own.

'Please, sit,' says the tiny girl who has brought them in. 'Be comfortable.'

Faith sits on what must be the teacher's chair, while Lovemore pushes her buttocks up onto the table next to it and sits swinging her legs, unsure and uncomfortable. It is not nice to see children who have to struggle.

The boy in the wheelchair wears glasses with very thick lenses that make his eyes look tiny. He smiles at them. 'You're friends of Miss Concilia, *sivyo?*'

Lovemore and Faith nod.

'We saw you coming from her car,' says the girl with plastic legs, pointing to the classroom's windows.

The tiny squashed girl without knees is perching on a very low stool. 'Miss Concilia is our friend.'

'Then we are the same,' says Lovemore, trying not to feel so different.

'We're at school, too,' says Faith. 'I'm in Standard Five.'

'Me too.' The girl taps the lower part of her legs, releasing a hard, hollow sound. 'I just got my new legs last week. *Eh*, I'm so happy! The old ones gave me too much pain.'

'They make legs for us here,' says the tiny girl on the low stool, 'and our shoes. Here in the compound.'

'There's a workshop,' says the boy in the wheelchair. 'Do you want to see it?'

Lovemore is worried that Concilia will not be able to find them if they go far. From her seat on the table, she has a good view of Concilia's car. 'Maybe next time. But thank you.'

'What class are you in?' It is the girl with new legs who asks.

'Form One,' says Lovemore. 'It's very difficult!'

'But you are lucky,' says the tiny girl, still smiling. 'Our school is just primary, it only goes up to Standard Seven.'

'Then we have to stop.' The boy pats the wheels of his chair. 'An ordinary secondary is too difficult for us to move around in.'

Lovemore feels dreadful. How could she have said that secondary was in any way difficult for her?

Faith comes to her rescue. 'How do you know Miss Concilia?'

'She comes to our school if somebody is upset,' says the girl with new legs. 'She helps us with our worries.'

'Nobody gives her a shilling,' says the boy in the wheelchair, 'not even Major.'

'She is our friend.' The tiny girl stands up from her low stool, adjusts her body a little and then sits down again. 'Does she help you with your worries?'

'Mm, but mostly our mama.'

Bibi is not Lovemore's mama. 'Our grandmother. Our parents are late.'

'Aah, sorry!' The girl with the new legs reaches out and takes Lovemore's hand.

'*Pole sana!*' says the tiny girl, standing up and doing her best to hug Faith in her chair, even though it looks like it is causing her pain.

'That is too sad.' The boy's eyes blink quickly behind his very thick glasses.

The tiny girl sits back down on her low stool, wincing.

The girl with the new legs does not let go of Lovemore's hand. 'So you are sisters?'

'Yes,' says Faith. 'We are sisters.'

Through the window, Lovemore sees Concilia heading towards her car. 'There's Concilia!' She slides down from the table, and the girl lets go of her hand. 'Do you want to say hello?'

'We can wave to her,' the boy is moving his wheelchair, 'but we mustn't bother her. Major says her time is precious even while it's free.'

Lovemore and Faith thank them for the talk and for their time in the shady classroom, and go to join Concilia at the car, passing on their way an angry-looking boy with no arm coming out of the left sleeve of his T-shirt, and another in a wheelchair who is blinking very rapidly as if to prevent tears from falling. Before getting into the car, all three of them wave to the three children gathered around the doorway to the classroom.

Concilia turns the car around, careful to avoid the two pink-skinned girls with yellow hair in the shade of another tree.

'Why are those girls here,' asks Faith. 'They have nothing wrong.'

'No. It's for their safety.' Concilia gives a kind of salute to the soldier at the gate of the compound. 'Men who are sick with AIDS can want to attack them because they think that doing sex with an albino will cure them of their sickness.'

'*Eh!*' say Lovemore and Faith. Needing some comfort against the idea of that happening, Lovemore reaches a hand back to Faith, who takes it and gives it a quick squeeze.

'And they are not safe from witches. Witches want to kill them to use their body parts for medicine.'

'*Eh!*'

'No. There is nothing wrong with *them*, there is something wrong in our society. As a society we need to open our eyes and look clearly at what is happening around us, look clearly at ourselves. But here albino children are safe. They are safe in this compound.'

After a few minutes, Lovemore hears the click of Faith's glasses case, and knows without needing to turn around that Faith is settling her glasses on her nose so that she can look clearly.

Sno-Cream is full, but when two young men see that Concilia is leaning on a stick, they give up their table and stand to finish their ice creams.

Lovemore looks at the menu. 'What can I have that doesn't have sugar?'

'Um … Lovemore …?' Faith frowns at her from behind her glasses.

'Yes?'

'Um … You can have sugar if you want.' She begins to squirm on her seat.

'No, I can't, there were ants in my cup.'

'No.' Faith is beginning to cry. 'No, I swapped them round. It was *my* cup.'

Concilia places a hand on Faith's shoulder. 'What are you saying, Faith?' Her voice is gentle.

'I'm so sorry, Lovemore!' Faith reaches for a paper serviette and tries to dab at her eyes, but her hand finds her glasses.

'We take them off when we cry,' says Concilia, holding Faith's glasses for her while she wipes her eyes.

'I didn't want it to be me with sugar. I didn't want it to be me who was different. I wanted it to be you. I'm so sorry.'

'It's okay.'

'No, it's not okay! You can have sugar, Lovemore! It's me who can't.'

'It's okay, Faith, I don't mind. Really. I was glad when it was me. I'm not used to sugar, we never had it much at home because buttocks are in my family. I don't want to have sugar.'

'You don't want to have sugar?' Faith's glasses are back on, and she is looking at Lovemore like she has said something ridiculous.

'No. I'm glad I don't have to have it. Really, you did me a favour.'

'Oh.' Faith looks and sounds the tiniest bit disappointed.

'But *you* should stop sugar, Faith.' Concilia is fanning her face with the menu. 'Starting now.'

'I like not having sugar,' says Lovemore. 'Let us not have it together.'

'You see?' Reaching across the table, Concilia puts one hand on Lovemore's shoulder and the other on Faith's. 'Now you two are the same and I'm different. You two can order something like fruit with cream, but I'm going to order something enormous covered in every possible thing. I'm going to have as much sugar as I can get, because I have a very, very big achievement to celebrate. Just for today, my hips can watch themselves.'

When Babu gets back from Chad, they have a special meal of boiled *matoke* and fried chicken, with a salad of tomatoes and onions and another of grated cabbage and carrot, all from Benedict's garden. Everybody's attention is on Babu rather than the salads, but Lovemore notices Benedict beaming with pride as his eyes sweep over them. When she catches his eye, she mouths the word *asante* to him, and his smile stretches even further when he mouths the word *karibu* back to her.

Babu is full of stories about desperate families who have fled from the war in the Darfur region of Sudan to desperate refugee camps in Chad, and about his work to help keep the children's schooling going in those camps. Lovemore listens carefully to Babu's words, genuinely interested in what he is saying, but after a while she finds herself slipping back into her old habit of listening only to the sound of Uncle Joseph in his voice. Very soon her mind takes her back home to Mwanza, and to another meal of *matoke* and fried chicken.

The smell of the pieces of fried chicken, spicy with *pilipili*, escapes from under the cover that is keeping them warm, making Lovemore's stomach feel like it is eating itself. She can hear the scrape of metal against melamine as Mama's cousin Sigsbert and their house girl Pritty eat their supper in the kitchen, and she wants to be in there, eating with them, but Mama does not want Lovemore to eat before Uncle Joseph arrives.

All they are doing is sitting around waiting. The jigsaw puzzle that Lovemore is busy with is tucked away on its polystyrene foam board under the couch, Mama's extra work is packed away in her bedroom, and her computer sits idle on its small table in the corner, its screen dark. They are not even listening to one of Auntie Agrippina's cassettes or to news on the radio, because they are waiting to hear the sound of Uncle Joseph's car.

Mama does not like to sit around doing nothing. It makes her anxious. She goes to the window, lifts a corner of the curtain and stares out into the night. Then she sits back down, only to get up a few minutes later to pace up and down their small lounge. Lovemore sits waiting at the dining table, her stomach aching for the fried chicken and the *matoke* in the two covered pots.

'Can we not eat, Mama?'

But Mama seems not to hear her, going to the window again and staring out. After a long time she lets go of the corner of the curtain and turns to Lovemore. 'He's not going to come.'

Lovemore is disappointed, because she does love spending time with Uncle Joseph, but she is also relieved, because now she and Mama can eat. She is so hungry!

But Mama does not let Lovemore eat. She calls Pritty and tells her to put all the pieces of chicken into one plastic bag, and all the *matoke* into another. Then she tells Lovemore to change her good clothes and shoes for something casual and easy to walk in, and Mama does the same. Sigsbert has to stop getting himself ready for his night out, and he has to walk with Lovemore and Mama to keep them safe.

Mama carries the bag of *matoke*, Uncle Joseph's favourite, and Lovemore carries the bag of fried chicken pieces. Mama has tied the handles of the bag into a tight knot, so Lovemore cannot steal a piece as they walk, no matter how desperately she wants to. There is plenty of light because the moon is over half full, and Mama is walking fast, marching like a soldier. Lovemore battles to keep up.

Sigsbert tries to chat with Mama, but Mama does not join in. When he asks her questions, her answers are short, and it is obvious that she is angry. Lovemore feels sorry for Sigsbert, because maybe he does not know that Mama's anger is for Uncle Joseph. Maybe he thinks that it is for him, even though he has done nothing wrong. Sigsbert is a young man and he is supposed to be spending his Friday night partying, not walking fast through the streets of Mwanza with an angry lady and her child. One day Sigsbert is going to marry Rose's big sister Lulu, and then he can settle down and be responsible, but now he should be partying. That is what he has told Lovemore many times.

Lovemore wonders if they are going to walk all the way to Uncle Joseph's house in Capri Point. That is so far! She is already tired, and her hunger is making it worse. Two dogs are following her, attracted by the smell of the fried chicken in her bag. Every now and then Sigsbert chases them away, but they always come back.

Sigsbert tries again with Mama. 'Glory, where are we going?'

Mama must have walked away some of her anger, because now she answers with more than one word. 'We're going to see Milton.'

'Milton? Lulu's uncle? At his workplace?'

'Yes.'

Milton shares a room with Godbless in Auntie Agrippina and Uncle Steven's house. Godbless sleeps in that room at night, and Milton sleeps in it during the day, because at night Milton does his night watch job in Liberty Street. They are not far from Liberty Street now. Lovemore does not understand why they are going there. Is it because Uncle Joseph knows Milton? Milton's best friend is Bismarck, the night watch at Nile Perch Plastics.

Liberty Street has every kind of shop in it selling everything you could ever want to buy. Milton's job is at a shop that sells anything that is made of plastic or melamine as well as pots and pans. In the day, a lady sits on the shop's wide veranda making clothes on her sewing machine. She made the nice dress that Lovemore was wearing for supper with Uncle Joseph tonight, and she is the person Mama goes to if ever she needs something new and smart. As they approach, Milton stands up from a chair on the veranda and reaches for his stick. Really, if anybody wants to steal anything from that shop tonight, all they need is a bigger stick.

'Milton!'

'Ah, Glory! And is that Philbert with you?'

Anybody who does not know Mama's cousins Sigsbert and Philbert well can easily confuse them, especially in the dark. But Lulu knows the difference, and Lovemore thinks that is probably all that matters to them.

'I am Sigsbert, Milton.'

'Ah! Sigsbert!' Milton shakes Sigsbert's hand, and also Mama's. 'Lovemore, is it not late for you at his time?' He pats the top of Lovemore's head. 'What are you all doing in the streets at this time?'

Something shifts in a dark shadow on the veranda, and Milton turns briefly to look.

'We brought some food for your extras.' Mama hands over the bag of *matoke*.

Lovemore does not want to hand over her bag because she feels hungry enough to eat every piece of the fried chicken that is inside it, but she gives it to Milton anyway. She knows about his extras; she has heard Auntie Agrippina saying that Milton gets more money from his extras than from his night watch salary.

'Thank you Glory! Thank you, Lovemore! They will be too happy. There are many tonight. The ones on the veranda, *eh!*' Lovemore can make out a pair of feet sticking out from the dark shadow on the veranda's floor. 'They have been sniffing. They will not wake tonight. But there are others on the roof.'

Milton's hand points up casually, and Lovemore looks up, straight into the eyes of a young child who is peering at her over the roof's gutter. The child looks like a girl, but Lovemore cannot be sure. What she does know for sure is that all of the children sleeping on the shop's veranda and on its roof have no home other than the streets of Mwanza, and that each of them has paid Milton some money for a safe place to sleep. Tonight, Milton will take care of them. Lovemore has heard him tell Mama that maybe they steal the money that they pay him, or maybe they beg it, or maybe they do a small piece of work for it, like washing a car. Milton does not care where their money comes from. It is his extra. His best friend Bismarck never gets any extra because no children want to sleep at Nile Perch Plastics, far out of town near the airport.

Milton tells the child who is looking down at Lovemore to wake the others, and slowly more heads appear above the gutter. Two children reach down to take the two bags that Milton stretches up to give them. Several voices say *asante*, then there is the sound of the bags being torn open, and a fight breaks out.

Leaving Milton to sort out the fight, Mama, Sigsbert and Lovemore walk home again, more slowly now because Mama's anger is gone. Lovemore tries not to think about feeling hungry, because she has a house to sleep in with her own bedroom and a comfortable bed all to herself. Sigsbert leaves them at their gate, turning straight back to make his way to Kirumba where Philbert will join him later after closing up Mama's business Friends in Deed.

The next morning, Uncle Joseph comes early to apologise.

'I am so sorry! Benedict was sick. *Eh!* I just couldn't get away.'

'Is there no telephone in your nice big house in Capri Point?'

'Glory, I am sorry, it just wasn't possible to phone.'

'Lovemore, tell Joseph what he missed for supper last night.'

'*Matoke* and spicy fried chicken,' Lovemore tells him.

'Ah, that is my favourite! I'm sure it was delicious.'

'Lovemore, tell him who ate his supper.'

'Street children ate it,' Lovemore tells him.

'Children without a father,' Mama adds. 'Or maybe their father lives in a nice big house in Capri point but he doesn't care about them.'

'They ate *our* supper, too,' Lovemore tells him. 'We didn't keep any for us.'

'Ah, Lovemore. What did you eat?'

'Just a slice of bread.' When they got home last night, there was nothing else in the kitchen that did not need cooking.

'Ah, *pole sana*. I'm sorry.'

'Life is hard for fatherless children, Joseph.'

Lovemore understands now what Mama was saying to Uncle Joseph, but back then she did not understand because Mama had not yet told her that Uncle Joseph was her father. All she knew then was that Mama's boss and friend Uncle Joseph had disappointed Mama – disappointed both of them – by not coming for their lovely supper, and that Mama was still going to be angry with him until after she prayed at Highway of Holiness.

Now, over this plate of *matoke* and fried chicken, Babu seems to have finished telling everybody about his work in Chad to help the refugee children from the Darfur region in Sudan, and Lovemore is sad to have missed what he said. She wants to ask what gift of wisdom he has brought for them from there, but maybe he already told them while Lovemore's mind was back home in Mwanza. She thinks of a way to ask that will not make her look silly.

'Babu, is there a *lot* of wisdom in Chad?'

'*Eh!* Your gift of wisdom! Thank you for reminding me, Lovemore. Truly, there is a lot of wisdom in Chad. It was hard for me to select just one piece to bring home for you, so I brought two.'

'That is very generous, Pius.'

'Thank you, Angel.' Babu helps himself to another piece of fried chicken. 'The one is very easy to understand. It is this. If you always walk down the same path, you will always go where you have already been.'

Grace lets her forkful of *matoke* rest on her plate. 'Ah, that one is too easy!'

'Too easy? But are you sure you know what is means? Faith?'

Faith struggles to finish chewing before swallowing. 'Um … say again?'

'It means we must try new things,' Lovemore tells her, 'otherwise we're not going to get anywhere.'

'Not going to get anywhere *new*,' Babu corrects her. 'Daniel? Moses? Are you listening?' The two boys nod their heads yes, though really they have been concentrating only on their fried chicken. 'There is more to discover in life than just football, see?'

'Yes, Baba.'

'Okay, here is the other one. This one is not too easy, I think. This one can take a very long time to understand. It is this. A tyrant is only a slave turned inside out.'

There is silence for some time after that, except for the sound of knives and forks on plates, and teeth on bones. Lovemore feels the same way she used to feel when she was still a bit too young to understand Auntie Agrippina's cassettes. Every time she thinks that she is about to grasp the meaning, it slips away from her again.

'Mm,' says Babu, nodding his head slowly. 'A tyrant is only a slave turned inside out. That is what they say in Chad.'

When Pius at last gave in and took Benedict to visit Ibrahim and his daddy, it gladdened Angel's heart. Before, when he had been working at the university, he had often met up with various professors for long discussions and debates, and Angel had never minded that he was out because he had always come back with his brain well exercised. But since he had begun travelling away for work, that habit had gone from his life. She had said to him several times that he should start spending time with his old colleagues again, but he had always said that he was too busy or too tired – and while he was certainly both of those things, Angel suspected it was really because he felt that he was away from home too much already, and that when he was home he should be at home.

With the cakes on the dining table still a little too warm for icing, and their icing already mixed, Angel navigated her way past Grace, Faith and Lovemore practising modelling in the passage, and shut the bedroom door behind her. There was something that she badly needed to do, something that she should have done a very long time ago – years ago in some instances. She had not realised quite how bad it was until Irene had come to help her to prepare for the photo that the Kilimanjaro Snow people wanted from her ahead of the second round of the competition.

Fatima had given her a very good price on some beautiful cloth tied and dyed in purple, pink and turquoise, as well as a smaller piece in the same turquoise with white, and a tailor near the market had fashioned the bigger piece into a full-length dress – comfortably loose while still suggesting a waist – and also hemmed the smaller piece to use as a head wrap. Irene was an expert at wrapping a head, and Angel had fully intended to be in her dress already before Irene had arrived. But her customer – one of the new ones who had come after Angel had been listed as a round-one winner in Kilimanjaro Snow's full-page announcement in the *Citizen* – had had a particularly long story to tell about what he wanted his cake to say, and it would have been unprofessional of Angel to rush him. So Irene had been with Angel in her bedroom when she was putting on her dress.

'Are those the underwears you are wearing, Angel?'

'Mm, they're my best.'

'Seriously? *Eh*, let me see what else you have.'

In Irene's nicely manicured fingers, every one of Angel's panties in the drawer had been embarrassing – old, stretched, not quite intact – her once-white brassiere grey, the black over-stretched.

'Seriously, Angel?'

Angel had blamed time, money, her business, the children and anything else she could think of, but her voice had wavered and she had failed to convince even herself.

'But no woman should have to put anything or anybody ahead of a decent pantie for herself, Angel. No woman should have to sacrifice for others to the extent of having no brassiere that would be proud to hold her money. I'm telling you, Angel!'

'You are right, Irene.' Angel had put on her new dress as quickly as she could. 'I'm going to start putting some money aside today.'

'But you have all that prize money from the competi—'

'Uh-uh, I haven't won it yet! I've only just got through round one!'

'Ah, Angel, you are going to win! Sit for me here. Glasses off. No, all of us have said. Besides, you *have* to win. Esther has prayed for it so hard that her faith will be badly tested if you don't.'

Irene had wrapped Angel's head expertly – if a little tightly – with a striking, wide and high shape that had somehow managed to make Angel's face look thin. Okay, not *thin* – but certainly less round. The photographer had focused on her head and shoulders only, and the neckline of her dress was not the kind that might allow a strap to show, so there had really been no reason at all for her to feel anything other than confident as she had sat in his studio – first with a screen of blue sky behind her, then with plain white – but a hint of shame had still lingered.

Now she stood in front of the open drawer, trying to sort what absolutely had to go from what could be made to last. In any case she would have to buy at least one new set before there was any real hope of any prize money, because how could she now stand comfortably and confidently in front of the judges, aware that her smart appearance was concealing such shamefully inferior underwears?

Underneath her brassieres in the drawer, her fingers found something hard. *Eh!* It was the small photo of Joseph that she had hidden away. She looked at it now as the girls in the passage paused in their modelling to laugh about something, and she recognised that she was no longer angry with her son. Disappointed – yes, still disappointed – but not angry. No. Somehow she had found it in herself to forgive him. The anniversary of when robbers had shot him dead in his house was next week, and perhaps now her grief that day was going to be a bit less complicated than she had feared. She wiped the glass of the small frame with the edge of her *kanga* and placed it on top of the chest of drawers, next to the matching frame that held a photo of Vinas.

The girls were still laughing, all three of them together. Whatever it was that Concilia had said to Faith when they had gone for ice cream had produced a big and lasting effect. Concilia had said that an intervention like they did for Stella would not have been an appropriate way to help Faith with her behaviour. No. Concilia had wanted to try something else instead. She had sent Angel an SMS text to ask if the Saturday morning would work – and that had been perfect, because Titi had been due a day off anyway. Angel had not known that there was going to be ice cream, or even that the end of Concilia's studies was going to need to be celebrated, so those were surprises that had helped Angel to pretend to be surprised that Faith and Lovemore were going to spend time with Concilia.

That day, Faith had come home and confessed to Angel that she had swapped her cup of urine for Lovemore's to make Lovemore the one who had to stop having sugar. She had apologised with very few tears, and afterwards she had made herself sit down at the table and write a letter about why she was ashamed of herself to give to her grandfather when he came home. Since that day, Faith had avoided sugar without whining too much, she had been more considerate of the others in the house, she had been friendlier towards Lovemore, and always – *always!* – her glasses had been on her nose. It was as if she had gone out for ice cream as one girl and come back as somebody else. Angel hoped very much that this new Faith was here to stay.

A soft knocking began at the door, and Titi was there with Pius's ironed shirts, and also with Angel's mobile phone, the small light flashing to show that an SMS text message was waiting to be read. It was from Agrippina, probably in reply to the message that Angel had sent her earlier today to thank her once again for her effort – and expense – with Nansi Ngeleja, the cake cheat in Mwanza. Angel had said in that message how blessed she continued to feel that somebody far away, somebody she had never even met, had gone so far out of her way to help her. She pressed the button on her phone now to read Agrippina's reply.

My dear, are we not neighbours in the village that is raising Lovemore?

Ah, Agrippina!

As Titi finished hanging Pius's shirts in the wardrobe and left the room, Angel hesitated briefly before slipping a hand into her brassiere – trying not to think about the state of the brassiere itself – to retrieve a tissue so that she could dab a tear from her eye. It was the kind of wisdom that Pius would like, but Angel would wait a while before sharing it with him. In Chad he had seen so many children scattered from their villages back in Darfur, destroyed villages that were no longer there to go back to. If it took a village to raise a child, how were the children in those refugee camps going to be raised? No. It would be wrong to show Pius Agrippina's message now, while the desperately sad things that he had seen in Chad were still reflecting in his eyes.

But Pius was a much happier man when he returned from visiting Ibrahim and Ibrahim's daddy with Benedict. He was full of excitement and very keen to talk. Lovemore happened to be practising her fast typing at the computer in front of Pius's big map of Africa on the wall, so Pius told her all about Ibrahim's daddy's pre-independence stamps, pointing to places on the map as he talked of the British and the Germans and the French and the Portuguese and the Italians and the Belgians, and about places that had once had names like Portuguese East Africa and Rhodesia and Upper Volta and Basutoland and Tanganyika.

Angel came to Lovemore's rescue. 'Pius, did you remember to get batteries for the small tape recorder?'

'*Eh!*' Pius slapped a hand to his forehead. 'I'll go now!'

But there was no rest for Lovemore, because almost immediately Benedict was beside her, chattering non-stop about all the kinds of birds that were under protection from crows in Ibrahim's back yard. Lovemore obviously did not want to hear about birds – she was not a girl who liked animals – and she was beginning to look at her brother like he might be a fish market at the end of a very hot day, when he told her that some of the tiny birds were just the tiniest bit bigger than butterflies, which somehow got her to smile. She showed him how to find pictures of the birds on the computer, and as soon as Pius was back, she slipped away from Benedict and headed for the girls' room.

Really, thought Angel as she pulled the batteries from their packaging, if Pius and Benedict were ever to find an interest in common, they would talk from morning to night. She slid the fresh batteries into Lovemore's mama's tape recorder, relieved that she could now tell it all the reasons she had to be grateful today.

Friday the 6th of June 1997 is the day I am never going to forget for as long as my life continues. The road was still a mess after the end of the long rains, and when I walked along it to go and meet the Nile Perch Plastics daladala I had to hop and jump across all the holes and ditches like in the hop-scotch game that Lovemore plays with her friends at school. I remember that as I was hopping and jumping part of me was being careful not to break a heel on my shoes, meanwhile another part of me was thinking about Joseph and about what we spoke about the week before.

Evelina was in the hospital again, this time she was already there for more than 3 weeks, and maybe this was the time she wasn't going to come home. Joseph said that when she was late he was going to drive her to her family in Morogoro for burial, and then he was going to continue the short distance to Dar es Salaam to see his own family. When he came back again he wanted me and Lovemore to go and live with him at his house in Capri Point. His church would let him marry me then because he wasn't going to be a divorced person, he was going to be widowed. He wanted us to be a family.

Those were the words I wanted to hear from his mouth for so many years! But they should have come from his mouth a long time ago, long ago when they still mattered to me. When they did come out, they were nothing to me, they meant as much to me as the sound of the fishing boats coming in means to the kind of Mhindi like old Mr Chowdary who eats only vegetables and rice.

From the day Joseph told me about him and the trader woman from Congo, even before I went for my own test and I got my own result, from that day I never let him touch me. That day I stopped loving him. For almost a year I tried very hard to make myself hate him, but in the end I couldn't hate him because he was half of our daughter and I couldn't make myself hate any amount of her. Another year went past with me not loving him and not trying to hate him, and now he wanted me and Lovemore to be his family in his house in Capri Point. I thought it was maybe a good idea so that Lovemore could learn to know him as her father, but I also thought maybe it wasn't a good idea because I didn't love him, I didn't even like him any more.

Just like the 2 Friday mornings before that Friday morning, I woke up feeling a bit different, a bit strange. It was still new to me to go to Group on Thursday evenings, and the Thursday evening before that Friday morning was only my third time. I was still too shy and too ashamed to speak, and I was still surprised by how much the other ladies spoke. When the daladala arrived at Nile Perch Plastics that Friday morning I wasn't surprised that Joseph's car wasn't already there. I had keys because after the second time we all had to wait outside for him to come late, I insisted to him that I must have keys. I let everybody in and we all began our workday. Before, when Joseph came late he wasn't more than 20 or 30 minutes late. That Friday morning, I phoned him at his house after 1 hour. He didn't answer, so I thought he was on his way.

After 2 hours I became angry. Since he came back from taking his and Evelina's children and the house girl to live with his parents in Dar es Salaam at Christmas, Joseph was becoming the kind of man who drinks alcohol each and every day. I told him his body was filtering beer like the swimming bladder of a Nile perch in England, but he told me he was still jogging and playing football, he was still fit and strong. I told him it was good that the younger Mr Desai wasn't there to see how did he look when he came to work some days. It was also very good that the younger Mr Desai wasn't there to see how was he managing the old warehouse.

After 3 hours I started to worry about him. What if he was sick? What if he crashed his car and now he was in the hospital? Just before lunch time one of the Nile Perch Plastics trucks went to the railway station to collect a delivery of plastic pellets from Dar es Salaam, and I went with the driver. The walk from the railway station wasn't far, but the hill up into Capri Point was steep. I remembered going that same way with Lovemore the day Joseph took his and Evelina's children to Saa Nane Island to see the animals, soon before he took them to stay with their grandparents in Dar es Salaam. Walking up that hill and thinking back to that day with Lovemore, I didn't feel good about myself. But what I did in the past is not something that I can change.

After the tennis courts on the right I took the road to the left, and there was Joseph's house with the big blue gates with the pattern of fish. Behind the gates I could see his car, so he wasn't in the hospital after he crashed it. I went through the gates and I knocked at the front door calling his name. He didn't answer, and I thought maybe he was lying sick or full of beer in his bed, and maybe his bedroom was at the back of the house. I didn't know the house, I didn't know which way should I go to get round to the back. I chose the way near where he parked his car because maybe the back door was near there and maybe he always used to park there to make it easy for his house girl to carry market things from the car into the kitchen. I found the back door a little bit open, and I knocked on it and called his name into the house. He didn't call for me to come in, but I pushed the door open and I stepped inside anyway.

Eh, what I saw inside that kitchen will stay in my mind for as long as my life continues! Joseph was lying on the floor with his eyes open but his eyes didn't move. I didn't move. It was only flies that moved, hopping all over the big stain on the floor near Joseph's head. For maybe ten minutes I didn't move. I'm not sure I could have moved if I tried. It was like my shoes were stuck to the floor, and my legs didn't feel like they belonged. I looked at Joseph. He was lying on his side, on his right, and on the side of his head near his left eye was a round black mark. Agrippina's TV was always on, anybody who visited her house couldn't help but see some things even if they didn't want to look, so I knew enough about how a shot person looks to know that somebody shot Joseph dead.

People talk sometimes about pilots being automatic, they make their plane fly without even thinking about it. That's how I was then, automatic like a pilot. Everything I did was something I did without thinking what was I doing and why was I doing it. I stepped round Joseph and I went into the rest of the house, the house where me and Lovemore were supposed to live. I found his and Evelina's bedroom, the bedroom where it was supposed to be me and him, and I found the lowest drawer where he kept his socks. When I found the right ones at the back of the drawer, I took all of them. My handbag was too small, so I looked for Evelina's biggest one and I put my small handbag and all of the socks in there. Then I went back into the kitchen, I stepped round Joseph and I went out of the house and out of the gate and down the hill, and just before the railway station I found a taxi coming from Tilapia Hotel that took me to the police station.

The police didn't have to ask me was I coming to them with empty hands? I walked in with 100 dollars clearer than clear in my hand, so 2 of them pushed each other to get to me first. I told them what I saw at my boss's house in Capri Point, and I took them to see. On the way I told them answers to their questions. Mr Tungaraza always left work a bit early to go and visit his wife in Bugando Hospital, and he did that yesterday too. His house girl was with his children in Dar es Salaam, so he had the habit to go for his supper at Tilapia Hotel because it was near. Maybe he came home after his supper and men were already in his house to rob his things, then when he came in they got a fright and they shot him, then because they shot him they got a fright again and they ran away.

When they looked, those police agreed with everything that I told them, they said Mr Tungaraza came home before the robbers managed to take too much. I didn't know the house, I didn't know what was there, I couldn't say what was missing. And I didn't know the phone number for Mr Tungaraza's parents, but I knew his father was a professor at the University of Dar es Salaam.

In the taxi on the way back to Nile Perch Plastics, I stopped being automatic like a pilot. My body began to shake and tears came to my eyes, then I began to struggle to breathe. The taxi driver helped me into the office, and I sat down in reception with Margaret shouting for Doris to bring me tea and everybody coming from the factory and the offices to find out what was it that happened? I felt maybe I was going to vomit, and when I thought about the word vomit I heard it in my mind like it started with a w, the way old Mr Chowdary said it to me when I ran to him that day and he led me to the washroom at the back of his shop because I looked like I needed to vomit out everything that upset me. I couldn't breathe or speak properly, so I couldn't phone the older Mr Desai in Dar es Salaam to tell him, the clerk who came from the factory in Dar es Salaam did that for me. The older Mr Desai said we must all lock up and go home early for the weekend, he was going to send us the younger Mr Desai from Kenya by Monday.

Everybody at Nile Perch Plastics thought I was shaking and crying and wanting to vomit because I saw our boss dead. Nobody there knew that I used to love him, nobody there knew that my child was his. Nobody there noticed that my handbag was much bigger than before. Nobody but me knew the real truth about why Joseph was dead.

Lovemore does not want to read any more. When she closes Mama's journal, it feels like her whole body is shaking.

Chapter 12

As the second round of the Kilimanjaro Snow competition approaches, Bibi becomes very nervous. She will be judged on just one wedding cake, so it is important for it to be the best wedding cake that she has ever made.

'What if the judges are *Wazungu*?' she asks, interrupting as Lovemore is trying to distract herself from the words in Mama's journal by helping Benedict on the computer. '*Wazungu* think that a wedding cake is supposed to be white, completely white.' A shudder runs all the way down Bibi's body. 'How can I make a cake that is completely white and love it in such a way that I will make the judges love it too?'

Lovemore and Benedict both tell her that her cake can have as many colours as she wants, and that it is going to be the most beautiful wedding cake in the room.

'How I am going to control my nerves?' she asks Babu when he phones the family from Ivory Coast in West Africa. 'How am I going to keep my hands from shaking?'

Somehow Babu manages to find the right things to say to her, and in no time at all she is telling him about something else.

'They have supplied only four packets of Kilimanjaro Snow to each of us for this round,' she tells everybody at supper. 'Does it mean they're expecting something small and simple? Am I thinking too big?'

Everybody assures her that thinking too big simply does not exist, and anyway, if it does exist, Bibi is not capable of it.

'But why have they chosen to judge a wedding cake?' she asks Ibrahim on the phone while Lovemore is typing something for her on the computer. 'Not every faith has a wedding with a cake. Are they not discriminating against Muslims and other non-Christians? Should I not phone the organisers and ask them to choose something else?'

Whatever Ibrahim tells her, Bibi does not phone the organisers.

Ibrahim is still at her service twenty-four six, even though she is not yet ready for a website because she has not yet chosen a name for her business.

'Titi, how can I make a wedding cake for a bride who doesn't exist? A bride I don't know?'

Struggling to concentrate on her books on top of Titi's top bunk, Lovemore can hear Bibi through the door that leads into the kitchen.

'Auntie, what if you choose somebody you know?'

'But I don't know anybody who is getting married.'

'Is Esther not engaged to be married, Auntie?'

'*Eh!* Esther? Esther is engaged, Titi, but is she ever going to be married? Ooh, uh-uh. That Kenneth? Each and every time that Esther tries to push him, he places his feet in a bucket of ice, he threatens to disengage. Ooh, no, Titi, if I make a cake for Esther's wedding, that Kenneth will run! He'll be gone. No. And I don't know anybody else who is getting married.'

'Maybe you can pretend, Auntie. You can pretend that somebody you know is getting married, and that you are making the cake for her.'

'You know, Titi, that is a good idea.'

'What about Concilia, Auntie?'

'Concilia? Ah. No. Not Concilia.'

'Why not, Auntie? One day she will marry.'

'Ah, no. Not Concilia.'

'She can find a man who doesn't mind her leg, Auntie.'

'It's not that, Titi. No. Concilia is simply not … she's not interested in … *eh*, Concilia is not interested in *colours!* Yes, colours. Always with her it is just browns and black.'

'That is true, Auntie.'

'But, Titi, what about you?'

'Auntie?'

'Let me pretend that it is *your* wedding!'

'Ah, no, Auntie, please.'

'But why not? You are the one who has given me this very excellent idea!'

'No, Auntie.' Titi's voice is suddenly firm. 'It was only last year that me and Henry—'

'*Ooh!* Titi! Titi, I'm so sorry! *Eh! Eh! Eh!* I have only been thinking about myself!'

Lovemore climbs down the small wooden ladder and goes through to the kitchen, ready for a distraction from her schoolbooks, desperate for a distraction from trying to un-read Mama's journal.

'Is everything okay?'

'Everything is okay,' Titi tells her.

'I've been selfish,' Bibi tells her. 'Titi had the idea that I should pretend to be making the wedding cake for somebody I know, and—'

'Ah, that is a very good idea, Titi!'

Titi smiles. '*Asante*, Lovemore.'

'Bibi, can it … Can it be me?'

'What?'

'Can you pretend that I'm grown up and I'm getting married?'

'*Eh!*'

Bibi and Titi look at each other and then at Lovemore before looking back at each other.

'Auntie, it is good practice for when she is grown.'

And so it is Lovemore's wedding cake that Bibi makes. There is a lot of discussing and a great deal of planning, and all of it helps Lovemore to lock outside of her mind what she read in Mama's journal. It also helps her to discover what she really likes. Mama would have planned a *Wazungu*-style wedding cake for her, all of it completely white, Lovemore knows that surer than sure. But Bibi helps her to see that colours are so much more beautiful than white. Lovemore is surprised to find that she does not want her dress to be white. She wants it to be a soft, pale blue with pale green ribbons woven through it, and she wants the flowers in her bouquet to be pink, pale purple and white. She can visualise it all so clearly, and she knows that one day it is going to happen because one of Auntie Agrippina's cassettes said that visualising something clearly is the way to make it happen one day. Over the next few days, Bibi does a huge amount of mixing and baking, and at last the big day arrives.

The judging is to take place in the hall of a private secondary school in the Tabata area of Dar es Salaam, on Saturday afternoon. It is not the hall of the International School on Msasani Peninsula, but Lovemore does not mind very much. Concilia comes for Bibi and Lovemore very early in the morning so that there is plenty of time to get through the traffic while the air-conditioning in Concilia's car keeps the five separate cakes cool, and by nine they are at the school's gates. Once they are inside with all the things that they have brought with them, Concilia leaves them so that she can get on with her day. She will be back to support Bibi through the judging later on.

Tables draped in white cloth line three sides of the hall in a U shape, and a teacher from the school is there to tell them which table is theirs. It is strictly alphabetical, so they have no choice. When Bibi begins piecing the cake together, she becomes a different Bibi from the one who was nervous and worried and insecure before. She is suddenly Angel Tungaraza, professional cake-maker, and Lovemore sees at once that she herself is not there to support Bibi or to calm her nerves: she is simply there to assist. Grace and Faith assisted yesterday afternoon by winding white ribbon tightly and neatly around the special metal stand for the cake that Bibi had a man at the Mwenge Market make for her, so already there is none of the ugly metal showing.

Slowly and carefully, Lovemore's wedding cake takes shape. The four smaller cakes circle the central pole of the ribboned stand, starting with the smallest of them at the top, then one slightly bigger lower down and a little way around and a little further out, and the same again until all four are perfectly in place, each tilted at a slight angle. Finally the large cake takes its place on the base of the stand, some distance from the central pole. Each of the pieces has the same design: round with the top surface the pale, soft blue of Lovemore's wedding dress, the sides packed round with long, slender leaves of different shapes and in different shades of green, the leaves extending above the blue surface, some of them bending back and away. Each cake looks like a beautiful, clear pool of water. Once each piece is in place, Bibi positions long strands of stretched sugar to look like water flowing down over the edge of each cake into the lower one and then into the next lower one, until finally the water flows down into the pool of the largest cake. On to the surface of that cake go water lilies in the same pink and white and pale purple that Lovemore will have in her bouquet, and finally Bibi positions sugar butterflies in darker, brighter colours – pinks, purples, blues, greens and white – on the ends of long wires at various points on the cake, the biggest ones flitting over the biggest cake, the smaller ones higher over the smaller ones. There are no fish under the water to turn Lovemore's stomach, there are no birds above it to scare her, and there is not the frog that Benedict tried to suggest.

Bibi is lucky that there are even butterflies, because Lovemore and Benedict were in charge of designing them and it did not go well at first.

'No, Lovemore, no butterfly has that colour pink. They never have pink, they have red.'

'But the cake isn't going to have red, it's going to have pink.'

'No, but butterflies don't have pink. Help me to look on the computer, Lovemore. I'll show you.'

There were many pink butterflies on the computer.

Benedict set about finding the name of each and every species of pink butterfly and where in the world to find it. Meanwhile, Lovemore waited on one of the couches with her geography book, keeping her mind busy by revising the two sections of the East Africa rift valley: the eastern section going from Lake Turkana in Kenya, through Lakes Eyasi and Natron and down to Lake Nyasa between Tanzania and Malawi; the western section passing through Lakes Tanganyika, Kivu, Edward and Albert. In between those two chains of lakes lay Lake Victoria.

'You see, Lovemore?' Benedict showed her his page of hand-written notes and drawings. 'There are no pink butterflies in Tanzania.'

'Ah, Benedict, it isn't a cake about Tanzania, it's a cake about my wedding. Maybe my wedding is even going to be in New York.'

'But the competition is national, for Tanzania.'

'Oh. Right. Do you think the butterflies have to look like real butterflies?'

'Mm. Butterflies are real.'

'Okay. Let's look on the computer.'

Most of Tanzania's butterflies were brown, orange, black, yellow – colours that were just not right for a cake that was going to be mostly blue and green – but there was the lovely blue kind that had flown over Mr Kapufi's wall to feed in Benedict's garden, there were the tiny white ones, and there was a nice green one.

At last Bibi put them right. 'Is this a cake for professors of butterflies at the university? No. Is Lovemore really getting married? No. It is a cake about pretending, about imagining.'

So together she and Benedict imagined the beautiful butterflies that dance across the finished cake now. Really, it is a very, very beautiful wedding cake. Standing back from the table as Bibi takes photos of it, Lovemore cannot help wishing that she really was getting married.

Bibi digs a tissue out from her bra and mops her forehead before telling Lovemore to stand guard over the cake while she goes to the washroom to change out of her T-shirt and *kanga* and into something much more smart. Lovemore has been so absorbed in watching her own wedding cake come together that she has not looked at anybody else's cake. Now, standing firmly in front of Bibi's table so that nobody has the chance to spoil her cake in a fit of jealousy before the judges get to see it, she casts her eyes around the room. At least half of the other cakes are mostly white with just a touch of another colour, and one is entirely white. How Lovemore wishes that she could be standing there in her wedding dress with her wedding bouquet so that the judges could see exactly how perfect her wedding cake is compared to all the others!

Bibi comes back from the washroom looking very smart in the same green satin dress with rhinestones around its neckline that she wore to Grace's Dialogue Night, and she takes a slow tour around the room, examining each of the other cakes closely and carefully. Very soon she is back beside Lovemore with her eyebrows almost meeting above her glasses, and Lovemore thinks that maybe Bibi has found a cake that she suspects of being in fact a cardboard box.

'Lovemore, count the cakes, please. There are supposed to be twelve.'

Leaving Bibi to guard their own cake, Lovemore walks and counts. There are twenty.

'But why are there twenty? I didn't know I was competing against nineteen, I thought I was competing against eleven.' Bibi's nerves are back, and she is talking much too fast.

'I don't know, Bibi.' Lovemore gives her some water and asks somebody to bring a chair. 'But there could be one hundred cakes here in this hall, and yours would still be the best.'

'You think so?' Bibi eases herself on to the chair, careful not to split her dress where it is tight across her buttocks.

'I know so, Bibi.'

Gradually the frantic activity around the tables comes to an end, and everybody is asked to wait outside during the judging. There are three judges, three very smart and serious-looking ladies, not one of them a *Mzungu* who is going to make the all-white cake win. There is a young man with them in a suit and tie, but he carries no clipboard as the ladies do, so he is clearly not a judge.

'That one is from somewhere outside,' Bibi whispers to Lovemore, nodding her head towards one of the judges, 'she's in the Diplomatic Spouses Group.'

The doors of the hall are closed, and everybody outside waits, not one of them breathing as deeply as they should.

A photographer and two men with a TV camera try to get into the hall, but they are stopped.

The judging takes a very long time, and more and more of the ladies waiting outside request a chair from the students who are on duty. One of the ladies is in fact a man, twenty-something, maybe even thirty. On his own with nobody to help him with his cake, he seems very quiet, though when Lovemore catches his eye he is quick to smile, the bright white of his teeth highlighting the pretty white daisies that pattern his lilac shirt.

SMS text messages come through for Bibi, but she is too focused on waiting for the result to read them, just asking Lovemore to tell her who has sent each one. Fatima. Esther. Grace. Stella. Benedict.

Concilia is suddenly beside them with Bibi's friend Irene, apologising for being late. 'Traffic,' they say, as a student brings chairs for both of them. They sit with Bibi and Lovemore, waiting quietly, Concilia holding one of Lovemore's hand as Bibi's clutches the other.

At last the doors of the hall open, and the young man in the suit introduces himself as Evarist Somebody from Something Sugar Company which is manufacturing Kilimanjaro Snow, the icing on the top. He introduces the judges, Mrs Somebody, Mrs Somebody, and Mrs Somebody Else. Nobody is interested and nobody is listening.

All that anybody wants to know is who has won. But Evarist goes on and on. Bibi and Lovemore nudge each other when they hear him say the numbers twelve and twenty, and they pay attention. Unfortunately, some of the regions of Tanzania have produced no winners of a high enough standard to continue into the final, so the decision was made to select two winners from the Dar es Salaam region because there were so many more entrants into round one from here. Evarist says that it is probably down to the number of households that are having ovens, and the few who are listening nod their heads and murmur their agreement. At last Evarist stops talking and hands over to one of the Mrs Somebodys to announce the two winners.

Everybody holds their breath. Everybody hears Mrs Somebody's speech only as blah blah very high standard blah blah extremely beautiful blah blah such fine craftsmanship blah blah very great honour, until they hear the word *winners*.

'In no particular order,' Mrs Somebody says, before looking at her clipboard, 'Mr Peter Mapashi ... and Mrs Angel Tungaraza.'

'Eh!'

There was no point at all in Angel even trying to go to sleep, because it was almost impossible for her to keep still. As bright as the lights in the lounge, the dining area and the kitchen were, the light that she was radiating herself was brighter still. She had been photographed by the *Citizen*, she had been interviewed for TV and radio, friends and strangers had congratulated her, and she had been hugged almost to not breathing by everybody in the family. *Eh!* It had been the most wonderful day!

Helping herself to iced water in the kitchen, she felt herself glowing with extra joy because the cake had been for Lovemore, her granddaughter. Her daughter Vinas had married in Arusha, where the groom's family had organised everything, so Angel had not made the cake for her daughter's wedding. That had been long before Angel had started her business, but still her cake for Vinas would have been much more professional than the one that had been there. It had been a bad sign, that wedding cake. It had not been nearly good enough for

Vinas – which was exactly how Vinas's husband had turned out to be. But Angel did not want to think about bad cakes and bad husbands tonight. No. Tonight was for rejoicing that she had got the chance to make the wedding cake that she had never made for Vinas – *and* it had won round two of the competition!

In the lounge now with her glass of water, she saw that there was an identical glass of water that she had already poured waiting for her on the coffee table. *Eh*, her thoughts were so giddy tonight!

Too restless to sit, she drank her water in front of the TV cabinet, looking at the photos there. How blessed she was that her grandchildren were giving her a second chance to be a good mother! Of course she had done her very best the first time round, but she had been young then. She could have said to Vinas, look, there have been rumours about this man and the female students he is training as teachers, are you sure that he is the man you want to love? But she had said nothing. She could have said to Joseph, look, this marriage to this girl Evelina is very rushed, why not go and settle in Mwanza, settle in your new job, then after some few months come back for Evelina and have a wedding that has been properly planned. But she had said nothing. Now she was blessed with a second chance to get things right with all these grandchildren. How empty the house would be without them!

Still unable to sit, she circled the dining table, trailing a finger around the edge of it as she did so, her mind going to how … well, not *happy* … comfortable? No, more than comfortable. How … affectionate … okay, yes … how *affectionate* the family's memorial for Joseph had been on the fifth anniversary of his death. After all that worry, it had been a truly lovely ceremony. Here is where Pius had sat to light his candle and to tell everybody one of his memories, a memory of teaching Joseph to ride a bicycle, and when the boy had mastered it, going inside to leave him to practise on his own, only to come back out later to find that Joseph had disassembled the bicycle to find out how it worked. Here was where Benedict had sat, lighting his candle and remembering for everybody the day that his baba had taken them on the boat to see the animals on Saa Nane island, and his baba had scrambled all over the rocks to catch a big agama lizard

– bright blue on its body, red on its head and shoulders – for Benedict to look at closely. This was where Lovemore had lit her candle and told everybody about how, when her Uncle Joseph – her *baba!* – had sat on the couch and slipped off his shoes, she had crawled under the couch and tickled his feet, making him chase after her and tickle her until they could both hardly breathe from laughing, and then he had sat with her on his shoulders so that she could not reach his feet again. Here Grace had remembered him taking her and her mama to get new dresses made by a lady who sewed on a veranda in a street called Liberty, and here Moses had remembered going with him to watch football at the stadium. Right here is where Angel had sat, lighting her candle with a smile as she had told them about how excited Joseph had been when he had come home from school one day with a lump of gold the size of a small guava that he had found on a pile of stones at a building site, gold that he was going to use to buy the whole world for his family. Then Pius had come home that evening and told him no, it was not real gold, it was something called fool's gold, a mineral called iron pyrite. *Eh*, Joseph had been so disappointed! But the next day he had sold it to another boy at school for a very high price!

The table fully circled, Angel went to the telephone-fax, picking up from beside it her wonderful congratulations fax from Pius. The telephone connection was good in Ivory Coast, so Angel had been able to let him know immediately by SMS text this afternoon that she had won round two – and when Concilia had got her home after all the cameras and microphones, this fax from Pius had already been waiting for her. She skim-read it again, unable to concentrate even on this with the excitement of her win still skipping dizzily through her mind, and the pride of it still swelling in her chest.

She was in the kitchen now, refilling her glass from the boiled water in the fridge, adding a few new squares of ice.

Eh, what a blessing Concilia was! Because of Concilia there were children asleep tonight with their bellies full and warm with sweet cake, children that Angel did not even know, though it was her winning cake that was in their bellies. Concilia always knew where to find the kind of people that others looked at without seeing, as well as the kind of people who needed to hide from others' eyes – the kind of people who most needed the comfort of cake. After dropping everybody at home, Concilia had taken part of the cake – the largest piece that had sat on the base and had the waterlilies on top – to a shelter for children who had no other home, and a smaller piece to a place where women whose husbands had been too violent could be safe. Angel had insisted that Concilia should also take the smallest piece – the piece from right at the top – for herself, and Concilia had said that she would take it for her mother, who was going to be very excited to have part of Angel's winning cake.

Of the final two parts of that cake, only one still remained, because the family had eaten all of the other with tea when Angel and Lovemore had got back. Okay, not quite *all* of it. Titi had ululated about Angel's win so loudly that Mr Kapufi had popped his head up above the back wall to find out what was happening, and Benedict had been feeling so happy and proud that he had very kindly given Mr Kapufi a small wedge of it for himself and Mrs Kapufi, even though he did not at all like what Mr Kapufi did to crows.

How was Angel ever going to sleep tonight? And how was she ever going to choose just five – *five!* – things to write down in her notebook? There were so many today! But surely there was no rule about *only* five? No. She would write as many as she liked. But perhaps she should watch a bit of TV first to see if that could settle her mind.

Going back into the lounge with her fresh glass of water, she saw the other one still waiting for her on the coffee table.

Eh!

Lovemore returns to concentrating hard on her schoolwork, going through things over and over again until she has memorised them perfectly. After each half hour of half-hearted help from Grace with her maths, she sits for another hour on Titi's top bunk trying to put her whole heart into understanding it by herself. She is friendly and polite and kind to everybody, but really she is only half there. Now that the excitement of the wedding-cake competition no longer stands between her and the words in Mama's journal, she feels Babu's absence particularly deeply, wanting him to be here at her side instead of far away in West Africa. Without him here, without even Uncle Joseph's voice to cling to, she feels unanchored, adrift, as if the shallow waters at Bagamoyo beach are suddenly treacherously deep.

She does not want to read any more of Mama's journal, but that is exactly what she cannot help doing.

When Joseph got shot his father came to take him for burial in Dar es Salaam, and the younger Mr Desai came back from the Samaki Accessories fish-leather business in Kenya to manage Nile Perch Plastics. I didn't meet Joseph's father, I didn't even know he was in Mwanza, it was the younger Mr Desai who helped him with everything. I stayed at home feeling sick for almost a whole week, I only went out for praying for Joseph's soul. When I went back to work at the end of the week the younger Mr Desai said he wanted to ask me for an advice, he said it was a very delicate matter. The house in Capri Point where Joseph lived with his family belonged to the younger Mr Desai, Joseph was renting it from him. But now Joseph was gone and Joseph's children were gone, they were living in Dar es Salaam with Joseph's parents, and the younger Mr Desai wanted his house back. He wanted to know did I know how was Mrs Tungaraza? He wanted to know did I think she was ever going to come out of Bugando hospital? Was there anything that she needed? It wasn't decent for a gentleman to visit a lady in the hospital when she wasn't his wife, so he wanted to know would I go and visit her? Would I find out about her family?

I already knew about Evelina's family, they were in Morogoro and they didn't want to come and see her ever since she got sick. But I didn't know how to tell the younger Mr Desai that I didn't want to visit Joseph's wife, so we went together that afternoon. I went to find her in the wards and the younger Mr Desai went to the hospital administration to ask about the other delicate matter. Bugando isn't like Sekou Toure hospital, at Bugando you have to pay, and the younger Mr Desai felt that he must pay for Evelina.

Her ward was right near the top of the building, it was hard for me to breathe from climbing all the stairs and also from being too too nervous. I didn't know what was she going to say to me when she saw me? I didn't know what was I going to say to her? I stood very still in the passageway for many minutes while many people walked past me, and then because I didn't want to make the younger Mr Desai wait for me, I knocked on the door and I stepped inside. It was a private room with just two beds and its own washroom, so the younger Mr Desai was going to be paying even more than he thought. The one bed had 5 or 6 visitors around it but the other had none. I wasn't sure which bed did I want Evelina to be in? If she wanted to say bad things to me then maybe it was better for us to be alone, but maybe if she had other visitors she wasn't going to say bad things to me.

Evelina was in the bed with no visitors, and she was asleep. Suddenly my hands felt very empty, I should have something for her, even just a nice cold soda, I should have asked the younger Mr Desai to stop at Friends in Deed on the way. I greeted the other patient and her visitors, and they smiled and said it was nice that Evelina had a visitor, her father-in-law came two days after but otherwise there wasn't anybody else in the week since her husband. Nobody had to say anything more than since her husband, because everybody heard on the radio about the robbers shooting her husband dead in his house in Capri Point, and 2 of those same visitors were there when the police came the Friday before to tell Evelina. They told me the shock wasn't good for her, she was down more and more every day.

I stood next to her bed and I watched her sleeping. I wasn't sure did I want her to wake up? I tried to imagine how would it be for me if I was lying sick in that bed in Bugando hospital without any visitor? And with my children far in Dar es Salaam and my husband late? Eh, how would that be for me? How would it be for me if I never had a job so there were no colleagues or friends from work to come and visit me? How would it be for me if I was far from where I went to school so there was no friend to come and talk to me?

Then I remembered how it was for me when my parents sent me to Mwanza for my schooling and I had no friend and my family was far in Ngara, and my eyes began to fill with tears. I closed my eyes and I let the tears run down my cheeks. Eh, I was too too surprised to find myself thinking back to that time, it was so many years ago. I opened my eyes and I took hold of Evelina's hand. It wasn't because I wanted to be holding her hand, it was because I wanted a hand to be holding mine. I closed my eyes again, and I let my tears fall.

After some minutes the hand that was holding mine squeezed it. I opened my eyes and I saw that Evelina was looking at me. Eh! There were tears in her eyes too. I let go of her hand and I looked in my handbag for my toilet paper and I tore off a length and wiped her eyes for her. She looked at me all the time, then she stopped my hand with hers and I thought maybe I did the *wrong thing, maybe she was going to try to hit me, but she pulled me closer and she took the toilet paper and she wiped my eyes for me. Eh!*

I helped her to sit up a little and to drink a few sips of water. Then I told her she mustn't worry about money because the younger Mr Desai was downstairs taking care of that, and I asked her was there anything she needed? She shook her head no. Then I asked her could I come and see her again? She nodded her head yes, so I said I was going to come again that weekend, and I squeezed her hand again as I said my goodbyes to everybody.

I cried all my way down all the stairs to the bottom, and I told the younger Mr Desai that Evelina wasn't ever going to go home to the house in Capri Point.

This time when Lovemore closes Mama's journal, she feels a little better. Mama was a kind person. She was a kind person even though she found Uncle Joseph dead in his house and acted like it was nothing, even though she never told Lovemore that she was the one who found Lovemore's baba dead.

Mama was still a kind person.

Ready for more of Mama's kindness, Lovemore opens the journal again and begins to read the next of Mama's entries.

I'm happy because the younger Mr Desai is going to stay in Mwanza now to manage Nile Perch Plastics. Somebody else is going to manage the fish-leather factory for him in Kenya, but he is still going to go and check on it every now and so often, just like he used to come and check on Nile Perch Plastics. I'm glad no new manager is going to come here. I like being the Personal Assistant to the younger Mr Desai, it is like it used to be when I was his clerk at the old warehouse, when we were still just a depot for the Tanzania Plastics factory in Dar es Salaam. I like listening to the way he talks, sometimes it reminds me of the time long ago when I used to work for old Mr Chowdary.

Those days working for Mr Chowdary used to be hard, but I didn't know then that my life was going to become harder, that I was going to throw my love away on a man who was going to throw my life away.

That is not something that Lovemore wants to read about, not now. Turning her head away quickly, she looks out of the window instead, and spends a few moments watching Benedict busying himself with a watering can in his vegetable garden. Still focusing on him and his tender care of his plants, she closes Mama's journal without even looking at it.

She really should turn her attention to her schoolwork, but right now her heart is just not in it, and her mind is too far away. Not knowing what else to do, she finds herself climbing down the small wooden ladder and going through the kitchen into the back yard, where Benedict is still busy watering.

'Are there any butterflies today?' she asks him, though she can see that there are none.

'Uh-uh. They haven't come for a while now. I think maybe they have a season.' Coming right to the edge of his garden, he puts the watering can down on the bare earth, next to a large metal bowl, which he picks up.

'Do you want to help me, Lovemore?'

'In the garden?'

'Mm. We can pick some tomatoes.'

'But I don't know how.'

'It doesn't matter. I can show you. Or you can just hold the bowl for me.'

'Let me hold the bowl.'

Lovemore steps from the hard, bare earth of the yard on to the soft soil between the tomato plants and a row of what looks like the green leaves on the ends of carrots. Some of the tomatoes are green, others are a kind of orange colour, others on their way to a deep red. Those are the ones that Benedict seeks out, pulling them gently but firmly from the plants and placing each of them into the bowl as if it is a precious treasure.

'We're doing a poem at school,' she tells him, not really knowing why. 'Me and Grace.'

'Yes?' He bends to check if a reddish one near the bottom of a plant is red enough. 'What's it about?'

'Um, there were six men, and they found themselves trapped somewhere icy cold, and they huddled round a fire to keep themselves warm.'

'*Eh*, that was not here in Tanzania!'

'Uh-uh, Miss Brown chose it. She's that *Mzungu* from England, the one from Dialogue Night.'

'Ah.' He adds another tomato to the bowl. It is fat and round and very, very red.

'Anyway, each of those men had a log of wood that he could have added to the fire to keep it burning, to keep them all warm, but not one of them would add his log because he had a problem with one of the others, and he didn't want to help that one to stay alive.'

'*Eh!*' Benedict straightens up and looks at Lovemore. 'What kind of men were those?'

'Stupid ones. Because if they didn't keep the fire going, every single one of them was going to die from the cold.'

'Mm. Is the bowl heavy?'

'No, it's okay. So we're doing the verses in small groups. My group's verse has a rich man who wouldn't add his log because he wanted to hold on to everything he had, and he was never going to do anything to help the poor man in rags sitting opposite him.'

'*Eh!*' Benedict is on his knees under a tomato plant.

'Grace is in another group, they've got the black man who wouldn't add his log because he wanted revenge on the white men.'

Benedict clicks his tongue against the back of his teeth, handing a red tomato up to Lovemore from under the plant. Lovemore takes it from him and adds it gently to the others in the bowl.

'Fenella's man wouldn't help because one of the others was from a different religion. And there are other verses, too. Anyway, in the end they all just sat there and died of cold, still holding on to their logs. The logs could have saved them all if only they'd stopped hating. So they didn't die from the cold without, they died from the cold within. That's what the poem says in the last verse. We all have to say that verse together, all the groups.'

Benedict adds a last tomato to the bowl and does a quick last scan of the plants. 'But that can't happen here, here there is no cold like that. What is it? Cold outside?'

'Cold without.'

'Cold without. No, we don't have that here.'

'Except on top of Mount Kilimanjaro.'

Lovemore thinks that the men in the poem could also have been trapped inside the big walk-in freezer at Uncle Steven's work, but she does not say that to Benedict. She steps back out of the garden and puts the bowl of tomatoes down on the hard bare earth next to the watering can. She is not yet ready to go back inside to her books. Benedict is on his knees amongst the cabbages now, pulling tiny plants out of the ground. Weeds, he tells her, plants that don't belong. Lovemore does not want to get her jeans dirty by kneeling, but she squats down on her haunches and copies what Benedict is doing.

They work in silence for a while before Benedict asks in a very quiet voice, barely more than a whisper, if Lovemore thinks that Mr Kapufi is cold within.

Lovemore considers his question carefully. 'Well, he kills things,' she whispers, 'so yes.'

'But also no, Lovemore, because he does it to save things, other birds.' Lovemore can see from the look on his face that the question is important to him and is troubling him deeply. 'So he *does* give his log.'

'But I think he hits a crow with it first,' whispers Lovemore, surprising herself by making both of them giggle.

Then Benedict says that it is exactly the kind of question that Babu would like to puzzle over and help them to think through, and they agree that when he is back they will ask him what he thinks, but only after Lovemore has recited the whole poem for Babu so that he can understand fully. They continue to weed and chat until a hoot at the gate tells them that a customer has arrived for Bibi, and Benedict rushes inside to get to his room and his library book, and Lovemore washes her hands in the kitchen sink before drifting back to the top bunk in Titi's room.

She has lost count of the number of times that she has heard Bibi say that she is not going to have another mouthful of cake because of her hips, and then Bibi says, okay, maybe just one more mouthful, the very last one. And then she continues having just one more mouthful, the very last one, until it has to be the last one because not a single crumb of cake is left. Afterwards Bibi is full of regrets because of her hips.

That is how it is for Lovemore now, not wanting to read any more of Mama's journal entry because it is upsetting her, but deciding to read just one more paragraph, then just one more. And then there is no more of that entry left to read, and she regrets that she has read it because she feels unsettled and uncertain all over again. At the end of the entry, there is a note to her from Mama:

Lovemore — Sometimes a good person can do a bad thing. Maybe they know it's bad or maybe they don't.

That is all that Mama has to say to Lovemore at the end of her long and very ugly story.

It is not enough.

Putting the journal aside, Lovemore goes into the kitchen and pours herself some of the boiled tap water that lives in the fridge. Next to the sink is an almost-empty tray of ice cubes, and she tips the two remaining melting cubes into her glass, where they clink with the shaking of her hand. They make the water so icy cold that it almost hurts to drink it, but she gulps it all down. Before she is even back in Titi's room, she has decided that she wants Mama to leave her alone now. She wants to lock Mama's journal away in the box inside the suitcase under her bed, and leave it there for some time.

But when she picks up the journal to do just that, she feels that she must first do the one thing that she has been dreading. All along, she has been afraid of reaching the end of Mama's journal, of having no more of Mama's words left to read. But now she wants Mama's words to stop. Paging right to the very end of the journal, she looks for the blank line marking the start of Mama's final ever entry.

Taking a very deep breath, she reads the last words that Mama ever wrote.

I know my goal and I have my plan. I have already started. For some time now I have been helping Pastor at every baptism. I am the one standing to my ankles in the lake, the one who guides each person one by one into the deeper water where Pastor and his assistant are waiting. I have my own white robes now, not like when I had my own baptism and I wore the white trouser and white top that old Mr Chowdary borrowed for me from a Mhindi lady. I step to the side and wait while they help the person to go backwards under the water then I go forward again to lead the person back to the shore where everybody is cheering and singing and dancing. Eh, I love that party, I can feel the Holy Spirit coming inside me.

I want the worms to come inside me too. The lake has many small snails, when you go into the water they can send small worms into your body to make you sick. The sickness is called snail fever or also bilharzia, it's in the water because the fishermen use the lake as their toilet. But what are they supposed to do? Where else can they urinate when they are out on a boat? The worms are just part 1 of my plan. Very soon I'm going to do part 2.

I'm going to stop eating, and I'm going to become weak. When I become too weak to go to work, I'm going to say the doctor says it's snail fever, it's bilharzia, I must have got it from baptising. Nobody will know the truth until it's too late. When I become even more weak, I'll go to die in Sekou Toure hospital because Lovemore must not find me late at home. I already asked Agrippina to take Lovemore if ever I have to go to the hospital. Agrippina also knows that if ever I go to the hospital and it looks bad for me, she must give Lovemore's papers to Mwalimu Mkuu Makubi and ask him to write a letter to Joseph's father at the University of Dar es Salaam to say he has a grandchild soon to be an orphan. Mwalimu Mkuu Makubi is educated, he will know how to write a good letter to a University Professor, he will know to put the school stamp to show that he is serious.

Lovemore's grandparents will take her — Joseph's other children with Evelina are already at their house. Lovemore will go in time to start her secondary schooling in Dar es Salaam then she will go to university and become a lawyer in New York. Here in Mwanza, I cannot give her that. I'm fine now, but one day I'll get sick. People are saying that soon the government is going to give us the medication for free — but I know the medication isn't right for everybody. It didn't sit well with Evelina, and Steven's friend at the fish-processing factory is struggling to keep it down, and two women at Group have stopped trying. I don't want that for me, I don't want it for Lovemore.

Nobody is going to know my plan and nobody is going to know my goal, not even Agrippina. I already told Agrippina that when it's over she must look under my bed for the box and give it to Lovemore, and that made her cry so hard that her buttocks began to shake. I held her and I told her no, I only meant some time in the future, I was only telling her now because who knows? The Nile Perch Plastics daladala could crash with me inside it next week and then Agrippina doesn't know there is a box for Lovemore under my bed.

Nobody is going to know because nobody is going to see me not eating. At work I'm going to be busy at my desk during the lunch break or I'm going to say I was too hungry earlier, I already ate, or I'm going to say I'm trying to reduce. At home I'm going to say a woman brought nice maandazi to Nile Perch Plastics, we all bought some and I ate too many, now I cannot eat. Or I'm going to say I stopped at Friends in Deed on the way home, I ate too many peanuts. I can have so many stories. If it happens that I have to eat in front of somebody, afterwards I'm going to vomit it out.

This is what I'm going to do. When it's over, everybody can say it was the snail fever that took me, nobody will need to say the word that nobody likes to say.

<u>Lovemore</u> — My parents couldn't hope bigger for me than they did, but I hoped bigger for myself and I made it happen. I hope bigger for you than anything I can give you myself. I know you will make it happen.

When she closes Mama's journal, Lovemore's hands are shaking badly, and her eyes are wet. There was something that Mama wrote at the front of the journal, on the list taped inside the front cover, the list of five things with only four completed. What was it? Lovemore finds that list now. There it is, right at number one:

1. Always remember that everything I did was for you. You were always everything in the world to me so I always wanted everything in the world for you. I loved you with all my heart since I first held you in my arms, and so did Joseph. Never forget this, Lovemore.

So this is what Mama meant.
    This is what Mama did for her.
    Because she wanted everything in the world for her.
    Because she loved her with all her heart.
    How is Lovemore supposed to feel now? Should she love Mama with all her heart for sacrificing everything – *everything!* – to give her a better life? Or should she hate Mama, because how can her life be

better without Mama in it?

It is almost too much for Lovemore to bear. And it is way more than she wants to think about.

As soon as she can, she locks the journal away in the box inside her suitcase under her bed. She wants to talk to Mama, but of course Mama is not there. She wants to talk to Auntie Agrippina, but not over the telephone-fax with other ears listening. She wishes that she could at least listen to all of Auntie Agrippina's cassettes again, all in a row, not even pressing pause when she has to use the washroom or when she needs to eat.

Three Sunday phone calls with Rose pass and Lovemore tells Rose nothing about what Mama wrote in her journal. The only way that she knows to keep Mama's words from dripping into her mind in the same way that the rainwater drips from the kitchen ceiling into the bucket is to fill her head with as much schoolwork as possible. She ignores calls from Grace and Faith to come and watch *Charmed* or *Friends* with them, she ignores Bibi's reminders that *Ally McBeal* is on, and she resists her sisters' pleading to *please* come to Magdalena's birthday party with them.

One afternoon, she is on her way back into Titi's room to carry on with her homework after using the washroom, when somebody begins banging at the gate. It is usually only Titi who is allowed to pass through the lounge when Bibi has a customer, but Titi has gone to the market with a shopping list. As quietly as she can, Lovemore opens the door that leads from the bedrooms and slips silently around the edge of the room without even raising her head to look at Bibi and her customer at the dining table at the far end.

At the gate, Benedict is suddenly beside her, breathless from running round the side of the house from his garden at the back, a small spade still in his hand. Together they open one half of the big green gate a small way, and Lovemore is surprised to see two *Wazungu* standing there, a man and a lady. Both of them look just as surprised to see Lovemore and Benedict.

'Oh!' says the man, his pink skin shining damply in the heat. 'I think we have the wrong house.'

'No, I'm sure we're right,' says the lady, her yellow hair flapping back behind her bare red shoulders as she moves hot air around her face with a fan woven from banana fibre.

'Can we help you?' Benedict asks.

'Yes, I hope so. Is this not the home of Professor Bogere? From the university?'

'No,' Lovemore tells the man, 'it's the home of Dr Tungaraza from the university.'

'Oh.' The man looks at his wife, and she clicks her tongue against the back of her teeth.

'Do you mean Professor Bogere from Uganda?' Benedict asks them.

'Yes,' both *Wazungu* say at the same time, looking at Benedict with their eyebrows so much higher than they were before.

'He rented our house while we were away,' Benedict tells them, 'him and his family. But now we're back.'

'Oh, I see.' The man's eyebrows sink back down on his shiny pink forehead. 'Do you know where they are now?'

'Mm, they're near. Um … if you go …' Benedict begins to point, and then drops his arm. 'Can I show you on the map?'

The *Wazungu* nod, and Benedict runs inside, leaving Lovemore at the gate. She is nervous around *Wazungu*. The only one she knows close up is Miss Brown, and she knows from Miss Brown that it is always important to be polite and to speak English clearly.

'I'm sorry we cannot invite you inside,' she tells them. 'Our grandmother is busy with a *customer*.' She emphasises the word so that they can understand that a customer is somebody very important, important enough to keep these visitors at the gate rather than politely inviting them in.

'Oh, no, that's okay,' says the lady.

'When she has a customer we have to stay in our rooms, we mustn't disturb her.'

'Oh? What … er … What kind of customer are we talking about?'

'It's *confidential*,' Lovemore tells them, emphasising the word so that they know not to ask any more. 'We're not allowed to tell anybody.'

'I see.' The man and the lady look at each other, then look away, their eyes bright, their mouths clamped shut.

'Everybody knows about her, customers come from all over to see her. She's almost the best in the whole of Tanzania.'

The lady stops holding her breath and smiles widely. 'Your *grand*mother?'

Lovemore nods proudly. 'There's a competition.'

'A *competition?*'

'Mm, in three rounds. She got through round one by sending in six photos—'

The man bursts out laughing. '*Photos?*' He must know how silly it is just to send photos.

'Mm. Bibi didn't like that, she is preferring face to face.'

'Of course,' says the lady, laughing as she uses a tissue to wipe a tear from her eye. Her pink face is looking very red, almost as red as her sunburnt shoulders.

'Face to face is always best.' The man is still laughing at the idea of sending photos.

'Yes. For round three they're going to give her a room at New Africa Hotel.'

Both of the *Wazungu* laugh out loud, and they are still laughing when Benedict arrives with the map. Lovemore does not know what she has said that is so funny, but maybe *Wazungu* are just like that. Babu has said that they drink a lot of beer, and Lovemore knows from Walk on Water, Auntie Agrippina's bar next to the lake, that people who are full of beer like either to laugh or to fight. She is glad that these *Wazungu* are not fighting.

Benedict shows them on the map how to get to where the Bogere family is staying now, tracing the way with a finger that he has not washed since working in his garden, a dark line of black under the end of its pink nail. He always puffs his chest with pride when he can tell people something that he knows and they do not. Uncle Joseph – his baba – was not like that, so he must have got it from his mama.

'I don't know the number of the house,' he tells the *Wazungu*, 'but I can show you how it looks.' He pulls a photo from the back pocket of his shorts and shows it to them. The man takes it while the lady puts on a pair of glasses.

'Oh, look, darling, here they are.'

The lady looks. 'Oh, yes! And their dog!'

'Madiba,' Benedict says.

'That's right! Madiba. He was just a puppy when we last saw him. Look at him now!'

'That's outside where they're staying now,' Benedict tells them, pointing with his dirty finger. 'This is their wall, it's yellow like ours, and this is their gate.'

'Red,' says the man, at the same time that the lady says, 'Orange.'

'Well, orangey-red,' says the man.

'Once upon a time,' says the lady. 'A lot of the colour's peeled off.'

'It's easy to find,' Benedict assures them, taking back the photo and the map.

The *Wazungu* are full of thanks as they climb back into the *bajaji* that has been waiting for them, and Lovemore and her brother close the gate together, Benedict bending to push the bolt into its slot in the ground while Lovemore slides the other bolt sideways into its slot on the other half of the gate. Benedict rushes back round the side of the house to get back to his vegetables, and Lovemore follows more slowly, wondering why she did not think to get to the gate by going through Titi's room and the kitchen, then round the side of the house, instead of disturbing Bibi and her customer by passing through the lounge. Bibi cannot have been pleased by Benedict coming into the lounge to get the map and to search through the photo albums for the right picture.

Lovemore is still moving slowly past the side of the house when everything seems to happen at once. It feels like somebody has taken a photo inside her head, the flash on the camera illuminating the darkness for just a second, as a sudden pain in her stomach doubles her over and a feeling that she might pass out forces her buttocks to the ground. For a moment she sits there, startled, not seeing any part of the yard that her eyes are looking at, not wanting to see anything that is going on inside her head. Then she curls into a ball on the bare earth, trying hard to focus on the pain and the dizziness, because those are the things that she can bear, those are things that somebody – Bibi, a doctor, anybody – can help her with, and because if she focuses on those things then she cannot also think about what is happening inside her head, where pieces are coming together like in a jigsaw puzzle and the picture that they are making is too ugly, too frightening, for her to look at, and if she has to look at it – really look at it – then everything is going to change, for ever.

She does not know how many minutes pass as she sits there in a ball, rocking herself back and forth, wishing that Mama could be there to hold her, wishing that everything could be different. Slowly she becomes aware that the pain and the dizziness have eased, and that she really must get up before Titi comes back from the market with Bibi's shopping balanced in a basket on her head, banging on the gate and bringing Benedict hurtling round from the back yard again. If he finds her there, he will ask her questions, and then Titi will ask her more questions, and then Bibi will ask her even more questions.

Under no circumstances must there be any questions from anybody at all.

Dusting herself down, she makes her way round into the back yard, where Benedict is concentrating so hard on tying some plants to upright sticks with string that he does not notice her as she slips into the kitchen. Back on Titi's top bunk, she pushes all her schoolbooks aside and closes her eyes tight, trying hard not to look at the picture inside her head that all the pieces have made.

But she is going to have to look. And everything is going to change, for ever. Because if Bibi and Babu ever find out – *when* they find out – what she did, they will never be able to forgive her. They will never be able to accept her in this house, this family. She knows that surer than sure.

Later, she gets out of eating supper with the family by pretending that she has a stomach ache. The stabbing pain that doubled her over outside has gone completely, but she bends and clutches her stomach in the same way that Rose's sister Lulu used to do every month when she tried to make Auntie Agrippina let her stay home from school. Bibi and Titi think that Lovemore's period might be starting, and Grace is upset because she wanted to be the first. They put Lovemore to bed in the girls' room, and Titi brings her a small bowl of fennel seeds to chew for the pain.

As soon as she hears the sounds of knives and forks on plates,

Lovemore slips out of bed and slides her suitcase out from under it. Unlocking the padlock with the key on its shoelace necklace, she takes out Mama's box. She knows without even trying that the whole box will be too big to fit into her schoolbag, so she chooses only a few precious things: Mama's journal; the photo album that Concilia gave her for her birthday turning thirteen, with all the old photos of her and Mama inside it; all four of the socks, fat and round like slices of a snake. Taking her purse from her suitcase, she unzips it and looks at the big roll of Tanzanian shillings that she has saved from her pocket money. There is no point in counting to see how much is there. The purse goes into her schoolbag along with what she has chosen from Mama's box and all the books that she will need at school tomorrow.

In the morning, Lovemore reports that she is feeling much better after a good night's sleep – though she has hardly slept at all – and that her period has not in fact started. Grace jokes that she is happy about Lovemore feeling better because now she does not have to walk to school alone, but Lovemore knows that Grace is really just happy that she herself might still be the first. Today is Grace's turn to have the phone that used to be Mama's, but there is nothing that Lovemore can do about that. If she asks to swap turns and have the phone herself, Grace is going to ask questions – and under no circumstance must anybody ask any questions. Lovemore makes herself eat breakfast because she cannot afford to feel weak or dizzy today, although, really, it is very difficult to swallow, and not just because her slice of bread tastes like a piece of polystyrene foam in her mouth. It feels like everything that she does not want to say – not even to herself – is sitting in her throat.

She gets through the first part of the school morning by being there without really being there at all. *Madame* Lumumba does not call upon her to say anything in class, which is as it always is. All of the extra French lessons that Mama sent her for have marked her out for *Madame* Lumumba as a girl who needs less help than the others, so no matter how much extra effort Lovemore puts in herself, she seldom gets the chance to shine in class. Normally that bothers her, but today she is glad of it. Sometimes it worries her that *Mwalimu* Chipeta seems to think that there is no point in asking her anything in Maths because she struggles so much, but today she is glad to be ignored. She pretends to giggle behind her hand with the other girls when *Mwalimu* Masabo gets so excited talking about how a solid state can change into a gaseous state without passing through a liquid state that his breasts bounce up and down like Pamela Pima's, but her mind is not even in the room.

At the end of break, she tells Grace that her stomach ache is back.

'Ah, no.' Grace looks more disappointed than concerned.

Lovemore gives her all of the books that they share. 'Please tell Miss Brown that I've gone to lie down.'

'Okay.'

Grace goes off to double English, and Lovemore pretends that she is going to the office to ask to lie down in the room for girls who are not feeling well, but instead she goes to the washroom. Inside one of the cubicles it is like she suddenly wakes up to what she is doing, and her heart begins to beat fast. She has never before done anything like this – she has never before even *thought* of doing anything like this. She has no idea how much anything is going to cost, but she is sure that one hundred American dollars is a lot of money, and that it should be plenty. Opening her schoolbag, she digs inside it for one of the fat round socks, and slides one of the notes out of it, folding it twice and checking to see that two folds make it small enough. Then she closes her bag and swings it up on to her back. She runs from the washrooms hoping that she looks like a girl who is running to class, and as soon as she is out of the school gate, she slows to a steady walk, expecting every second to hear her name called out by a teacher or by *Mwalimu Mkuu* Moshi or by one of the senior girls.

The urgent drumbeat of her heart pumps fear throughout her body, shouting at her to run, but she forces herself to walk, because nobody who sees her must guess from her pace that running is exactly what she is doing. Nobody who notices the sweat beading at her temples and dampening her dress must think of anything other than the late morning's heat as its cause. She tries to breathe deeply but her chest feels tight. Everything that she does not want to say sits inside her throat, threatening to choke her.

She must be clever about choosing a vehicle. Not a private taxi, because it will battle to make its way through the endless traffic jams clogging the city's roads. Not a *daladala*, because the other people inside it will look at her and they will ask too many questions. Not a *bodaboda*, because sitting on the back of a motorbike will let everybody see her, and somebody might recognise her. To be safe, she must get into a *bajaji*, even though nobody who wants to be safe will ever choose to travel in one of those.

As she gets nearer to the *daladala* stand, the dusty verges of the busy tarred road fill with even more stalls and kiosks. Unable to think of eating, she ignores the pyramids of pineapples and mangoes and the delicious smells of fried *sambusa* and *maandazi*. A young man shouts to her that he has phones on a special, and for the briefest moment she thinks about buying one. She could if she wanted to – she has the money – and it would be good to be able to phone ahead to say that she is coming. But no, she must not delay. She needs to get away from here as quickly as she can.

Outside a kiosk a little way ahead stands a *bajaji* that was maybe once red, or that maybe still is red underneath its thick covering of brown dust. A grey-haired man stands next to it, one hand on its roof, the other around the bottle of soda from which he is drinking, his head tipped back. As she approaches, he empties the last of the soda into his mouth and hands the bottle to a young man leaning against the kiosk. Then he pats his large stomach and lets out a loud belch, making the young man holding his empty bottle dip his head and laugh. The grey-haired man laughs too, patting his stomach again.

Lovemore reaches him as he is about to get back into the *bajaji*, and doing her best to look and sound calm, she asks politely if he will take her to the airport. His eyes narrow to slits as he looks her up and down. She knows that questions are forming in his mind as he takes in her school uniform and her school bag: Why is she not at school? Why does she want to get to the airport? Why is she by herself?

But only one question comes from his mouth: '*Una pesa?*'

'*Ndiyo.*' Yes, she has money.

If she had a bra, her money would be tucked in there. But she is not quite big enough yet to need one, so she unclenches her fist and shows him what has been concealed in there since the other side of the school gate, the side she is supposed to be on right now, in double English with Miss Brown. Creased and damp from her sweat, the note is still very obviously one hundred US dollars. The man's eyes are suddenly very big, and she tells him it is his if he can get her to the airport very quickly.

He bustles her into the back of his *bajaji*, the part that has two wheels and a seat wide enough for two, almost throwing himself into the front part that has only one wheel before starting the engine and setting off along the dusty verge, accelerating past the impatient vehicles beside them on the tarmac and sending pedestrians scattering. The shady roof of the little vehicle and its open sides cool her as she slips her schoolbag off her damp back. There is space for it on the seat beside her, but she puts it on her lap, winding her arms through its straps and holding on to it tightly.

The *bajaji* turns off the tarred road and begins a short cut along streets littered with bumps and dips that lift her buttocks off the back seat then slam her back down, only to lift her again. Every turn to the left or the right flings her sideways, making it hard to keep hold of her bag. Each time the driver stops briefly at an intersection to check for traffic, the dust cloud behind them catches up, making her cough and sneeze. She wishes now that she had paused to buy water.

At last they are back on tarmac, hurtling down Nelson Mandela Road and slipping off it onto the verge whenever the flow of traffic begins to slow and stutter. For a moment she wishes she had taken the time to buy one of the phones that the young man had on a special, so that she could speak to Rose and Auntie Agrippina. But part of her knows that it is probably better not to tell them that she is on her way. Auntie Agrippina would definitely phone Bibi.

They have turned on to Nyerere Road now, and they are making their way towards Julius Nyerere International Airport. If Lovemore had a passport, she would buy a ticket to somewhere international, somewhere far away like New York. That was what Mama always planned for her. Running away from the Tungarazas was never part of Mama's plan, but when they find out what Lovemore did, Babu and Bibi will want her gone anyway, the further the better. They will never forgive her. Going back to Mwanza is a step backwards, but right now she has no other choice. Auntie Agrippina and Uncle Steven will take her in. Rose and Lulu will be her sisters. Nobody in that family will hate her.

After the *bajaji* driver has dropped her off and slipped her hundred-dollar note into his pocket, she makes her way to the airport washroom. She has sweated every drop of moisture out of her body, so she does not need the toilet, but she does need some privacy. Behind the cubicle door, she opens her school bag. How much does a ticket to fly from Dar es Salaam to Mwanza cost? Two hundred dollars? A thousand? She has no idea. She does not want to have to open her bag in front of anybody who might see all of her money, so she takes out her purse of Tanzanian shillings and folds just eight hundred US dollars into it, tucking them underneath the roll of Tanzanian shillings that she has saved from her pocket money.

Before leaving the washroom, she splashes some water onto her face, dabbing it dry with a piece of toilet paper. Then she swings her school bag onto her back and goes to find the ticket office, clutching her purse to her chest. On the way, she stops to buy a bottle of cold water and drinks from it thirstily. It hurts as she swallows, as if the water is struggling to get past the words that she does not want to say, the words that are sitting in her throat threatening to choke her.

When the ticket-office man asks her age and she tells him that she is thirteen, the man shakes his head.

'Only an adult can buy a ticket,' he tells her, looking over her shoulder. 'Where is your mama?'

'Late,' she tells him. 'My mama is late.'

'Ah, *pole sana*,' he says. 'Sorry. Are you here with your baba?' He looks over her shoulder again.

'Uh-uh,' she says, looking down as she shakes her head. 'My baba is late, too.'

'Ah, *pole sana*. But who is here with you? Maybe your aunt?'

'My aunt is in Mwanza,' she tells him. 'It's why I need to go there.' It is not too big a lie. Auntie Agrippina is not actually her aunt, but she and Mama *were* like sisters. She tries again to show the ticket-office man the dollars in her purse, but he shakes his head no again.

'I cannot sell a ticket to a child,' he tells her again.

Tears are beginning to build up in her eyes as a ticket-office lady comes to see what is going on. The ticket-office man turns his head away and explains to the ticket-office lady in a soft whisper, and all the time the ticket-office lady's eyes are upon Lovemore, one eyebrow rising slowly. Maybe the ticket-office lady will understand. She tries to show the ticket-office lady the dollars inside her purse.

But the ticket-office lady's eyes are hard. 'Where did you get that money? Did you steal it?'

The question hits Lovemore like a slap, and she pulls back her purse, clutching it to her chest.

'What is your school?' the ticket-office man asks her.

'Let us phone your *mwalimu mkuu*,' says the ticket-office lady.

If they phone *Mwalimu Mkuu* Moshi, Lovemore is going to be in very big trouble. The drumbeat of her heart becomes more urgent, and fear pumps throughout her body, shouting at her to run. But the last thing she wants is to be chased by security.

'*Samahani*,' she says politely as she backs away slowly. 'Sorry.'

Already two more people have moved ahead of her, adults who can buy tickets from the ticket-office man and the ticket-office lady, and she turns to go.

But go where?

She returns to the washroom and splashes water on her face again. There is no toilet paper left now, so she fans her face dry with her purse while she thinks. She cannot stay here at the airport. If the ticket-office people refuse to sell her a ticket to fly, there are other ways. The road between Dar es Salaam and Mwanza has not been good for some time, so going there by bus or *daladala* would take forever, and all along the way somebody could stop her and try to bring her back to Dar es Salaam. There is only one other choice.

Outside the airport building, she finds a taxi-driver and asks him to take her to the railway station. The taxi-driver is kind, turning the air conditioner up high in his big vehicle that can drive smoothly over any kind of ground, and making sure that her seat belt is on and that she is comfortable in the seat next to his.

'My daughter is your age,' he tells her as he uses a card to lift the beam so that his taxi can leave the parking area. 'Form One? Form Two?'

'Form One,' she says, hoping that he is not going to ask about her school so that he can try to take her there instead of to the railway station.

'Ah. Photosynthesis. Diatomic elements. Irrational numbers. All those things.'

'Yes. And volumes of cones. Those things are too hard.'

His left hand goes up to the side of his head and he blows a high-pitched whistle. '*Eh!* I want to run away if Tunda asks me for help with any of that! What are those things even for? My goodness me!'

She smiles, surprising herself.

'Tunda is my daughter, huh? By the way, my name is Nelson.'

'Nelson like Mandela?'

He laughs as he brakes hard behind a line of traffic. 'Nelson like Mandela.'

'I'm Lovemore,' she tells him, realising too late that maybe a lie would have been better. But what can he do with her name?

'Lovemore? That is a good name.' He negotiates the narrowest gap between a bus and a *daladala*. 'Do people love you more?'

She shrugs. She has never really thought about what her name means. Nobody is going to love her at all when they find out what she did.

'*Eh*, these jams!' He looks at his watch. 'What train are you hoping to meet?'

'I'm going to Mwanza.'

'Mwanza? But, *eh!* There's no train going to Mwanza today.'

All the air comes out of her lungs in a rush, and she slumps down in her seat. She is suddenly too exhausted for any more panic.

'I have water,' he says. They are waiting at traffic lights now, and he reaches under his seat for two small plastic bottles that are slippery and wet with cold. He hands her one. 'Come, let us keep cool.'

She thanks him, breaks the seal on the bottle and takes a sip, battling to swallow. Nelson seems kind, but maybe he is lying about the train to Mwanza. Maybe he just wants to take her back to her school, or even to the Tungarazas' house. She is about to ask him to take her to the railway station anyway, when he suggests it himself, just in case the railway schedule has changed.

When at last they reach the station, he refuses just to drop her, insisting that she must wait in the taxi while he runs in to check. Sokoine Drive is busy and hot, and he wants to leave the engine running and the air-conditioning on so that she can stay cool, but that would just be inviting somebody to steal his car. He does not say, but maybe he thinks that she might even steal it herself. She has to admit to herself that if she knew how, and if the road to Mwanza was in a better state, she would slide across into his seat and do just that. She has already done something a thousand times worse.

What is she going to do if there is no train to Mwanza today? Where is she going to go? By this time, everybody will have gone home from school and the gate will be locked. Further down Sokoine Drive from the railway station is St Joseph's, but what would be the point of going there? In no time at all somebody there would be on the phone to Bibi – and she cannot go back to Bibi's house. Not now. Not ever.

There is no train today, but Nelson has written down on a piece of paper that there will be a train tomorrow at five in the afternoon and also one on Sunday at the same time. He has also written that it will take forty hours for the train to reach Mwanza. He gives her his business card and says that she can call him and he will fetch her and bring her back to the railway station then.

'Let me take you home,' he says.

But she has no home. Not any more. She will never again be welcome at her grandparents' house.

There is only one other place in Dar es Salaam that she can think of to go. Exhausted, she tries to remember the route that Benedict's finger showed her on the map, and she does her best to direct Nelson there through the traffic.

Chapter 13

Those days working for Mr Chowdary used to be hard, but I didn't know then that my life was going to become harder, that I was going to throw my love away on a man who was going to throw my life away. If I could go back in time I would still love Joseph and I would still have Lovemore, but when Joseph's wife was carrying their second-born I would ask the younger Mr Desai could I not go and get a job with the older Mr Desai in Dar es Salaam? Then I would still be alive today.

Once upon a time, Joseph was a good man. He never once beat me and he never once beat his wife. OK he wasn't honest to his wife — but that was because she trapped him into marriage by pretending to be pregnant with his baby when the older Mr Desai asked Joseph would he like to be manager if they upgraded the depot in Mwanza into a factory? Joseph wanted to come because he was only deputy-manager in Dar es Salaam, but Evelina didn't want him to come without her.

Joseph was never a handsome man, but still he looked nice. He was tall and strong. When he spoke, people believed him, they wanted to do what he said. Everybody at the factory respected him, he never had to shout. Agrippina once said he should have been a pastor, or at least a priest. Maybe she was right, but still he was very good as a manager.

It was after he took his children to stay with their grandparents in Dar es Salaam that I saw he was changing. When I think about it now, maybe he started changing even before then but I failed to see it. In the beginning he tried to hide it, but as he got worse he didn't care and the bottle of Konyagi stopped going back into his drawer, it stayed on his desk for anybody to see.

One afternoon I saw that there was less and less Konyagi in the bottle each and every time I went into his office. When everybody else got into the Nile Perch Plastics daladala at the end of the day I told them to go without me because Mr Tungaraza still had work for me. Then I took a glass of water and a teapot full of Tanica coffee into Joseph's office and woke him up. He tried to push me away at first, but after he drank a cup of Tanica he started to walk up and down and to talk angry nonsense. He pointed at the January photo from the calendar, the photo of the whole of Lake Victoria from high up in the sky.

Him — This lake! Eh, this lake!

Me — Joseph, don't poke at the glass with your finger, Doris will have to clean it.

Him — Do you not see, Glory?

Me — I see you drawing the shape of the lake on the glass, I see your finger making the glass dirty.

Him — This lake is dirty! Can you not see it? Look at it, Glory! Do you not see it is a deep wound in our land?

Me — It is a lake, Joseph.

Him — No!

Me — Yes. It is a lake full of water, and the water is full of fish.

Him — It used to be full of fish, many kinds of fish. Then somebody from Europe put Nile perches in our lake. That fish was never from here, it never belonged here. Now it has colonised our water, cannibalised most of our native fish, the small ones that used to keep the water clean by eating all the algae. Now the water isn't getting oxygen. It's dying. Those foreign fish are killing us, Glory!

Me — Those Nile perches are feeding us, Joseph. Me, you, everybody in this factory, everybody in the fish-processing factories, every fisherman on the lake, what jobs will all of us have without those fish? Can you not see that those fish are our life?

Him — Hah! They are maggots in this rotting wound!

Then I told him to stop poking at the glass with such force because what if he broke it and cut himself? I poured him some more Tanica from the pot and he sat down at his desk to drink it. I tried to make him talk about normal things, things from every day like invoices and plastic pellets and Lovemore's schoolwork and the latest small business that Agrippina wanted to spend her abundance on. Joseph's mind was starting to become clearer, but I could see that it was somewhere else. Then he began to talk about where it was.

Him — Glory, there is something I have done. I don't want to tell you about it but I don't want it to sit inside me.

Me — What? What have you done? Have you been with another dried dagaa trader-woman from Congo? With another woman of any kind? Because you know it is too late to hurt me with such stories, Joseph. The only thing we have between us now is our daughter.

Him — Eh, I know that, Glory. The story inside me is not about any other woman.

Me — Then tell it to me.

He took a deep breath of air and he knotted his hands together and he began to fidget on his chair. I remembered then the Saturday afternoon when he came to my house after football and he fidgeted like that and I thought he was going to tell me he was mine now, but instead he told me the worst thing a man can tell a woman, the thing that made me stop loving him. I remember thinking that night in his office with just the two of us there that he couldn't tell me anything worse than he told me that Saturday afternoon. But I was wrong.

Him — I'm serious, Glory, people are saying that our lake is going to die. The lake is our life, and if it dies it will be the death of us. What other work can we get in this place? How will we feed ourselves? How will we feed and educate Lovemore? Eh! I was thinking about that when I was drinking at a bar in Kirumba after work one day. A man I didn't know, a Congolese, he bought me a beer, he asked was I the one with space to rent in a warehouse near the airport? I said yes, I asked him did he want to rent a unit for something? He asked could he rent it for just in case? He asked it with a laugh so I laughed with him. Then he asked me about security and I told him we have a night watch and a day watch and also a marabou stork that chases people like it's a dog. After he bought me another beer he asked me to go to the washroom with him, and he took a fat roll of $100 notes from inside his jacket and asked me was it enough to rent the very back section of the warehouse, the private unit with its own roller door? It was too much money, too too much, but I said yes and I took it because the lake is dying. I said he could come the next day to complete the forms and he laughed again and said he could see I was a man of honour and men of honour need only a handshake.

Me — Eh! But is that far unit of the warehouse not empty?

Him — It is empty! Except sometimes for just a few hours or maybe just a day. Then there are wooden crates in there.

Me — Wooden crates? With what inside?

Him — If I tell you, you will not believe me.

Me – I used to believe everything you told me, even the lies.
Him – Don't start that story again, Glory. That was all your fault, coming here with your breasts and your buttocks.
Me – My breasts and my buttocks were here even before you came here, Joseph. You are the one who started that story.
Him – No, but this is a different story. You will not believe it.
Me – Tell it to me anyway. Tell me what is inside those wooden crates.
Him – Eh! How can I say? Let me say . . .
Me – What?
Him – Let me say tools.
Me – Tools? For what?
Him – Let me say an industry.
Me – What industry.
Him – Eh! The biggest industry in Africa.
Me – Joseph, I am not a university professor like your father, I don't know what is the biggest industry in Africa. Just tell me straight.
Him – I am talking about war, Glory.
Me – War? Tools? Tools for war? Joseph, are you talking about what I think you are talking about?
Him – Yes.
Me – Eh! Eh! Eh! They told you? They showed you?
Him – Uh-uh. I looked. You know when we put those division walls in the warehouse we put a door from the main part into each unit. The door into that far unit has no handle, it has just the bolt on the main warehouse side to keep it shut. If you enter that back section from the big roller door on the outside, all you see is a side wall made up of wooden sections, if you don't know to look you don't know that one of those wooden sections is a door into the rest of the warehouse. Bismarck told me one morning that men were there the night before, they came in two big pick-ups and drove right inside that division and later they drove out. They had keys for the padlocks so Bismarck didn't worry. I went in through that wooden door at the back and I saw the crates. I suspected but I wasn't sure. Less than a minute with a crowbar and I knew.
Me – Eh! Guns?
Him – Yes.
Me – In our warehouse?

Him — Yes. But only for a few hours, and only three or four times. Most of the time that part of the warehouse is empty.

Me — But guns? Here in Mwanza?

Him — I think maybe they come sometimes in the planes that come empty from Europe to fetch the frozen fillets. I don't know. But how else are guns going to come here to Mwanza?

Me — But why are they coming here to Mwanza? There is no war here.

Him — There is war all around us, Glory. Those guns are for Congo, for Angola, for Sudan, for Somalia, for anywhere with a more difficult airport than Mwanza.

Me — Eh! You have brought guns and wars to our warehouse? Joseph! How could you do that?

Him — Glory, I have done something more.

Me — Something more? What?

Him — Where is my Konyagi?

Me — Uh-uh. If you are going to drink something it is Tanica or water. What more have you done? Tell me, Joseph.

Him — Eh! I cannot tell you.

Me — I can tell the younger Mr Desai that wars are in our warehouse and that you put them there.

Him — No! You must tell nobody!

Me — Then tell me everything that I must tell nobody. Tell me what more you have done.

Him — Eh!

Me — Tell me.

Him — Glory, I have taken some of those guns.

Me — What?

Him — Last time after they brought crates, I went in when there was just me inside and Bismarck outside. I reversed right into the main part of the warehouse so Bismarck didn't see. I took one gun from each crate, I nailed everything shut afterwards.

Me — Joseph! Where has your mind gone? Why?

Him — In less than twenty-four hours I had a buyer, I had more American dollars than I ever saw before.

Me — But dollars for guns are stained with blood!

Him – I know. It's not something that I don't know. But those dollars will feed us when our lake dies, those dollars will make Lovemore into a lawyer in New York.

Me – Joseph, do you think those men are going to understand about why you took their guns? Do you think they are going to care that you have a daughter who wants to be a lawyer? They are going to shoot you dead!

Him – They didn't even notice, Glory! And why will they suspect me? Do they see me driving a new car? No. Do they see me wearing a new suit? No. I am living my life like nothing has changed. The only change is one they will never see, and that change is that my socks are full of dollars.

Me – Your socks?

Him – It's a security trick I learned from my Auntie Geraldine in Bukoba. The safest place to keep your money is rolled up inside a sock at the back of the drawer with all your other socks. And your sock drawer must always be the lowest one. If it's the top one somebody can open it fully and see that something is inside a sock right at the back. But nobody ever pulls the bottom drawer out as far as it can come, because their feet are in the way and bending low and pulling is too uncomfortable. No house girl is ever going to find your money inside a sock at the back of the lowest drawer.

Me – Eh! But Joseph, you did a very bad thing. Do you not feel bad inside yourself?

Him – I feel very bad inside myself.

Me – Are you not afraid?

Him – I was afraid when I was doing it. Yes. I was very afraid. I could hardly contain my bowels.

Me – But it's finished now? You're not going to do it again?

Him – Glory, you can bring me a Bible and ask me to swear on it that I'm not going to do it again.

Me – Good.

Him – You can ask me to swear it, but I cannot swear it.

Me – Eh!

Him – The fear excited me, Glory. It excited me. What am I supposed to do? You are refusing to excite me now.

Me – Don't try to blame me for this!

Him – No. The fear excited me. And the money too.

Me – Joseph, they will kill you! Tell them they can no longer use our warehouse! Don't steal from them again! Did your parents raise you to do this? Did they raise you to be such a bad man?

Him – Am I a bad man for wanting a good future for our child?

Me – No. But–

Him – But nothing. I'm just doing my job plus extra for Lovemore. Grace, Benedict and Moses are with my parents, their grandfather will do his job plus extra for them. People do their job plus extra for their children. You do your job here plus you do typing at home plus you have Friends in Deed, you do your job plus extra for Lovemore. Agrippina has all her businesses, she does her job plus extra for Rose and Lulu. Everybody does their job plus extra.

Me – Not everybody. Steven just does his job.

Him – Hah! Steven? Steven who is afraid every day to go too near to a freezer? That is who you are holding up to me as a good example of a man? He is your good example of a father? Look at him there in the calendar photo, dressed up in plastic like a baby that might wet itself!

Me – Eh! Steven does good honest work, he doesn't harm anybody.

Him – Hah! Look at him there in his yellow plastic gloves, putting those fillets into those polystyrene foam boxes for their flight to Europe. Where do those boxes come from, Glory?

Me – You know where, Joseph, we make them here at Nile Perch Plastics.

Him – Exactly! We turn tiny balls of plastic into polystyrene foam boxes and polystyrene foam trays and polystyrene foam cups and polystyrene foam anything a customer wants. Do you think we do good honest work that doesn't harm anybody?

Me – Of course.

Him – Hah! Those street children who crawl through Mwanza like insects, they take the polystyrene foam that we make and they melt it into glue for sniffing. When a child sniffs it he is no longer there, he is like a doll made from rags. Anybody can do anything to him, they can sodomise him, they can kill him. Girls, too, they are homeless on our streets almost as much as boys. We make what makes it easy to rape them. We are all responsible for that, every one of us here! So don't try to tell me there was never anything bad or dangerous here at Nile Perch Plastics before I brought those other things to our warehouse.

Bismarck knocked on the window of Joseph's office then, he wanted to know *was everything OK? I was too glad that he knocked, because eh, what Joseph was saying was making me feel too too uncomfortable. Was I really responsible for those things happening to those children? Part of me wanted to go and say prayers about it at Highway of Holiness, but the other part of me wanted to go and hold my own child. I went home in a daladala that was coming from further along the airport road. I didn't want to go with Joseph in his car, I didn't want to sit next to him. Really, I didn't even want to sit next to myself.*

<u>*Lovemore*</u> *— Sometimes a good person can do a bad thing. Maybe they know it's bad or maybe they don't.*

Closing Mama's journal, Bibi puts a shaking hand inside her blouse and reaches for another of the tissues tucked inside her bra. She takes off her glasses and dabs at her eyes before using the same tissue to wipe the lenses. She never looked old before, but now she does, her face grey, her round cheeks sagging.

Concilia puts a hand on Bibi's knee. 'I know it must be a shock, Angel.'

Bibi closes her eyes and shakes her head slowly from side to side, and many minutes pass in silence. Lovemore has no idea what to do or say. She feels maybe she should offer Bibi a cup of tea, but they are at Concilia's house and offering tea is Concilia's job.

'My son,' says Bibi, her voice quiet, her eyes still shut, her hands still slowly polishing the lenses of her glasses. 'My own son. My Joseph.'

'It's a shock, Angel.'

Bibi opens her eyes. 'They shot him dead.' She puts her glasses back on, and tapping at the cover of Mama's journal where it rests on her lap, she looks at Lovemore. 'Your mama was right. They shot him dead.'

Nodding her head yes, Lovemore looks down at her bare feet, which are sticking out from under the *kanga* that Concilia has lent her because all she has is the school uniform she arrived in late yesterday when nobody would sell her a ticket to fly to Mwanza and there was no train, and this was the only place she could think of to come.

'Why is Pius away at a time like this? Why?'

'Angel, it is only a time like this because this happens to be the time that Lovemore read that entry in her mama's journal and became afraid.'

'Oh, Lovemore! You ran away because you were afraid?'

Lovemore nods her head yes again. 'I'm sorry, Bibi.'

'No, stop those sorries, Lovemore, please. I'm the one who is sorry.' Bibi's hand drums on her chest above her breasts. 'I'm sorry that you came to read a story that is too hard even for an old bibi like me, it's much too hard for a girl who is only just a teenager. How are you going to read that story and then everything is fine like before you read it? How are you going to understand it?' Bibi gulps in some air and lets it out in a deep, long sigh. 'I want Pius to understand this, I want him to read this story.'

'Bibi—'

'But no, it's your mama's private journal, her private letter to you.'

'Bibi—'

'I didn't want to read that story myself, you know that, it's only that Concilia said I must and you said it was okay.'

'Bibi—'

'Now, how can I ask for Pius to read that story? It's your mother's private—'

'Angel, stop. It's okay. Lovemore and I have already talked about this. I'm going to take her to photocopy that entry for Pius to read.'

'*Eh!*' Bibi's face lights up, as much as a face that has suddenly become old and grey and exhausted can.

'And later on, if she reads any other entry she feels she wants to share, I can take her to photocopy that for you, too.'

'Bless you, Concilia. Thank you, Lovemore.' Bibi takes some banknotes from her bra. 'Let me give you something for the cop—'

'No, Angel!' Concilia pushes Bibi's hand back towards her breasts. 'It's okay.'

Shrugging, Bibi slips the notes back inside her bra. 'I'll owe you then. You can just—'

'No, Angel.' Concilia's voice is firm. 'It's me who owes you.'

'*Eh*, Concilia! But not forever!'

'Yes, forever.'

'It was just a cake.'

'Ah, Angel, you know better than anybody that a cake is not just a cake. A cake is never just a cake. No, they let me photocopy at the university's health centre anyway, I do bits and pieces to help out there. It's no problem.'

'Thank you.'

'No problem. Now. I think we need some tea.'

Concilia gets up, and leaning on her stick, she pulls Bibi to her feet. Bibi puts Mama's journal down on the coffee table, from where Lovemore snatches it up and holds it to her chest. She does not like that anybody else has touched it, has read a piece of it, but she knows that Concilia was right, that Bibi really did need to read that part. And after reading that part and having a cup of tea, Bibi might be ready to hear why Lovemore really ran away. She tucks the journal back into her schoolbag before joining Bibi and Concilia in the kitchen.

'I can't believe this is my first time to be inside your kitchen,' Bibi is saying.

'That is because you spend too much time inside your own!'

'It's small,' Bibi says, looking around her as Concilia measures three mugs of water into a pot, 'but I think for one person it's okay.'

'It's perfect for me. I have everything I need. Oven, fridge, sink, cupboards.' Concilia spoons milk powder and plenty of sugar into the pot of water. Lovemore does not mind the sugar because Concilia has already said that sugar is good when things are bad, and when things are bad there are more important things to worry about than buttocks and hips. Concilia places the pot on the top of the oven, switching on one of the plates.

'Electric?'

'Mm.' Concilia adds teabags, a few fat cardamom pods and a stick of cinnamon.

'Electric is not good for cakes.'

Concilia smiles. 'And I am not a baker! Your business is going well, Angel, that gas oven of yours never seems to get a rest.'

Like most of the other things in the Tungarazas' house, Bibi's oven is not new and shiny. Two of its knobs at the front have even broken off and been replaced by parts that do not belong, one a silver something and one a gold something. The kitchen floor is uneven, so the flattened cover of a matchbox holds up one of the oven's feet to make it level. It is not the kind of oven that belongs in a nice big house in Capri Point back home in Mwanza or on Msasani Peninsula here in Dar es Salaam, but it keeps Bibi's business going and it keeps everybody in the house well fed, so Lovemore does not mind.

Anyway, ovens are not at all important right now. Lovemore is aware that they are choosing to talk about things that do not matter, because what they need to be talking about matters too much.

'I'm sorry I didn't bring cake,' says Bibi. 'I thought I was just coming to fetch Lovemore and take her home.'

'Aah, you thought you could come to my house without having a cup of tea? After all the cups of tea you have made for me?'

Bibi smiles. Lovemore tries to smile with her, but she is too nervous about what she still needs to say.

'Lovemore, that key there,' Concilia points to a silver key hanging on a small hook next to the fridge, 'it's for my mama's back door. She'll be out at work now, so you can just go in. See if she has any biscuits for us.'

Lovemore takes the key off its hook. It is on a ring from which a bright yellow smiley face hangs. 'Where must I look?'

'There's a high cupboard above the fridge, she hides them from herself there. You might need to stand on one of her dining chairs.'

Lovemore goes out of Concilia's back door and walks the few steps to Mama-Concilia's back door. Inside the kitchen, she tries at first without a chair. She can get the cupboard open, but she cannot see inside it or reach for anything that might be in there, so she goes from Mama-Concilia's kitchen into the next room to find a dining chair. Like at the Tungarazas', the dining area is part of the lounge. There are photos in frames all over the walls, and Lovemore cannot help looking.

There is a big wedding photo, which must be Concilia's parents. Concilia calls this house her mama's, not her parents', so maybe her baba is late now. Tucked into the corner of that frame, on the outside of the glass, is a small photo of another wedding, a black man with a *Mzungu* bride. Then there is a big photo of Concilia from her waist up, wearing a university hat and gown, holding a rolled-up degree certificate and smiling very widely. That degree certificate is now in a frame of its own on the wall at Concilia's, right next to another degree certificate from a university in South Africa.

One day Lovemore is going to have degree certificates of her own, and there is going to be a photo of her on her graduation day exactly like this one. The only thing that is going to stop her smile from being just as wide as Concilia's is that her mama will not be there to see it.

There are so many photos of so many different people. Some of them have faces a bit like Concilia's, so maybe they are cousins and aunts. There is one girl who could almost be Concilia when she was younger, except that she is winning some kind of race, the ribbon breaking as she runs through it ahead of another girl. There is another photo of the same girl standing next to the same couple from the big wedding photo. Maybe Concilia has a sister, or maybe that couple are an uncle and aunt, and the girl is a cousin. She is very like Concilia, only she is slimmer and she does not need a stick to stand with.

The biscuits! Lovemore must not keep everybody waiting. Putting one of the dining chairs in front of the fridge, she steps up onto it and chooses a packet of pink wafers from the cupboard.

When she locks Mama-Concilia's kitchen door behind her, she can hear Bibi and Concilia talking in Concilia's kitchen.

'My son? Did that? Uh-uh.'

'But look at why he did it, Angel. He wanted to be sure he could provide for his family—'

'His other family! Is it not already enough that he did that? Is it not already enough that he gave us another grandchild and never told us? That we had to learn about her only last year when her school head sent us her birth certifi—'

'I'm sorry, Bibi!'

'*Eh!*' Both of them swing round to look at Lovemore where she stands in the doorway, and Concilia raises her hand to her mouth, dropping the stirring spoon into the pot of simmering tea, where it disappears completely.

'Lovemore!' Bibi looks like she is going to start crying again. 'I didn't mean—'

'I'm sorry, Bibi!' Lovemore does not know what else to say, standing there clutching the packet of pink wafers to her chest.

Bibi comes to her and holds her tight. She wants to hold Bibi back, but she cannot free her arms. Even as she begins to cry, she worries that some of the pink wafers are getting crushed between them.

'My anger is for my son, Lovemore, not for you.' Bibi speaks into Lovemore's hair, and Lovemore smells the cocoa butter on Bibi's neck, the same cocoa-butter smell that Mama used have. 'He kept you from us all those years. All those years we could have loved you. My anger is for him, not for you.'

Lovemore sniffs loudly, badly needing a tissue. When Bibi hears why she really ran away, Bibi will have plenty of anger for her. But Bibi does not let go of her until Concilia says their tea is ready, and will Lovemore help her with pouring because there is a spoon somewhere inside the pot that is going to fall out and make a mess.

Bibi puts some of the pink wafers on a plate, and they go back into Concilia's lounge with their tea. It is a small lounge – because Concilia's house is really just a small house in her mama's back yard – and the lounge is also Concilia's office. It is where people come to talk to her if ever they have worries or anything they need to talk to somebody about. There is no dining table, but there is a desk in one corner with the two degree certificates on the wall above it. There are no photos on the walls like at Mama-Concilia's, but instead there are posters that Concilia has made herself. One has a photo of a *Mzungu* with metal pieces a bit like machetes instead of the lower parts of his legs. He is running in a race, and the big words that Concilia has put under the photo say: *Don't tell me you can't run just because you have no legs*. Another poster has a photo of another *Mzungu* with glasses, slumped down small and old in a wheelchair with all kinds of equipment around him. The words underneath it say: *Don't tell me you can't work out how the world works just because no part of your body works*. There is a young man pedalling a bicycle with his hands in the same way that Ibrahim does. *Don't tell me you can't ride a bicycle just because your legs don't work*. A big poster on the back of the front door, waiting for people to see it on their way out, says: *Of course you can*.

Concilia was very patient last night with all of Lovemore's can'ts.

'I can't go back to Babu's house!'

'I can't let Bibi read this!'

'I can't tell her, Concilia, I just can't!'

'No, I can't eat anything.'

'I can't sleep. I'm sure I can't.'

But she did sleep, a little. Concilia pulled a foam mattress out from under her bed just as Lovemore used to do when Rose used to sleep over, and together they made up a bed for Lovemore on the floor of Concilia's lounge. Concilia made warm milk and honey for both of them, and she sat with Lovemore until Lovemore could stay awake no longer.

Now Lovemore helps herself to a tissue from the box on the coffee table and blows her nose, while Bibi takes a tissue from inside her bra and wipes her eyes before putting it back. Adjusting her glasses, Bibi looks at Lovemore's chest wrapped tightly in Concilia's *kanga*.

'Soon you will get a brassiere of your own for tissues.' She is too old-fashioned to shorten the word. Rose's bibi is just the same. 'Grace is built like a pencil, it's going to be a long time before she needs a brassiere. I know the best shop. I took my daughter Vinas there.'

Bibi reaches for her tissue again, and Concilia puts a hand on Bibi's knee. Lovemore feels dreadful. Bibi's daughter is late, but nobody ever speaks about how or why – which probably means that she was sick in the kind of way that Mama would underline in her journal, sick in the kind of way that nobody likes to say when it is their own family. Now Bibi has just found out why somebody shot her son dead. Lovemore and her sisters and brothers are all orphans – well, maybe Faith and Daniel are not really orphans, maybe their baba is alive somewhere, but anyway he has been gone from their lives a long time, so they may as well be orphans. *Orphans* is the word for children who have lost their parents, but what is the word for what Bibi and Babu are? What is the word for parents who have lost their children? Is there a word? There should be. Lovemore must try to remember to ask Miss Brown.

Anyway, Bibi is already sad and shocked and angry and disappointed, and Lovemore is about to make it even worse. She gulps at her tea and gives Concilia a look that asks for help. Concilia gives her a look that says it is going to be okay.

'Angel, there is something more that Lovemore would like you to know.'

Bibi finishes blowing her nose. 'Something more? Something more that is bad about Joseph?'

'Uh-uh, Bibi. It is bad about me.'

'Bad about you? But you are not to blame for anything that happened, Lovemore. I told you—'

'Angel, please listen to Lovemore's story. She needs to tell it.'

'Okay. But—'

'No buts, Angel. Let us listen to her story from beginning to end while we drink our tea.'

Lovemore takes another gulp of her tea, and then she begins. 'It was a Thursday night, I remember that because Mama wasn't home, she was at Group.'

'Group?'

'Let us listen, Angel.'

'Mama went to Group each and every Thursday night. It was a new thing for her, I think she had gone only a few times already. She used to come home from work and Pritty would—'

'Pretty?'

'*Angel!*'

'Sorry.'

'Pritty would have supper ready early for Mama every Thursday, she used to eat quickly then go off to Group. I used to go to my friend Rose. Some Thursday nights I slept over at Rose's, but that Thursday night I didn't. I don't remember why. Anyway, Rose and her cousin Godbless had already walked me home, and I was there with Mama's cousin Sigsbert. He was talking with Pritty in the kitchen, and I was in the lounge doing a drawing. I heard a voice calling, *"Hodi"*, but the voice sounded far, and nobody was knocking on the door. I went to the window and I moved the curtain, then I saw that there was a big vehicle outside, big like those ones that can go straight over any bumps or dips in the road, not like ordinary cars that have to drive around those things slowly or they'll break. It was a rich person's car, a car for somebody with a lot of abundance.

'The car door was open, and I could see the shape of Bismarck standing next to it. He was the one calling *"Hodi"*, and I knew him because he was night watch at Uncle Joseph's work and he lived near to us. He was friends with Rose's Uncle Milton, so I went out to say hello. He wanted Mama, but she was out at Group, so he said maybe

I could help him. Did I know where Uncle Joseph lived?

'I went to Uncle Joseph's house once with Mama – not to go inside, just to stand outside the gate and look, just to see the kind of nice house I could have if I worked hard at school and made something of my life.'

Lovemore does not want to say the real reason why Mama took her there – and anyway, she did not know the real reason at the time that Bismarck came. 'So I knew where it was. I told Bismarck how to go there, but I didn't know the number of the house. I tried to describe the gate, it was blue but not solid like a wall, it was blue bars with a pattern of fish. Then I remembered I had made a drawing of it. That day that Mama took me to see it, she went to church later and I sat with my crayons and I drew it from my memory. So I went inside and I looked through my drawing books and I found it. I tore out that page and I gave it to Bismarck. He gave it to the men in the car and the men drove away. They left Bismarck behind, and he was angry because now he had to look for transport back to Nile Perch Plastics.

'I went back inside and went on with my drawing, waiting for Mama to come home. Sigsbert and Pritty were still talking in the kitchen, and when Mama came home she was upset and she went straight to bed, so I never told her about Bismarck coming and looking for Uncle Joseph. I forgot all about it. I only remembered when those *Wazungu* came to your house, Bibi, those *Wazungu* who were looking for the people who rented your house when you were all away in Rwanda and Swaziland. You were busy inside with your customer. Benedict showed them on the map where those people moved to, but he didn't know the house number so he showed them a photo of how the gate looks like.

'*Eh*, Bibi, that was when I remembered, and then I remembered Mama coming home the next day and saying that robbers had shot Uncle Joseph dead, and Mama and I were so upset, I never thought then about those men in the car with Bismarck the night before, but now I can't stop thinking about them.' Lovemore is struggling to breathe, but she makes herself continue to the end. 'Bibi, I am the one who told them where to find Uncle Joseph.' She begins to sob. 'I am the one who killed him!'

Bibi pulls her up out of her chair and holds her tight again. This time Lovemore's arms are free to hold Bibi just as tight. 'I'm so sorry, Bibi!'

'*Shh.*'

'I killed my baba! It's me who shot your son dead!'

'Uh-uh. *Shh.*'

'I'm so sorry, Bibi.'

'*Shh.*'

They hold each other tight for a very long time, and they do not let go until Concilia says softly that fresh cups of tea are ready and somebody needs to help her to bring them from the kitchen.

Bibi goes into the small washroom to use the toilet and to wash the tears from her face, then Lovemore does the same. The tea is warm and milky and spicy, with plenty of sugar, and it tastes good. Now that the story is out of her, Lovemore's throat feels clearer, but what she did still sits inside her like one of the large boulders on Mwanza's hilltops.

'You were only eight years old,' Concilia reminds her.

'You didn't know what was going to happen,' says Bibi. 'You couldn't know.'

'They came to your house with Bismarck. You knew him, he wasn't a stranger.' Concilia already said it to Lovemore last night, but Lovemore needs to hear it again. 'If they had come on their own, would you have helped them?'

'Uh-uh. I mustn't talk to strangers. I would have called Sigsbert to talk to them. But Sigsbert doesn't know Uncle Joseph's house.' Lovemore's hand starts to tremble, and her tea begins to spill. 'Sigsbert couldn't kill Uncle Joseph.' Putting her mug down on the table, she takes a tissue from the box. She wants to mop up her spilled tea, but she needs the tissue for her eyes instead.

'Stop it, Lovemore.' Bibi's voice is firm as she wipes the table with another tissue. 'Do you think that you were the only person in Mwanza who could tell Bismarck where Joseph lived? He was an important somebody, the manager of an important business. It was going to take Bismarck just ten minutes to find somebody else who knew Joseph and knew where he lived. Maybe even just five minutes.'

'She's right, Lovemore. We spoke about this last night.'

Lovemore nods her head yes, feeling their words chipping away at the boulder inside her.

'You were trying to help,' says Bibi, 'and helping somebody is a good thing to do.'

'It's a very good thing to do,' agrees Concilia. 'Even Bismarck was just trying to help.'

'*Eh!*' Bibi's hands fly up to her mouth. 'Where is Bismarck now? Did they shoot him dead too?'

'Uh-uh. But he left Nile Perch Plastics. Mama stayed home for some days after she—' Lovemore stops herself. She does not want to say that it was Mama who found Uncle Joseph dead in his house, and that Mama stepped round him as if it was nothing. 'After she lost Uncle Joseph she was sick at home, and Rose's Uncle Milton, he was Bismarck's friend, he came to tell Mama that Bismarck had gone back to his family in Tabora because he was upset about Uncle Joseph being late and he didn't want to work for the younger Mr Desai.'

'Maybe they scared him,' says Bibi.

'I think so,' says Concilia.

'*Eh*, how did I raise a son who could get involved in something like that? Me? And Pius? How did we raise a son who could do that?'

'Remember his intention, Angel. He wanted to be able to provide—'

Bibi interrupts. 'Uh-uh, Concilia! Talking about why he did it, that is just like sprinkling a layer of icing sugar over what he did. We can hope that the icing sugar will make it look like something sweet and nice, something good. But in our hearts we still know exactly what is underneath.'

'You are right, Angel, but I think he genuinely feared that the whole fishing industry was going to collapse.'

'*Eh*, Concilia, but how was the lake going to die?'

Lovemore suddenly remembers. 'The lake *did* die, Bibi.'

'What? Lake Victoria is dead?'

'Uh-uh, but it did die. It died twice. It was after Uncle Joseph was already late. The first time, it died of cholera. There was a bad cholera, it was everywhere in East Africa. The people in Europe, they said the cholera was in our lake, they didn't want our fish any more. All the fishing stopped, except maybe the small-small fishermen, and the fish factories almost stopped, except for some small orders from countries that didn't mind about our cholera. Rose's baba, Uncle Steven, he works in a fish factory, his job was suspended and he had to sit at home watching TV. Some days he got work at a small factory in somebody's back yard, a factory for fish for East Africa. But he was used to the hygiene code in the factories for fish for Europe, so he didn't like that small factory, he said it wasn't clean. Mama said some jobs at Nile Perch Plastics almost had to be suspended, but after six months the people in Europe said the lake was better, and everybody's work started again.'

'I remember that big cholera,' says Bibi. 'It was a hard time in all the towns on the shores of Lake Victoria, even for my family back in my home town of Bukoba.'

Lovemore manages just the hint of a smile, suddenly remembering that Miss Bukoba was runner-up when Miss Mwanza – Rose's sister Lulu – was crowned Miss Lake Victoria.

'We didn't make it back to Bukoba over this past Christmas time,' says Bibi. 'We had been planning to pick you up in Mwanza on the way there, then Pius thought about it and decided we shouldn't go. He said it was too far to drive all the way from Swaziland where we were coming from, especially with the microbus starting to have problems. He said we should just settle ourselves back into our house in Dar es Salaam, and then he would go to fetch you.'

'Probably a very good idea, Angel. It must have been hard enough for Lovemore to meet everybody in your big household here, I don't think she could have coped with all your and Pius's uncles and aunts and cousins in Bukoba too.'

'That is what Pius said.'

'I'm sorry you didn't go to Bukoba, Bibi.' Lovemore does not want to be responsible for one more bad thing.

'No! It's forgotten! I'm only talking about Bukoba because we are talking about the lake. You said it died twice.'

'Yes, Bibi. The second time it died, it died of poisoning. Some fishermen started to make a short cut by using poison to catch the fish, they poured poison in the lake and the fish died and floated up. Then they could just collect the fish from on top of the water, they didn't have to dive down or bother with their nets. But the people in Europe found that the poison was inside their frozen fillets, so they banned all our fish and everybody's work was suspended all over again. Mama said the younger Mr Desai tried his best, but he had to suspend some jobs at Nile Perch Plastics because it was nearly a year before the people in Europe wanted to buy fish from our lake again. There were parties all over Mwanza when the lake came back to life.'

'You see, Angel, Joseph knew that the fishing industry was vulnerable. He was trying to plan ahead. It's just that he chose a bad plan.'

'Hmm.' Bibi does not sound sure.

'Just like Lovemore chose a bad plan in trying to run away to Rose and Agrippina instead of coming straight to you or straight to me. It was a bad plan, that's all.'

Lovemore looks at her feet. 'I'm sorry, Bibi.'

'*Eh*, Lovemore, please stop apologising! You are new in our family. How could you know for sure that you are safe here with us, that we will never push you away or put you out of our house? I hope you know that now?'

Lovemore manages another small smile. She does know that now. It feels good. It feels safe. The boulder that was inside her feels like a small rock now. Until now, she has thought that she will never tell, but now she wants to.

'Bibi, I have Uncle Joseph's socks.'

'His socks?'

'The socks with his money in. Mama left them for me with her journal. I have them.'

'With the money in?'

'Yes.'

'*Eh!*'

'Do you know how much it is?' It is Concilia who asks.

'Uh-uh. I didn't look. I didn't count. I only took some of it yesterday for my ticket to Mwanza. But nobody would let me buy a ticket, so I still have it all, except for what I gave the *bajaji* driver. I think it's a lot.'

'*Eh*, you are not like Grace! Grace would have bought every shoe in Dar es Salaam already.'

Lovemore manages to smile. 'Faith too. Moses and Daniel would have bought the National Stadium.'

'Benedict would have bought a farm,' says Concilia, 'or even the Serengeti National Park.'

Bibi begins to laugh. 'And he would have bought my business from me so that he could manage it. He would be my boss! Imagine!'

All of them are laughing quietly now, and Lovemore can almost forget that she has Uncle Joseph's money because those men shot him dead and she helped them to do it. And she can almost forget what Uncle Joseph did to get the money. Almost.

Back home at the Tungarazas' house, Bibi says that Lovemore deserves a treat to help her to relax, and she takes her into the washroom attached to Babu and Bibi's bedroom. It is like a washroom in a nice big house in Capri Point or on Msasani Peninsula, only without being shiny and new. It has a shower – a proper shower with hot and cold water that comes down on you from above – just like in the girls' washroom and the boys', and it also has a bathtub. Bending low over the tub, Bibi stops the hole with a plug that has been hanging on a chain, and she opens both taps. Lovemore notices that the taps are not gold, and she also notices that she does not mind that they are not.

Bibi goes into her bedroom and returns with a pink bottle. 'A lady gave me this,' she says, struggling to unscrew its lid, 'as a thank-you for a cake.' Lovemore helps her to get the lid off, and Bibi pours some of it where the taps are starting to fill the tub. 'I've been saving it for a treat.'

Hundreds of little white bubbles begin to form in the water, and a lovely perfume floats up and fills the washroom. Bibi opens the small window as the mirror above the washbasin begins to cloud over, then she bends and uses her hand to spread the bubbles along the full length of the tub, checking that the temperature of the water is right.

'This is where my Pius loves to relax, but not with bubbles and scent.' She smiles, and Lovemore smiles with her. 'When he comes home after being away, this bathtub is all that he wants.'

'I'm sure he wants you, too, Bibi! And the children.'

'Ah, yes. But here he can close the door and be alone.'

Lovemore knows how it is to want to close the door and be alone. Is that just because she grew up having her own bedroom back in Mwanza?

Or is it something she inherited from her babu before she even knew that he was her babu?

Titi brings Lovemore her towel from the girls' washroom, and Lovemore unwraps herself from Concilia's *kanga* and gives it to Titi for washing. She will wash her pantie herself as she does every evening. Bibi turns off the taps and they leave her alone, closing the washroom door.

Very carefully, Lovemore puts one foot into the tub and then the other, holding on to the side so that she does not slip in the bubbly water. She has never before stepped into a bathtub. Before coming to this house, she had never before washed in warm water. She stepped up from scooping cold water from a bucket in Mwanza to standing under a warm spray of water in the shower here in Dar es Salaam, and now she has stepped up into a bathtub, even without going all the way to New York, or even just as far as Msasani Peninsula. Gently, she lowers herself into the warm water, giggling as the bubbles tickle her skin. It feels so good! She scoots her buttocks forward a little and leans back, resting on her elbows so that the water can flood over her stomach and her budding chest. Then she shifts herself back, moving from side to side on her buttocks and elbows as if they are feet, until she can rest her head and shoulders against the end of the bathtub. There she lies, willing the warmth to seep into her and dissolve the small pebble that she can still feel inside her, willing the perfumed bubbles to wash away what Uncle Joseph did and what she did to him.

When she is at last out of the bath, Lovemore finds that Bibi has gone in the old red microbus to fetch Faith and the boys from school. Bibi lost time on her orders yesterday while she panicked about Lovemore and phoned almost everybody in Dar es Salaam to ask was she there, until Concilia phoned her to say that Lovemore was with her and that she was going to sleep over, and more time has been lost this morning at Concilia's. Feeling that she must do something to help Bibi to catch up, Lovemore has Titi show her how to sieve icing sugar and blend it little by little with soft butter, finally beating it hard to make sure that there are no lumps. Bibi can add the colours herself later.

Titi is slicing a large pineapple into neat round circles for when the children are home. She has already told Lovemore that this is

Lovemore's home, that this is Lovemore's family, that Lovemore does not need to run away. Now she tells her more.

'Me, I used to miss Mwanza. I missed it too much when I first came to live here with Grace and Benedict and Moses. *Eh*, for me it was too hot here!' She places the slices in a neat pattern on a large plate, then starts to peel a fat, heavy mango. 'I can be honest and say that I thought about just going back home to Mwanza.'

'But you stayed.' Lovemore pours some more of the Kilimanjaro Snow into the sieve.

'Yes. I am here.'

'Why? Why didn't you go?'

'Because what did I have there? My cousin. My two friends. That's all. Here I had this job and my room. Here I had the children. And, *eh*, the children needed me then! Their parents were back in Mwanza, their friends were back in Mwanza, their mama was in the hospital back in Mwanza. Here they had their grandparents, but everything was new for them. It was only me that wasn't new for them. Now what if I left them? Uh-uh.' She shakes her head as she adds slices of bright orange mango to the large plate of yellow pineapple. 'Auntie would have to get a new house girl, and that was going to be too much new for them.'

'You are very kind, Titi.'

Titi shrugs, rinsing the mango from her hands under the tap. 'Then after some few months, everybody needed me when the police came here looking for Uncle to tell him his son was shot dead in Mwanza.'

The sieve jerks in Lovemore's hand, sprinkling some icing sugar on to the counter top instead of into the bowl. 'My baba,' she says, 'only I didn't know it then.'

'*Eh*, it was a bad time! Uncle went to Mwanza for the body. Auntie went to pieces. Then they needed me when we all went to Morogoro for Mama-Grace's funeral.' Titi gets some milk out of the fridge. 'Me, I don't mind if they need me here. This is my home now. This is my family. And I do go back to Mwanza. When everybody goes to Bukoba they leave me in Mwanza for some holiday. I think this Christmas time they can leave us in Mwanza together.'

Lovemore stops beating the icing sugar and butter. 'You think?' She can spend time with Rose and Auntie Agrippina! And Lulu. Maybe

Rose can make a party so that Lovemore can see everybody from school again – even Katherine. She can visit Sigsbert and Philbert, though she does not know where they live now. Mama gave them Friends in Deed, so Lovemore can find them there. They will know where Pritty is working now.

Titi is measuring mugs of fresh milk and water into the big pot. 'You can visit me there at my cousin's house.' She stops measuring and smiles widely. 'There is no fence or gate there for us to look at each other through.'

Lovemore puts the bowl down on the counter top, her face suddenly hot. 'You remember me?'

'Yes.' Titi goes back to measuring. '*Eh*, now how many did I count?' She clicks her tongue against the back of her teeth.

'My mama—'

'No, you don't have to say. I know.' Titi gives up measuring and pours more milk straight into the pot.

'You know?'

'I didn't know then, but I guessed. I only did primary, but I know things from outside school. I know when a lady comes with a child and stands outside a house, she is saying something to somebody inside that house even if she is saying no words.'

Lovemore sighs. 'It wasn't nice, Titi.'

Titi shrugs again. 'Love can happen to anybody. It happened to me with Henry when we were in Swaziland, and Henry already had a wife.'

'Ah, Titi!'

'It can happen to anybody.' The hoot of the microbus sounds at the gate, making Tit's eyes suddenly wide. '*Eh!* We are not ready!' She turns from the pot next to the sink to the oven and back to the pot again, desperately wiping her hands on the kitchen cloth as she turns in circles.

'Go!' says Lovemore, giggling at Titi's sudden panic. 'I'll make the tea!'

Titi pulls on the piece of washing line and the door to the lounge flies open as she rushes through the house to go and open the gate.

When Lovemore opens her eyes, the room is quiet except for the soft sounds of somebody else's breathing. Not sure where she is, she lies still while her eyes adjust to the darkness. Slowly, the greyish crown of a mosquito net takes shape close above her, and she recognises that she is on the top bunk in Titi's room. She is still in the clothes she put on after her bath, and a thin blanket is covering her. She remembers Bibi coming home with the children from primary, and she remembers Grace coming home later from secondary with all the work that Lovemore missed – but nothing more. Reaching out a hand, she feels the shapes of her schoolbooks lying next to her.

She must have fallen asleep, and they decided not to wake her. Or maybe they tried to wake her, but they could not. She feels that she has been very deeply asleep. But for how long? Is it nearly morning? When she swallows, her throat feels dry.

Moving very slowly and quietly so as not to wake Titi, she battles silently through the folds of the mosquito net and climbs down the small wooden ladder. She turns to make sure that she has not left an opening in the net for any mosquitoes to go through and give Titi malaria, then she quietly eases open the door that leads into the kitchen. Bright moonlight through the uncurtained window shows her Titi's last round of dishwashing drying on the rack next to the sink. She takes a glass from there, and is turning to the fridge for the jug of boiled water, when she hears voices.

She stands completely still, listening. She hears her own name spoken in Bibi's voice, and then Babu speaks, his voice not quite as clear. A thin strip of light outlines the door into the lounge, the door that does not close properly because of its washing-line handle. Silently, she puts the glass down on the counter top and moves closer to the door.

'We need to get some kind of savings account for her, to keep her money safe. I can do that when I get home.' Babu is on speaker. Bibi must still be busy with her cake.

'You're right, Pius, it doesn't matter how the money came, it's her inheritance from her mama. *Eh*, Pius! I've just thought!'

'What?'

'That bomb that blew up the American embassy here, here in Dar es Salaam!'

'What, you are thinking our Joseph even contributed to that?'
'I don't know, Pius, but—'
'Stop it, Angel!' Babu's voice is firm. 'Bombs and guns are two different things entirely.'
'Yes, but the same kinds of people—'
'No! Don't let your mind take you to thinking even worse of our son than we have to. The facts alone are already bad enough, already enough of a shock.'
'You are right, Pius. But as much as it's a shock to us, think of the shock to Lovemore, especially thinking it's her fault.'
'No, no, it's not her fault. Surely she knows we don't think that?'
Hearing them say that to each other rather than to her, Lovemore does know it.
'I told her, but you must tell her, too. *Eh*, Pius, you are right. She is too young to read a journal with stories like that. Concilia suggested she should put it away until she's older. Can we not convince her to do that?'
'We can suggest it, Angel, but the decision is hers.'
'I know.'
Lovemore hears a sound like Babu is clicking his tongue against the back of his teeth, then there is silence. She wonders if the phone line has died. If that has happened, could Bibi come into the kitchen for a glass of water? Could Lovemore get back through the door into Titi's room in time for Bibi not to know that she has been listening to a private conversation?
The sound of a muffled sob reaches her through the small gap in the door.
'Ah, Angel, don't start again.'
Bibi sniffs loudly. 'Joseph! The son that we raised!'
'It's not—' Babu clears his throat. 'It's not how we raised him, Angel, not at all. We raised him with a very different set of rules.'
Lovemore's mind jumps to the list of Home Rules on the other side of the wall behind the fridge, and she remembers learning them by heart when she was trying not to see the flamingos on the screen. *Always be honest. Count your blessings. Bear each other's burdens. Forgive and forget. Be kind and tender hearted. Comfort one another.*

Keep your promises. Be supportive of one another. Be true to each other. Look after each other. Treat your friend like you treat yourself. Love one another deeply from the heart. Obviously Uncle Joseph failed to follow the first rule about being honest, but which of the others did he disobey? Lovemore is not sure – and she cannot think about it now, because Bibi is speaking.

'But we raised him, Pius. We raised him and he did that.'

'I know. Do you think I'm not feeling it like a machete through my heart? Do you think I'm not feeling it like an F on my student essay? *Eh*, Angel! And I'm far!'

'You are far.' Bibi blows her nose.

'I was far when Joseph was growing.'

'Yes.'

'He was six when I went to Germany for my Masters, twelve when I came back with my PhD.'

'You came nearly every year to see us, twice I even came to see you.'

'But he was twelve before I was a father to him, Angel.'

'You were far for your studies so you could get a better job, so you could provide better, so you could be a better father.'

'But I was far.'

'Yes.'

'And now I'm far again.'

'Yes.'

'And now there are six children with their father far.'

'Yes.' Bibi sighs.

'Angel, we must find another way.'

'Yes.'

'We need to be together as a family.'

'Yes.'

'But, *eh*, these short contracts are good money, money to put away for their future.'

'But it's the same again, Pius, it's you somewhere far so the children can benefit. Only now the children are your grandchildren and you are all these decades older.'

'We must find a way. Grace must get to university, for what I don't yet know. That girl is much more clever than she knows. And Lovemore needs plenty of study if she's going to practise law in New York.'

Listening in the kitchen, Lovemore feels dreadful. Bibi and Babu are apart because of her. The family used to go with him to where his work was when he had contracts for a year at a time. But now she is in their family, and she is just one too many. And Babu is working more, when he should be working less and preparing himself for his retirement, and that is because Lovemore wants her university fees paid so that she can be a lawyer in New York. It does not feel right.

'Benedict doesn't want university,' Bibi is saying, 'he's chosen a job with animals that doesn't need any degree.'

'That's what he thinks now, and really his marks aren't good. But sometimes when somebody finds what he loves to do, suddenly his marks can become excellent. I've seen that myself with students.'

'Moses and Daniel won't need university, they're both going to be David Beckham.'

Babu laughs. 'Those two!'

'Ibrahim says when I get my website, I can—'

'Don't say you can get even more business, Angel, you're already sitting up late into the night working on a cake. You're not a young girl any more!'

'*Hah!*'

Babu laughs. 'You know what I mean. What time is it there? Almost midnight?'

'Mm. And there?'

'Just before nine. I have an early breakfast meeting in the morning, I hope I can have a good night of sleep. *Eh*, this has been such a big news.'

'I couldn't sit with it inside me until you came home.'

'No, no, you were right to tell me now. I hate that I'm far.'

'Me too.'

'We'll have a long talk when I get home.'

'Yes.'

'I must try to sleep now. And you must get to bed soon.'

'Mm, I will.'

'Promise?'

'Promise.'

'Goodnight, Angel.'

'Goodnight, Pius.'

Lovemore worries that Bibi might want a glass of water now, but she wants a glass of water herself, so she does not want just to rush back to Titi's room. She moves quietly back to the door to Titi's room and waits near it. If Bibi comes into the kitchen, she can pretend that she has just come in herself.

After a few minutes, she goes to the fridge and pulls it open roughly so that the things inside it jangle.'

'Titi?' Bibi's voice calls from the lounge.

Closing the fridge, Lovemore picks up her still empty glass and goes towards the door into the lounge.

'Bibi?' Tugging on the washing-line handle, she pulls the door open. 'You're still busy?'

'Lovemore! You're awake! You were so fast asleep.' She smiles, but Lovemore can see that she has been crying.

'I need to drink water, Bibi, do you want some?'

'That will be nice. Thank you.'

Lovemore returns to the kitchen and comes back with two glasses of water, hooking a toe around the door to pull it open. She sits down at the table.

Bibi's cake is looking beautiful, its surface a smooth pale pink dotted with flowers in light purple, blue and white.

'Nearly finished,' says Bibi, moving the telephone-fax machine from the dining table back to its place next to the computer, and scooting the wire linking it to the phone jack out of the way. 'How are you feeling?'

Lovemore has not thought about it before Bibi's question. 'I'm tired,' she says, noticing that the boulder that was inside her is now as light as a few grains of sand.

'Yes. Concilia said you should expect that.' Bibi drinks some of her water, then she looks around at the crumpled tissues on the table top. Standing, she gathers them up. 'Let me just wash my hands before I continue.'

Lovemore decides not to ask about the tissues or the phone. Bibi must have had the phone on speaker so that she could work on her cake and talk to Babu at the same time. Maybe they do that often while Babu is away. Lovemore suddenly wishes that her mama could have met Bibi. They would have liked each other. They could have had conversations together while doing things with their hands. Mama could have been at the computer typing a document for somebody while Bibi was at the table turning sugar into flowers, and all the time they could have been talking or listening to news on the radio or paying attention to one of Auntie Agrippina's cassettes. Lovemore could have sat with them afterwards, practising her American accent.

But would she have wanted to? Would she have wanted to sound like an American? *Does* she want to? Is there really anything wrong with sounding like a Tanzanian? With sounding like Josephine Lovemore Lutabana Tungaraza?

Being a lawyer in New York was Uncle Joseph's idea for her – and she knows now that Uncle Joseph's ideas were not always good.

Back with clean hands, Bibi sits down at the table and begins to place more of the sugar flowers on the cake.

'Bibi, remember that you told me Uncle Joseph—'

'Your baba,' Bibi reminds her.

'*Eh*, I'm sorry!'

'*Sawa*. You're tired. It's okay.'

'You told me that my baba didn't want to go to university but you and Babu wanted him to go?'

'Especially your babu!'

'Yes, but then you said Babu understood that each bird must fly on its own wings.'

'Mm-hmm.'

'Bibi, how does a bird know when it's flying on its own wings?'

Bibi looks up from her cake, a lilac sugar flower poised delicately between a finger and a thumb. '*Eh*, I don't know. Is it even possible for a bird to fly on another's wings?'

Lovemore thinks about it, uncomfortable with talking about a bird. 'I don't know.'

Bibi places the flower in exactly the right place on the cake. 'I mean, maybe it *can* only fly with its own wings. Because how is it going to make another bird's wings work?'

'You mean it must stay on the ground? Without flying?' Lovemore tries hard not to think about the enormous marabou stork that ran after her all over the Nile Perch Plastics compound, but the harder she tries not to think about it, the clearer it is in her mind.

'I suppose. A bird is supposed to fly. Now how is it going to fly if it doesn't want to use the wings that God gave it?'

'I suppose.'

'But let us leave these questions for an educated somebody like your babu, or like Concilia. I'm not an educated somebody myself, and it's late and both of us are tired. Come round this side and help me to make this cake beautiful.'

Lovemore goes round to the other side of the table. 'It's beautiful already, Bibi.'

'Then let us make it more beautiful together.'

And that is what they do, taking turns to add beautiful pale flowers and green leaves until every piece looks like it is exactly where it should be. When they have finished, Lovemore feels like she and her mama have just finished putting a jigsaw puzzle together.

Chapter 14

In the morning, Angel would not allow herself to leave her bedroom and begin her day without first writing her list in her notebook. Last night had been the first night since beginning the habit that she had broken it. Really, at the end of such a day – the day when she had found out that her son had done something so much worse than cheating in his marriage and hiding his firstborn child from his parents – how could she possibly have climbed into bed and written about being grateful?

But this morning, after a night of shifting between light sleep and deep thought, her mind was just a tiny bit clearer. First of all, she was grateful to Concilia for being a safe place for Lovemore to go. Concilia was like a daughter to Angel, that was how good a friend she was. She was like family. But really, Concilia must stop believing that she was going to owe Angel for the rest of her life, simply because the first cake that Angel had ever made for Mama-Concilia had caused that particular effect. Many of Angel's cakes had caused effects. But Angel could not think about her cakes right now, because she had a list to write before the chaos of breakfast and getting the children to school began.

She wrote for number two that she was grateful that Pius had been in his hotel room in West Africa when she had phoned him last night. He could so easily have been out at a business dinner – and then what would Angel have done? She had needed very badly to share with him the shock and shame of why it was that their son had been shot dead in his house. Pius had been there, on the end of the line, and she could not give thanks enough for that.

She could not give thanks at all for Joseph – not right now. But she could write for number three that she was grateful that Grace, Benedict and Moses had already been safely here in Dar es Salaam before Joseph had begun his nonsense there in Mwanza. What if those men had gone to Joseph's house when the children had been there? How many more bodies would Pius have had to fetch from Mwanza? That thought sent a shudder right through Angel's body. Number four on her list was that she was grateful that Joseph had not been at Mama-Lovemore's house when Bismarck had taken those men there. What would Lovemore have witnessed then? Would Lovemore even be here, now? Angel shuddered again, and moved on quickly with her list.

Number five was that she was grateful to the police in Mwanza, because they had decided that robbers had been to blame, because they had never discovered the truth about who had shot Joseph dead and why. If people were to know the truth, the shame for the Tungaraza family would be too great to bear. Who in Africa would want to employ Pius as a consultant if they knew that his son had been involved in supplying guns for Africa's wars? Who would want to order cakes from the mother of a gun dealer?

But Angel had worried over these thoughts for most of the night already, and now she must stop, put them away in the drawer with her notebook, and take a few deep breaths before heading out of the bedroom and into a busy Friday morning.

On Saturday afternoon, Lovemore sits at the dining table with her geography textbook and the big box of pencil crayons in twenty-four colours that Moses got for his birthday turning eight. He would have preferred to get a new football, so it means nothing to him if somebody else wants to use his crayons.

Rain is pounding at the tightly shut windows, making the air inside feel heavy and much too warm. Lovemore has positioned the standing fan to blow cool air onto as much of the room as possible, sweeping round from Daniel and Moses who are watching sports on TV to just the edge of the dining table where Lovemore is working. She does not want the full force of it disturbing her papers.

She has printed out from the computer an outline map of the world, and she is trying to make sense of the chapter on climate in her geography book by putting the twelve different climate zone maps together.

In the book, the maps are just black-and-white drawings, and they are all on different pages. She wants to see them all together and in different colours, so that she can compare them and learn them properly.

She has already drawn the Equatorial regions as they appear in her book and coloured them in with red crayon, as well as the Hot Deserts, which she has made yellow, and the Cool Temperate Interior regions, which she has made pale green. Now she adds the Tropical Grassland regions (Savannah or Sudan type), choosing to do them in blue so as to make a nice purple where they overlap with the red of Equatorial. Where Tanzania is on the map is now almost entirely purple because of the bit of Equatorial red that spreads east from the Congo Basin into the western part of Tanzania, and the thin strip of Equatorial red down Tanzania's coast in the east. In the centre it is Tropical Grassland blue.

There is a sudden roar of applause from the TV, and Moses and Daniel leap up from the couch, Moses jumping up onto it and punching his fist into the air while Daniel pulls the front hem of his T-shirt up over his face and runs around the lounge bumping into things.

Moses shouts the word *goal* stretching it to make it last for many seconds.

'Yes! Yes!' The shout is loud from behind Daniel's T-shirt.

Lovemore reminds them that Titi is taking her nap and that Benedict is in bed with a bad cold, and just seconds later Benedict comes through the door from the bedrooms and tells them to keep quiet because they are in the lounge and not at the National Stadium.

Before Benedict goes back to his library book and his bed, Lovemore asks him to help her quickly in the kitchen. There she has him hold a small pot under the leak in the kitchen roof, just inside the back door, while she lifts the plastic bucket that has been collecting all the rain that has dripped through so far. She empties it out into the sink and then puts it back down on the floor. Benedict moves the pot aside, and they wait for the dull *plink* of a drop in the bucket to be sure that it is in the right place.

Then Benedict stands staring through the kitchen window into the rain-swept back yard. He does not look at all well.

'Are you worried about your vegetables?' Lovemore whispers, so as not to wake Titi on the other side of the door – though the rain itself is already more than loud enough to do that.

He nods sadly. 'And the crows.' He begins to sigh, but his sigh turns into a cough that sounds full of bubbles.

Lovemore feels sorry for him, standing there sick and burdened with worries for the whole family while Babu is away. 'Mr Kapufi won't be out killing them in the rain,' she tells him quietly.

'I suppose.' He manages a small smile.

For a few moments they stand there in silence, staring out of the window together.

At last Benedict speaks, his voice a whisper. 'You know, when I heard that you were coming, that I was getting a new sister, I wanted you to be somebody who likes birds and animals. Somebody like me.' He sigh-coughs again. 'It's only me who likes birds and animals here.'

Lovemore can feel his loneliness standing like another child between them. She wants so very much to reach out for his hand, but he has just coughed into it. 'I'm sorry,' she whispers.

He shakes his head quickly. 'No, it doesn't matter. You listen when I tell you things, you look when I have things to show.' He sniffs loudly, his nose sounding like it is badly clogged.

'You showed me how lovely butterflies are.'

'Yes.' He turns to her, a small smile playing across his dry lips. 'I'm glad you came, Lovemore. I'm glad you're here.'

'Me too,' she tells him. And she means it.

Then she surprises herself by taking a deep breath and asking him to help her to stop fearing birds – just the small ones – and by suggesting that maybe possibly perhaps he could one day take her to see the saved birds in Ibrahim's yard. Even as she makes the suggestion, she is not sure how much of it is about wanting to show some kindness to Benedict, how much of it is about facing her fears in the way that one of Auntie Agrippina's cassettes says to do, and how much of it is about creating an opportunity to see Ibrahim. But it does not matter what it is about, really, because the smile that Benedict turns to give her lights him up to the full extent possible for a face that is grey with illness and puffy with congestion.

They stand together watching the rain for a few more minutes before

Benedict breaks their silence.

'You mustn't run away again, Lovemore, see?'

'Okay.'

'Okay.'

Letting Benedict get back to his room, Lovemore gives the pot a quick rinse in the sink before resting it upside down on the dish rack while she reaches for the cloth. As she does so, she notices Bibi's shopping list on the counter top, and a word on it jumps out at her.

Fishcake.

Feeling a little shaky, she begins to dry the pot, trying not to let her mind go to fish. But her mind insists on going there, and Lovemore is suddenly back in Mwanza.

Mama is angry with her. She has graduated from Standard Five eleventh in her class even after all of the extra that Mama has sent her for. She has worked her absolute hardest, she really has, but still she has come only eleventh. The shame of it is eating at her. Eleventh is bad. Eleventh is not in the top ten, and Lovemore is always supposed to be in the top ten. Lawyers in New York are never eleventh.

'Do you want to be nothing in your life?'

'No, Mama.'

'Do you want to live like somebody who is uneducated?'

'No, Mama.'

'Like somebody who has nothing?'

'No, Mama.'

'Do you know what life is like for those people, Lovemore? Do you?'

'No, Mama.'

'People who don't even know that there is something called abundance. Do you know what their lives are like?'

'No, Mama.'

'Can you imagine?'

'No, Mama.'

'Then we are going to go and look. We are going to go and look at what kind of life is waiting for a girl outside of the top ten.'

Rain has already fallen earlier, and the sky is still heavy with more. They both squash on to a *bodaboda*, Mama sitting sideways on the back with one arm around the driver, and Lovemore uncomfortable between his legs, her hands next to his on the handlebars. Filled with shame for doing so badly, for disappointing Mama despite everything that Mama has done to help her, she cannot stop herself crying. While the wind in her face dries her tears before they can even fall, the noise of the engine covers the sound of her sobs. In no time at all, her feet in her nice sandals are covered in mud.

When they get off, the air is thick with smoke and a rotting smell that goes right down Lovemore's nose into her stomach, making it turn. Asking the driver to wait, Mama marches her through the mud towards endless rows of tall wooden stands. They look like bookshelves, only there are sticks instead of shelves and the upright parts are branches cut from trees without any tidying at all. Nearby is an enormous, untidy pile of what is left of Nile perches and tilapias after the factories have taken off everything that is useful: heads joined to tails by bones that are almost completely bare. Lovemore knows from Uncle Steven that the factory workers are supposed to take everything off, every tiny scrap of flesh, but it is not always possible, especially when they have to work very fast. What is left of the carcass is called the frame, and people wait outside the factories every day to buy the fish frames. Not every factory sells the frames to the people; Uncle Steven's does, but some send them away for grinding up into fishmeal for feeding to animals.

A boy dressed in rags is adding to the pile of fish frames, emptying them out of the back of his *trolli*, while a too-thin woman wrapped in a filthy old *kanga* loads some into a big plastic bowl and lifts it onto her head. Flies from the enormous pile of frames follow the bowl on the woman's head towards a row of wooden stands. Mama pulls Lovemore along behind the woman, holding a tissue over her own nose and mouth, leaving Lovemore to breathe in the filth and the stench. The boy with the *trolli* shouts, clapping his hands and running at a marabou stork that is interested in the pile of frames. Lovemore holds on to Mama, her stomach heaving.

They stand and watch as the woman puts the heavy plastic bowl from her head down in the mud and lifts the fish frames one at a time to balance each one across the sticks where already row after row of very old fish leftovers hang.

'To dry,' says Mama from behind her tissue.

Lovemore's stomach is heaving from the smell, and when she turns her head to the side to try to escape from the flies that are interested in her face, she sees a skinny, sick-looking dog lifting its leg and urinating onto the enormous pile of fish frames. Dropping to her knees in the mud, she bends and gags. The woman's bare feet are right near her face, the stinking mud oozing up between her toes like bad diarrhoea, and she sees that the fish frames in the woman's bowl are covered in fat little worms. When she heaves and vomits right at the woman's feet, the woman simply carries on with what she is doing, as if somebody vomiting right near her feet is no more disgusting than anything she is already dealing with, and when the woman bends to lift another worm-filled carcass, Lovemore sees that her eyes are as dead and as cold as the eyes that are rotting in the heads of the fish.

Mama helps Lovemore to stand, wiping her mouth with her tissue.

'*Bibi*, are you disturbing my workers?' A man with a machete is walking towards them. An ugly scar runs down the side of his face.

Mama greets him. '*Mambo, Bwana*. I have just brought my daughter to look at what kind of life will she have if she doesn't work hard at school.'

The man looks at Lovemore through red eyes, his scarred face swollen with beer like the faces of the fishermen Lovemore has seen around Walk on Water, Auntie Agrippina's bar.

'I see. That is a very good lesson. *Sivyo?*'

Lovemore does not want to look at him. 'Yes, *Bwana*.'

'*Sawa*. Here you can work for me drying. But if you want, you can smoke. *Tuende*. Come.'

Lovemore and Mama follow him through more mud, mud that sucks Lovemore down like the bottom of the lake sucks at Uncle Steven's late wife and baby. The man leads them back past the huge pile of fish frames where he shouts and shakes his machete at some marabou storks that are trying to make a meal of the rotting fish carcasses sprayed with dog's urine, past countless sets of shelves where he shouts at women who are hanging up frames to dry, and on to where other women with tired, weeping eyes look up at Lovemore through plumes of smoke as they kneel to poke at fires beneath long, low brick ovens covered with rusting strips of corrugated iron.

'You can come and work for me any time,' says the man. 'Even now.' He runs the back of a dirty finger down Lovemore's cheek, and she begins to cry, not just from the smoke.

'Let her try hard at school first, *Bwana*. If she fails, she can come here.'

'*Sawa, Bibi*. I am here.'

He shouts at the women then, and Mama takes Lovemore back to the *bodaboda*, where the driver is chewing on a fried fish head and trying to dodge the drops of rain that are beginning to fall. Lovemore's stomach heaves all the way home, some vomit dribbling down the front of her dress and pooling on her skirt where it rests between her legs. Shrinking back from the rain stinging her face, she feels the driver's chest and crotch much too close behind her.

Back home, they take turns to wash, first Lovemore and then Mama, soaping themselves all over and scooping cold water out of the big bucket in the washroom to clean it off. The mud comes off easily enough, but Lovemore feels it is going to be a long time before the smell of that place leaves her hair and her skin.

'Do you see now, Lovemore? Do you see how people have to live when they have no education?'

'Yes, Mama.'

'When they have no chance of any abundance?'

'Yes, Mama.'

'And so? Now that you see, what are you going to do?'

'Mama, I'm going to try harder at school.'

'And?'

'I'm going to be in the top ten.'

'Always?'

'Always, Mama.'

'Good girl.'

Mama holds her tight then, and Lovemore knows surer than sure that everything she has just said to her mama is true. She is going to work harder than anybody else at school because she is never going to have a job with rotting old fish leftovers here in Mwanza. She is going to be a lawyer in a nice clean office in New York. She is going to tell Rose about that place, too, because Rose has not come in the top ten either, she is number fifteen. Lawyers in New York are never number fifteen.

The next day Pritty fries some tilapia for their supper, and when Lovemore sees it on her plate, she cannot help seeing small fat worms crawling all over it, she cannot help smelling smoke and rot and decay coming up off it. Heaving over the toilet bowl, she knows that she is never going to be able to put any piece of fish into her mouth ever again.

Swallowing hard over the sink now, Lovemore finishes drying the pot that Benedict held under the leaking kitchen ceiling while she emptied out the plastic bucket. She helps herself to a small glass of water from the jug of boiled water in the fridge, opening and closing the fridge door gently and quietly so as not to make any noise that might wake Titi, and returns to her map.

Grace and Faith are at Prisca's party for her birthday turning fourteen.

It is perfectly safe for them to be there, because Dickson will definitely not be there with Prisca's brother. Not long ago, Prisca came to school bubbling with news.

'Oh my God! Scholastica!' she said, as a small group of girls gathered around her. 'Her sister Euphrasia has learned that the baby is a boy!'

'But how?' asked Magadalena. 'I mean, is the family not cut off?'

'Supposed to be, but somehow Euphrasia learned. The story has an aunt, the aunt's friend, then somebody's girlfriend,' Prisca's hands moved this way and that like she was a traffic police directing vehicles at a busy intersection, 'then a boy called Venance, and then his cousin, and then a girl called Margaret, then a Lillian, then a Gaudacia, then finally Euphrasia heard.'

'Eh!'

'No, save your *ehs!*' Prisca's eyes were bright. 'There is more! I told my brother—'

'He's the baby's father!' declared Fenella, and Prisca tried to silence her by placing a hand over Fenella's mouth.

'No! My brother told Dickson—'

'*Dickson* is the father!' said Mary.

Magdalena sucked in her breath. 'I *told* you!' She glanced around at all of them, a look of triumph on her face. 'Did I not tell you?'

'What did Dickson say,' Lovemore asked Prisca, 'when your brother told him it's a boy?'

'Well, now you can say your *ehs*, because now Dickson wants to look for Scholastica to see does her baby look like him!'

'*Eh!*' said all of the girls, including Prisca herself, and then most of them said *eh* again, some of them – including Grace – with their heads tilted sadly to one side.

'Only because it's a boy,' said Fenella, and all of them nodded in agreement, the girls with tilted heads straightening them quickly before joining in.

'Mm. But my brother said Dickson cannot just ask Baba-Scholastica where is she. Number one, Baba-Scholastica will refuse, and number two, he will kill Dickson for impregnating his daughter!'

'*Eh!*'

Ooh!'

'Uh-uh!'

'Now how is he going to find her,' asked Grace. 'It's impossible.'

'But when you are in love,' Lovemore told all of them, 'a mountain becomes a meadow.'

'Aah,' said most of them, some of them – including Grace – tilting their heads sadly to the side.

'Do you not remember, Grace? That was Babu's gift of wisdom for us from Ethiopia.'

'*Eh*, you listen to him?' Grace looked shocked. 'Enough to remember?'

'He says a lot of interesting things. Important things, too.'

Prisca interrupted them. 'My brother said Dickson is going to ask his geography *mwalimu* for help with knowing where do they grow pyrethrum, because in one of those fields he will find Scholastica with her baby on her back.'

Then all of the girls seemed to speak at once, new sentences beginning before old ones had even finished.

'Maybe he'll bring her here to be his wi—'

'*Eh*, but how will he take care of her and his baby with only his soda mon—'

'Exactly! And he's not yet done with school him—'

'But he doesn't love her! He's only going to see if it's his s—'

'Yes, when it could still be his daughter, he didn't care about finding Scho—'

'What will she do when Dickson finds her? I mean, what if she doesn't see that he doesn't lo—?'

'Ooh, who is advising her that side? Who is—'

'She can get an advice from Dear Auntie at *Fema* magaz—'

'But how is Dear Auntie going to find her out there in those pyrethrum fiel—'

'*Eh*, life is too complicated for her!'

'Too complicated!'

'*Eh!*'

'Ooh!'

'Uh-uh-uh.'

All the girls continued to talk about the story of Dickson and Scholastica at every possible moment throughout that day, and it was only later at home that Lovemore was able to speak to Grace about it alone in their bedroom.

'You see, Grace? Did I not tell you to save your love for a better kind of boy than Dickson?'

'Did you tell me?' Grace's thumbs were busy on the keypad of Mama's old phone, still sending the story to others.

'Be serious, Grace. This is important.'

'Just sending.'

Lovemore waited, thinking about how Uncle Joseph had loved her – loved her with all of his heart – without caring if she was a girl or a boy; about how complicated life must have been for her own mama; and about how Scholastica's mama had maybe wanted the whole world for her, but now all Scholastica had was pyrethrum and a baby. At last Grace put the phone aside and looked up.

'Grace, I don't want your life to be complicated like Scholastica's. I don't want your good brain rotting in a pyrethrum field.' Suddenly Scholastica's pyrethrum field looked to Lovemore exactly the same as the place for drying and smoking discarded fish frames in Mwanza, and the disgusting smell of smoke and rot hit the back of her throat. 'I want better than that for my sister.' The words came out of her like a sob.

'Ah, Lovemore,' Grace sighed, reaching for Lovemore's hand. 'I want better than that for myself. It was only that Dickson made my face feel hot.' Smiling a little sadly, she licked a finger and touched it to her cheek. '*Tsss!*'

Anyway, now Dickson is too busy with looking for Scholastica to go to Prisca's party for her birthday turning fourteen, so Faith has no need to be embarrassed about pretending to be Grace and inviting Dickson for supper. Bibi has dropped Grace and Faith at the party before going to visit a friend until it is time to collect them again. Bibi did not say which friend, so it could be Esther, the one who is always praying, or it could be Fatima, the one who dyes beautiful fabric for clothes, or it could be Irene, the one who also has her grandchildren in her home, or it could be Stella, the one with white hair who used to fall asleep here, though she has not done that for some time. But since Bibi won round two in the competition, she has had many new customers, and she has barely found a moment even to speak to any of her friends on the phone. Even now there is baking and decorating that Bibi should be doing instead of taking a break, so Lovemore is sure that the friend she has gone to see is probably Concilia, because Lovemore has given Bibi many worries to talk through with somebody.

Prisca invited Lovemore to her party, too, but Lovemore needs to catch up on her schoolwork instead, because missing two days of secondary is like missing two weeks of primary. There is so much to do!

She is also hoping that Rose will phone. It was Rose's turn last weekend, but last Saturday Rose was busy at Auntie Agrippina's party at Three Times A Lady Beauty Saloon, which Auntie Agrippina was re-launching after giving it a complete makeover, and last Sunday the power was down in this part of Dar es Salaam, and the telephone-fax at the Tungarazas' only works when the power is on, so Rose sent an SMS text message to Mama's old phone to say that she would have her turn again this weekend. Lovemore is looking forward to telling her that she almost came to see her when she ran away on Thursday, only nobody wanted to sell her a ticket.

She colours the Mediterranean regions orange, then chooses turquoise for the Cool Temperate Interior regions (Steppe type). There are small patches in South America and South Africa where her turquoise is going to overlap with whatever colour she chooses for Warm Temperate Eastern Coast Margin (China type), so she opts for pink which, with the turquoise, will make a different kind of purple overlap than the overlap of red and blue across Tanzania.

The sounds coming from the kitchen now tell her that Titi is up and making tea. When Titi emerges from there with five mugs on the old tin tray, Lovemore has only two more regions to colour in. Titi puts the tray on the dining table, and Lovemore clears her things out of the way so that nobody can spill anything on her map.

Daniel and Moses come to join them at the table, and Daniel shouts loudly for Benedict.

'*Eh*, switch off before he comes!' Moses rushes back for the remote. 'We don't want the story that power isn't free.'

'Quick!' says Daniel.

But Benedict, when he comes, does not look like he has any energy for bossing anybody. All three of the boys gulp their tea down quickly and go back to what they were doing, leaving Lovemore and Titi sipping slowly at the dining table.

Lovemore puts her mug down and steadies her stomach with both hands before she asks.

'Titi, what is fishcake?'

'Fishcake?'

'Mm. I saw it on Bibi's list in the kitchen.'

'Oh, that is where she plans our meals for the week. Probably she wants me to make fishcakes for when Uncle comes home. He loves the fishcakes that I make.'

Babu will be back from Burkina Faso in West Africa on Wednesday, and Lovemore is longing to see him. But not if it means fish. She makes a face, and Titi sees.

'*Eh!* Don't worry, you can't see that a fishcake used to be a fish! Nobody is going to make you eat it. I take some mashed Irish potatoes, and I mix in some onions chopped fine-fine and some small pieces of fish, fish that I already cooked before. Also some garlic, some salt, then

I beat an egg, sometimes two, and I mix everything together. Then I roll it into balls,' an invisible ball moves between her hands, 'and I make each ball flat.' She squashes the invisible ball between her two palms. 'Then I fry. I think I can make them for Uncle's lunch when you are at school. But if it's the evening, I can make without fish for you, just potatoes and onion.'

Lovemore smiles, relaxing her hands on her stomach. 'Thank you, Titi. *Asante.*'

'Uncle isn't going to mind if you eat at the coffee table. I can eat there with you. Me, I don't mind to have just potato cakes.'

'*Asante*, Titi.'

Titi shrugs her shoulders, smiling. 'Me, I don't mind.' She looks out of the window. 'Eh, this rain! What am I going to do about the washing?'

Lovemore is about to tell her some of the sentences she has learned from her geography book about the heavy rain in this region being usually convectional if the test question is about the Equatorial climate, or, if the test question is about the Tropical Grasslands climate, it's because of the prevailing on-shore trade winds and to do with the migration of the Doldrums belt, when the phone begins to ring.

She jumps up quickly to answer it.

'Lovemore!' says Rose.

'Ah! How are you?'

'Fine, my sister. Good. And you?'

Lovemore sits down on the chair at the computer table. 'Very fine. How are Auntie Agrippina and Uncle Steven?'

'Everybody is fine. How about all of yours?'

'Everybody is fine. Babu is away.'

'Still?'

'Yes. He was in Ivory Coast first and now Burkina Faso till Wednesday.' Lovemore's eyes drift up to the big map of Africa on the wall, hovering over the fat bulge of West Africa. 'You know what, Rose, this week I nearly—'

'Katherine wants to say hello.'

Lovemore says hello to Katherine, and finds out that everybody in Katherine's family is well. Then Rose is back on the line.

'Ah, Lovemore, you should be here with us!'

'I nearly came—'

Laughter bursts from Rose, and from Katherine, too, in the background. 'We're acting out all our teachers! Katherine can do *Mwalimu* Kilonzo perfectly, but my *Mwalimu* Shuma is the best.'

Lovemore does not know *Mwalimu* Kilonzo or *Mwalimu* Shuma. 'Our physics and chemistry teacher still needs a bra,' she tells them. '*Mwalimu* Masabo.'

'That man?' Rose reminds Katherine about Lovemore's science teacher, and both girls in Mwanza laugh.

Lovemore smiles, but she is not in the mood for laughing with Rose and Katherine over the phone. She wants Rose to be there alone, listening to Lovemore's story about running away. Lovemore cannot tell Rose why. Of course not. She has not even told Grace or Faith or Titi or any of the boys. It has to be a secret between her, Concilia, Bibi and Babu, because nobody must know that she is the daughter of a man who was helping with wars, and Grace, Benedict and Moses do not need to know that about their baba.

Titi takes the tray of empty mugs into the kitchen, leaving Lovemore to talk and giggle with Rose and Katherine about silly things, things that mean nothing, until Lovemore lies about having to go because her Bibi is calling her.

When they have said their goodbyes, Lovemore sits quietly in front of the blank screen of the computer. What if somebody had let her buy a ticket, and she had gone to Mwanza? How would that have been? She would have used some of the dollars from Uncle Joseph's socks or some of the Tanzanian shillings from her purse to take a taxi from the airport, past Highway of Holiness church, past the turn-off to Nile Perch Plastics, past Friends in Need, all the way to Auntie Agrippina's house. All of them would have been excited to see her at first. Auntie Agrippina would have squashed her in a big embrace, and Rose would have jumped up and down squealing with delight.

They would have talked without stopping for maybe an hour or two, and then what? Their lives are so different now. They are at different schools in different cities, and the easy everydayness of their friendship has been lost. She and Rose are always going to be friends, but they are further apart now than just the distance between Mwanza and Dar es Salaam.

With a sadness in her heart, Lovemore goes back to her map and her colours.

Just as she promised, Concilia takes Lovemore to the university to photocopy part of her mama's journal for Bibi, the part about what Uncle Joseph did that made somebody shoot him dead. Compared to Mwanza, which is bumpy with hills and boulders, Dar appears to be smooth and flat with only one hill. The university sits on top of it, and Concilia drives Lovemore all the way up, pointing out places that Babu must know well.

Babu did his first degree not here but at Makerere University in Uganda, and then he went to Germany for his Masters, staying there even longer until he could come back as Dr Tungaraza. Lovemore knew all that even before she knew that Dr Tungaraza was her babu, because Uncle Joseph always used to boast about him. During all of Babu's time away in Germany, Bibi stayed in their home town of Bukoba on the western edge of Lake Victoria, where their families could help her with raising the two children, Joseph and Vinas. They moved to Dar together when Babu got his job at this university. Maybe they even started out in one of the staff quarters that Concilia is pointing out.

After they park, Concilia removes a nice new five hundred Tanzanian shilling note from her purse and gives it to Lovemore. 'Here. See if you can find this building.'

On one side of the pale green note is a dark green buffalo. Lovemore turns it over. The building pictured there has a huge, gently curved arch at the front, with another arch like it around either side of the front. The rounded roof curves over each of the arches, looking like a small cluster of enormous bubbles. There is also a big green snake curling itself around a pole, and there is a background pattern of dhows. The building itself is very unusual. Flattening the note against Mama's journal, she looks around her. She cannot see the building anywhere.

'Where is it?'

'You find it. But don't go too fast, don't leave me behind.'

Lovemore enjoys exploring, finding her way around the campus where she is going to be a student one day. She feels excited enough to run, but she knows she must not. Every time she turns round, there is Concilia a few metres behind her, leaning heavily on her stick and laughing. At last she finds the building, exactly like it is in its picture on the banknote.

'This is Nkrumah Hall, named after Kwame Nkrumah who led Ghana to independence. He was a big believer in pan-Africanism, so I'm sure you can guess who holds him as a hero?'

'My babu?'

'Mm. *Mwalimu* Julius Nyerere opened this building himself. Who knows? Maybe your babu was here back then to see it happen.'

They do their photocopying in an office at the health centre, and then they head to where Concilia wants to show Lovemore the view of the city from the top of the hill. Lovemore can see a white-haired lady already there with a man in a wheelchair, and as they get nearer she recognises the lady as Bibi's friend Stella.

Concilia and Stella greet each other warmly, then Stella introduces both of them to Mr Chiza, the elderly man in the chair.

'I've brought a group,' Stella tells them, looking much more alive than she ever did when she was sitting fast asleep on the couch at the Tungarazas'. 'We are six today.'

'That is very good,' says Concilia, smiling. 'Are you enjoying the views?'

'Yes! Yes!' Mr Chiza tells them, his eyes twinkling like the stars reflected in Lake Victoria. 'I haven't been to this campus since my days as a student! *Eh*, I feel young again being back here today!'

Four others join them, all of them elderly, two of them slightly bent over sticks, and Stella introduces them.

'We were just saying, Stella,' one of the ladies says, her voice sounding frail, 'what a breath of fresh air you have brought into our lives.'

Stella gives them all a very big smile. 'Ah, no, actual—'

'Absolutely. It is too good to get out like this,' says one of the men, 'out of the house.'

'Out from under our families' feet,' adds the lady with the frail voice.

'And always such an interesting outing,' one of them tells Concilia and Lovemore. 'Places nobody thinks to take us.'

'*Eh*, is Stella not *stellar*?' asks Mr Chiza, joining in as everybody laughs at his joke.

Stella's smile looks very much like the smile of a girl in love as she pushes Mr Chiza's chair and leads her group away from the view.

Concilia watches them go, her smile very wide, before she turns to show Lovemore the view.

'You see? You can see all the way to the Indian Ocean. Have you put your feet into it yet?'

'In the sea?' Lovemore feels a shiver running all the way down her body.

'You don't want to?'

'Uh-uh. It's got fish in it.'

Concilia laughs. 'And sharks! How about the lake? Did you go in there?'

'Uh-uh. It's got snails and worms.' Lovemore swallows hard. 'And fish.'

'Ah, I know what you need! Come!' Concilia leads her to a gateway in a wall, where they can see a big swimming pool full of clear water, bigger than the swimming pool at Tilapia Hotel back in Mwanza, probably even bigger than the pools at the nice big houses in Capri Point.

'*Eh*! It's beautiful.'

'I'm sure there are pools more beautiful in New York.'

Lovemore sighs, feeling tired at the very idea of New York.

'Do you know swimming?' Concilia asks her.

'Uh-uh. How about you?' The question is out before Lovemore even has time to think. Can a polio swim?

Concilia does not seem to mind. 'I used to love it! I was always in this pool. But let us not pay to go in just to cool our feet. Let us find some shade to sit in. I have water for us.'

They find a shady place to sit on the ledge around the base of a sculpture of unusually tall people put together from metal pieces, and drink their water in silence, watching the students come and go. After a while, Lovemore realises that she has stopped thinking about herself one day being one of those students and has started to think about something else.

'Concilia?'

'Mm?'

'Your cake … the one that Bibi made for you …'

'The deaf alphabet?' One of her hands begins to shape a letter.

'Uh-uh, the one that makes you feel you owe Bibi something.'

'Ah, that wasn't for me, it was for my mother.'

'What was it?'

'Well, it wasn't the most beautiful cake your bibi ever made, but it was the first of her cakes that I ever saw, so I thought it was wonderful.'

Lovemore thinks back to the first of Bibi's cakes that she ever saw, the beautiful orange heart that said WELCOME LOVEMORE in yellow letters.

She asks again. 'What was it?'

'Ah, you know that your bibi's cakes always come with a story?' Lovemore knows. She nods her head yes. 'So I have to tell you the story first. I have a brother, younger than me, very clever. A bit like your babu. Anyway, after his degree here, he was chosen for a scholarship in England for his Master's.'

'A lot of congratulations to him.' Lovemore is going to be chosen for a scholarship too, she is going to make sure of it. That way her babu will not need to pay.

'Thank you! So off he went, and my parents always understood that he was going to come back here and work in finance. Finance is in our family, both of my parents are executives in banking. Anyway, while he was in England, he fell in love.'

'Ah, that's nice.'

'Yes. But my parents never liked the girl, they couldn't accept her.'

'No?'

'She's a Chinese.'

'A Chinese?'

'Mm, from Hong Kong. And after his Master's my brother went to Hong Kong with her, to work there. That made my mother hate her even more, because she took her son far away from here, away from *her*.'

Sipping her water from the plastic bottle, Lovemore thinks how determined her own mama used to be that Lovemore must marry a man far away from here.

'And my father wasn't impressed because she wasn't in finance, her Master's was in languages. So then my brother said he was going to marry her, he was going to bring her home for an engagement party with all his friends and family. The wedding was going to be with her family in Hong Kong, so my mother couldn't even organise it.'

'But she didn't like that girl. Why would she want to organise the wedding?'

'Ah, Lovemore, wait until you are a mother yourself, then you will know that mothers always want to organise the wedding. Ask your bibi. Your bibi organised Joseph's wedding here in Dar, but Vinas's wedding was far away in Arusha, and the groom's family did everything. Even the cake!'

'Even the cake? *Eh!*'

'I know! I think that upset your bibi more than it upset her that the man just wasn't right for her daughter.'

'I'm sure that cake wasn't good.'

'Ooh, ask her to tell you!' Concilia laughs. 'Anyway, my mother said she would organise the engagement party, and then of course she had to have a cake. She asked around and heard that Angel Tungaraza was the person to go to.' Lovemore finds herself smiling, proud to belong with Angel Tungaraza. 'So she went to your bibi, and your bibi gave her tea and listened to the story about the Chinese and the languages and the picture of my brother's life just not looking how it was supposed to. My mother didn't know how the cake should look, so she left that up to your bibi.'

Lovemore's bibi always knows exactly how a cake should look. 'What did she make?'

'Ah, it was perfect! It was a pile of different shapes in different colours.' Lovemore closes her eyes, trying to see it. 'Triangles, squares, balls, stars, oblongs, every kind of shape. Blues, greens, yellows, oranges, purples – you name it. Clear colours, but not bright. Not pale, though. And sitting on top of that jumbled pile of shapes was a big red heart, such a bright red that it was all you saw. It was only when you went to look carefully that you noticed all the other shapes under and around it. The story of the cake was that none of the other shapes and colours mattered because love was more important than anything. And you know what, just for that night, just for that party, that was how everybody felt. Apparently my father even said that in his speech.'

Lovemore is about to drink some more of her water, but the word *apparently* stops her. 'You weren't there? At the party?'

Looking uncomfortable, Concilia shifts her weight on the ledge. 'I was there for a short while, just for a bit. You see … the thing is, I was one of those shapes, those other shapes that my family didn't approve of.'

How could that be? 'Because you weren't in finance?'

'Ah, no.' Tipping the plastic bottle back, Concilia drinks the last of her water.

'Is it … Concilia, is it because …' Lovemore does not want to say the word *polio*. She finds a way to dance around it instead. 'Is it because you need a stick?'

Concilia smiles. 'In a way, I suppose it is. Let me tell you the rest of the story about your bibi's cake. Come, walk with me.' They walk slowly, Lovemore clutching her mama's journal to her chest, with the big brown envelope containing the photocopied pages sticking out. 'You see, before that cake, my family hadn't spoken to me for a long time.'

'*Eh!*' But Concilia is so easy to talk to!

'They used to be proud of me, even though I wasn't interested in finance. I did very well here, here on this campus, and they let me follow my dream of going to Cape Town in South Africa for my Master's. I graduated there with a distinction.'

'Ah, a lot of congratulations!'

'Thank you! But then I disappointed them. I didn't come back, I stayed there to work. You see, part of my parents' problem with my brother was that he was disappointing them in exactly the way that I had already disappointed them. Lovemore, let us go a different way, there are too many steps here.'

'Okay. Do you mean you fell in love?'

'Yes!'

'He was a Chinese?'

Concilia laughs, but her laugh does not sound happy. 'Even worse! He was a *she*.'

'What?' Lovemore is not sure exactly what Concilia is saying.

'Ah, Lovemore, I am not the kind of woman who wants a boyfriend.' Glancing around her, Concilia drops her voice. 'The truth is that I am a lesbian.' Concilia uses the word that others would dance around. 'In fact I met a girl even before I went to Cape Town. There was a conference here in my final year, it was for post-graduate students from all over Africa, and she was here for it. She was near the end of her Master's, and she encouraged me to go for my Master's in Cape Town so we could be together.'

'You loved each other?'

'Yes. People here don't understand it, they don't like it, they don't allow it. It's a kind of different that isn't accepted here, not in our courts, not in our churches.' Concilia shakes her head. 'Girls loving girls is a kind of love that Tanzanians cannot accommodate in their hearts. But that girl told me it wasn't like that in South Africa. All the old apartheid laws there that used to tell you who you could love and who could love you, those laws were gone. Now anybody was welcome to love anybody, even to marry anybody. So I went and I did my Master's, and all the time we were falling more and more in love. After I qualified and started working, we found a place and moved in together. Lovemore, here is some nice shade, let us sit.'

They sit, and Lovemore tries to imagine telling her own mama that she was going to marry a girl instead of a boy. Mama would definitely rather be late. 'Was it worse for your mother than your brother's Chinese?'

'Ooh, I didn't tell my mother! I told nobody here! Here people cannot accept it!'

Lovemore knows about girls liking girls. It is on TV. But it does not happen here. Not in Tanzania.

'Your mother found out?'

'Yes.' Concilia looks in her big handbag. 'I have more waters. Would you like one?'

It is very hot, but Lovemore is fine. She shakes her head no. 'Thank you. Who told her?'

'Ah. Well.' Concilia sighs, hesitates. 'To tell you that I would need to tell you a part of my story that is very hard. I think it is too hard for a girl who is only thirteen.'

Lovemore sits a little straighter to make herself look taller, older. 'Is it hard like my baba's story?'

'Ooh, no!' Concilia's eyebrows shoot up and she reaches for Lovemore's hand. 'Not as hard as that. No. Nobody died.'

'Then tell me, Concilia. Please.'

Concilia sighs, silent for a few moments while she thinks. 'Well, okay. I mean, you may as well get used to hard stories if you're going to be a lawyer in New York.'

Is Lovemore really going to be a lawyer in New York? She is a lot less comfortable with the idea than she used to be. But still she wants to hear Concilia's story.

'Tell me.'

'Okay.' Concilia takes a deep breath before she begins. 'Well, it turned out that being welcome to love anybody in South Africa was only words on a page, words in their new constitution. But words on a page don't always change how things are, Lovemore, that is something you will have to know as a lawyer. Sometimes words on a page are just words on a page. There are men in Cape Town who don't like women to love each other. It makes them feel unnecessary. And, *eh*, men don't like to feel unnecessary! Anyway, one night a group of men who felt unnecessary got together, and after some beers they decided they wanted to teach us about what we were missing by not liking men. They came and attacked us in our home.'

Lovemore clutches Concilia's arm, her heart beginning to beat faster. It is like a story on TV. 'They … they …?'

'They raped us. All of them.' Concilia drinks some water then dabs her lips with a tissue. 'All of them. And both of us.'

Tears come to Lovemore's eyes, and she searches for a tissue in the pocket of her jeans. Before she can find one, Concilia gives her one from inside her big handbag.

'It's not something to cry about, Lovemore. Not any more. After some time, somebody helped me to see that I wasn't a victim, I was a survivor, and after some more time I learned to stop calling myself a survivor because calling myself a survivor still said who I was in terms of what they did to me. Now what they did to me is just something they did to me, it's not who I am. Though I can't forget it, because the weight of them did this to me, too,' she pats her left thigh, 'broke my pelvis, messed up my hip.'

So it is Concilia in the photos on Mama-Concilia's wall, winning a running race, standing without a stick. Concilia was never a polio like *Mwalimu Mkuu* Makubi at Lovemore's school back in Mwanza.

Concilia pats her thigh again. 'But this is not what they intended. What they intended was to make us think that being with a man was really nice, that we had been mistaken to love each other, that we had loved each other simply because we were ignorant of how nice it is to love a man.'

Lovemore shakes her head slowly, trying to imagine a man attacking her like that to make her see that a man is nice. Maybe afterwards she would rather choose to fall in love with a girl instead. But her mind races quickly around the girls at school, and she cannot imagine falling in love with a girl instead of a boy. She cannot imagine wanting to kiss a girl. No, if a man did that to her, maybe she would rather just choose to be by herself.

'There are men who think like that, especially around Cape Town. They think that girls who love girls are doing wrong and need to be corrected. Those men tried to correct us through violence. But, really, they could have tried any other means and still we would be the same. We didn't choose it. It's not how we choose to behave, it's how we were born. They couldn't correct me, but I have to thank them because they gave me the subject for my doctoral studies. My thesis is about corrective rape. I'm going to be known as an expert in that subject.'

Lovemore's response is automatic, and it comes with no joy at all in her voice. 'A lot of congratulations.'

'Thank you!'

'But your girlfriend, Concilia …'

'Ah, our love couldn't survive it. It was too much. After it happened, an ambulance took us both to the hospital, and the hospital found out my next of kin from the university. They phoned my mother and immediately she flew to Cape Town. I was in surgery when she came, so the police told her what had happened. She didn't want to meet my girlfriend. She left as soon as she knew I was going to be okay. Really,

I think she thought I got what I deserved.'

Lovemore's mind goes to Miss Brown's poem about the cold within, and an image comes to her of Mama-Concilia holding on to her log of wood and refusing to add it to the fire to save Concilia from the cold without. Concilia herself is not like that at all. Concilia would add her own log to save absolutely anybody.

'Anyway, I registered for my doctorate and I did my fieldwork research, but after some time I came to realise it was too hard being in Cape Town after everything that had happened, so I came back home to finish my doctorate here by distance. My mother wouldn't let me into her house so I stayed with a friend.'

'A girlfriend?'

'No! Here that could put me in jail.'

'But that's not fair!'

'Ah, Lovemore, the world is not a fair place. And you should be glad of that, because if everything in the world was fair there would be no need of lawyers and you would be out of a goal.'

Lovemore considers that. 'I suppose.'

'But let me finish the story of your bibi's cake.'

'Oh, yes.' Lovemore has almost forgotten about the cake.

'For the longest time I never heard from my mother or my father. I kept in touch with my brother, and I learned from him that our father had transferred to a bank in Dodoma but our mother hadn't transferred with him. My brother was sure that there was trouble between them because of his Chinese, and I didn't want to tell him I was sure it was because of me, because I didn't want to tell him about me. I was afraid that he wouldn't accept it, and I didn't want to lose him too. Then he was going to bring his Chinese here for their engagement party, and I knew our mother wasn't going to invite me to that, so I made up some excuse about his party and I said I would see him and his fiancée the next day. But, you know what? When our mother collected the cake from your bibi, and when she heard the story that the cake told, she phoned me and she said I could come to the party! But only for a little while, and I mustn't let my father see me because he just couldn't accept who I was.

'So that cake brought a kind of peace between my mother and me, and after that we met and talked, and she said I still wasn't welcome to stay in her house but she was going to build a small house for me in her back yard, and she also helped me to buy my car. Of course I had to go and thank this Angel Tungaraza who had made that cake!'

'My bibi!' Pride swells in Lovemore's chest.

'Yes. She was a new mama then to Faith and Daniel, though Grace, Benedict and Moses had already been with her for some time. And now she's a new mama to you!'

Lovemore does not feel like Concilia needs to be corrected. Bibi *is* a new mama to Lovemore, though she is not Mama.

'In a way, I felt like she was a new mama to *me*. She didn't reject me like my own mama did, she already knew about girls like me from her travels to Germany when your babu was studying there. We started to become friends, but very soon the family went off to Rwanda. When they were back for a very short time before going off to Swaziland, we fell straight back into talking like it was only the day before that we had seen each other. I was so happy when she came back here to stay! Sometimes I wish she could really be my mama.'

'You would be my big sister.' Lovemore smiles at the idea.

'Yes! Just not your auntie, see? I don't want to feel old.'

Laughing together, they get up to walk again, making their way slowly back towards the car. Lovemore remembers Bibi telling her to ask Concilia what it means that a bird must fly on its own wings, and Concilia says it means that you must do what it is you were born to do; you must be who you were born to be.

'Like me,' Concilia says. 'The way I was born, I like girls. I can't change that. I can *pretend* to like boys, I can even marry a boy to try to make my mother accept me, to try to make my church accept me. But I will know, and God will know, that those are not the wings He gave me. It will make many people very unhappy, not just me.'

Lovemore can see that it is important to be who you are. 'But how do you know what work it is that you were born to do?'

'Ah, that can take some time, and you are still young to know that for sure. You can still change your mind, many times. There's another saying that I like. Do you know Albert Einstein?' Lovemore shakes her head no. 'Old *Mzungu* with a big moustache and crazy hair. Bad hair. Really, he needed some braids or at least a good treatment. You can find a picture of him on the computer. Anyway, he was a very famous scientist. He said that everybody is a genius, but if we're going to judge a fish by how well it can climb a tree, that fish is going to live its whole life believing that it's stupid. Lovemore, what is that face for?'

'Sorry, Concilia. I don't like thinking about fish.'

'Okay, let's change it. Let's say ... let's say that if we are going to judge an elephant by how well it can play a guitar, that elephant is going to live its whole life believing that it's stupid. I can see by your face that that is better.'

Lovemore is smiling now. 'An elephant is not made to play a guitar!'

'Exactly! But is that elephant stupid? No! It's simply doing something that isn't right for it. Probably somebody has given it a guitar, or somebody has told it that guitarists have a very good life.'

'But the guitar is not right for the elephant.'

'Not right at all.' They are at the car now, and Concilia is digging in her large handbag for the keys. 'Now, if somebody had given the elephant a *piano*...'

Lovemore giggles at the idea of an elephant trying to play a piano with its huge feet. Then an idea comes to her. 'They should have given it a trumpet!'

'You see? Now you understand what that man with the bad hair was talking about!'

All the way back down the hill, they giggle about the idea of an elephant trying to play a violin or a marimba or a *zezi* or a *kinubi*, and in between giggles, Lovemore thinks about what music she is built to play herself. Is she really made for being a lawyer in New York, or was that just another of Uncle Joseph's bad ideas? Is she going to fail at it and spend her life thinking that she is stupid like an elephant that was never supposed to be able to play a guitar? She is glad that she is giggling with Concilia, because she does not want to think about it too much right now. Already it feels like she has borrowed a jigsaw puzzle from the Indian ladies' toy library, a puzzle that she knows well because she has put it together over and over again, but somebody has swapped some of it with pieces from another puzzle and it is simply not possible for her to make that same familiar picture again.

Giggling with Concilia is much better than thinking about how uncomfortable that feels.

Chapter 15

WHEN BABU gets back from Ouagadougou in Burkina Faso, he is much happier than he sounded on the phone all the way through his time in Ivory Coast. In Ouagadougou he attended something pan-African, and anything pan-African excites him because it brings all the countries in Africa together. This was a conference that ran alongside an exhibition and market of all the traditional crafts from Africa's different countries. There was leatherwork from Morocco, basketwork from Namibia, beadwork from South Africa, cloth from Ghana, soapstone carving from Zimbabwe, and just about every kind of beautiful thing you could imagine from just about every country on the big map of Africa on the wall above Babu's desk, except for the countries that are too busy with war. Grace and Faith are not happy that with all those lovely things to buy, Babu has brought them only a piece of wisdom. But Lovemore does not mind.

'In Burkina Faso,' he tells them, 'this is what they say. If somebody washes your back, you yourself should wash your stomach.'

'What does it mean, Baba?'

'You tell me, Faith. Now that you are wearing glasses, you should be able to see if you just take the time to look.'

'Aah, Baba!'

'Think for a moment, Faith.'

Lovemore thinks that she understands. 'Babu?'

'Mm?'

'Does it mean that you mustn't just depend on others to help you, you must also help yourself?'

'Yes! Exactly! Give this girl a medal!'

Smiling very widely, Lovemore sits up a little straighter.

'That is your kind of wisdom, Pius. You don't want all these countries in Africa to depend on aid from outside.'

'Not if they're doing nothing to help themselves, Angel. Soon they will forget how to wash their own stomachs.

'And Ivory coast?' asks Grace.

'Côte d'Ivoire,' Babu corrects her.

'What do they say there?'

'Ah. Now. In Côte d'Ivoire they say that the death of an old man is like a library burning down.'

That is an easy one for everybody to understand, even Faith. They all sit nodding in agreement until Benedict speaks up.

'But not every old man, Baba, not Mr Kapufi on the other side of the wall.'

'Is he still upsetting you?' Benedict nods his head yes. 'But you know that those crows are pests, killing everything. You know that by getting rid of crows Mr Kapufi is helping to save all our other species, just like Baba-Ibrahim.'

'But …' Benedict's face looks a bit like Lovemore's used to when she wanted so very much to understand one of Auntie Agrippina's cassettes but she was still too small.

'Ah,' says Babu, looking carefully at Benedict. 'I think this is a problem about understanding means and ends. But these things can be difficult to explain, and now is not the time. For now let me simply ask you this. Is killing crows the only thing you know about Mr Kapufi?' Benedict nods his head yes. 'You don't know what work he did before retiring?' Benedict shakes his head no. 'You don't know if he went to university or what he studied there?' Benedict's head continues to shake. 'Then how do you know what kind of library he carries in his head? How do you know what knowledge will be lost when he is late?'

'Pius, please, let us not talk about old men becoming late. Tell us rather about your work in that country.'

'Ah, that was even sadder than old men becoming late, that was about children being slaves.' Shaking his head, Babu clicks his tongue against the back of his teeth. Everybody does the same, until Benedict speaks up.

'You were buying child slaves to save them Baba? Like the Holy Ghost Fathers in Bagamoyo?'

Babu smiles sadly. 'No, no. But I was helping to organise schooling for the children who lost their childhoods when they became slaves on the cocoa plantations of Côte d'Ivoire. Maybe there are as many as half a million of them, some even from across the border in Burkina Faso or Mali. Many of them were sold to traffickers, others were sold direct to the farmers from families who are living in poverty.

'You're not going to sell us, Baba?' Moses clings on to Daniel.

'Don't be silly,' Benedict tells them. 'We're not living in poverty.'

Lovemore remembers what she thought when she first came here to this broken house in the rusty, cracked old microbus.

'First I would sell my kidney,' says Babu, 'and ever other possible organ. No child of mine is ever going to do work like that, cutting down cocoa pods with sharp machetes, then slicing the pods open in their bare hands,' Babu makes his open left hand look like it is holding something big and fat, while his right hand hits down upon it with an invisible machete. 'Carrying back-breaking loads day after day, working as many as a hundred hours every week, for no money, just a little bit of food to keep them going. Endlessly getting the seeds out of the pods for processing into chocolate, chocolate that they don't even know exists.'

Lovemore does not want to ask, but she has to. 'Are they in chains, Babu?'

'Uh-uh! And maybe it is worse that they're not!'

'Pius, what are you saying?'

'I'm saying that they don't even know that they're slaves, they don't seem to think that anything is wrong with the way they live. Angel, they just don't know anything else! They don't know that it's not normal to spend their lives doing heavy labour for no reward. Many have been working like that for many years, they started when they were small and they're still children today. It's all they know. To them, there's nothing wrong, there's no injustice in their lives. It's simply normal.' Babu shrugs his shoulders, raising both hands in the air, palms up. 'Even the farmers think there's nothing wrong, they're happy to show any visitor their child slaves at work. If those slaves were in chains, surely they would try to break free!'

'Babu, I think they *are* in chains.' Lovemore is feeling the same way that she felt on the beach at Bagamoyo, where people in chains laid down their hearts before walking across the water to the boats. 'Chains they cannot see.'

'You are right, Lovemore.' Shaking his head again, Babu clicks his tongue against the back of his teeth some more.

'Tell us the good part, Pius.'

'Ah. Yes.' Babu straightens his back a little. 'The good part is that a protocol was signed by everybody in the cocoa industry last year to put an end to child slavery in the industry within five years. Not that any farmer I spoke to has ever heard about that protocol, let alone signed it. Anyway, I was helping an organisation that aims to prepare those child slaves for their freedom by giving them some schooling. *Eh*, there is so much work to be done!'

'Thank you for helping them, Babu.'

'Ah, Lovemore.'

'It isn't fair, Babu, it isn't right!' Something is welling up inside Lovemore, but she does not yet know what it is. Anger? Pain? Maybe it is both.

'I think we have a lawyer in the house!' declares Babu, just as his mobile phone begins to ring. Looking at its small screen, he excuses himself and goes through the door leading to the bedrooms to take the call.

Lovemore decides on another law that she and Rose will make when they are lawyers – *if* they are lawyers – a law saying that chocolate made from cocoa on farms where children are slaves must say *Made by Child Slaves* on its wrapper. But she is not entirely sure that she will remember to tell Rose to add it to their list, because her eyes are on the door leading through to the bedrooms and she is feeling very concerned for Babu. He has not yet spent any time in his bedroom – he just went to use the washroom very quickly after the taxi brought him home – but Lovemore knows that if he sits on the bed while he talks on the phone, or even maybe if he walks around inside the bedroom, he is going to notice the big brown envelope on top of the small, low cupboard on his side of the bed. If he opens that envelope, he will find inside it the photocopied pages from Mama's journal – and he does not need that extra pain on top of seeing all those children as slaves.

Lovemore has not read anything new in Mama's journal since

jumping ahead to the final entry then locking it away. She knows that Concilia is probably right, that she probably should just lock it away again until she is older. But she wants to lock it away with a better memory of it in her mind, so she needs to read just a little more. Opening it at random, she finds a blank line that marks the end of one entry and the beginning of another. The entry that follows seems to be about Mama's family. Mama never spoke about them much, and now that Lovemore knows that Mama had a sister called Edna, she would like to know more.

My family home is the village of Ngara in the north west of Tanzania at the border with Rwanda. My family land was always for bananas and beans but after the trouble with banana weevils in the Kagera region they switched to beans and groundnuts. Now the land is for beans, groundnuts and artemesia. Some Wazungu came and asked my family did they want to grow artemesia? Now the Wazungu help my family with seedlings and then they buy my family's artemesia harvest, they are using it to make a medicine for malaria.

Ngara is where I was supposed to live my life, but my father gave me the name Glory and my mother gave me the name Matumaini. In English Matumaini means hopes and expectations, it was because my mother had hopes and expectations for me that were bigger than growing beans and groundnuts like all my big sisters did after their primary schooling. There was no boy among us, so when I finished my primary my parents decided I could do secondary too, and they sent me to my uncle here in Mwanza, and he was going to pay for my schooling.

But that is not how it was. My uncle was a fisherman, he lived away from home at the fishing camp on an island in the lake, so it was just me and my uncle's wife and her grown children at home. Auntie said my father sent me there to be the house girl, she said my mother was lying to me about schooling, there was no money for that. And why should they pay for a girl to go to secondary when even their own sons never went?

I didn't know cooking or cleaning because our own house girl always did those things. Auntie hit me when I cooked badly, so I learned to cook better. She hit me when I cleaned badly, so I learned to clean better. She hit me when I cried, so I learned to swallow my tears. After a few months I learned to be very quick and very quiet, and she learned not to see me.

When I went shopping for her, I started cleaning for old Mr Chowdary, the Mhindi general dealer near the market who told me what spices to put in my cooking to make it nice. I dusted and cleaned all his stock nice and quick and quiet, and after some weeks he stopped telling me he didn't have a job for me and he started to pay me every time I cleaned. After some more weeks I started to help his customers if I was there cleaning and he was busy talking to somebody on the phone, and after some more weeks he left me alone in his shop if he needed to go out for a short time. But it had to be just a short time because I was only out at the market for Auntie and I needed to get back, I needed to have the food ready before Auntie got back from her work of frying fish heads to sell.

He was a good man, Mr Chowdary. It was him I ran to in his shop when Uncle came home from the fishing camp full of beer and tore my dress and my pantie. Mr Chowdary asked me did I want to sleep in the storeroom at the back for some days? Some days became many days, and in the end I never went back to Uncle and Auntie. Mr Chowdary started to teach me his business, how to count his stock and when and how to order more, how to write an invoice and when not to write an invoice because nobody needed to know.

Then he asked me would I like to go to school? School was still my hope and my expectation, it was why I was saving my wage. Mr Chowdary said he was going to pay my fees if I promised to work in his shop every afternoon and evening so that he could sit at home with his feet up drinking chai and being the old man that he was. Right from the beginning of Form I me and Agrippina became friends, but I never saw her outside of school because I had my job. I left school after Form 4 because I didn't need university, my new hope and expectation was to be a clerk in a big business one day. I used some of my wage to pay for lessons in typing, and after 3 months I got my certificate. But Agrippina continued with school because she was going to be a teacher.

Two years after I finished at school Mr Chowdary said he was too old now, he wanted to go and be with his brothers in Kenya, they wanted to exchange him for two of his nephews who were going to come and make his shop big. But Mr Chowdary wasn't going to go until I had my job as a clerk in a big business. He spoke to the older Mr Desai who came from Tanzania Plastics in Dar es Salaam to set up the depot in Mwanza that the younger Mr Desai was going to run. Mr Chowdary told the older Mr Desai I was a very excellent clerk and I even had a certificate, the older Mr Desai couldn't ask for any clerk better than me.

That was the job that I got, at the Tanzania Plastics depot in Mwanza. At first it was just me and the younger Mr Desai at the warehouse on a big piece of land off the road to the airport, and a man who drove the truck for deliveries. People in Europe were starting to like Nile perches from our lake because they were running out of their own fish called cod, and people in Mwanza were starting to set up factories to turn the Nile perches into frozen fillets for the people in Europe. Me and the younger Mr Desai were supplying what the fillets got packed in for their flights to Europe.

When the fish factories got bigger and busier, the older Mr Desai came from Dar es Salaam with his calculator, and he and the younger Mr Desai decided it was going to be better to have a Tanzania Plastics factory in Mwanza instead of just a Mwanza depot for the Dar es Salaam factory. So they built a factory on the same piece of land where the warehouse was, and some big machines came in trucks from Dar es Salaam. They called the new factory Nile Perch Plastics, and they sent a machine expert and a manager and a clerk from the Dar es Salaam factory to work in it. I didn't mind that they sent another clerk because I wasn't a clerk any more, I was the personal assistant for the new manager they sent.

The manager's name was Joseph Tungaraza. I didn't love him from the first day because we were too too busy, but by the end of the first month I knew I was going to do anything for him that he asked.

Lovemore never knew about Mama being sent to Mwanza as a house girl. It helps her to understand why Mama always wanted her to achieve so much, so that Lovemore was never going to end up as just a house girl herself. Maybe a lawyer in New York was the furthest thing away from a house girl in Tanzania that Mama could ever imagine. Lovemore tries to imagine coming here to Dar es Salaam only to find that she was expected to be her grandparents' house girl. *Eh!* That is too hard. What she found here was not at all what she expected, but she has already been so much more fortunate than Mama ever was.

Very soon Babu will be going away again, just for a short time and just nearby, to Tanzania's neighbour to the south. Mozambique is hosting a symposium on technology that is appropriate for Africa, and the President is sending Babu there so that he can come and report back on technologies that can help Tanzania to develop. Babu's work has been becoming more and more interesting to Lovemore. At first, it was only the sound of Uncle Joseph in his voice that she listened for, and it did not matter at all what his words were actually saying. Now, she is full of questions even before he goes.

She wants Babu to go with better thoughts about Mama and Mama's journal in his head, and she would like to find a nicer, less shocking entry to photocopy for him to read before he goes. Mama was kind to Uncle Joseph's wife Evelina near the end, so maybe an entry about Evelina will do. Maybe something nice about the mother of Grace, Benedict and Moses will help Babu to forget anything bad about their father, his son Joseph. Using the scanning skills that Miss Brown has taught the Form Ones, Lovemore manages to find an entry that has Evelina's name in it many times.

It was me who helped the younger Mr Desai to clear the Tungaraza family's things from his house in Capri Point. Joseph's father already took the few things he wanted, just some papers, the photographs of the children growing up and one or two other small things that could remind him of his son. The boys' clothes we took to Kuleana, the home for boys who used to live on the streets, and Joseph's and Grace's clothes went to a shop that sold used. I didn't want Grace's clothes for Lovemore, that wouldn't be right, but I took a small suitcase of Evelina's things to my house.

Two days a week the younger Mr Desai let me work through my lunch hour then leave work early so that I could go to visit Evelina in the hospital. He always wanted to know how was Mrs Tungaraza doing? He never asked me what was she sick with, it was something that everybody knew without anybody needing to ask or to say. I went to visit her on Saturdays too, and every time I went I took her a nice cold soda and some of what Pritty cooked for us at home, maybe some rice and beans or some matoke and tomatoes or a piece of tilapia with boiled Irish potatoes or some slices of pineapple, mango, pawpaw and watermelon.

They always reminded us in Group that we weren't going to stay well or get well without eating good food, and I wanted Evelina to get well. At first she didn't want to eat, and then she wanted to eat but she couldn't, and then at last she could. She was getting stronger every time I saw her, so it was a shock to me the day I went to her room and her bed was empty. There were noises in the private washroom, but the woman who came out of there wasn't Evelina, she was the daughter of the patient who was sleeping in the other bed, she told me Evelina's bed was empty when she came. Eh! Part of me was thinking was Evelina late? Another part of me was thinking did she get better and go home to her house in Capri Point? I didn't tell her yet that she couldn't go home. My heart began to beat hard in my chest like I was climbing up all the hospital stairs again, and I ran to find somebody who could help me.

A nurse led me right to the far end of the corridor where the doors opened on to a wide veranda that went all the way round each and every level of the hospital. Evelina was there, leaning against the low concrete railing. It was only a little higher than her waist, she could easily climb over it if she wanted, and the ground was too too far below her. Eh! I ran to her side and I held her. Look, she told me, look how beautiful, and I stood holding her while we both looked. The hospital is on a hill so it's already high, and so many many stairs and levels up we were higher than high. Beyond the hospital's grounds Mwanza spread out below us, and then there was the lake. Down on the ground nobody can see how big is the lake, but up there we could see it going on and on and on.

I asked her was she OK, was she not cold? But she told me no, it was nice for her to be standing in fresh air instead of lying in her bed. Then she showed me the cement basins where patients could do their washing, and she told me she came out to wash her pantie but she got tired half way, so she left it. I reminded her that she didn't have to wash her own pantie, after every time I visited I took her things home with me for Pritty to wash and I brought them back for her fresh and clean. I twisted the water out of her pantie and we went back inside to her room. She managed to eat some of the eggs and spinach I brought for her without me helping her, then she told me the doctor said maybe she could go home very soon. That was when I told her that the younger Mr Desai was back in his house in Capri Point and she was going to come and live with me in my house. She began to cry and she asked me why was I helping her? I told her when you have daughters who are sisters then you are each other's family, it doesn't matter what happened before.

I held her while she cried, then I asked her did she know it wasn't me *who did this to her? She nodded her head and she said Joseph told her, and she asked me did that Congolese trader woman kill me too? I told her yes, I was no longer my daughter's like she was no longer her children's. She cried too much then, she told me she didn't want her children seeing or remembering her so sick.*

Then the patient in the other bed started to vomit, and I rushed to help the daughter with a bucket and a cloth, and when the daughter fell to pieces I thought no, no, no, this is not how I am going to go, Lovemore is not going to spend her days looking after me like she's a nurse. <u>NO</u>.

Maybe this will help, thinks Lovemore. Babu will see that Mama-Grace was not alone at the end. He will also see that Mama-Lovemore was not the one who killed everybody, which will help him to think better of Mama – and he needs to think better of Mama because he does not think that she was right to leave her journal for Lovemore to read. Okay, he will see that everything was Uncle Joseph's fault, but already he knows that Uncle Joseph was guilty of so much worse. Lovemore carries on reading.

When Evelina came home to live with me and Lovemore I gave her my own bed. It was nothing for me to sleep in Lovemore's room on the mattress from under her bed, or to sleep in Lovemore's bed when she slept over at Agrippina's to be with Rose. The younger Mr Desai called me a good woman and Agrippina's mother called me an angel of God. But Agrippina called me mad.

Her – Are you crazy? She is going to be in your bed! You were in that same bed with her husband!

Me – Yes. But my love for her husband was late since long before her husband was late. It was only me in that bed for a long time.

Her – But you broke her marriage!

Me – Uh-uh, I never broke it. He never left his marriage for me.

Her – But you wanted him to!

Me – Yes, I wanted him to for a long time. But that was long ago. Anyway, he's late now, it doesn't matter.

Her – It doesn't matter? How do you know it doesn't matter to her? How do you know she isn't going to take a machete to you in the night?

Me – There is no machete in my house.

Her – OK, a knife. She can plunge a knife into your heart like you and her husband plunged a knife into hers.

Me – Eh, Agrippina, she is still weak. If she goes to the kitchen and she finds a knife and she carries it into Lovemore's bedroom, she is going to be too tired to lift it, forget about plunging it.

Her – But are you not trying to help her to become stronger?

Me – Yes.

Her – Then she will become strong enough to plunge it!

Me – Uh-uh, she will never plunge it. Who is going to look after her without me? Where is she going to stay without me?

Her – Eh! But Philbert or Sigsbert must sleep in your lounge room, they must pull the sofa across the door into Lovemores room.

Me – Philbert and Sigsbert already have the job of looking after Friends in Deed, they cannot have the job of night watch too.

Her – Then maybe I should send Godbless to sleep in your lounge room.

Me – Godbless? Are we talking about the same Godbless who is Steven's nephew and lives in your house? Because that Godbless is a too too thin young man, when he carries his Bible to church it looks like he is struggling with the weight of a Nile perch the size of a man! What is he going to do to protect me and Lovemore in the night? Place his Bible on the floor in such a way that Evelina will trip over it while he sleeps?

Her – Eh, now you are making me laugh!

Me – Worrying about Evelina is something to laugh at, Agrippina. Really, no knife is going to be plunged in my house.

Her – OK. But I'm going to give you the cassette about gratitude and also the one about forgiveness, you must make sure that Evelina listens.

Evelina tried to listen but at first she wasn't able to concentrate for long. When she got a little better at it, I went to speak to the priest at the church where she used to go with Joseph and her children. He came to pray with her at my house, and then he talked with her like I asked him to. Then he came and knocked on the door to Lovemore's bedroom where I was waiting, and he asked could we help Evelina to phone to her mother in Morogoro? He and Evelina spoke on the phone to her mother for a long time, but I didn't mind about the cost. Then he asked her like I asked him to, did she not want to *phone her children in Dar es Salaam? But she cried too much to the point of collapsing like she did every time I tried to talk to her about them. When the priest came again 2 days later, Evelina was ready with the small suitcase of things that I took when I helped the younger Mr Desai to clear the house in Capri Point. Inside one side of her bra was some money from the younger Mr Desai to help her on her way. Nobody wanted to say that it was funeral money. In the other side was some money from me. I didn't want to say that it was from Joseph, from one of his socks.*

We all went together to the bus stand in the priest's car. When Evelina tried to step up into the bus to Morogoro, she was too weak, the priest had to help her by saying encouraging words and I had to help her by pushing her from behind. I got her up on to the second step, then I stepped up on to the first step behind her to help her up to the third. That was when she stopped trying and she fell back on me, and I fell backwards from the bus. Me and Evelina knocked the priest off his feet, and then we were both on top of him on the ground. Eh! Suddenly we were like a delicious grilled tilapia on a mound of ugali and the people at the bus stand were like hungry street children rushing to us and pulling us apart. They helped us to stand and to brush the ground from our clothes, and then we saw that Evelina couldn't stand, it was like she was asleep. I don't know how many pairs of hands helped us to carry her back to the priest's car. I looked for her small suitcase, but it was gone.

We put her on the back seat with her head in my lap and while the priest was driving fast to the hospital I put my hand into her bra and I told the priest to take her to Bugando instead of Sekou Toure because she had money. Even after we admitted her she never woke up.

The fare for the late is much more expensive than the fare for the living. The money the younger Mr Desai gave to Evelina struggled to pay for hiring the covered trailer, and the money I gave her struggled to convince the driver to attach it to his daladala. He wasn't going to tell his passengers what was in the trailer, but passengers always know, and they don't like it when the late are following them all the way to where they are going. Evelina's mother was going to wait for her at the daladala stand in Morogoro, she was going to ask Joseph's father for funeral money for his grandchildren's mother.

Lovemore is not entirely sure that this is the best entry for Babu to read, but Concilia will know for sure. When nobody is listening, she will find Concilia's number in Bibi's book of names and numbers, and she will use the telephone-fax to call her to arrange a time. When that time comes, she will walk to Concilia's small house in the back yard of Mama-Concilia's house, following the way that Benedict traced for her on the map of Dar es Salaam when she was still new in this house, the way she knew to lead Nelson the taxi-driver, when nobody would sell her a ticket to fly to Mwanza and there was no train.

Till then, Lovemore is not going to read any more of Mama's words, and afterwards she will lock the journal away inside Mama's box inside her suitcase under her bed. Mama will wait for her there, until Lovemore is ready.

Pius came out of the washroom smelling of toothpaste and soap, and instead of going round to his side of the bed, he perched on the edge of Angel's side and tried, very gently, to take the photocopied pages out of her hands.

'How many times do you need to read about our son losing his way, Angel? Surely once is already too many!'

Angel held on tight, not letting him take Mama-Lovemore's words away from her. 'Ah, Pius, our eyes have been on Joseph because our pain is there. But we missed this here,' Angel showed him on the page, pointing. 'Here Mama-Lovemore wrote that Evelina trapped him into marriage by pretending to be pregnant!'

'*Eh?*' Pius took the page and read.

'You see? She didn't want him going to live in Mwanza without her.'

Shaking his head, Pius let out a long, slow breath. 'And so, Angel? Do you want me to be disappointed in the mother of three of our grandchildren as well as their father? What good will that do us? What good will it do *them*?'

Angel thought about it. She had been hoping to have a conversation with Pius about Joseph and Evelina's hasty wedding, and about Mama-Evelina, who had declined to come to Dar es Salaam from Morogoro for Joseph's funeral but had taken advantage of Angel's phone call about the funeral arrangements to ask about Evelina.

Mama-Evelina had no longer been speaking to her daughter because AIDS had come to her daughter's house. And Mama-Evelina a single mother, with Evelina her only living child! Angel had been hoping to have a conversation with Pius about those things, but perhaps she would leave it, talk it through with Concilia, rather, some other time.

She let Pius slide the pages from Mama-Lovemore's journal back into their brown envelope and hide it away in the chest of drawers. After closing the drawer he lingered there, his back to her, and Angel wondered if he was perhaps looking at the small photo of Joseph on top of the chest, next to the one of Vinas in its matching frame. Was he thinking about putting that away in one of the drawers, too? But both photos were still there when he came to his side of the bed and settled down with his papers.

Angel wrote down in her notebook that she was grateful that his back was straighter now than when he had first returned from West Africa, his shoulders further back. She did not like to see him coming home weighed down by what he had seen. He had been like that, too, when he had first got back from helping those refugee children in Chad, so Angel knew that it was the slave children in Ivory Coast who had bent him low this time. Of course, he had gone on to that exciting pan-African conference in Burkina Faso straight from Ivory Coast, so his spirits should have been higher by the time he got home. But Angel did not want to believe that coming home to what Joseph had done could have sunk him down into himself in the same way that refugees and slaves had. No. She did not want to believe that at all.

Suddenly Pius was throwing down his papers, swinging his legs out of the bed and heading back to the chest of drawers.

'Pius?'

'What are we doing, Angel?' The brown envelope was in his hand.

'Eh?'

'Why are we keeping this?'

His question surprised her, and she could not think of any answer at all, let alone a good one.

'Do we want to keep reading it and re-reading it until we know it by heart?'

'No, Pius, of course not.' It was possible that Angel already knew parts of it by heart.

'Do we want it to be sitting in our house like a grenade that one of the children might find?'

'*Eh!* Pius! No!' It was not a story that any of the other children should read – especially not by chance. And anyway, it was from Lovemore's very private book.

So Angel lit her bedside candle, and together they went into the washroom, opening its window wide. Then, one by one, Pius held each of the pages by one corner over the bathtub while Angel touched the flame to it, and when it burned too close, Pius let it fall. When every page was gone, Angel rinsed the soot and ash down the drain of the bath until nothing at all was left.

They got back into bed, then, Pius on his side with his papers, Angel on hers with her notebook. After a minute or two, she decided to count one of her blessings out loud instead of just writing it down, and she reached across to Pius, squeezing his shoulder lightly.

'I'm grateful that your next trip is not to somewhere far,' she told him.

'Me too,' he told her softly, taking her hand from his shoulder and planting a kiss on the back of it before returning to his reading.

He would be going only as far as their southern neighbour, Mozambique – though the symposium would be in the capital, Maputo, which was right at the southern end of that country, next to Swaziland where they had lived last year. *Eh*, last year seemed such a long time ago now! So much had happened since.

She wanted to say that to Pius, but she could see that he was concentrating hard. Glancing across at what he was reading, she saw that it was about the kinds of technologies that their President was sending him to Mozambique to investigate.

'You mean computers?' Grace had asked him at supper a few nights ago.

'Ah, no,' Pius had said, 'not computers.'

'But computers are technology. We do information and communication technology at school, and that's computers.'

'But computers need a wall socket and electricity, and most of the people living on this continent don't have things like electricity or wall sockets.'

'Babu, I think some don't even have walls.'

'That is true, Lovemore, that is true. Something that you have to plug in is not always appropriate everywhere in Africa. Here we don't always need big expensive things that come from outside and then break because the climate is wrong for them and nobody has been trained to fix them, or nobody can afford to buy what is needed to fix them or even to keep them going. That is not sustainable. Sometimes what we need is not a billion-dollar dam that displaces thousands of people and is already inadequate before it is even halfway built. Sometimes what is more appropriate is a simple pump that children can work without even knowing they are working a pump, because it is the roundabout that they are playing on, and as they spin round and round on it, it is pumping water up out of the ground into a tank that leads water to the taps in their homes.'

As Pius had become more excited about his subject, Grace and Faith had begun to roll their eyes, and Moses and Daniel had begun to fidget. Only Lovemore and Benedict had truly listened. Angel herself had tried hard to concentrate, but her mind had slipped away to the cake that she would start baking the next morning for the *mwalimu mkuu* at the private secondary in Tabata where she and Peter Mapashi had won round two with their wedding cakes. Ever since her very beautiful winning cake had been on TV and in the newspaper, more and more new customers had been looking for her – and so far they had not objected to the higher prices that Pius had advised her to charge because of demand and supply.

Angel had continued to think about her business rather than focusing on Pius's words to the children about technologies, until the word *oven* had brought her back. Lovemore had just asked him a question.

'But how can maize leaves in a bag cook something, Babu?'

'They insulate. First you dry the leaves, then you stuff them into bags that you sew to a particular pattern. You heat your pot of beans or whatever on the fire, just until it's boiling, then you put your pot, with its lid on, into your bag. The maize leaves keep your pot hot, and the heat keeps your beans cooking. Now you no longer have to tend your fire and watch your pot for hours, so you are free to go to a literacy class or whatever else you want to do to improve your life. When you come back later your beans are cooked through and still hot.'

'And Baba, you've used less wood, you haven't been burning your fire for all that time.'

'Exactly, Benedict. So you're sustaining the environment.'

'For the animals and birds.'

'Mm. And the people.'

'Pius, can you bake a cake like that?'

'Ah, no, Angel. But you can bake in a solar oven that is like a box.'

Angel's mind had drifted then to Nansi Ngeleja and the wedding cake made from a box that had won round two in Mwanza.

Now, sitting in bed with her notebook, it broke Angel's heart that Pius would not be back from Mozambique in time for the final round of the competition. But at least he would be back a day later, and he could congratulate – or comfort – her then. Angel felt in her bones that he would be congratulating her, but she was very, very nervous, and she did not want to allow herself to believe. She could at least write down that she was grateful that the design for her cake was now finalised, and that she knew exactly how many pieces of what size to bake to make up the whole cake. It was going to be more work than any cake before had ever been, and it was truly very complicated – but nobody else in the Crystal Room at New Africa Hotel would have a cake that was in any way like it.

The idea for her cake had come – indirectly – from Joseph, though she was not quite willing to write that she was grateful to him for that. Pius had already begun to make a philosophy about what Joseph had done, with the help of a piece of Tanzanian wisdom that said that to get lost was to find the way. Joseph had got lost – very badly lost – but he had never had the opportunity to find his way again. Pius was beginning to become certain that Joseph would have found his way, eventually, but Angel was not so sure.

What she was sure of now was that she was grateful that two of Joseph's children – the two who liked most to be alone – had sat together for a long time at the computer to find and print for her the pictures that she was going to use to get her cake exactly right. When Lovemore and Benedict were together, they were quiet and serious – unlike Moses and Daniel with their constant energy and activity, or

Grace and Faith with their talk and attention hopping from here to there like locusts. Really, Angel and Pius must try to think of more things to ask Lovemore and Benedict to do together.

The last thing that Angel wrote tonight was that she was grateful that Pius had blocked some time in his diary for them all to go in the microbus to see their extended family in Bukoba when the schools closed for the holidays. They would stop in Mwanza on the way so that Angel could meet Agrippina, the new friend she had only ever talked to on the phone. *Eh*, she was looking forward to that! Lovemore had said a few times that she thought Angel and Agrippina would like each other's company very much – and maybe when they were face to face it would feel like the right time for Angel to ask Agrippina some of the questions that she had been sitting on about Mama-Lovemore. At least she knew now that Agrippina's best friend since school had indeed been a good woman, a moral woman who had tried to make Joseph stop doing wrong.

Lovemore could stay with Rose and Agrippina in Mwanza if she wanted, or she could come to Bukoba to meet everybody else. Titi would stay in Mwanza, spending time with her cousin there. On their way back through Mwanza from Bukoba, everybody would be gathered back together in the microbus, all nine of them.

Pius and Angel were still talking about what would happen after that. This past Sunday in Saint Joseph's, Angel had prayed for their President to be so impressed with Pius's report on technologies that were right for Tanzania's development, that he would decide to offer Pius a very good job right here in Dar es Salaam.

Smiling at the thought of how nice that would be, she turned to share her idea with Pius, but his article was lying slack across his chest, and he was beginning to snore very softly.

Chapter 16

IN THE final round of the Kilimanjaro Snow competition, as in the wedding-cake round, Bibi is allowed only one assistant to help her to put together her cake that represents Tanzania. Lovemore does not want to be chosen, because of Bibi's choice of cake, but everybody else wants to be chosen, because they will get to sleep in a room at New Africa Hotel with Bibi for two whole nights.

'Please choose me, Mama,' says Grace. 'Have I not known your cakes for longer than anybody?'

'I've known them just as long,' says Benedict, 'and, Mama, I'm the one who found all the pictures for you for your cake! Please let me help!'

Actually, Lovemore and Benedict found the pictures together on the computer, but Lovemore says nothing. And the idea for the cake was hers – well, hers and Benedict's – but she does not remind Bibi of that.

'I can hold your icing syringe for you, Mama,' says Faith, 'like a nurse helping a doctor on TV.'

'Please choose me,' says Moses. 'It was me who washed our football so you could look at it for the football cake, the one that helped you to pass round one.'

'But it's my football, too,' says Daniel, pushing Moses aside. 'Mama, I can watch sports on the big TV screen at the hotel and come and tell you the scores while you are working.'

Even Titi wants to be chosen. 'Auntie, do you not need somebody who can clean up for you as you go?'

Lovemore says nothing, and still Bibi chooses her. It is because she is good at puzzles, good at putting pieces together, and also because she knows better than anybody else exactly how Bibi's cake should look when it is finished.

On Thursday evening Lovemore finds the card that Nelson gave her when he thought he was going to come and fetch her in his taxi to take her back to the railway station for the train to Mwanza, and she calls him from the telephone-fax. He says that he remembers her, though Lovemore is certain that he is only pretending, and he agrees to come for her and Mama at five on Friday afternoon. At quarter to five he is there, reversing his big, air-conditioned vehicle into the front yard and parking it next to the old red microbus. The microbus is bigger and it has more space, but it is like an oven and it would spoil Mama's cake long before it got to the Crystal Room at New Africa Hotel.

After folding flat the seats in the back of his vehicle, Nelson goes inside to look at everything that Bibi needs to take. It is all spread out over the dining table, and the coffee table too.

'All of this, Auntie?' Nelson puts his left hand to the side of his head and blows a high-pitched whistle. 'My goodness me!'

'And those, too,' says Bibi, pointing to the two small bags that she and Lovemore need for two nights in the hotel.

Shaking his head, Nelson whistles again. 'This is two loads, Auntie. Otherwise let me call my brother, he is also driving taxi.'

'Air-conditioned?'

'Of course, Auntie, very nice vehicle, just like mine.'

'Okay.'

While they wait for Nelson's brother to make his way to them through the traffic, they load up the back of Nelson's taxi, carefully positioning the parts of the cake so that none of them will spoil, and making sure that the different parts of the enormous cake board are flat and secure. The last of it goes into Nelson's brother's vehicle, and everybody gathers in the front yard to wave them goodbye until the judging tomorrow. They will be safe enough in Titi's care, with Benedict in charge as the man of the house. Bibi travels with Nelson's brother so that Lovemore can go with Nelson. Lovemore has been alone with Nelson before, so Bibi knows that he is not going to try to do anything funny to her, which is Bibi's way of dancing around a word that Concilia would actually use.

At the hotel, Evarist from the sugar company is there to greet them, and many pairs of eyes look at them and at everything that they have brought with them. Finalists from outside the Dar es Salaam region have already been there since last night, spending the day today doing any last-minute baking in the ovens of a catering college, and all the finalists are interested in looking without appearing to be interested in looking. Evarist tells them that they can leave things in the Crystal room overnight if they want to, but Bibi is worried about sabotage, so everything goes up to their room with them to be kept cool by the air-conditioning.

They could go and eat in the restaurant, but Bibi would rather not have to dress up, so they order some lamb curry over the phone and a waiter brings it to their room, which is definitely the kind of room that you would find in a nice big house in Capri Point back in Mwanza or on the Msasani Peninsula here in Dar es Salaam. Bibi takes the tray from the waiter at the door, not wanting to let him enter in case he steps on something and ruins everything.

She pushes her pieces of lamb around on her plate. 'What if they laugh at my cake, Lovemore?'

'Bibi, has anybody every laughed at one of your cakes?'

'Well, no. But nobody has ever seen *this* cake.'

'Nobody ever saw any of your other cakes until they saw them, and then they never laughed.'

'But what if I forget my speech?'

'It's not a speech, Bibi. It's just telling everybody why your cake represents Tanzania. And you know why it does.'

'But there are going to be TV cameras!'

'Yes. And there was a TV camera at round two, and you spoke into the man's microphone without any trouble.'

'But they didn't show me talking on news.'

'News only had time for one minute about cakes, Bibi. And when that lady interviewed you for the radio, your words came out just fine.'

'But she was asking me questions then. This time I have to give a speech.'

'It's not a speech, Bibi. It's just telling everybody why your cake represents Tanzania. And you know why it does.'

Competitions just do not sit well with Bibi's nerves.

After her shower in the lovely washroom, Lovemore sees that Bibi is sitting up in her bed, writing in a small notebook.

'You don't have to write a speech, Bibi.'

'Ah, no, Lovemore, it's not a speech.'

'Are you writing a journal, like my mama?'

'No, no. I just like to remind myself at each day's end the reasons why I'm grateful today.'

'Okay, Bibi.' It sounds like something that one of Auntie Agrippina's cassettes might suggest. 'Try to get some sleep, see?'

At four in the morning, Bibi is in reception with her badge saying FINALIST, asking for the Crystal room to be opened, and Lovemore is there with her badge saying ASSISTANT and the first load of Bibi's things from upstairs. Even with the porter's trolley, there are several more loads. Around the edges of the room, fifteen tables draped with white cloths make a U shape, with plenty of space between each table and the next. Already there is a small label on each table, and very quickly they find the one that says TUNGARAZA, ANGEL, and underneath that, DAR ES SALAAM. They can see at once that Bibi's table is not going to be big enough, even though it is the same size as every other table. While an extra table is fetched and the other tables are re-spaced, Bibi and Lovemore look for the table with the label saying NGELEJA, NANSI, and underneath it MWANZA. The table is three away from Bibi, down the same side of the room and just before the U makes a turn. It is going to be difficult to keep an eye on that table to check for any signs that the cake is in fact a box. There is nothing yet on that table, though some of the other tables bear the beginnings of other finalists' creations.

As Bibi goes quickly to work, Lovemore sees all of Bibi's nervousness disappearing. Together they cover the white tablecloth in swathes of the cloth dyed in different shades of blue by Bibi's friend Fatima, bunching it high towards the back of the two tables. On top, they arrange loosely the wide netting that Bibi had a lady at Mwenge market knot for her using white string. Next come the four big cake boards, which they line up level with the front edge of the two adjoining tables, each of them already covered in sugar paste that makes each look like it is made up of planks of wood running from front to back. The joins between the boards look the same as the joins between the planks on the boards.

'Drink water, Bibi,' Lovemore tells her before they start on the cake itself. 'Sit for five minutes.'

'Ah, Lovemore, what I really want is a cup of tea!'

'I can bring you tea, but I think you must also eat breakfast.'

The room is beginning to buzz with quiet activity now, and finalists are at work at nearly all of the tables. Nansi Ngeleja's table is still bare.

'Go and eat your breakfast, Lovemore. Bring back something small for me.'

'Okay, but you must sit for five minutes and drink water.'

'Okay.'

The breakfast buffet in the restaurant is not like anything that Lovemore has ever seen before. There is so much food! Meats, beans, tomatoes, onions, chapattis, pancakes, fruits – everywhere Lovemore looks there is more and more. A round man in a tall white hat tells her that he can cook eggs for her in any way that she likes, but there is just too much to choose. She settles for a slice of bread and butter and a glass of mango juice, recognising as she sits at one of the tables to eat that she is not feeling very comfortable in her stomach. Perhaps last night's lamb curry was not fresh, or maybe she has got caught up in the nerves of the competition. She wants more than anything for Bibi to win, or at least to be first runner-up or even second runner-up. But what if Bibi gets nothing, comes nowhere? How will anybody be able to comfort her then, especially with Babu still away in Mozambique? For sure Bibi would not want to spend tonight here in this hotel.

When she has finished her breakfast, Lovemore takes a cup of tea and a nice fat *maandazi* in a paper serviette to Bibi, and it is very obvious that Bibi has not sat for five minutes or for any time at all. She has lined up all of the separate enormous pieces of the cake and built what is unmistakably a Nile perch the size of a man. Okay, not a man the size of Babu, but still a man. Lovemore swallows hard, telling herself that it is just a cake. Bibi is now hiding the joins on the underside of the fish by smoothing on some more of the shiny, gold-coloured sugar paste. She will conceal the joins on its side and back with separate silvery scales to match the ones that already cover the rest of it, but first Lovemore tells her to sit and have her breakfast.

They sit together, watching the other finalists and their assistants at work, knowing that they are being watched, too.

'Bibi, did Nansi Ngeleja come yet?'

'*Eh*, I don't know, I've been too busy.'

Standing up for a moment, Lovemore looks over to Nansi Ngeleja's table. It is bare. 'Maybe they know she cheated.'

'Then why is there a table with her name?'

'I don't know, Bibi.'

Bibi finishes her tea and her *maandazi*, and they sit for a minute more while they breathe deeply in and out. Bibi knows about breathing to calm yourself even without listening to any of Auntie Agrippina's cassettes, and Lovemore is glad of the breathing because there is a Nile perch on the table behind her and her stomach does not feel right.

When Bibi was trying to choose what cake to make, she asked everybody at home to give their suggestions of what would say Tanzania. But for everything that any one of them suggested, Bibi said no, it was too obvious. Somebody else could easily choose the same idea, and the judges would not bother to choose between two similar cakes, they would rather choose a cake that was more original. So all of them tried even harder to think of what else might say Tanzania. Without really wanting to say it, Lovemore suggested that maybe what said Tanzania was its fishing industry, its fish. Benedict said yes and Titi said tilapia, then Lovemore began to say Nile perch just a fraction of a second before Benedict began to say it, and when they both finished saying Nile perch at the same time and Bibi said *eh*, Lovemore and Benedict looked at each other and high-fived each other even before Lovemore had a chance to feel nauseous.

Bibi and Lovemore stand up from their breathing, and Bibi asks Lovemore to assist by going around the room and looking at all the other cakes. Lovemore makes an effort to remember them in as much detail as possible so that she can report back properly to Bibi. There is a cake the shape of the outline of Tanzania with the design of the Tanzanian flag across it. The flag has a simple design – a triangle of green in the top left corner, a triangle of blue in the bottom right corner, and a bar of black between them running across from the bottom left corner to the top right corner with a thin stripe of yellow along either side of the black – and the cake itself is very simple. There is a Mount Kilimanjaro rising high from the green of the cake board, with a dusting of white snow on its top and many tiny sugar animals around its base. Another cake is a two-dimensional picture of some animals – an elephant, a lion, a giraffe, a zebra – with Mount Kilimanjaro in the distance.

Peter Mapashi, the other finalist from the Dar es Salaam region, has made a cake that shows perfectly the chaos of a traffic jam. Its surface is crowded with cars and *daladalas* and *bodabodas* and *bajajis* and there is even a bus. Angry faces and fists stick out from every window. It is a very exciting and colourful cake – but perhaps it is a cake about Dar es Salaam rather than a cake about Tanzania. One cake looks exactly like a *tingatinga* painting, the lovely style of painting that Mr Tingatinga began. One school holiday Mama sent Lovemore for art classes, and one of the things they had to learn was *tingatinga* painting. Your colours have to be bright and your drawings simple, which is easy enough when you are still a child. This *tingatinga* cake has two leopards – a mother and her baby – very bright yellow with black spots, against a bright red background. There are bright blue flowers as well, and some simple birds with long tails. Benedict will know what kind of birds they are, but Lovemore does not want to look at them too closely.

Another cake has been shaped into the long, thin, two-dimensional outline of another bird. Fearing that it might be a marabou stork, Lovemore looks only as far as what the finalist is piping onto the cake board: CRESTED CRANE, National Bird of Tanzania.

The tanzanite ring cake is not at all impressive. The metal part of it is a dull grey sprinkled with the ordinary kind of silver glitter that Lovemore and Rose used to use for pictures when they were small, and the big tanzanite stone on it is simply a bright blue sprinkled with ordinary blue glitter. Nobody who eats a slice of this cake is going to feel at all well. Lovemore has always liked tanzanite, the beautiful blue stone that comes only from Tanzania – and only from the hills around Arusha and Kilimanjaro – but Mama always said that diamonds were better because they were more international.

The ferry cake looks complicated and professional, and although it is probably the ferry that links the island of Zanzibar to mainland Tanzania, it reminds Lovemore of Uncle Steven's first wife sinking on the ferry in Lake Victoria together with their baby. The dhow boat cake is simple and beautiful. There is a lovely cup of tea on a saucer, which Lovemore wants to pick up and hold, though it is much bigger than a real cup. Floating on top of the tea in the cup are a clove and a cardamom pod made of sugar, while a sugary stick of cinnamon rests on the saucer in place of a spoon for stirring.

There is a good two-dimensional portrait of Julius Nyerere, Tanzania's first ever president, and there is a good two-dimensional Uhuru Torch, shimmering with the right kind of edible gold. The last cake is a pair of brown hands pulling at the chain that is wound around them, breaking one of its links. Babu would love it – and Lovemore loves it, too – because a slave is setting himself free, but Bibi will surely not be impressed by the standard of the work.

Walking back towards the table where Bibi is working, Lovemore is surprised. The Nile perch looks very real, but it also looks beautiful. She does not want to let her eyes linger on the pale pink inside its big open mouth, or on the black of its eyes, but now that Bibi has added the golden fins to its sides and the spiky silvery ones to its back, it is a very impressive cake indeed, one that Lovemore actually wants to look at.

'*Lovemore!*' Bibi whispers, jerking her head in the direction of Nansi Ngeleja's table. 'She's here!'

'You've seen her?' There is nobody standing next to that table.

'Uh-uh, just her cake. Go and look and tell me if it's cake or cardboard!'

Nansi Ngeleja's cake is a big map of Africa with each of the countries in a different colour. The shape of Tanzania zooms up out of it as if you are looking at it with a magnifying glass, and stands about as high as the length of a ruler – the thirty-centimetre one, not the smaller fifteen-centimetre one – above the rest of the cake. It is easily four or five times bigger than its place on the map, and it tapers down to fit into that original space. It is not a cake on a hidden stand, it is just a level surface that tapers down. It cannot possibly be made of cake because that small base shape would never support its weight.

'That is exactly what I thought,' says Bibi, when Lovemore gets back to her. 'You wait here. I'm going to look for Evarist.'

'But what are you going to tell him, Bibi? We don't know for sure that it's not cake.'

'I'll simply tell him what we heard about her Mwanza Region cake and ask him to look carefully at this cake. *Eh*, but I'm hungry, Lovemore, do you not want lunch?'

Lovemore is surprised to find that so much time has passed. 'You go, Bibi. Bring me something small back.'

'No, no, I'll just go to the washroom and find Evarist, and then you can go and bring me something small back.'

When Lovemore uses the washroom before she has her lunch, there is a very small smear of blood on her white pantie. She is sure that it was not there the last time she came to the washroom.

Eh!

But she does not want to tell Bibi, not now. Bibi has so much else to think about. Packing a wad of toilet paper inside her pantie, she goes to the restaurant where there is another big buffet. She chooses a piece of chicken and some chips, and is about to find a small table on her own when an arm reaches out and stops her.

'Sit with me,' a friendly looking lady tells her, showing Lovemore her badge saying FINALIST. Lovemore sits. 'You're the big fish, *sivyo*?'

'Mm.'

'I'm the cup of tea.'

'Ah, I love that one!'

'Thank you! I'm from the Arusha Region, actually from Arusha itself.'

'We're from here, the Dar es Salaam Region. Are you by yourself?'

'Mm, I used the other ticket for a seat for my cake, brought it already finished.

They eat their lunch together, chatting about the different cakes.

Then the cup-of-tea lady leans in towards her. 'Tell me,' she says, lowering her voice, 'that one, the map of Africa.' Her right hand hovers about the length of a ruler above her spaghettis. 'Can a cake do that?'

Putting her chicken leg down, Lovemore leans in, too. 'Me and my bibi, we think it's not a cake.'

'Ooh!' The cup-of-tea lady's eyebrows move further up her forehead as she lowers her voice even more. 'What is it?'

'We don't know,' Lovemore tells her, 'but maybe it's a box.'

'A box? *Eh!* I suppose.'

'My bibi reported it to Evarist, but all he said was her allegation was noted.'

'Ah. Probably that means the same as he doesn't intend to take an action.'

'Mm, that's what my bibi said, but she isn't happy. She isn't going to accept if that lady wins a prize, because winning by cheating can damage the reputation of all cake makers who are professional.'

'Exactly!' says the cup-of-tea lady, trying to balance some spaghettis on her fork.

'So if that lady wins a prize, my bibi is going to challenge her to cut her cake and serve out slices.'

'Ooh, I'm with your bibi!'

Lovemore glances around her to make sure that nobody else is listening. 'Even if that lady doesn't win, I think I'm going to knock her cake over by accident. But I didn't tell my bibi that!'

'Ooh!' A smile spreads across the cup-of-tea lady's face. 'I'm with you! We can do it together!'

The cup-of-tea lady reaches her right hand across the table, and Lovemore quickly wipes the chicken grease off her own with a paper serviette before they shake to agree.

After her lunch, Lovemore goes back to the washroom to look at the wad of toilet paper inside her pantie. There is not a mark on it. Then she takes Bibi a plate with the same choice of chicken and chips that she chose for herself because there is way too much else to choose from.

Bibi has finished the Nile perch completely, and she is beginning to tidy away all her bits and pieces under the floor-length white tablecloth. Lovemore finishes up for her while Bibi nibbles at her lunch, nervous again now that she has stopped being busy with her cake.

One of the hotel waitresses comes around handing out programmes for the afternoon. All the finalists need to be done completely by two forty-five – less than half an hour away – at which time they should leave the room and let the official photographer come in to take photos. A note on the programme assures the finalists that the photographer is a professional who will not touch anything or knock anything over. At three fifteen the judges will enter the room, and throughout the judging period the photographer's pictures of all the cakes will be displayed on the large screen in the area outside the room, where tea will be served. At three forty-five the finalists will be invited to re-enter the room, along with representatives from the media, and to tell the judges why they think their cake is a good representation of Tanzania. This will be played live on the big screen outside. After that the room will be cleared while the judges confer one last time before the winners are announced.

Bibi abandons her lunch and takes some photos of her cake.

'That must go on your website, Bibi.'

Bibi rolls her eyes. 'If I can ever name my business.' She glances at her watch. '*Eh*, I must go upstairs and change! Look at me!'

The room begins to empty as everybody finishes their tidying up, but Lovemore sits guard over Bibi's cake until she is asked to leave so that the photographer can come in.

Outside the room, Bibi's friend Stella is getting a cup of tea for her wheelchair friend Mr Chiza, while Bibi's friend Esther is making sure that the others in Stella's elderly group are taken care of. Lovemore has been wandering around the lobby area for quite some time, willing the minute hands on every watch and clock in the hotel to speed up, when her sisters and brothers arrive with Titi, Concilia and an older lady in a smart suit who looks slightly familiar.

'Lovemore, this is my mother,' Concilia tells her.

'Mama-Concilia!' Lovemore shakes her hand, recognising her now as the lady in some of the photos on her own lounge wall. 'I am happy to meet you!'

Mama-Concilia smiles and says hello.

'We needed two cars to bring everybody,' Concilia says, 'and Mama wanted to come anyway to support her favourite cake-maker.'

'That is Angel Tungaraza, of course,' says Mama-Concilia. She is friendly but a little distant, as if she is standing on the other side of a fence made of strong iron palings. She tells Lovemore about all the people that she has sent to Bibi as customers. While they are talking, Lovemore sees Bibi's friends Fatima and Irene arriving.

'There she is!'

Bibi is coming towards them in the same *kitenge* outfit that she wore to meet Lovemore at Julius Nyerere International Airport all those months ago. Everybody hugs her hello – everybody except Mama-Concilia, who simply shakes her hand – and Lovemore tells all of them that Bibi's cake is truly beautiful.

'Even though it's a fish?' Grace asks her.

'Even though,' says Lovemore.

While everybody is getting tea and Bibi is busy greeting all the friends and customers who have come to support her, Lovemore whispers into Grace's ear that she has become the first.

'You mean …?'

Lovemore nods.

'When?'

'Today!'

Grace rushes off to the washroom to check whether she herself is not perhaps the first, and Faith goes with her.

Evarist takes five judges with him into the room, and when the doors close, the cakes appear one by one on the screen. There are plenty of chairs, but they fill quickly, leaving many to stand behind, crowding around to see. A TV camera films them watching. Lovemore has already seen all the cakes, so after a while she goes to the washroom again to check if anything more has happened. The tiniest hint of a smudge has appeared on her wad of toilet paper. When she returns, she has lost her seat.

At last Evarist invites the finalists and the press and TV cameras in.

The noise of everybody shouting good luck is so loud that nobody can possibly hear their own wishes from their own friends and family, and then a silence falls as a moving image appears on the screen. The other Tungaraza children rush to the front where they sit cross-legged on the carpeted floor, but Lovemore prefers to stand behind the rows of chairs because she is not entirely sure what will happen in her pantie if she sits like that.

One after the other, finalists introduce themselves and tell the camera how their cake represents Tanzania. The nice cup-of-tea lady is talking about the importance of tea in the everyday lives of Tanzanians and about spicy tea coming to Tanzania with the Indian traders and railway-builders, when two hands place themselves gently on Lovemore's shoulders. She turns to look.

'Babu!'

'*Shh!*' he whispers into her ear as they hug each other. 'I think we are supposed to be quiet.'

'You're back!'

'I finished up early so I could get back here in time.'

'Does Bibi know?'

'Uh-uh. I wasn't sure I'd make it.'

'She's in there now.'

'Ah.'

Everybody claps for the nice cup-of-tea lady as the camera lingers on her cake, and Lovemore decides that the next time everybody claps she will tell Babu her news. Not the news about what is happening to her body today – obviously not that news – but her other news, the one she is sure that Babu will like. She has been thinking about it for some time, building the idea up slowly in her mind, and now she is ready to tell Babu. She wants to tell him before they know if Bibi has won or not, because after that – either way – the time will not be right. Lovemore has not yet told Rose, but Rose will not mind too much. Rose is already dancing around the idea of maybe becoming a physics and chemistry teacher, without yet having the courage to say it out loud to Lovemore.

When everybody is clapping for the Julius Nyerere cake, Lovemore tells him.

'Babu, I have a news.'

'Yes?'

'I don't want to be a lawyer in New York.'

'*Eh!* No?'

'Uh-uh. I think I want to work here in Africa. I want to help people to have their human rights.'

'*Eh!* He knocks on his chest with his right fist. 'Do you feel it here?'

Lovemore knocks on her own chest. 'I feel it here.'

Babu hugs her tighter than tight. '*Eh*, you are a true daughter of mine! I'm so proud of you, Lovemore, so very, very proud.'

'Thank you, Baba.'

And there the word is, out from her own mouth.

Baba.

Baba with an *a* at the end in place of a *u*.

For the first time in her life, she has called a man *Baba*. He is her grandfather, not her father, but it does not feel wrong. In fact, it feels completely right.

Baba wipes a tear from the corner of one eye, but Lovemore does not know if it is because she called him *Baba,* or because he is happy that somebody else in his house cares about the same things that he cares about, or because he is relieved that he will not, after all, have to find the money for Lovemore to become a lawyer in New York.

'We're about half way,' she whispers to him. 'Bibi asked to go last.'

'Going first is better,' he whispers back. 'Get it out of the way.'

'Wait, Baba, you'll see.'

Lovemore pays very little attention to the rest of the cakes, waiting only to see Nansi Ngeleja's cake on the screen. But it does not come before

Bibi's enormous fish appears, and then Bibi is beside it, telling the camera her name and saying that she is a grandmother in Dar es Salaam.

'This is a Nile perch from our biggest lake,' she says, 'Lake Victoria. This fish is part of a very big industry for us, an industry that employs and feeds and clothes many thousands of Tanzanians. In life, this fish can be this big, or sometimes bigger still. The Bible tells us that Jesus fed thousands with just five loaves and two fishes, and that it was a miracle. When I look at a fish this size, I think that the miracle was only about the loaves.'

The people outside the cake room clap and laugh, and Lovemore can see that there is laughter inside the cake room, too, because the image of Bibi on the screen is wobbling up and down.

'Ah, Angel,' Baba says quietly to himself.

'The Nile perch has not always been a Tanzanian,' Bibi continues. 'It came here from outside, but we welcomed it and we made it our own. That is how we are as Tanzanians, we welcome others.'

People clap again, and there is even some whistling.

'Now,' says Bibi, 'Kilimanjaro Snow calls itself the icing on the top. That is very good, but I'm sure the people at Kilimanjaro Snow know that icing is not only for on the top. I want to show you the icing inside so that you can see that the Nile perch is now Tanzanian through and through.'

Everybody sits a little straighter and stands a little taller to look at the screen while Bibi takes a large knife and cuts right through the fish a short distance back from its head. Nobody can see what Lovemore knows, that Bibi is cutting exactly where one board meets another. Putting the knife down, Bibi slides the board with the head part on it a little way out before turning it to face the camera. Inside the body of the fish is the Tanzanian flag, green sponge and blue sponge, with a diagonal band of black sponge between them edged on both sides with a thick layer of bright yellow icing.

Nudging Lovemore with his elbow, Baba whispers, 'Have we made that fish our own, or has it has eaten us up?'

The crowd in front of the screen is on its feet, shouting, whistling, ululating and clapping. Inside the cake room they can surely hear the noise, because Bibi stands quietly, patting the piece of *kitenge* cloth wrapped around her head with one hand. When the noise finally dies down, Bibi says that everybody is welcome to have a piece of her cake when the competition is over, and that there is surely enough.

'Ah, Angel,' Baba says again, clapping along with everybody else.

Outside the room again while the judges make their final decisions, Bibi is so happy to see Baba that when they hug she bursts into tears, wetting the front of his shirt as her tears roll down below her glasses. All the Tungarazas crowd around, excited to see Baba, excited about Bibi and the competition.

While they wait for the judges' decision, Lovemore goes quickly to the washroom. The hint of a smudge on her wad of toilet paper is just the tiniest bit larger.

At last the doors open, and Evarist is there with the five judges and their clipboards. A silence falls. He thanks everybody for their patience before introducing himself, another man in a suit and a smartly dressed lady, both of them from the sugar company, and all five of the judges. Lovemore is sure that nobody is listening to their names because everybody is just waiting to hear the result.

'I have just one short announcement to make before the winners are announced,' Evarist says, as people shift impatiently on their feet. 'Our judges have judged only fourteen cakes instead of the fifteen that are in the room.' Bibi and Lovemore reach for each other's hand. 'Very unfortunately, one of the cakes was disqualified when it was found to be made not of eggs, flour, butter and, of course, *sugar*,' he pauses, smiling, 'but of polystyrene foam.'

There is laughter and indignation, and Bibi and Lovemore look at each other, their eyes shining. Lovemore looks around for the cup-of-tea lady, who is looking around for her. When their eyes meet, they exchange knowing nods and smiles.

Then a movement catches Lovemore's eye. 'Bibi, look!'

Two smartly dressed ladies are pulling their suitcases behind them, bending low as if to make themselves too small to be seen, keeping their eyes down as if they cannot see or hear the large crowd that is there for the competition.

'*Hah!*' says Bibi. 'One of those is Nansi Ngeleja!'

'Cheat!' they both say together as the two ladies pass through the lobby looking like dogs that have messed indoors and know they are going to be hit.

Then it is the turn of one of the judges, the same one who announced the winners of Bibi's wedding-cake round. She gives the same speech: blah blah very high standard blah blah extremely beautiful blah blah such fine craftsmanship blah blah very great honour. At last she says the word *winners*.

'Second runner-up, with her very beautiful cup of tea, is Mrs Somebody from Arusha Region.' Everybody claps and cheers while the nice cup-of-tea lady from Arusha Region is photographed receiving her prize basket as her cup-of-tea cake shows on the large screen.

Not one of the Tungarazas moves a muscle.

'First runner-up, with her very beautiful ferry boat, is Mrs Somebody from Somewhere Region.' Everybody claps and cheers while Mrs Somebody from Somewhere region is photographed receiving her prize basket as her ferry-boat cake shows on the large screen.

Not one of the Tungarazas breathes.

'And the winner of the Kilimanjaro Snow national cake-decorating competition, with her very beautiful, inside and out, Nile perch fish, is Mrs Angel Tungaraza from Dar es Salaam Region.'

Lovemore is suddenly in tears. When she looks, she sees that the others are, too, even Titi and Concilia and Mama-Concilia, and every one of Bibi's friends.

While Bibi is cutting pieces of her cake to go on the small plates that a waiter has provided, somebody who takes a piece says, '*Asante, Bibi-Keki.*'

Slowly some others begin to say it, too.

'You are a worthy winner, *Bibi-Keki.*'

'*Bibi-Keki*, by far your cake was the best.'

'You are the only one who knows that cake is meant to be eaten, *Bibi-Keki. Eh*, what is the point of a cake that you just look at?'

'Your speech got me here in my heart, *Bibi-Keki*, here in my heart.'

'So you are *Bibi-Keki* now,' says Baba, taking a small piece for himself. 'I suppose you may as well be the grandmother of cakes since you are already the grandmother of six children.' He gives her a tired smile. 'Six that we know so far.'

'Don't, Pius. Just don't.'

Moving away from them to let them talk, Lovemore overhears Evarist talking with the other two from the sugar company, the man in the suit and the smartly dressed lady. They are looking at Bibi.

'Really,' Evarist is saying to them, 'I think she'll be perfect.'

'Though how is her hair under that *kitenge*?' the lady asks.

'Black,' says Evarist, 'I saw it earlier.'

'At her age it must be dyed,' the lady says.

'She can be convinced otherwise,' the other man in the suit says.

'Maybe if she grows out her roots so her parting is white on top,' the lady suggests.

'Perfect!' Evarist says, and the other man nods.

'There you are, Lovemore!' Concilia takes Lovemore's arm and leads her out of the room. 'Listen. We think your babu should—'

'He's my baba now.'

'Seriously?'

'Mm. It just happened.' Lovemore feels herself smiling very widely.

'Aah!' Concilia hugs her with the arm that she is not using for her stick. 'So your baba should have the room here tonight with your bibi, and I can take you home with me. What do you think?'

Lovemore is still smiling. 'Perfect.'

'Good. Is there anything you need from the room?'

Lovemore thinks about her few items of clothing and shakes her head no. She is a different person today, not the girl who came here yesterday with those clothes in a small bag, but a young woman instead. A young woman who has made her new baba very proud.

Titi is waiting patiently in the lobby with Benedict and Mama-Concilia, but Grace and Faith have gone to look for Moses and Daniel.

'They'll be watching football on a screen somewhere,' Lovemore says, and that is exactly where she finds them.

Benedict makes sure that they stay in the lobby while Lovemore and Concilia fetch Bibi and Baba away from Bibi's friends. Bibi is trying to assure Baba that he no longer needs to avoid Stella because Stella has found a new man to give her the attention she needs, and Baba is commenting that poor Mr Chiza cannot run away.

Bibi has placed the head and the tail ends of the Nile perch together on one of the boards. 'There's enough on this board for a very big party,' she says.

'Then we must have one,' says Baba. 'Tomorrow afternoon. Tell all of them to invite their friends, Lovemore.'

'Really, Baba?'

Baba nods his head yes. 'We need to celebrate your bibi's win. *And the fact that they have asked her to be the face of Kilimanjaro Snow!*'

'Eh!'

'Ah, Angel, I'm so very proud.' Concilia reaches for Bibi's hand and gives it a squeeze.

'I don't know what it means yet.'

'And there is still some negotiating to be done,' says Baba.

'Please ask your mother to come to the party, Concilia. It's so good to see you two out together.'

'Invite her yourself,' says Concilia, 'she's waiting to help me to drive everybody back home again.'

'*Eh*, she is the one who helped you?'

'Mm, but don't say anything. By the way, Pius, you're sleeping here tonight, in the room with Angel. It's all arranged.'

Bibi and Babu smile at each other, and then at Lovemore and Concilia. Lovemore pins her ASSISTANT badge on to Baba's shirt so that he can have his supper and his breakfast for free.

'Come and say goodbye,' says Concilia, leading them to the lobby, where Benedict and Titi are struggling to carry all of Bibi's prizes. Lovemore helps the two of them to take everything to the boot of Concilia's car. The picture on the heaviest box shows a mixing machine – not the small kind that you hold in one hand as it beats or whisks, but the very big kind that sits on the counter beating into its own bowl.

'*Eh!*' says Benedict, as they pack it into the boot. 'Mama will not want to use this!'

'Ooh, no, Auntie doesn't like things to be modern.'

'But she must try to modernise,' Lovemore tells them. 'I think with this machine a cake can be beating itself while she decorates another or talks with a customer.'

Benedict nods his head yes as he takes the last box from Titi and puts it in the boot. 'It can help her business to grow.'

'It's going to grow now anyway,' says Lovemore, 'now that she's won the competition.'

'*Eh*, she will need this machine!'

'Can we not help her to be comfortable with modernising, Benedict? You and me? Together?'

Benedict smiles. 'Okay. Let us find ways.'

'And me,' says Titi. 'Me, I want to modernise.'

'We'll help you, too,' Lovemore tells her with a smile, and Benedict smiles, too, as he closes the boot and presses a button on Concilia's keys to lock it with a beep.

'But only in the kitchen, see? Me, I don't want computer.'

After all the goodbyes in the lobby, Mama-Concilia has already driven off from the parking area with Benedict, Grace and Faith, and Concilia is about to drive off with Lovemore, Titi and the two youngest boys when Lovemore spots a familiar figure out on the road.

'Concilia, is that not Ibrahim?'

Concilia peers through the evening's darkness. 'Yes it is! Quick, call him.'

While Lovemore runs towards him, Concilia hoots several times. Ibrahim sees Lovemore and cycles up to her with his hands, the small torch strapped on to his crash helmet shining into her eyes.

'You are out late, Ibrahim.'

He smiles at her. 'I am at my clients' service twenty-four six.'

'Yes. I have news, well three pieces of news.'

'Ah.'

'News number one is that Bibi has just won the Kilimanjaro Snow cake-decorating competition!'

Letting out a whoop, Ibrahim claps his hands together loudly. 'Very well done to her!'

'News number two is that she has a name for her business now!'

'At last! What is it?'

'*Bibi-Keki!*'

'*Bibi-Keki,*' he says quietly to himself a few times, his head beaming the torchlight from his crash helmet in every possible direction. '*Bibi-Keki!* That is truly an excellent business name! Very good, I will start the work tomorrow.'

'Maybe start it on Monday,' Lovemore tells him, 'because tomorrow afternoon we are having a party to celebrate, and you and your daddy must come for tea and some of the winning cake. Our baba is home from Mozambique.'

'Ah, a party? That is a very good news number three!'

'I think maybe Benedict is going to invite our neighbour over the wall, the one who is killing the crows.'

'Ah! Excellent! Very good!'

Lovemore is quiet on the journey back to the house. So many thoughts are running through her mind. Bibi will have many things to write in her notebook tonight, many things to be grateful for – but maybe she will write them tomorrow, because Baba is there with her tonight. Baba gave them their gift of wisdom from Mozambique just before the last of their goodbyes at New Africa Hotel.

'In Mozambique,' he told them, 'they say that an anthill that is destined to become a giant anthill will become one, no matter how many times it is destroyed by elephants.'

Lovemore feels sure now that she is destined to become a giant anthill, not because Mama always told her that she must be a lawyer in New York, but because she knows now the kind of giant anthill that she wants to become. It does not matter what Uncle Joseph became. That was his destiny, not Lovemore's. Mama's parents sent Mama away to be just a house girl, but Mama chose a different destiny for herself. Lovemore is choosing her own destiny now, and her new baba is going to guide her with an abundance of wisdom, the most precious gift that any father can give, whether his house is nice and big in Capri Point or on Msasani Peninsula, or whether it is past its better days. Maybe there will be a way for Baba to stay home with them here in Dar es Salaam, or maybe he will take all of them with him to a longer job somewhere else in Africa. Lovemore does not really mind what happens. She has broken free from what Mama and Uncle Joseph expected, and now she is finding her own way.

'It's clearing,' Concilia says, meaning the traffic.

'It's clearing,' Lovemore agrees, meaning everything else.

Gratitude

MY THANKS go to the many people who helped as I researched and wrote this book, especially Vinas Bgoya in Ngara, Tanzania, whose friendship has sustained me across many countries for over thirty years.

In Mwanza, I'm grateful to: Peter Onyango of Kuleana Centre for Children's rights for all he does to help the street children there; Vicki Randell of Caretakers of the Environment Tanzania (now Cheka Sana Foundation) for sharing her experience of working in child safety there; Dr Robert Peck for showing me around Bugando Medical Centre; Pastor Eugene for showing me around Highway of Holiness church; Josephat Kamugisha of AMREF for outlining the extent of AIDS counselling there; Engineer Richard Katarama for showing me around his fish factory; and Martine John (MJ) for his excellent taxi-driving and his many useful connections.

In Dar es Salaam, I'm grateful to: Margaret Muganda for her friendship and connections; Lulu Rwekaza and Rehema Mugasha for showing me around the University of Dar es Salaam; *Mwalimu Mkuu* Mkuna and the teachers and pupils of Msasani Primary School for giving me access to their wonderful work integrating deaf, blind and autistic children into 'normal' schooling; Hugoline Tillya, Orthopaedic Technician at Matumaini School of Hope for the disabled, for giving me an overview of his and the school's important work; *Mwalimu Mkuu* Emil Rugambwa and Director Albert Katagira of Tusiime Secondary School for their insight into secondary schooling in Dar; the staff of *Fema* magazine – Femina HiP, particularly director Dr Minou Fuglesang, Lilian Nsemwa and Constancia Mgimwa, for filling me in on the magazine's work and the state of HIV/AIDS education in Tanzanian schools; the Rt Rev Eusebius Nzigilwa, Auxiliary Bishop of Dar es Salaam, for giving me his time and having St Joseph's Metropolitan

Cathedral opened up for me; and Nelson Daniel Lija for driving me around Dar and taking me to Bagamoyo.

And in London I'm grateful to my indefatigable agent, Christine Green, for her advice, support and belief in me throughout the creation of the trilogy *Baking Cakes in Kigali*, *When Hoopoes Go to Heaven* and *Kilimanjaro Snow*.

Printed in Great Britain
by Amazon